Wiregrass Country

Wiregrass Country

A Florida Pioneer Story

by

Herb & Muncy Chapman

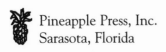

Pineapple Press, Inc.
Sarasota, Florida

Inquiries should be addressed to:
Pineapple Press, Inc.
P.O. Box 3899
Sarasota, Florida 34230-3899

Library of Congress Cataloging in Publication Data

       Chapman, Herb.
         Wiregrass Country / by Herb and Muncy Chapman. —
     1st ed.
        p.   cm.
        ISBN 1-56164-164-2 (hc. : alk. paper) — ISBN 1-
     56164-156-1 (pbk. : alk. paper)
        I. Chapman, Muncy.   II. Title.
       PS3553.H2835W5 1998
       813'.54—dc21   98-24079
                                        CIP

First Edition
10 9 8 7 6 5 4 3 2 1

Composition by Stacey Arnold
Map by Justine A. Rathbun
Printed and bound by Maple Press at York, Pennsylvania

For our children, Jill, Margy, Melinda, and Lee,
who, like wiregrass, have their roots firmly implanted
in the soil of Florida

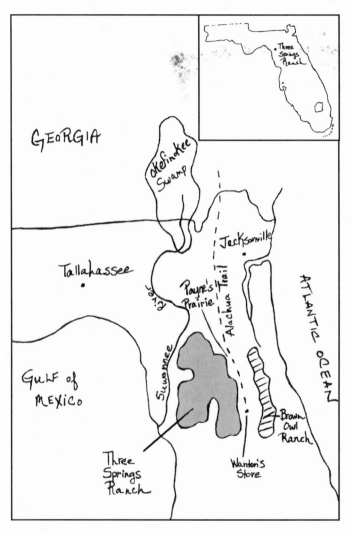

North Central Florida Territory, 1835

Preface

FOLLOWING THE REVOLUTIONARY WAR, lawlessness increased drastically throughout the Southeast. The Harpes, Mike Fink, John Murrell, Sam Mason, and others pillaged settlements and murdered travelers along the Mississippi River and on the Natchez Trace. Ruthless outlaws and renegade Indians rustled cattle, burned settlers' barns and homes, and killed early settlers along both sides of the Florida-Georgia border. The McGirts, Jesse Fish, John Linder, Francisco Sanchez, and other outlaws were well-known and feared in the Florida Territory.

In 1835, before the official start of the Second Seminole War, widespread disorder and violence ran rampant throughout the Territory. Marauding outlaws, renegade Indians, and family feuds fueled fires of hostility and danger in the Territory. Seminoles fought to protect their land from settlers encroaching from the North and their cattle from rustlers coming down from Georgia and Alabama. During the 1830s and 1840s, travel was extremely dangerous, and men carried arms to defend themselves and their belongings.

Many early pioneers lost their possessions and even

their lives. Those unable to adapt to the subtropical conditions, or to succeed economically in the Territory, often moved on to other places. A few strong survivors persevered, and from this nucleus of hardy pioneers emerged several cattle ranches that served as the foundation of the present-day Florida cattle industry. Drawn together by their hardships and their struggles to protect their ranches, these rugged pioneers developed strong family values and a spirit of kinship with their neighbors that still prevails across the land, in families whose roots lie deep within the Florida soil.

Wiregrass Country tells the experience of one such family during a three-month period in late 1835, just before the Second Seminole Indian War.

1

TREFF BALLOWE WATCHED the murky waters of the Perdido River slide beneath the deck of the ferry as the Alabama riverbank receded in the distance. Ahead, the familiar sight of piney woods and thick palmettos seemed to welcome his return to the Florida Territory.

He felt a slight jar as the ferry made contact with the landing and put one hand on his horse's rump to steady himself. Holding the reins in a loose grip, he led his pony onto dry land and tightened the cinch straps of his saddle. Then, swinging his long, lean body into the saddle, he said, "Come on, Rojo. We're going home!"

Riding eastward, Treff pulled down the soft cotton brim of his hat to shield his eyes from the morning sun and headed for the sheltering shadows of the woods. He relaxed in the saddle, confident in Rojo's sense of direction toward the Three Springs Ranch.

Holding the reins in one hand, he used the other to pat his left shirt pocket, reassuring himself that his letter from Ace Dover was still inside. He had read that message at least six times in the last three days, yet he still did not understand its meaning. The only thing that he did understand was a great urgency to return home as quickly as possible.

He stroked his horse and felt the moisture on his flanks. "All right, Rojo, we'll stop for a short rest when we get to Chico's hacienda. We should be there around dinnertime." The faithful horse, seeming to understand his master's words, lifted his head and picked up his pace.

Five years ago, Treff had traded two of his best cows to a Choctaw Indian for this dark red pony that had since become his best friend and constant companion. Treff still marveled at the good fortune that had brought the two of them together. The short-coupled, muscular horse was larger than most found in the Florida Territory and was ideal for driving the wild Spanish cattle like those Treff and his crew of cowhunters had delivered to Mobile three weeks earlier.

Treff and his horse followed a narrow, winding Indian trail, a path he often traveled between Mobile and his home in the Territory. The shade of the dense woods offered welcome relief from the warm September sun, and Treff filled his lungs with the refreshing familiar scent of pine trees.

Happy to be heading home, Treff grew languid and drowsy, letting his thoughts drift toward the family he had called his own for the last fifteen of his twenty-five years. But his reverie was soon broken when suddenly, without warning, Rojo tossed his head high, twitched his ears forward, and gave a loud snort.

Acting on reflex, Treff grabbed his new rifle and threw himself from the saddle, rolling into the thick brush by the side of the trail.

This quick movement, he later realized, was responsible for saving his life. The loud crack of a rifle shot exploded the air around him. A bullet tugged at the shirt sleeve of his right arm and scorched his heavily muscled shoulder at the precise moment he catapulted from the saddle. Another second's delay would have allowed the bullet to find its target square in his chest.

Breathing hard, he rolled deeper into the bushes and peered between the stiff palmetto fronds, hoping to identify his attackers. His keen blue eyes darted from left to right, seeking a barricade that would shield him from view. Spotting a fat pine log, he crawled behind it and hunkered down to watch the action.

Nearby, he heard an ugly chuckle and a nasal twang boasting, "You shore hit that feller straight up, Smitty."

"Mebbe, mebbe not," a gruff voice growled. "We need to be keerful, case'n he's still alive."

"Aw, you knocked him plumb out of his saddle, Smitty. He shore won't be needin' that purty little red hoss no more." The shorter of the two men slapped his hand against his leg in joyous anticipation. "I'm shore gonna like havin' that hoss fer myself."

"Squint, the horse is nice all right, but I'm a hell of a lot more interested in them saddlebags. This coot just took a herd of cattle to Mobile. Don't you realize what that means? He must have gold in them bags."

"Smitty, I'll give you half of my share of any gold we find, fer that pony. A man only gets a hoss like that once in a lifetime an' I been waitin' sixty years fer mine!"

Rojo stood silent and motionless as he had been trained to do, but his ears and tail twitched nervously. As the approaching voices grew louder, Treff peered through the bushes for a better look at his attackers. Two men on horseback edged toward Rojo as clouds of dust mixed with dry leaves swirled around their horses' hooves.

As the two drew closer to his hiding place, Treff silently adjusted his rifle so that it centered upon the men.

"Squint, I seen that feller before. I knowed if we waited long enough that coot would come back. He al'us comes this way," the taller of the two outlaws was saying.

When they reached Rojo's side, Squint raked his eyes over the ground in a complete circle and frantically exclaimed, "He ain't here, Smitty. Where the hell is he?"

"Over here, fellows. I'm right over here," Treff declared in a low, even drawl. "And you both better reach for some clouds."

In an instant, the two outlaws spun their horses and reached for their guns. As Smitty pulled up his pistol, Treff fired his rifle. His bullet hit the outlaw's hand, knocking his pistol to the ground and almost unseating him from his lunging horse.

Smitty's screams and curses echoed through the pine forest. "You've done ruint my hand! All the bones is broke. I ain't never gonna be able to use this hand again!" He struggled to regain control of his horse.

Still concealed by the pine log, Treff replied, "You're lucky I didn't blow your head off, after you tried to bushwhack me. Now both of you get down from your horses."

"I ain't about to get down," Squint shouted with false

bravado. That red pony was too pretty to give up without a struggle.

Treff fired again. This time his bullet hit Squint in his right arm and almost caused him to fall from his saddle. Before Squint could regain his balance, Treff had his rifle reloaded.

"Oww! Why'ja do that fer, you damn idjit?" Blood seeped through Squint's cotton sleeve, changing it from dirty gray to red. A stream of profanities poured from his lips. "It's a good thing fer you that I can't see where you're hidin', you yellow-bellied coward. You done messed up my right arm, but I shoot pretty good with my left hand, and I ain't soon forgettin' what you done to me."

"Don't you fellows understand English? I said for you both to hit the ground. Do it now!"

"We can't with only one good hand each," Squint protested.

"Fall off if you need to, but get down before I help you some more," Treff ordered. He was fast running out of patience.

The two outlaws struggled off their horses, still trying desperately to locate Treff among the trees.

"Drop your gun belts and move away from your horses." After the two outlaws grudgingly obeyed, Treff stood and emerged from his hiding place. "Now get over there, sit down on that rock, and take off your boots," he ordered.

Squint didn't intend to let this young upstart tell him what to do. "No way kin you make me take off my boots," he said.

But before the words completely left his mouth,

Treff answered by shooting the heel from one of his boots.

"You ruint my boots! How kin I walk with the heel gone from one of my boots?" Squint whined, his show of courage fast disappearing.

"If you don't start doing what I say, you won't be able to walk at all! Now shuck those boots!"

Smitty and Squint pretended to try to remove their boots. They made a great show of difficulty, exaggerating their injuries to stall for time while furtively watching for an opportunity to outsmart their captor. Using his left hand, Squint fingered the knife hidden deep inside his right boot.

Without further warning, Treff's rifle spoke again and Smitty's hat flew off his head and landed in a patch of palmettos. "If you don't hurry up and do what I told you, the next bullet will be lower."

"Man, have a little heart! How kin we take our boots off with only one hand?" Squint pleaded, changing his voice to a more conciliatory tone. "You gotta come over here and hep us."

"Help each other, but get those boots off now. I don't have time to waste worrying with the likes of you."

Squint and Smitty finally recognized that it was time to give up. Sitting on the ground, they shucked their boots and their bare feet hit the sand. While the outlaws struggled with their boots, Treff scooped up their guns from the ground and tied them in back of their saddles.

"Now stand up and move back," Treff commanded. As the men complied with his orders, Treff picked up the two pairs of boots.

Something shiny dropped from Squint's boot and landed in the sand. Treff bent to pick it up. "A knife! No wonder you didn't want to take off your boots. Well, I'll just have to take this along with me." Treff put the knife in his saddlebag.

He tied one pair of boots to each of their saddles, beside the guns he had already attached.

"You two fellows need to go back to Alabama and stay there. If I ever see you in the Florida Territory again, I'll shoot you on sight. If you start walking today, you might get back home by the end of the week." Treff gathered the reins of their horses and mounted Rojo.

"You can't leave us here," Smitty screamed indignantly.

"I can and I will," was Treff's calm reply. "You're lucky you're not dead. I should string you up to that oak tree, but I've got no time today to waste on the likes of you. Someday I may be sorry that I'm letting you go."

"We didn't mean no harm," Squint protested. "We wasn't really goin' to do nothin'. Can't you take a little joke?" He tried to laugh, but the sound was weak and unconvincing.

"Since when did murder get to be a joking matter? I've got a perfect right to kill you both here on the spot, but I'm giving you a chance to live if you can make it back to Alabama alive." Treff turned Rojo toward the east.

"Come back here. You can't steal our horses. That's agin the law!"

"I'll leave your horses with the sheriff in Pensacola and tell him they belong to Squint Mobley and Hawkeye Smith. I'm sure he would like for you to come and claim them."

Smitty's mouth dropped open and his eyes bulged. "How do you know our names?"

"I've been knowing about you two for a long time," Treff replied. "You've been robbing travelers on the postal route for more years than I've been old enough to ride. I'd better not see you in the Territory again." Without further words, he left the two barefoot outlaws screaming threats and curses as he led their horses away. Looking back, Treff could not suppress a smile.

"Rojo, I don't know how in the heck we're gonna get these horses to Pensacola. Maybe we'll meet someone heading that way."

Leading the outlaws' horses, Treff moved through the Florida Territory under the warm September sky. In spite of his urgency to return home, he resisted an impulse to push Rojo into a faster pace.

Rojo was now eight years of age, and Treff knew that, besides being alert and intelligent, his horse was strong enough to travel thirty-five or forty miles a day without showing signs of fatigue. But except for the meeting with Squint and Smitty, he and Rojo had been traveling non-stop from before daylight until after dark since leaving Mobile. Still nine or ten days from the Three Springs Ranch, Treff was well aware of the threat of exhaustion in this hot, humid weather, to himself as well as his horse.

The two strange horses were unaware of their former owners' problems and trotted along in happy oblivion, relieved to be freed from the burden of riders. Rojo led the way with his head held high, asserting his role as leader.

Treff continued to follow the wilderness path, winding his way through the pinewood forest. His throat was parched and his stomach grumbled. He could hardly wait to reach the comfortable hacienda of his friend, Chico Leon.

Working beneath the shade of two moss-covered oak trees,

Chico did not hear the approach of the three horses. He used a faded blue bandanna to wipe the sweat that ran down his caramel-colored cheeks and bent to hammer another shoe on one of his recently purchased horses. A refreshing southwest breeze drifted up from Pensacola Bay, helping to cool the muscular, dark-haired Spaniard. He turned back to the fire and picked up his hammer. Chico was a meticulous man, never satisfied with anything less than perfection when it came to fitting his horses with proper shoes. Absorbed in his work, he was unaware of a visitor until he heard the clang of metal beaten against the iron triangle hanging by the gateway to his hacienda.

Surprised, he looked up in sudden apprehension, but quick recognition of his blond-haired friend brought a wide grin to his leathery face.

"*Buenos tardes, mi amigo*. It is good to see you! Welcome to my humble abode. *Mi casa es su casa*. Get off your horse and stay for a while."

Treff Ballowe stepped down from his saddle, and the two men embraced. "Chico, it's great to see you again! I stopped here last month when we passed this way, taking that last group of cattle to Mobile, but you weren't around."

"No, señor. I heard you were here, and I'm sorry we missed each other. We were north of here chasing a band of outlaws. They've been robbing travelers and stealing cattle from some of the new settlers from the Alabama Territory. We are trying to put a stop to them."

"I've heard tales about that. Did you catch 'em?"

"No, señor. They are a slippery lot, like a bunch of

17

damn rattlesnakes. Most of them escaped. We killed one and captured another one who was wounded during the chase, but we lost the rest when they headed east toward the Blackwater River."

"How many got away?"

"Five, we think," Chico replied. "The one we captured told us their gang was led by an *hombre* from Mississippi and places to the west, name of Abe Zink. Ever hear tell of him?"

"Not that I recollect. Where is this wounded man now? I'd like to ask him a few questions myself."

"Ah, but unfortunately, that is not possible," lamented Chico, shaking his head. "He is dead. We had a frontier jury that decided he should pay for his gang's last robbery, which killed the Calvins and both of their children."

Treff shook his head. "That might be the same bunch of outlaws that tried to steal cattle from the last herd my men and I drove to Mobile. We had to fight off a mean group who ambushed us along the way. Fortunately, no one was seriously hurt, but more and more outlaws seem to be crowding into the Florida Territory, bent on robbing and killing settlers and travelers. As a matter of fact, I've just had a run-in with a couple who might have been part of the group that attacked us on the way to Mobile. They knew I had just sold a bunch of cattle."

"Is that where you got the extra horses?" Chico asked.

"Yes, and I probably should have ended their thievery the same way your frontier jury would have. It wouldn't be the first time I've had to resort to that kind of justice, but I decided to give them time to think about their actions by letting them walk all the way back to Alabama without their shoes on. I'll bet the sandspurs are giving them a fit." The steely glint in his blue eyes revealed his lack of sympathy.

"They would not have been as generous with you. Perhaps you should have dealt with them more harshly!" But in spite of himself, Chico smiled as he pictured the two outlaws trying to walk barefoot through the woods. Then, suddenly remembering his manners, he put down his iron tongs and said, "Come inside, Señor Treff. Let's have something to eat and drink. You look as if you could use some rest and food, and perhaps a little liquid refreshment."

"Thanks, Chico. I'm glad for a chance to stop, and it's always good to visit in your home, my friend. But first let me give my horse some feed and water, and give him a chance to rest and cool while we visit. This is our first stop since leaving Mobile day before yesterday. Do you think I could leave the other horses here, for someone to take to the sheriff in Pensacola?"

"That will be no problem, my friend."

"Good. Tell the sheriff the horses belong to Hawkeye Smith and Squint Mobley. He knows who they are. Tell him he can add my name to the list of people they've tried to kill. They aren't likely to come his way, but at least he can have a laugh thinking about their barefoot journey to Alabama."

Treff tied the outlaws' horses to a hitching post.

"I'll have my men take care of them," Chico assured him.

Treff removed Rojo's saddle and put him in a stall with hay and grain and a bucket of cool water. Then he followed as Chico led the way through the courtyard and into the cream-colored stucco house. They were met in the foyer of the spacious hacienda by an elderly Spaniard who took their hats.

"Arturo, show Señor Treff where he can refresh himself and then arrange for us to have lunch on the patio. Maybe we can talk him into spending the night with us."

Treff followed Arturo down the wide hallway to a large bedroom at the back of the house. Wide, uncurtained windows were open to the fresh breeze that drifted in from the south, off Pensacola Bay. Arturo crossed the room and lifted a tall pitcher from the oak washstand. He poured cool, clear water into a clay basin, and handed Treff a coarse linen towel. "Can I be of further service, Señor?"

"No, Arturo, not just now. Thank you for your kindness."

The old servant bowed with dignity before he left the room.

As soon as Treff heard the door close, he unbuttoned his shirt and draped it over a chair to dry. He splashed the cold water over his face and then his bare chest and arms, and immediately felt at least partially renewed and invigorated. He took a deep breath and filled his lungs with the refreshing salt air. Then he dried himself and sank into a chair to collect his thoughts. It felt so good to relax, but he could not permit himself the luxury of lingering. He picked up his shirt, making sure his letter was still safely stored in its pocket, and slipped it over his chest. He smoothed his hair with the palms of his hands and went to find his friend.

"Out here on the patio, *mi amigo*. I am anxious to get

word of your family." Chico had met the Dovers over twenty years ago when the young family first settled in the Florida Territory, and they had remained good friends ever since.

"How are Señor and Señora Dover? It has been a long time since we have seen each other."

Treff settled his long, lanky body into one of the comfortable patio chairs. A frown creased his forehead as he thought of his foster parents. He took so long to answer that Chico feared he had asked a sensitive question. Finally, Treff shook his head and confessed, "Chico, truthfully, I just don't know. They were both fine when I left them, but . . ." Treff thought of the message he carried in his shirt pocket and almost shared his concern with his friend, but decided instead to wait until he knew more details. "I've been gone for several weeks, so I don't know how to answer your question, but I'd have to suppose that they're both well, thank you." Treff beamed what he hoped was a convincing smile that shielded his anxiety.

In spite of his worries, Treff found that it was indeed good to sit at the table and relax. Arturo brought huge platters of steaming food from the kitchen and put them on the round mahogany patio table. Steaks as thick as a man's arm, tortillas filled with red beans and hot peppers, and an impressive assortment of fresh garden vegetables were downed with gusto by the two hungry men, as they laughed and talked and drank what seemed like gallons of strong, black Spanish coffee.

At last, Treff leaned back in his comfortable chair and sighed. "That was a mighty fine meal, Chico. The best I've tasted since leaving home last month. My only regret is that I won't get to see your family this visit. Did you say they're in Pensacola?"

"Si, señor. Claudia took all five niños and went to visit her parents, but they will be back tomorrow. She will be very disappointed if she does not get to see you. Are you sure you cannot stay?"

"Chico, I really wish that I could. I'm sorry that I won't be able to see them this time. It's always hard to leave your comfortable home and your warm hospitality, but I'm afraid it's urgent that I get back to the TSR as soon as possible."

Chico walked with him to the horse barn and helped him saddle his horse. "Adios, my friend. Vaya con Dios."

"Thank you, Chico. Thank you for everything," Treff said as he swung himself into his saddle. "I wish that you and your family could come to our place for a visit. Perhaps you might come for our annual open house this fall."

"Gracias, señor. We would like that very much, but it would be a long trip for Claudia and our five children."

"Well, give it some thought, Chico. You know you are always welcome at the Three Springs Ranch."

"Mi amigo, be very careful! Abe Zink is still in the Territory. Remember also the recent Indian raids that have killed many of the cattle belonging to our neighbors."

With the parting words of Chico echoing in his mind, Treff turned his horse to the east and continued his journey toward home.

2

REVITALIZED BY THEIR STOP at Chico's ranch, Treff and Rojo moved through the woods with renewed vigor. The shortest and quickest way home lay less than two days' ride to the south, where the land sloped toward the Gulf of Mexico. Another popular trail was the Jacksonville-Pensacola mail route which ran parallel to the Georgia-Florida border. But with Chico's words of warning still ringing in his ears, Treff chose a hidden path that had been traveled only by Indians for many years.

The narrow trail meandered eastward through the northwest portion of the Territory, and was concealed by a thick virgin stand of pine trees and heavy underbrush.

Rojo followed the path easily, as if guided by some mystic instinct passed down by earlier generations of Indian ponies. And as his horse followed the trail, Treff's thoughts returned to Mobile where he had spent the last three weeks.

❖   ❖   ❖

In Mobile, those who sought to do business with Treff Ballowe always knew where to find him. He chose to stay at the Oaks Hotel, mainly because of its central location. Though small and unpretentious, the place was clean and furnished Treff with the modest comforts he sought, not the least of which was an excellent dining room.

Four days ago he had been sitting in a rocking chair on the front porch of the hotel, exchanging small talk with three other guests while waiting for the clang of the dinner bell. Mockingbirds and whippoorwills warbled songs from the moss-laden oak trees, and the lingering scent of spent magnolia blossoms hung sweet and heavy on the evening air.

Treff's curiosity was piqued by a young man carrying a crumpled fold of white paper. He climbed the wooden steps onto the porch and asked in an uncertain voice, "Can somebody here tell me where I can find Mister Treff Ballowe?"

Treff did a quick appraisal of the man. He did not appear to be armed. He was clean, and his plain cotton clothes gave him the appearance of a sailor or a manual laborer of some sort. Satisfied that this stranger meant no harm, he said, "I am Treff Ballowe. What can I do for you?"

"Sir, my name be Lenny Samuels. I jes' arrived in port on a barge carryin' timber from the Apalachi region of the Florida Territory. Mister Dover, from the Three Springs Ranch, heerd we was coming to Mobile, and he asked me to deliver this-here letter to you. He said it was very important and he told me not to give it to nobody else but you."

"How did you know where to find me?"

"Mister Dover, he told me you usually stayed at the Oaks Hotel, so I come here to look fer you."

"I'm much obliged," replied Treff, reaching for the paper. "Did Ace say anything else?"

"No, sir," Lenny replied. "He jes' kept tellin' me how important it be to git this to you."

Their conversation was interrupted when a plump black woman wearing a white apron over her calico dress stepped out onto the porch and clanged the big iron triangle that served as the dinner bell.

"Won't you join me for supper?" Treff asked, hoping for a chance to learn more about Ace and the rest of his family.

Lenny did not hesitate. "That would be mighty nice. The food on board the barge ain't been too good lately."

Seated across the dining room table, Treff was amused by the amount of meat and potatoes Lenny packed away. The food on board ship must have been pretty bad, or else this young sailor had not eaten a square meal for a very long time. While Lenny was busy stuffing himself, Treff opened and read the letter from Ace, not once but twice. Frowning, he refolded the paper and tucked it safely into his shirt pocket.

Finally Lenny's plate was clean. He put down his fork and looked across the table at Treff. "Mister Dover said you always stayed at this-here place, and now I know why. I shore do thank you for lettin' me eat with you," he said, using the sleeve of his shirt to wipe the gravy that dribbled down his chin.

Smiling, Treff pushed his chair back from the table

and the two men stood and shook hands. "Lenny, what do I owe you for delivering this message?"

"Not a cent, sir. Mister Dover done paid me in advance, and anyhow, that fine meal would be payment enough!"

On the front porch, Lenny thanked his host once again and started down the steps. "Reckon I better git myself back to the barge. We're fixin' to deliver that timber by the end of the week." With a look of satisfaction on his face, he ambled off toward the waterfront, while Treff went upstairs to his room to study his puzzling letter from home.

While in Mobile, he had bought eight of the new breech-loading rifles from Europe he'd been hearing about, and enough ammunition to last until he came this way again.

Treff had planned to spend the entire month in Mobile, to arrange delivery of another group of cattle to market and to settle his financial accounts. After paying two months' wages to his foreman, Cotton Smith, and his cowhands, he had sent them back to the ranch with some badly needed supplies, seven of the new rifles, and part of the gold received for the delivered cattle. Three Springs Ranch was over four hundred miles from Mobile, and Treff needed to stick around long enough to make some important business contacts before returning home. And he wanted to find out more about that new Colt revolver he heard was being produced.

But Ace's mysterious message had quickly changed all of his original plans. Leaving unfinished business behind, he rode out of Mobile before daylight the next day and, except for his run-in with Squint and Smitty, and a brief stop at Chico's place, he and Rojo had been riding hard ever since.

Even without Chico's warning, Treff knew that dangerous outlaws constantly roamed back and forth between southern Alabama and Georgia and the Florida Territory, rustling cattle, terrorizing settlers, and robbing careless travelers. He carried two saddlebags partially filled with gold received from the cattle sale, and he did not intend to have any of it stolen during this trip. He was not anxious to meet anyone on his way back to the Three Springs Ranch, especially in light of the mysterious message he carried in his pocket. If only Ace had explained his problems instead of leaving everything hanging in the air!

Rojo turned his head toward an inviting patch of grass, and Treff understood the horse's unspoken plea. "All right, old boy. You deserve a little treat." Treff slid out of his saddle to let Rojo rest and graze, while he relaxed his lean, muscular body against the trunk of an oak tree. He removed the letter from his shirt pocket and read it once again, still trying to find answers to the questions that bothered him about the short, cryptic note:

> Tre—
> We have a serious problem and need your help. If Lenny Samuels is able to find you please come home as soon as possible. <u>Be careful!</u> —Ace

It was not like Ace to be so secretive. Perhaps he was worried that the information might fall into the wrong hands. But Treff had made several trips to Mobile in the past and never before had Ace sent for him to come home early. He tried to imagine what might be wrong at the ranch that was important enough to cause him to leave his business unfinished. Whatever it was, he knew Ace well enough to be certain that this was something major and that he must get home as quickly as possible. He did not ever want to let Ace down. He owed a lot to Ace Dover. Without his help, Treff would probably not even be alive today, and neither would his brother, Ten.

As it often did, his mind wandered back to that terrible day when he and Ace first met. He could still smell the smoke from the flames that had destroyed not only his home, but all the hopes and dreams and everything dear to the hearts of two helpless young boys.

Treff and his brother were born in the foothills of the Blue Mountains in North Carolina. In 1821, when his parents learned that Spain had deeded the Florida Territory to the United States, Charles and Alice Ballowe decided to take their two young sons and move south to settle in the rich grasslands of the Utinara region of the Territory.

Early one morning, soon after settling in their new log home, Treff pulled on his younger brother's arm. "Ten, let's go to that turkey roost we found the other day.

Maybe we can shoot us a turkey for supper."

"Yeah, let's go. But let's don't tell anybody. Let's just sneak off and surprise 'em. Pa'll sure be proud of us if we can bring home a turkey!"

The boys stole quietly through the thick woods surrounding their cabin until they saw their prey.

"Look, Ten. Up in that big oak tree! There's three of 'em roosting on that low limb." He put his finger to his lips to remind his younger brother to keep silent.

As quiet as two field mice, the boys crept up behind the unsuspecting turkeys. Just as Ten was drawing a bead on the largest one, the air seemed to explode with shooting and whooping in the distance, and the noise was coming from the direction of their home!

Forgetting the turkeys, both boys ran as fast as they could, back toward their home and parents. But as they approached their clearing, they stopped and gaped in horror as they watched their small cabin, engulfed in angry orange flames, seem to dissolve before their eyes. Brightly painted Indians, led by a tall, young, one-eyed warrior, rode around the burning house, shouting and waving in celebration.

Treff and Ten were terrified, knowing almost surely that their parents had been killed. Their first impulse was to rush ahead and try to help them, but what could they do? Common sense told them that there were too many Indians for two young boys, ages ten and eight, to fight.

In desperation, Treff took charge. He grabbed his younger brother by the arm. "Quick, Ten, hunker down in the middle of that palmetto patch and keep quiet." The boys lay flat on the ground and tried to cover themselves with dirt and leaves, almost afraid to breathe lest they be found.

The renegade band of Creek Indians circled through the woods for what seemed like hours, looking for two young boys known to live in the cabin. Strong boys would make good slaves. The Indians would be proud to return to their camp bearing two such prizes.

Ten and Treff did not move a muscle. Minutes seemed to stretch into hours. More than once they felt the ground tremble and heard the Indian ponies circling their palmetto patch, but they buried their faces deeper into the dirt and remained motionless.

Because the ground was dry and covered with leaves, the Indians were unable to find footprints leading to the boys' hiding place. Frustrated, they raced through the trees, their ponies disturbing any remaining trace of tracks that might have led them to their prize. Treff held his brother down as the Indians continued their search. Suddenly he felt the ground shake as another group of horses rapidly approached. His heart beat wildly and his hopes sank. Were more Indians coming to help look for them? But to his surprise, the Indians suddenly turned and raced away without looking back. Later the boys were told that the Indians were apparently frighened away by the sound of the approaching horses' hoofbeats.

Ace Dover led his band of cowhunters toward the burning house. He had come that day to welcome the family of new settlers and to offer a helping hand. He and his men were sick at heart when they found the cabin burning and realized that the family must surely have perished in the fire. They were surprised when the two children emerged from their hiding place.

In dazed shock, the dirt-covered boys crawled from the bushes, their cheeks wet with tears. Without a word, Ace Dover slid off his horse and wrapped Treff in a tender bear hug and let the boy sob onto his chest until there were no tears left. Ten, too, was held and comforted by one of Ace's cowhands, a big, burly man whose own cheeks were streaked with tears.

"I should have shot those Indians," Treff moaned. "They killed our Ma and Pa."

"It's not your fault, boy," Ace assured him. "Now, don't you ever go thinkin' that. There was nothing you could have done except get you and your little brother killed. You did the right thing, son. You're a brave boy."

It was hard for the two boys to realize that their parents were dead. Ma and Pa were the only relatives they had, and now they had no one. Their only possessions were the clothes they wore and the guns they had taken turkey hunting. The Indians had even stolen their two horses and killed their hound dog.

"What're we gonna do, Treff?" a grief-stricken Ten asked.

Treff put a protective arm around his brother's shoulder and tried to sound more confident than he felt. "Never mind, Ten. Don't you worry. I'll think of something."

But Ace Dover took immediate control of the situation and, after burying the charred remains of the father and mother, he took the boys home to the Three Springs Ranch, east of the Suwannee River, where his wife, Amaly, welcomed the boys with open arms. Amaly's maternal instincts were as wide as her ample bosom, and she never questioned Ace's decision to bring the children home. The Dovers raised Treff and Ten along with their own two sons, eleven-year-old Jeremiah and nine-year-old Rusty, often forgetting that the two Ballowe boys were not their own flesh and blood.

And the Dovers had a daughter, too. Marvelous Dover, at seven years of age, refused to admit that she could not do everything as well as her four big brothers. With a stomp of her foot and a shake of her bouncy red curls, she emphatically declared, "I may not be a boy, but I'm just as good as a boy!" Once, when one of the cowhands jokingly told her that she could turn into a boy by kissing her elbow, the tenacious child had almost broken her arm trying to twist it into a position within reach of her lips.

Treff had to admit that his sister really did seem able to do almost anything her brothers could do—sometimes better. A skilled rider, she could mammy calves, brand, hunt cows, and shoot a rifle. And she understood as much about the cattle business as any of her brothers—maybe even more.

At age fourteen, she chose a name that she felt suited her personality and made her feel important. "I would like to be called Marv," she announced one day, and she had been known by that name ever since.

The five children, now grown, were all actively involved in managing the vast family ranch, which had grown in size just as the children themselves.

❖   ❖   ❖

Even today, Treff could still see the one-eyed red warrior in his mind, and by night the vision often invaded his dreams. Treff could never erase that afternoon from his memory, nor did he want to until justice was done. Since then he had heard many times of the Indian called He-with-One-Eye-of-an-Eagle and had learned that the warrior led a small band of renegade Creeks who still roamed southern Alabama and Georgia. Treff hoped that one day that bunch would make the mistake of coming back to the Florida Territory. He had an old score to settle with their leader!

Rojo's smooth gait, coupled with the warm sunshine filtering through the cypress and pines, had a hypnotic effect on Treff. Reminiscing about Ace and the rest of his family had effectively served to drain some of the tension from his mind and body, and he struggled to avoid dozing in the saddle, but the letter in his pocket stimulated him to remain alert and on the move.

Ace was the only person who ever called him Tre, and then only when he was troubled or serious. Whatever problem was bothering Ace must surely be a big one.

Without warning, Rojo lifted his head, flared his nostrils, and twitched his ears. Apparently, he had been spooked by something in the pine trees on the right side of the path. Putting his hand on the horse's neck to calm him, Treff's keen eyes scanned the bushes but saw nothing except cabbage palms, briars, and palmettos. He pulled gently on the reins, bringing Rojo to a stop, and eased himself from the saddle. Dropping the reins to the ground, he lifted the two heavy saddlebags and hid them under a clump of palmettos. Then, slipping his rifle from his saddle, he moved on soundless feet through the thick underbrush to discover what had disturbed his horse.

At first glance, he detected nothing unusual. He put his ear to the ground, but the earth was still and silent. He slipped from tree to tree, pausing each time to look before moving again, but still he found nothing that would have startled his horse. Perhaps Rojo had been spooked by a wild animal that was scared away by their intrusion. The sun was inching its way toward the western sky and Treff decided there was no need to delay his journey further.

Just as he started to retrace his steps, he heard a low moan coming from somewhere in front of him. He hunched his body and crept forward until he came into a small clearing beneath an oak tree. A man lay propped against its trunk, his shirt caked with dried blood. Obviously wounded and suffering intense pain, the man seemed oblivious to Treff's approach, and jumped when Treff asked, "Do you need help?"

Treff saw the man instinctively reach for his gun. From his position, Treff could not see that the stranger's holster was empty and he did not wait to find out. "Don't touch it," he cautioned, pointing his rifle toward the man.

"Who are you?" the injured man asked. "How did you find me? I sure didn't hear you coming. You must be part Indian."

With his blond hair and blue eyes, Treff had never before been mistaken for an Indian, but he had been taught long ago how to move quietly and invisibly through the woods. He had spent almost his entire life out of doors, and the only man in the Florida Territory who could best him as a hunter and tracker was the Indian who had taught him.

Kneeling to examine the man's wounds, Treff asked, "What's your name? What happened to you?" But his questions went unanswered as the stranger slipped in and out of consciousness.

Treff handled the man gently as he examined his wounds. He had been shot in the right shoulder. Treff could see where the bullet had entered the back of his shoulder and come out at the front, passing completely through the man's body. His shirt was glued to his flesh with coagulated blood, and the angle of his left arm left little doubt that it was broken.

The wounded man opened his eyes and mumbled an explanation. "I was bushwhacked . . . shot in the back just before dark . . . two thieves. I think just yesterday—not sure." Between broken sentences, the man paused to draw air into his lungs and gain strength to continue. "Broke my arm when I fell from my horse. They thought they had killed me so they took my gun . . . money, too. Left me here. I've been too weak to get up." The tremendous effort of speaking left him limp and breathless. He slumped against the tree trunk. After a few moments, he continued. "Until you came along, I figured this was where I would die. Last night I could hear wild animals. I knew if they found me I wouldn't be able to defend myself, with a broke arm and no gun."

Tearing the man's neckerchief in half, Treff placed a bandage on each bullet hole and, by using the man's belt to hold the bandages in place, he was able to protect the wounds and prevent further bleeding. Breaking some straight branches from a myrtle bush, Treff set and bound the man's arm to hold it straight and still.

Once more Treff asked, "What did you say your name was?"

"I didn't say . . . but it's Hank O'Mara," the man haltingly replied. "I own the HO-Bar Ranch over near the Yellow River." O'Mara squeezed his eyes, trying to focus his thoughts. ". . . other day I lost about twenty head of cattle. Their trail came this way—and I followed to look for 'em. Maybe the guys who shot me are—same rascals who stole my cattle."

"Did they steal your horse, too?"

"I don't know. I haven't seen him," Hank muttered.

Taking up his rifle, Treff said, "I aim to go look for your horse. Maybe he's somewhere close by."

It took almost an hour of searching through the woods, but finally Treff found the horse about a half mile away, its reins tangled in bushes so that it could not move. Disentangling the reins, he mounted the pony and rode back to the place where he had left Hank propped against the tree.

"I reckon this is yours?"

Hank nodded, and Treff dismounted and tied the pony's reins to a low limb. Then he gathered some wood for a fire, boiled some coffee, and found some jerky and biscuits in Hank's saddlebags. This man needed to eat if he was going to be strong enough to ride.

After they had eaten, Treff asked, "Do you feel like you can ride?"

"I think so," Hank replied, "but I'll need help getting on my horse because of my arm."

"How far are we from your spread?"

"About a three-hour ride yesterday. Probably a little

longer today though, in my condition," Hank answered.

"Rest here while I get my horse," Treff said. "Then I'll come back to help you." He picked up his rifle from the oak tree and went back to where Rojo was munching grass, waiting patiently for his master.

Treff stopped to look and listen before he reclaimed his two saddlebags. He did not wish to suffer the same fate as his new acquaintance. When he was sure there was no one else around, he tied the leather bags in back of his saddle, mounted his horse, and returned to help Hank.

"Okay, Hank. Let's get you back on your pony."

Treff lifted and pushed until Hank, still groaning in agony, was firmly mounted, and the two of them headed toward the Yellow River. Treff realized that he would be backtracking, and he hated wasting precious hours, but he couldn't leave Hank alone. The man was too weak, scarcely able to sit straight in his saddle. Treff had trouble just keeping him awake and alert enough to guide them toward his home.

By the time they arrived at Hank's small cabin, darkness had begun to roll in. They were greeted by his foreman, Pato Bevis, who cast a suspicious eye in Treff's direction and raised the rifle in his hand. "What is it, señor? Has this man caused trouble for you?"

"Don't worry about him, Pato," Hank assured him, "Treff saved my life and we will always be in his debt."

Pato relaxed his aggressive stance and the two of them helped Hank from his saddle. They carried him inside the cabin and placed him on a bunk. While Treff got some water from the river to clean Hank's wounds,

Pato started a fire in their small iron stove and began to cook supper for the three of them.

"Don't fix anything for me. I'm not hungry," Hank protested.

"You must eat in order to regain strength and recover from your injuries," the foreman insisted.

"Pato is right, Hank. You need a good hot meal in your belly."

Although Pato prepared a robust supper, Treff did not linger over it. As soon as he ate a few bites and downed a cup of strong coffee, he stood and made his apologies for a hasty departure. Even though there was no moon and the sky was as black as tar, he bid them good-bye and started east. Rojo saw well at night, and Treff wanted to make up some of the time he had lost.

He had no way of knowing then that Hank O'Mara was to play an important role in his future.

3

WATCHING THE YOUNG SPANIARD drop anchor in Havana Harbor, Captain Caleb heaved an audible sigh of relief. He remembered many happy trips to Havana, but this had not been one of them. He hated the stinking cattle he carried on his boat! From the cabin of his steamer, he looked down on the cargo of milling, bawling animals he had brought from the Florida Territory and considered himself lucky to have arrived safely, with no loss of cattle or crew. During most of the trip, strong winds and heavy rains had kept eight- to ten-foot swells on the sea, making the cattle unusually restless and hard to manage, in spite of the small individual pens that kept their weight spread evenly across the flat-bottomed paddlewheeler. The quiet waters of Havana Harbor were a welcome sight.

Turning to a husky sailor, the Captain barked his orders: "Ramon, lower the rowboat and go get the cattle buyers. Juan and I want to unload these cattle as soon as possible."

As the young sailor hurried to carry out his orders, Caleb muttered under his breath, "Why did that damn Hurley Post have to go and get hisself hung? That just messes up everything."

Two years ago, Hurley Post had involved him in the cattle-smuggling business, and the venture had proven very profitable indeed. The idea was simple enough. Cuba did not have enough beef to supply their demand, and the Cubans were willing and able to pay well in order to obtain it. Wild cattle were plentiful in the woods and marshes of the Florida Territory, and Cuban buyers had been known to pay as much as two ounces of gold per head, delivered to Havana.

Caleb had spent his entire life on the waters surrounding the Florida Territory. He was as skilled as the captains of the large Spanish galleons that traveled from Mexico to Spain and as clever as the pirates who plundered the coastline. He preferred to work the west coast of the Territory because it offered deeper harbors and fewer reefs than the eastern side of the peninsula. Barring unusual developments, he could reach Havana, sell and unload the cattle, clean his boat thoroughly, take on a load of wood for fuel, and return to his hidden harbor near Pine Level in the south Florida Territory, usually in only ten to fourteen days. And each time he made the round trip to Havana, he knew he could always count on Hurley Post and his small band of outlaws to have another group of four- and five-year-old steers ready for immediate loading upon his return. This enabled Caleb and his crew to load a new group of cattle and clear the coastline quickly, leaving no evidence of the stolen cattle. There had been many such trips to Havana during these past two years, and as a result, Caleb had amassed a small fortune. What would happen now, he wondered, without Hurley to rely on as a source for cattle?

Caleb tried to haul about three hundred steers on each trip, but this time his cargo numbered scarcely more than two hundred head. Last week, when he reached the Florida Territory and docked at his hidden pens to pick up the next load of cattle, he and Ramon had been greeted by a very agitated Juan Diego.

Juan had served as Caleb's first mate for the last two years. The young Spaniard's soft voice and mild mannerisms seemed to provide a calming influence on the nervous wild cattle, and Caleb was happy to have him back onboard for this trip. Last week, when Caleb had made his previous trip to Havana, Juan had stayed behind to visit his sick mother, and Caleb had missed his help.

Caleb had scarcely docked the boat near Pine Level last week when Juan ran up to him, his eyes widened in alarm. He spoke in a frantic jumble of words, a mixture of English and Spanish.

"Captain Caleb, we have *muy malo* trouble!"

"What's the matter, Juan?"

"Hurley and his cowhunters got caught stealing cattle from a holding area near Hopper's Prairie, owned by the MP Ranch. The owner of the ranch, Señor Pablo Munez, he was very angry."

"Where is Hurley?" Caleb had asked.

"I only man to escape," Juan replied. "The other four are hanging from a big oak tree near where they got caught."

41

Caleb had been more than a little worried over this turn of events. If Pablo and his cowhands got Hurley and his boys, they were probably on the lookout for him, too. Caleb surely did not want to end up hanging from an oak tree, nor did he want to leave without loading the cattle gathered during his absence.

"Do you think you and I can load these cattle on the boat?" he had asked Juan.

"Señor, we have Henry, our big ox, with the steers. He will lead the steers onboard. It will be easy."

"Good! Let's get these cattle aboard and get out of here as quick as possible. There's no telling what Hurley told the MP Ranch boss, hoping to save his own neck. We sure don't want to get caught with these cattle."

Captain Caleb had worked with cattle as a young man, and Juan was an excellent cowman. Although the job was not quite as easy as Juan had predicted, four hours later the two men had managed to herd the last of the cattle onboard, and the steamer had slipped quietly away from the coast without being noticed.

There were only 213 steers in this group, hardly worth the trip to Havana if the gold had to be split fifty-fifty with a partner. But Caleb no longer had a partner, he reminded himself, so he could well afford to make the trip with a smaller load. There were, after all, certain advantages to having Hurley out of the picture.

Now that he had reached the safety of Havana Harbor, the smoother waters helped ease Caleb's anxieties, even though he knew that the most difficult part of the trip might still lie ahead. Dealing with Cuban cattle buyers had to be done very carefully. He had learned the hard way to bring the buyers to the boat and never to unload the cattle until he had his payment locked in the secret safe below decks.

Caleb strained to peer across the dark water, hoping to catch sight of Ramon's boat bringing the cattle buyers. He was impatient to complete this deal and return to the Florida Territory to start looking for his old friend, Abe Zink. Abe might be just the man Caleb needed to replace Hurley Post and supply him with cattle for the Cuban trade.

Caleb recognized an urgency to do as much smuggling as possible during the next few years. During a recent trip to Fort Brooke, he had run into an old friend in Tres Amigos Saloon, Captain Andy Hooks.

"Caleb, things are changing in this country," his friend told him. "Just last week I heard a rumor some people are trying to make the Florida Territory a state, part of the United States."

"I sure would hate to see that happen, Andy," Caleb mused. "Army troops and settlers would come swarming into the Territory like buzzards after a dead horse's carcass. Things would get way too crowded."

Caleb did not voice his major concern, that additional army troops would keep a close watch on the movement and activities of ships, and smuggling would become much more difficult and dangerous. Too, Caleb feared that if the Territory became a state, big cattlemen would likely start shipping large numbers of cattle to Cuba, and with more cattle available to Cuban buyers, the profit from smuggling might not offset the danger involved.

Yes, Caleb decided, he absolutely must find Abe Zink

without delay. There were lots of wild cattle in the Territory, free for the taking, and Abe knew where to find them. Many had been lost by Seminole Indians when they fought settlers for their land. Other cattle had been abandoned by the Spanish as they moved from place to place. And when wild cattle were not readily available, Abe Zink and his men were not reluctant to rustle to get what they wanted.

Caleb was anxious to get his share of these cattle before someone else beat him to them. He had told Juan more than once, "A fella has got to take advantage of opportunities of the moment, but he needs to know when it's time to move on to something else."

At last, Captain Caleb heard the rhythmic sound of oars bringing the small boat with the cattle buyers. Peering through the slight fog that had settled over the harbor, he watched the group ease alongside the cattle boat. Straightening his hat, he went to meet them.

"My friends, it is good to see you again!" he exclaimed. His white teeth gleamed through his wide smile. "Here, let me give you a hand."

Ramon had brought three buyers to the boat, and Caleb anticipated a lively sale if he could entice them to bid against each other. He had sold cattle to each of them during previous trips, and he was familiar with their needs as well as their wiles. They would try to keep the price down by refusing to compete with each other, and then split the cargo later, after the cattle were unloaded. But Caleb hoped that, with such a small load of cattle this trip, the buyers might be induced to become more aggressively competitive.

Shaking hands with each man, he greeted them warmly. "Señor Garcia, Señor Gomez, Señor Patilla, welcome aboard the *Honey Bee*. May we serve you some coffee or a shot of whiskey, perhaps?"

Pleasantries were exchanged, but the cattle buyers declined the offer of drink, choosing instead to examine the cattle.

"We were very fortunate to have found larger cattle for you this time," Caleb boasted, standing aside to give the buyers a better view of his cargo. "Quite possibly the very finest stock you have ever seen. Not wanting to crowd such valuable animals, and recognizing your appreciation of quality, we decided to bring only two hundred thirteen head. It is your good fortune that we were able to bring such fine cattle. The only one not for sale is Henry, our big ox."

Each buyer examined the cattle with solemn diligence. With Juan serving as a translator, Señor Patilla began the bidding by indicating that he could pay one and one-half ounces of gold per head.

"Come, come, Señor Patilla! These are some of the finest steers we have been privileged to bring you," Caleb said. "Surely you will agree that they are a real bargain at three ounces of gold per head."

Señor Patilla shook his head and looked back at the cattle. The three men huddled together and whispered. Finally Señor Gomez said that he could go as high as one and three-quarter ounces a head.

Caleb sensed that perhaps things could become more interesting and asked Juan to keep talking with the buyers. Thoughtfully rubbing his chin, Señor Garcia indicated that he might concede that the steers were worth two ounces per head.

Caleb forced a laugh. "I am sure you are making a joke with me, no? But I tell you what I will do, gentlemen." He gave them a smile with all the warmth of a brother. "You are all my very dear friends, and because of that I will make you a special offer. You may have the steers for two and one-half ounces of gold per head!"

After considerable discussion, Señor Patilla finally offered Caleb two and one-quarter ounces. "I must be insane to make such an offer!"

Caleb feigned hurt and disappointment at such a low bid. He shook his head, but at last he said, "My friends, consider this my gift to you, that I allow these prize animals to go for such a ridiculously low price. If we were not friends, I would be insulted with such a deal."

Not one man among them smiled, each trying to project the impression of having received the short end of the stick. Yet secretly each man felt proud and happy that the deal was even sweeter than his most optimistic expectations.

As soon as the gold was lifted from the rowboat and stored in the safe below deck, Captain Caleb pulled up anchor, moved next to the dock, and unloaded the steers into the Havana cattle pens.

"When will we see you again?" Señor Patilla asked through the interpreter.

"It may be four weeks before I am back with the next load. I need to do some repair work on the boat."

After the buyers left, Juan cleaned the boat and loaded fuel for the trip home.

Two nights later, as the steamer inched its way out of the harbor, Caleb stood on the deck and watched the lights from Havana gradually fade in the distance. There were changes in the wind, and now he must plan for the future. But first he must find Abe Zink. He would start his search along the waterfront saloons as soon as he reached Mobile.

Caleb had no inkling yet that finding the outlaw would prove much easier said than done.

4

FROM THE MOMENT Drag Johnson rode his stolen horse onto the Brown Owl Ranch, he sensed that he might have struck pay dirt. And when Zeke Mongol, owner of the expansive ranch, invited him to "stop and rest for a spell," he was sure of it. What better place to begin activating the plan that had rattled his brains for the last four years? Prison life gave a man plenty of time to plan and think about his future, and going back to that damn Mississippi rat-hole of a prison was definitely not part of Drag's plan.

He had already served time for rustling only a few measly head of cattle. Next time he'd go big-time, and he didn't plan to get caught, either. He was older and wiser now, and any man clever enough to escape from that stinkin' prison was sure as hell smart enough not to get caught a second time. Drag had far better ideas for his future than that! What's more, he felt confident that his carefully calculated plan was absolutely safe and foolproof.

He lay on the hard horsehair mattress in the Brown Owl bunkhouse, his feet hanging several inches over the end of the six-foot bed. His sun-darkened frame was lean and rugged, his bulging muscles a dubious reward from his recent months of hard labor, sun-up until sundown, rain or shine, clearing and widening the Natchez Trace.

Small wonder that his nights on the narrow cot in his cramped, smelly cell had been spent planning and dreaming of the day he would make his getaway—the day he would start riding down the road to riches. Was it just blind good luck when that road seemed to run right into the Brown Owl Ranch? No, it was more than luck, Drag decided. Luck was something that happened by chance, but coming here was not by chance at all, in spite of what he'd told his host. It was his own clever planning that had brought him here.

It all began coming together the night he escaped from prison. On a stolen horse, Drag had moved stealthily through the woods to Georgia, with the idea of rustling a few cattle to get his starter-stake. He had enjoyed moderate success, and the money had been fair, but rustling alone was slow, hard work, and carried the risk of his getting caught and returned to prison.

The sale of a few head of stolen cattle to an old Georgia farmer gave him his big inspiration. When he heard the cracker-man say he was heading to the Florida Territory, Drag decided he ought to take a look at that place himself.

He was especially curious about a little town in the northeast corner of the Florida Territory. Named for President Andy Jackson, Jacksonville was said to be a busy center where large numbers of cattle were moved across the St. Johns River on their way to the Savannah market.

When Drag first rode into town, he found nothing to impress him. There were the usual string of saloons, gambling halls, a general store, and a blacksmith shop. Cowhunters wandered up and down the boardwalk looking for ways to relax as they stopped on their way home carrying several months of pay in their pockets.

Having traveled the last few days in the woods with nothing to eat but some jerky, Drag felt hungry for a good meal. He looped his reins around the horse rack in front of the Four Amigos Café and ambled in through the double swinging doors.

Drag chose a table toward the back of the room, with a good view of the street. He ordered a T-bone steak, thick and rare, and sat down to study the other patrons in the café.

Julio, the server, brought a cup of coffee to the table, sloshing some of it on his greasy apron. "Yer new around here, ain't ya?"

Drag took his time in answering. "Yeah, I guess you could say that." He gulped the lukewarm coffee. "Say, you got any idea where a fella might find a card game in this here town?"

Julio thought a minute before answering. "You might check in the Cowhunters Saloon, across the street and down four buildings. Sometimes there's some guys in a game. You can get a room there too, if you want."

Drag could use some quick cash, and a card game might be an easy way to learn something about the territory and pad his pockets at the same time. He finished his meal, paid the man four bits, and went in search of the Cowhunters Saloon.

He spotted it easily by the many horses hitched out front, a sure sign of a bunch of cowhunters inside, downing a few drinks before heading home. He pushed through the doors and swaggered up to the counter. "Got a room?"

Without looking up, the clerk nodded. "Private?"

"Yeah, private."

"Number Four, upstairs, second door on the left. Four bits in advance."

Drag plopped his money on the counter and picked up the key. Then he sauntered over to a nearby table where four men sat clenching their cards close to their chests. Drag pointed to an empty chair. "Stud poker? How about settin' in?"

Without answering, the dealer included him in the next hand. There was little conversation as the men played four or five hands. The stakes were modest, and no one seemed to win or lose much.

The cowhunter on Drag's left was a sour-looking man with a jagged scar on his chin. The other men called him Snake Leggitt. Snake lost more than the others but seemed unconcerned about it. Once, after throwing in his cards, he said, "Them Injuns shore do have nice cattle. I shore would like to git my hands on a couple hundred, but it be too dangerous. Them damn Injuns is attackin' anybody that messes around with 'em."

"Snake," his companion said, "you wouldn't know what to do if you had two hundred cattle. All you be knowin' is how to ride a hoss and brand a calf, and you don't do that too good."

Drag smelled opportunity. "Bartender, set these fellers up with another round of whiskey." He figured a few drinks might loosen some tongues, and he liked the way the conversation was beginning to turn.

As the game wore on, Drag won a few dollars and lost a few, but his net winnings were enough to buy several more rounds of whiskey. The cowhunters either didn't realize or didn't care that he used their money for the rotgut.

"Snake," Drag finally dared to ask, "where did you see them Injun cattle?"

"I seen a passel east of the Ocklawaha River, about three days south of here. Then once I seen a big bunch by the old Cuscowilla settlement of the Seminoles. Them cattle sure was wild, but they had lots of grass, and they was fat as hogs in a corn patch."

Snake turned to one of the men who had been playing his cards in silence. "Toke, didn't you tell me you seen a big bunch of cattle down around the end of the Alachua Trail?"

Toke Bannon sat slumped over his cards. He was badly in need of a bath, and the straggly, unkempt, black-speckled beard that covered his swarthy face seemed a likely nest for varmints. His belly sagged over his gun belt with muscles that had turned to fat. His clothes were covered with dirt, exhibiting the probable residue from weeks of riding without washing, but in spite of his unsavory appearance, he seemed to be the leader of this motley group. Drag noted the gun on his hip and suspected he might have a knife hidden either in one of his boots or perhaps between his shoulder blades.

Toke did not respond immediately. His black eyes glared at Snake a long time before he answered. "Yeah, I did, but they warn't Injun cattle. Them belonged to the Brown Owl Ranch."

One of the other card players complained about his cards and folded. "I'm fixin' to head back to the swamp."

"Wait up 'til I git some bacon and flour at the store and I'll go with you," his friend said.

Toke said, "You three fellers go on back to camp. I'll be back tomorrow. I can't stay too long in this here place or I might be spotted by that damn marshal that comes down from Savannah. He ain't been around fer awhile, so he's likely to show up any time now."

After the three hands left, Drag and Toke sat at the table and had another drink. Without warning, Toke looked hard at Drag and said "You been in prison, ain't ya?"

Despite his best efforts, Drag could not hide his star-tled reaction. How did Toke know about that? What gave him away? Who was this man, and just how much did he know?

Drag tried to evade the question. "Why would you think a thing like that?"

"I can usually spot an ex-con. You don't fit with the other people. You're wearing new clothes. You're too clean to be a cowhunter, too well-dressed to be a farmer, and your hands are too calloused to be a storekeeper or banker. I think you ain't been out of prison too long."

Drag adjusted his belt to bring his gun closer to his

hand before he asked, "What's it to you? Who are you, anyway?" He tried to buy time to decide how to answer Toke without revealing too much.

"I ain't the law," Toke assured him, "and I ain't no bounty hunter. I got me a group of men livin' on a place called Black Oak Island, up in the Okefinokee Swamp. We like it there 'cause the law don't come to the swamp. We make money any way we can. After we do a job, we go back to the island and wait awhile afore comin' out. We plan everything careful, and so far we been lucky."

As Toke continued to talk, Drag's mind worked furiously. Suddenly he became very interested in Toke Bannon. This could be the missing part to his plans. He needed someone to do the rustling, while he only supplied information. The whole operation needed to be a well-guarded secret. He sure didn't want to go back to prison, yet he didn't know any way to get money except by stealing. He needed someone willing to work with him on a fifty-fifty split. But how could he know if Toke was dependable? What if he double-crossed him? Toke sounded like a good deal, but Drag wanted to know more about this man before exposing his master plan.

"Why are you worried about the marshal spotting you?" he asked.

"I kilt a man up in the Carolinas, and they've got some rewards posted. They ain't got no picture of me and not too good a description, so most folks don't know me. But there's a Marshal Mizell from north Georgia that does know me. He keeps lookin' for me. He comes this far south about twict a year. I hear tell he won't be happy 'til I hang from a tree limb."

Toke looked around the room and lowered his voice to a whisper. "I been with these three fellers fer about two years. We stay hid in the Okefinokee while we plan our next work. After we come out and do our job, once in awhile we stop in a place like this fer some fun and female company, but we don't stay long. They's a lot of travelers on the Alachua Trail and we rob a few of 'em. We steal a few cattle when we git a chance. We don't git rich, but we have a good time, and so far we ain't been caught."

"Do you know the cattle trails to Savannah?" Drag asked.

"We taken cattle there two or three times," Toke replied, "but I worry about that Marshal Mizell when I'm in Georgia. Most of the time we're able to get rid of just a few head in St. Augustine, but I worry about the law when I'm down there, too."

"Have you ever been south of here? Ever get down to Fort Brooke? Would you be able take a herd of cattle to a loading dock down that way?" Drag asked.

"No, I ain't been further south, but I ain't never seen a herd of cattle that I couldn't take someplace." It was apparent that Toke liked to brag about his cattle-stealing successes as long as the law was not around. "I even sent a couple of loads to Cuba. Now, that's a good deal, 'cause you git the cattle out of the Territory where they ain't seen. I got connections with a smuggler," he boasted.

"Let's go upstairs where there's not so many ears," Drag suggested.

The two men moved upstairs to Room Four and talked until almost daybreak. Finally Drag decided to lay out his plan. "I need a partner that can help me sell some of these wild Spanish cattle, and maybe some stolen cattle. When I locate cattle that can be picked off, I need someone that can take 'em to market and get rid of 'em fast. I would tell where to git the cattle each time, and where to sell 'em, but I wouldn't be connected with you except to plan the next job. I'm willin' to pay well and split the money fifty-fifty. My partner won't get filthy rich, but he could pull in a lot more than you and your crew make robbin' a few travelers."

"Would we have Injuns to fight?"

"Maybe, but most of the time I think not. But those Indian herds have been raided a lot lately, and they're fightin' for their land and cattle. If there was two or three hundred head someplace that could be gotten easily, you'd have to move the cattle fast and get 'em out of Indian territory. It's possible there might be some trouble."

"I'll have to talk to the boys. They worry about Injuns."

Drag decided they had talked long enough. He needed sleep, and besides, the smell of his future partner was becoming too much in the small room. "Okay," he said. "I'm gonna be around this area for about a week. If you decide you like the deal, meet me at Cap's eatin' place across the street, one week from tonight. Come alone. Don't bring your boys. If you come back, we'll decide then how we're gonna work the deal. If you don't show up, I'll know you ain't interested."

Toke stood and opened the door to leave. "By the way," Drag snarled, "I'll kill anybody who tries to double-cross me or who tells anybody who I am."

❖ ❖ ❖

Sure enough, Toke showed up in Cap's place one week later, just as he promised.

"I see you made it," Drag said, noting that Toke still wore the same dirty clothes and smelled worse than ever!

"Yep," Toke said noncommittally.

"Let's walk outside where we can talk private," Drag suggested, wanting to surround his new partner with some clean, fresh air.

"Better yet," Toke suggested, "let's ride up to my place on Black Oak Island. Won't nobody bother us there, and we can palaver about this deal without worryin' about other people."

So the next few days were spent in Toke's territory. Drag tried to think of some way he could make Toke "accidentally" fall in the river, but that opportunity never presented itself, and Drag finally conceded that accepting Toke as he was would be part of the price of working with him.

As they discussed their plans, the biggest problem seemed to be how Drag could contact Toke without raising suspicion.

"Tell you what," Drag decided. "I'll meet you in Jacksonville two weeks after the next full moon, and we'll make our final plans."

The two men shook hands, and Drag rode away, happy to fill his lungs with the fresh country air.

❖ ❖ ❖

After leaving Black Oak Island, Drag had spent the next week in the saddle, looking at cattle, talking to travelers and cowhunters, and trying to pick up as much information about the Florida Territory as he could.

As he had traveled southward along the Alachua trail from Georgia, Drag had heard a lot about a place called the Brown Owl Ranch. It was said to be a large ranch containing over 250 sections of land. They were able to carry more cattle than most ranches that size because they grazed some of the excellent grasslands formerly belonging to Seminole Indians. Reportedly, the Brown Owl headquarters was located on the western edge of the long ranch.

He had decided that his best bet would be to try to get a job at the Brown Owl Ranch, and he set out to find their headquarters.

Three weeks later, as he lay in his bunk at the Brown Owl Ranch, Drag thought about the days following that meeting with Toke Bannon in the Okefinokee Swamp and how satisfactorily his plans were progressing.

When Drag first rode onto the ranch, he had been careful not to mention that he had already secretly examined and assessed the eastern portion of the ranch. Zeke Mongol's unexpected hospitality seemed almost like an omen to Drag, convincing him that he was moving in the direction that Lady Luck was leading.

Now, sprawled on the hard bunkhouse mattress, he listened to the raucous, jovial jawing among the cowhands who had just finished their day's work. Someone across the room strummed a guitar and sang a sad, plaintive ballad.

Drag felt very pleased. If things continued to move according to his plans, he would one day be recognized as an important cattleman in the Florida Territory! He would have his own ranch, and cowhands such as these would answer only to him.

It occurred to him then that he should find a wife, preferably a daughter of a prosperous and highly respected cattleman; someone who could help him meet the right people. Together they could plan ways to help him grow and become a powerful figure in the new territory. He needed to lose his past identity in this new frontier and become a successful man, strong enough to defeat competition for land and cattle.

It seemed to Drag that there were cattle everywhere, just waiting for the strongest man to claim them. He needed a partner to take possession of the cattle after he located them, and Toke Bannon seemed to be just the man for that job. If rustling became necessary, Drag would not be involved in the actual stealing of the cattle. Surely no one could ever pin the rap on him, and he would never have to worry about going back to prison. That was all part of his brilliant, fool proof plan for wealth without risk.

Drag was suddenly jolted back to the present by the sound of the Brown Owl dinner bell and Zeke Mongol's loud voice echoing across the yard: "Come and get it!"

When Zeke Mongol called his men to supper, the bunkhouse emptied quickly, and Drag jumped right in with the gang. He hadn't had a decent meal in a week, and he was mighty hungry. He slung his long legs over the side of the bunk, ran his fingers through his thinning blond hair, and started for the house.

As he entered the eating area, Drag was surprised to see that all of the men wore guns. He had left his own shootin' iron in the bunkhouse.

Zeke smiled when he saw his guest cast a questioning look around the room, eyeing the guns worn by his men. "We been having trouble with rustlers," Zeke explained, "and the bloody Indians are bad right now. We started this ranch ten years ago and had to fight renegade Indians for several years. Then, for a long spell, we had good relations with the Seminoles, and things were quiet. But lately the rustling has started up again, and we've had a few cattle killed. The last time we took a herd to Savannah we lost about sixty head of cattle on the way and had one man killed."

Zeke did not tell his guest that he felt sure most of his rustling problems were coming from outlaws hiding in the Green Swamp area just south of the Brown Owl Ranch. He kept these thoughts to himself.

Zeke had been successful in solving his own problems for more years than he could count on both hands. His brand of justice was swift and harsh. If rustlers continued to steal his cattle, he would catch them. When he did, he wanted his men armed and prepared to deliver justice. Too, they needed to be ready if their headquarters were attacked by Indians. Zeke and his men would not be caught with their pants down!

Drag, wanting to learn as much as he could about the

ranch, tried to project only a casual interest as he prodded his host for information. "Do you have a family, Mister Mongol?"

"Just call me Zeke. No, I never had time for a wife, and I don't have any children that I know of. I had a sister back in London, but I don't even know if she's still alive, it's been so long since I've been there."

"You have quite a lot of men working for you," Drag observed.

Zeke eyed him suspiciously and took his time in responding. He helped himself to a cup of coffee from a chipped blue enamel pot. "Our land runs about a half-day's ride to the north, south, and east. It takes a lot of men to protect our cattle and land. Besides, it's getting near time to catch and mark calves." He purposely avoided telling Drag that some his crew were gunmen, hired more for their skill with a six-gun than a rope or blacksnake whip.

"Most of the crew have been with me several years," Zeke continued. "They're good cowhunters; they know how to use a gun and they like the challenge of building a ranch in this wild country."

He scratched his head and paused to size up his guest. Visitors were always welcome at the Brown Owl Ranch, but Zeke wanted to know more about this fellow. Was he just a traveler going south, looking for a job, or was there something more beneath the rough surface of this stranger? Zeke had a gut feeling that he needed to learn more about the man who called himself Drag. "Where are you heading for, Drag?"

"I'm just drifting through, trying to decide what to

do," Drag replied. There had been ample time in prison to concoct his story, and now he lied without flinching. "I've been out in Texas working on a ranch for several years, but Mr. Gomez sold his land and cattle to some Yankee, and I decided to get on my horse and come see what this new Florida Territory was all about. I got a friend near Fort Brooke that keeps pushing me to visit him. I might head down that way for a spell."

"Are you looking for work?"

"Depends." Drag did not want to sound too eager.

"Can you handle a gun?" Zeke asked.

Drag thought about Toke Bannon and his men hiding on Black Oak Island up in the Okefinokee Swamp, and coughed to cover up his smile. "Yessir, if I have to defend myself I can. I ain't never been one to use a gun except when needed." No need to tell Zeke that the last time he "needed" it was when he held up that Yankee traveling down the Natchez Trace on his way to New Orleans. He had stolen the man's horse and used his money to buy the clothes and supplies he needed before hastily heading for south Georgia.

"We might be able to use another man in the southern part of the ranch to replace the one killed on our last cattle drive to Savannah," Zeke said. "The pay is thirty a month and keep. Al Green is foreman of that division. I warn you, he expects a full day's work, but he's a fair man."

"I need a grubstake to take me on down the state. It might be okay to stay and help you out just until the end of branding season and then decide what I want to do." Drag pretended to be wrestling with his decision.

Zeke still didn't feel easy about this man. He wanted

to learn what made him tick. There was something about his story that did not seem to add up. Until it did, Zeke would not be in a hurry to commit himself by offering the man a job, although he sure could use the extra help.

Instead, he bought himself some time. "Al will be coming back into headquarters tomorrow. He does the hiring for that part of the ranch. If you decide you want to stick around and talk with Al, you're welcome to spend the night in the bunkhouse. One of the men will show you where to put your horse and saddle. You can make yourself comfortable until Al gets here."

"Thanks," Drag replied. "I reckon as how I might as well stay around to talk with him."

Zeke beckoned across the room to a lean, freckled-faced man who sauntered over to the table. As a manner of introduction, Zeke said, "Cal Whitney here is the foreman of the north part of the ranch. This is Drag Johnson, Cal. Show him where he can put his horse and gear for the night. He's gonna sleep in the bunkhouse tonight. He wants to talk with Al Green tomorrow."

Drag pushed away from the table and followed Cal outside. "This is mighty neighborly of you-all," he said. He unhitched his horse from the post and followed Cal out to the barn. Cal pointed to an empty stall. "You can put your horse in here. Hep y'self to the hay and grain there. It's kept for the crew to use."

"I'm much obliged," Drag offered, but Cal had already stepped out into the night. This pleased Drag, who was not accustomed to being given such unrestricted freedom.

After storing his saddle in the barn, Drag rubbed his

horse down and gave him a generous portion of the grain and hay. Unaccustomed to eating grain, the animal ate like a starved bear just coming out of hibernation. Drag held no special affection for the horse, but it did need to last him for a spell, so he was happy to have a little free feed to give him.

Returning to the bunkhouse, Drag climbed onto the same upper bunk he had used earlier and checked to make sure his gun had not been moved. Satisfied, he lay on his back, his head cradled in the palms of his clasped hands and his eyes focused on the knotty cypress rafters. He listened to the harmonizing voices of the cowboys, accompanied by the strum of their guitars, and felt pleased with the recent turn of events. It would be a stroke of luck if he could work on this ranch for a few months. He could discover exactly where their land began and ended, where their cattle grazed, and what lay beyond their southern boundary, and he could get to know Zeke's men.

Perhaps in time he might even have an chance to work on other parts of the ranch. He liked the fact that Zeke blamed his cattle rustling on Indians and outlaws in the Florida Territory. That kind of thinking would keep Zeke and his men on a wild goose chase, far away from the Okefinokee and Toke Bannon. And Toke Bannon was a very necessary part of Drag's long-range plan.

Too bad that Zeke Mongol didn't have a good-looking daughter! That part of his plan would have to wait.

5

TREFF'S ITCH TO GET HOME intensified with each slowly passing mile. Eight days had gone by since he had helped Hank O'Mara reach his small spread, and since then he had steadily ridden east. He continued to favor the hidden Indian trails rather than the better known paths between Pensacola and Jacksonville. Mail coaches from Pensacola, as well as most travelers in the northern part of the Florida Territory, chose the postal route south of the red hills when heading east or west. This popular route ran parallel to the Alabama-Georgia border and would have been much faster than the paths Treff followed, but in spite of his sense of urgency, Treff felt safer and more comfortable in the dark, secluded woods.

Two days ago, as he approached the Apalachicola River, he had been forced to temporarily abandon the secret paths and cut to the well-worn trail that led to the ferry.

He gave a gentle tug on the reins of his horse.

"Come on, Rojo. You deserve another rest and maybe a little treat, too."

As though he understood his master's words, Rojo turned his nose south and then east toward the river, stopping of his own accord when he reached the landing across from Bill Mitchell's small store and café.

Bill, a long-time friend of Treff and his family, owned and operated a lucrative business which included a ferry that crossed the Apalachicola River. Travelers from both directions kept the ferry in almost constant demand, and Treff knew that Bill Mitchell would be an excellent source of information.

Treff slid off his horse and unhooked an old iron bell that hung on a limb of a nearby cypress tree. He rang the bell hard and waited. In a matter of moments, he saw the big, clumsy barge separate itself from the east bank and begin to inch its way across the murky water.

"Why, Treff Ballowe! I ain't seen you in a coon's age!" The proprietor jumped off the ferry with his right hand outstretched. "Git aboard here and tell me what you been a-doin' since I seen you last. We'll go over to the café and get us some grub."

Grinning, Treff grabbed Bill's hand and pumped it. "Man, you don't know how good that sounds! I've been living on cold biscuits and jerky for the past six days!"

"Well, we can shore take care of that! Bring your horse and let's git started. I been hankerin' to talk to you ever since I heard you was a-comin' this way."

Treff was puzzled and a little alarmed. As he loosened the girth strap on his saddle, he asked, "Who told you I was coming?"

"Your men stopped in and got some grub a couple of weeks back," Bill said. "Told me they left you in Mobile tendin' to business. Said you'd probably be along directly, so I been on the lookout fer you ever since."

"Were all my men okay?"

"Yeah, but they had trouble with some Creeks back west a bit. Said they managed to settle without a fight, though. It seems like they had to give the Injuns some grub, so that left them short on rations themselves. They shore was a hongry lot when they rode in here."

Treff was relieved to know that his men had made it back this far, at least. "I'm sure you fixed them up with enough rations to get them the rest of the way home, Bill. If there's money owed, I'll settle with you before I leave."

As the ferry drew close to the east bank, both men anchored their feet on the slippery planks to brace themselves for the jolt against the landing. "Go on up to the café, Treff. As soon as I hitch this thing up here, I'll come up and fix our grub."

Treff led his horse off the ferry and across the sandy yard. He unfastened the saddle and lifted it from Rojo's back, just as Bill walked up behind him. "Can I borrow a brush for my horse and buy a bag of grain?" Treff asked.

Bill pointed to the barn. "Use anything you want, and take all the time you need. Whenever you git done, I'll be in the café stirrin' us up some grub."

After he brushed his horse and filled a bucket with feed for him, Treff walked inside Mitchell's Café and General Store to find Bill and settle the rumblings of his own hungry stomach. Bill specialized in hearty meals for traveling people, and Treff, draping his legs over a chair, sighed in happy anticipation.

"From the looks of that horse, it 'pears you been travelin' pretty steady," Bill observed. "I didn't expect to see you fer at least another week."

"Is anything unusual happening around this part of the Territory?" Treff asked. "While I was in Mobile, I received a message from Ace asking me to come home."

"Well, they's a few new settlers from Georgia and the Carolinas that's settled in the red hills. Some have brought along their livestock, and I hear rumors that He-with-One-Eye-of-an-Eagle and some other bands of Indians been rustlin' and killin' cattle belonging to them people," Bill replied.

Treff's blood boiled every time he thought of that one-eyed redskin who led the attack that had killed his parents. He hoped that some day he would have a chance to settle the score with that Indian who wore a patch over his left eye!

"Another thing," Bill continued, "I been hearin' how the Seminoles is startin' to git riled up over losin' some of their grazin' lands in the central part of the Florida Territory, and they're startin' to fight the new settlers that's movin' in."

"Have you heard anything from the Three Springs area?" Treff questioned. "We've always had good relations with the Seminoles, so I don't think they would cause a problem for us."

"No, I ain't heard nothin', but your ranch is so big that things happen all the time that we don't never hear nothin' about."

Treff was about to reply, but their conversation was

interrupted when a seedy herd of people straggled into the café.

"Kin I hep you?" Bill asked pleasantly.

"Yessir, I reckon you kin, if'n you're the feller that runs that ferry."

Treff was disappointed by the interruption of his visit with Bill, but perhaps these travelers could add something to the meager information he had thus far managed to gather. He turned to the tall, scruffy fellow who appeared to be the leader of the group. "Where are you folks heading?" he asked.

"We-uns is headin' toward Pensacola and then to the southern part of the Louisiana Territory," the man replied. "The wife has family south from New Orleans and we be on our way to see what it's like out yonder."

"Me an' the kids like what we see in this here land," his wife added, "but Pa here has a hankerin' to move on. We hear a lot of good things about that-there place." Several ragged children clung to her tattered skirt.

"Have you met with any trouble along the way?" Treff prodded, but the taciturn man only mumbled some indistinguishable words into his beard. He moseyed out the door, pulling his wife by the arm, and his fellow travelers straggled along behind them.

Bill pulled a few chips of rock candy from a jar and shoved them into his pocket. Those poor kids didn't look like they had ever tasted many treats. He followed the group out the door and down to the landing.

Treff followed along to help load the horses and wagon onto the ferry and offer assistance to the women and children. When all their belongings were loaded, the group filed on board. As they pulled away from the bank, Treff waved and hollered, "Good luck. Be watchful when you pass through the country north of Pensacola. There's a lot of outlaws out there."

As soon as Bill started across, Treff went in search of Rojo and found him contentedly nibbling grass behind the store. He saddled the horse and gave him a few more strokes with the stiff brush, and Rojo nuzzled him in appreciation. Treff was convinced that his horse had more sense than most of the people he knew.

By the time Bill returned from his trip across the river, Treff and Rojo were ready to ride.

"They was a very interestin' group of people," Bill said of the travelers he had just ferried across the river. "They was all of one family. That skinny lady was the wife of the tall man with the beard, and they brung along three younguns and both sets of grandparents. They're fixin' to start a newspaper."

"I wish them luck," Treff said with some misgiving. "They're sure going to need it!" After settling his account, Treff swung his leg over the saddle and reached down to shake Bill's hand. "Bill, it's been good to see you, and I wish I had time for a longer visit. Thanks for the good grub. I hate to eat and run, but Rojo and I best be traveling on. It's still a good ways to the TSR."

"I understand," Bill replied, "but I shore wish you could stay over fer a spell. A body gets lonely out here along the trail. Course, we see a heap of strangers every day, but that's not the same as old friends. If you could stay awhile, maybe we could do a little huntin'. We could shore use some fresh meat for the families around here."

"Maybe next time," Treff called as he rode away. "Good luck, Bill," he hollered over his shoulder.

As Rojo loped through the woods, Treff whistled to break the monotony. Although he remained alert and on constant guard, he encountered nothing that aroused his apprehension. The tall pines and occasional oak trees provided a cool canopy of shade for the horse and rider, and both were glad to be heading toward home.

But in spite of his serene surroundings, Treff was more than a little concerned about the things Bill had told him and about the earlier report from Chico. He took care to keep below the tree line and to avoid hills wherever possible. He kept an especially sharp lookout when he approached places that seemed conducive to ambush, and he slowed to examine any areas where he suspected that outlaws or Indians might hide. Was he delaying his journey needlessly by being overly cautious?

Treff usually made it his practice to stop during the middle of the afternoon. He would find a grassy place where Rojo could graze, and there he would build a small fire, boil some coffee, and cook his daily meal. After he ate, he was always careful to put out his fire and cover the area with leaves and sand to erase any evidence that he had stopped there. Then he would ride on until dark.

By old habit, he let no one know where he slept while traveling in the wilderness. When he found a safe place to sleep, he would stop for the night and, under the cover of darkness, lay his bedroll several miles from his fire and far away from the trail, thus sheltering himself from outlaws or malevolent strangers who might travel through the dark woods by night.

As the afternoon sun cast eastern shadows, Treff began to look for a place to stop, but a vague sense of uneasiness kept him moving. Treff had spent his entire life in the wilderness and was used to relying on his senses to alert him to possible danger. He learned long ago that men who failed to pay attention to their basic instincts often did not live long enough to talk about them. It was that kind of gut feeling that continued to plague Treff ever since he left the Apalachicola River. "Rojo," he said, "I'm not sure what it is, but I just feel like something is wrong. I keep feeling like someone is watching us." Rojo gave a snort which seemed to indicate his validation.

Several times during the day, Treff had hidden in the scrub and made a careful search of his back trail, but so far he had been unable to pinpoint anything. He had seen no unusual flight of birds that would warn of the presence of people, and putting his ear to the ground had revealed no strange noises or tremors. The air was still and quiet; almost too quiet. Treff observed that Rojo's ears twitched and that he seemed a bit nervous, but perhaps the faithful horse was only reacting to his master's unwarranted apprehensions.

This would be their last night before reaching the Three Springs Ranch. Surely no harm would come to them this close to home. Yet even as Treff tried to cast aside his suspicions, something inside of him seemed to sound a persistent alarm warning him to proceed with utmost caution.

As if in answer to his unasked questions, a sound of gunfire erupted, faint but distinct! Rojo heard it too, and his ears shot up. The sounds came from the direction of the Gruber place near the Pensacola mail route about three miles north. Treff touched his heels lightly to Rojo's flanks, and the pony needed no further urging to change directions and surge forward toward the noise.

The gunfire was irregular and intermittent, but horse and rider never slowed. They had covered about half the distance to the mail trail when Treff recognized the noise of running cattle. The gunfire sounded much louder now and definitely emanated from the Gruber homestead. Then he heard the dreaded whooping of Indians, the same sickening sounds he had heard on the day his parents died, and he realized that they were trying to either steal or kill the Grubers' cattle, and perhaps the family itself.

Taking his new rifle from its scabbard, Treff slipped from his saddle, ground-hitched Rojo, and crawled into a palmetto patch to see how many Indians they were up against. His heart beat wildly! Perhaps this might give him the chance he had waited for, the chance to see He-with-One-Eye-of-an-Eagle, to meet that devil face to face and settle the score!

John Gruber and his son were crouched behind a pile of logs, trying in vain to stop the vicious Indian attack. Even though the two men had managed to shoot a couple of Indians off their horses, they were badly outnumbered, with little chance to save their small herd of cattle.

Treff had been favorably impressed with the performance of his new rifle when he encountered Smitty and Squint. Now he could only hope and pray that the expensive weapon continued to give him the advantage.

This was another good time to put it to the test. Drawing a bead on the stomach of one Indian, he pulled gently but firmly against the trigger. The impact from the bullet knocked the Indian backward, but he held tight to the reins, pulling the horse over backward as both man and horse fell to the ground.

As the wounded Indian scrambled into the bushes, leaving his horse flailing on the ground, he looked back to learn the position of the extra gun and gunman. It was in that brief moment that Treff saw his victim's painted face clearly, and saw that he wore a patch over his left eye! There was no mistaking that evil face. He-with-One-Eye-of-an-Eagle was still alive and well, terrorizing the area with his marauding and pillaging!

Holding his horse on the ground as a shield, the one-eyed chief signaled some of his braves to attack the palmetto patch that provided Treff's cover. As the band of warriors bore down on him, Treff fired again and again and saw another Indian fall to the ground. He felt an arrow graze his leg but paid it no mind.

Across the yard, Tim Gruber yelled, "Pa, there's somebody hiding over there in them palmettos. I think he's trying to help us."

"I ain't never heard a gun sound like that, son," John Gruber replied. "Whoever it is shore is welcome. He knocked down the leader of them there Injuns with his first shot. Keep pourin' the lead to 'em, son. We need to hep that feller."

With the Indians' attention momentarily diverted to the palmetto patch, John and his son intensified their shooting. John shot one Indian and watched him fall from his horse before he felt the shock of an arrow hitting his right shoulder. Despite intense pain, he continued to fire alongside his son.

The unexpected renewal of fire power, coupled with the thundering sound of Treff's new rifle, finally caused the perplexed Indians to turn back and ride away without the Grubers' cattle, leaving four coppery bodies lying motionless on the blood-soaked ground.

As the band of Indians began to retreat, Treff's one-eyed nemesis crawled from the bushes and threw his leg over the side of his fallen pony. Before Treff could turn his rifle, the horse scrambled to his feet and raced away with his master clinging fast to his back.

Ignoring the throbbing pain in his leg, Treff lunged from his hiding place with only one thought in mind: catch the red devil and make him pay for his crimes. Only vaguely aware of the blood soaking his pant leg, Treff refused to stop until his knees buckled under him and he fell to the ground.

Treff was furious with himself! He-with-One-Eye-of-an-Eagle was getting away! After fifteen years of hoping to find the murderer and avenge his parents' death, he had only wounded him. If he had only seen that eye patch before he fired, he would have aimed at the red devil's heart instead of his stomach, and He-with-One-Eye-of-an-Eagle would now be dead! Treff's own wound was of little consequence to him at the moment, except that it had kept him from giving chase to his enemy and thwarted his long-awaited chance for revenge.

The arrow wound in the fleshy part of his left leg did not seem serious, but apparently Treff had lost more blood than he realized, because, when he tried to stand, his head whirled crazily.

John and Tim Gruber jumped from behind their log barricade at the same time that Treff tried unsuccessfully to stand. "Who is that feller?" John Gruber asked his son.

"John, Tim," Treff called. "It's me, Treff Ballowe." He made another futile attempt to stand before admitting, "I guess you're going to have to help me get out from the middle of these dang palmettos."

John Gruber, with an arrow still protruding from his right shoulder, hurried to help his friend, and young Tim was close behind. Leaning on each other for support, the three of them struggled through the woods toward the house.

They were halfway home when Maud Gruber met them. She took one look at the injured men, threw up her hands, and hollered, "John, stop! What in heaven's name do you think you're a-doin'?"

She made John sit down on a cypress stump. "Let me git a look at that thing," she said, gently fingering the end of the arrow that was anchored in her husband's shoulder. "You're lucky that thing is only in the fleshy part of your arm," she said. "Sit still and let me get some whiskey for you."

Hurrying to the house, she grabbed a bottle of whiskey and some clean rags and ran back to where her husband still sat dazed on the tree stump. "Here, honey, drink this. It'll make what we got to do a mite easier on you." While John had a couple of drinks, she examined Treff's leg and used a piece of rope to stop the bleeding.

"Treff, we be mighty beholden to you for helpin' save

our cattle. Our neighbors has had their livestock slaughtered by Injuns. We think these was prob'ly the same ones."

Beginning to feel better, Treff asked her, "Are your other children safe?" The Grubers' other two sons were both younger than Ten and Treff were when their parents were killed. Treff remembered how the Indians liked to steal children to use as slaves.

"Yeah," Maud said, "We have a special cupboard we use for storin' the corn we crack for bread. The boys are hidin' in the corn bin, safe as two little ole boll weevils." While she talked, she tore strips from an old cotton shirt and used them to bind Treff's wound. "That's a deep cut there, but you're plum lucky that arrow didn't lodge in your leg. If we can keep it from bleedin', it should heal all right."

She turned her attention to her husband, who sat on the cypress stump drinking whiskey and singing, his pain temporarily numbed and his words slurred by the effects of alcohol.

Maud very carefully removed his shirt, slipping it over the arrow. After pouring a generous shot of whiskey over his wound, she picked up a sturdy stick from the ground and placed it firmly between her husband's teeth. "Just clamp down on that, honey, and I'll try to do this the easiest I can," she told him, and he complied without argument.

"Treff, you and Tim are gonna have to hold John while I try to push this arrow the rest of the way through the muscle." Seeing her son cringe and pale, she tried to reassure him. "It's the only way, Tim. It's better than tryin' to pull it out. Now, you gotta be a man and hep me."

Clenching her teeth, Maud gathered her courage and gripped the arrow with both hands. She used all of her strength to push the arrow, and John let out a blood-curdling scream, letting the stick fall from his mouth to the ground, but the arrow did not move! Treff in his weakened condition found it almost impossible to restrain the tortured man, but with Tim's help they managed to hold him steady for another try. Pushing harder than she believed possible, Maud began to feel the arrow move just a tad.

Perspiration was running down her forehead, stinging her eyes and blurring her vision. She reached into her apron pocket and pulled out a remnant of the torn shirt she had used for bandages and mopped the sweat from her face. Blessedly, from a combination of shock and alcohol, John had passed out and offered no resistance at all when she resumed her task. This time, a hard, sudden shove pushed the arrow head through the flesh. "Gimme your knife, son," she commanded, and Tim quietly obliged. Maud cut the shaft of the arrow and gave a mighty tug to pull the rest of the arrow out. "Thank God that job is done!" she murmured, as she again wiped rivers of sweat from her face.

Treff helped her clean the wounds with whiskey, and she bound them tightly with the rest of the clean rags. "Now we gotta get him in the house. Where's Tim got off to?" she asked, looking around.

"Here I am, Ma. I'm comin' back to hep." She saw her son then, bending over a patch of palmettos, sheepishly using the back of his hand to wipe the vomit from his lips.

The three of them carried John into the cabin and

put him in the only bed in the small house.

After getting John settled, Treff went back outside to recover his rifle from the palmetto patch and bring Rojo up to the cabin. He reckoned he ought to bury those four dead Indians lying out there in the yard, but he didn't have the stomach for it right now, and he thought Tim had been through enough for one day.

He was halfway back to the house when he heard a low moan. After watching the warriors fall, it had not occurred to him that even one of them might have survived. He had thought all four of the Indians were dead, but if one of them was still alive, it gave him a new idea. Perhaps there was a golden opportunity for him here after all.

Turning the wounded man over, Treff saw that he had been shot in the right shoulder. In Creek dialect, Treff asked, "What is your name?"

The Indian glared at Treff with a mixture of hatred and fear in his eyes, but said nothing.

Treff continued to prod. "Which pony is yours?" The Indian still did not respond, but Treff noticed him glance at a pinto standing near the cabin.

Quietly approaching the pony, Treff was able to get close enough to grasp the reins and bring the pony over to where the Indian lay solemnly watching.

"How would you like to get on this horse and ride away?" Treff asked.

This grabbed the Indian's attention, as his eyes lit up with a spark of hope mixed with unmistakable distrust. What sort of white man's trickery was this? After a moment of hesitation, the Indian nodded guarded assent.

"We will help you on your horse soon," Treff promised, "but first I wish to give you a message to deliver."

When the injured man did not respond, Treff shouted at him. "Do you understand me?"

Again the Indian nodded his head.

"Good. Then this is my message. Tell the one who calls himself He-with-One-Eye-of-an-Eagle that Treff Ballowe is the man who shot him. Tell him I said he is killer of children, old people, and cattle, but that he is a coward who is afraid to face me. I am the Utinara Kid that he could not find when he killed my mother and father many years ago. I am still alive, and one day I will wear the feather from his hair. He is like a sparrow in the sky. He is nothing. I am the strongest! One day I will put another bullet in his weak body to go with the one he now carries."

The Indian's eyes filled with a hatred that overpowered his fear, and his anger loosened his tongue so that at last he spoke. "He-with-One-Eye-of-an-Eagle will kill you one day." He growled the words between clenched teeth.

"The only way he could ever do that would be to shoot me in the back. He is afraid to meet me face to face. He knows the Utinara Kid will wear the feather taken from his dead hair," Treff replied. He knew that the insult would present an irresistible challenge to the leader of that band of Indians. He hoped it would drive him to a degree of anger that would cause him do something foolish, and when that time came, Treff would be ready and waiting.

Tim, hearing voices in the yard, came out to see what was happening. Without another word, Treff and Tim slung the Indian onto his pony. They found a scrap of rope to tie his feet under the belly of his horse, making sure he would not fall off even if he passed out on his way back to his people.

Treff slapped the Indian's pony on the rump and watched them ride away toward the sheltering darkness of the pine forest.

6

"MARV!" HER MOTHER CALLED. "Rise and shine!"

Marv stirred slightly at the sound of her mother's voice, but she was reluctant to leave the comfort of her soft feather bed. It was the first time all week she had been able to enjoy the luxury of sleeping in her own room. She had been overseeing the Leon all week, filling in for Treff in the southern division while he was away. Although housing on the outlying divisions was adequate, there was just no substitute for her own bed and pillow. She buried her face in her goose-down pillow and drifted back into her interrupted dream.

"Marv, breakfast is ready," her mother called, louder this time. "Come and get it." Hearing no response, she raised her voice yet another notch. "Marvelous Abigail Dover, don't make me call again!"

Marv's feet hit the floor. Whenever Mama used that tone and called her Marvelous Abigail Dover, it signaled serious business and usually brought an immediate response. This time proved to be no exception.

Marv might be able to ramrod a crew of cowhunters all week out in the prairie country of the Leon Division, but when she came home on the weekends she knew who was boss of the Dover household.

After splashing cold water on her face and running a comb through her thick russet hair, Marv pulled on a plaid gingham dress and hurried down to breakfast.

Marv paused at the head of the table and stooped to plant a kiss on her father's cheek. "Good morning, Daddy."

Ace Dover was a hard-driving man, still in his prime at fifty years of age. Strands of silver crept around the edges of his red hair, but he was lean, unbent, and could fight his weight in bobcats. He could still outwork most of his cowhands, going strong after most of them sagged with fatigue, but when it came to his only daughter, he was as soft as a wad of cotton. "Good morning, little darling. We're mighty happy to have you back home."

Marv moved to the other end of the long dining table and kissed her mother's cheek. Then, circling the table, she took her place between Rusty and Ten. Across the table, her oldest brother, Jeremiah, sat with his wife, Cissy, and their three-year-old twins, Brad and Curry.

"Hey, look at the princess, strolling into breakfast in the middle of the morning," Ten said, with a smile on his long, tanned face.

"That's all right," Jeremiah added. "It just gave us more to eat. It's too bad you didn't get up on the first call."

"Yeah," Rusty chimed in, not wanting to be outdone by his brothers. "I just polished off the very last biscuit, heaped up with Mama's scrumptious guava jelly. Wish I'd of thought to save you one, Sis."

Marv's green eyes twinkled as she purposely ignored her brothers' friendly jibes. She smiled and said, "Cissy, how did you ever get mixed up with this family? There sure is a lot of hot air in this room."

Cissy, a pert, vivacious brunette, was born on a ranch near Cow Ford, before the little town on the St. Johns River became known as Jacksonville. Jeremiah had met her at a frolic one evening and married her only two months later. They had recently celebrated their fifth wedding anniversary, and the twins were the Dovers' only grandchildren.

"They kept all that hot air hidden until Jeremiah and I took the big step," Cissy said. "You'd think after they saw how good it turned out for Jeremiah, they might have been inspired to find wives themselves."

"I keep hearing about this one and that one," Marv replied, "but nothing ever happens! Maybe their reputation has finally scared all of the girls away."

It was a special time when all the family could be together, but because of their individual wide-spread responsibilities, it seldom happened. Today the one empty chair at the table was a stark reminder of Treff's absence.

"Francesca," Amaly called, "please bring another plate for Marv. She's put in a hard week. I expect she's extra hungry this morning."

Sunday morning breakfast at TSR was always a lavish affair. Bacon, eggs, hot fluffy biscuits, and rich fresh milk were served on Amaly's prize china and crystal brought from West Virginia years ago in carefully padded barrels.

After living on sweet potatoes, cornbread, sourdough biscuits, and jerked beef all week, Marv looked forward with happy anticipation to Amaly's good Sunday vittles, as well as a chance to catch up on all the family happenings during her absence.

"Daddy, when do you expect Treff to get back from Mobile?"

"We've been expecting him every day," her father replied. "The rest of the crew have been back about three weeks. If he got the note I sent him, I figure he should be here by now."

"I hope he hasn't run into trouble," Amaly worried aloud. "I know Treff is always careful, but things have sure been turned upside down with the increasing unrest between the army and the Indians to the east and south of us."

"Don't worry your pretty head about Treff, Amaly. That boy knows how to take care of himself."

Ace let his eyes linger on his beloved wife. The years had been good to Amaly. A charming Southern lady, Ace thought, who still resembled that beautiful city girl he had married thirty-two years ago.

Dealing with frontier life in the Florida Territory for the last twenty years had not been easy for her, Ace knew, but her strong yet tender personality had provided the glue that bound the Dover family into a close and devoted group.

Twenty years ago, Ace and Amaly, with their three

small children, had moved to the Florida Territory from West Virginia to claim a grant of 192,000 acres on the western boundary of Timucua, given to them in 1815 for service to the Spanish government.

When they reached Cow Ford on their way to their new home, Ace told them, "We better spend the night here so we can replenish our supplies. This may be the last chance we have, and from where we're headed, it would be a long trip back."

While shopping for supplies in Boody's General Store, Ace told the proprietor, "We need to hire a couple of good ranch hands. You wouldn't know of anyone, would you?"

Ed Boody took his time in deciding on a reply, sizing up the unfamiliar face, but finally he said, "A trail herd come through here t'other day and several of the cowhands decided to stay. You might check the Two-Bit Saloon."

"Amaly, I'm going across the street. You stay here and pick out whatever you think we'll need for the next month, and maybe Mister Boody will help you load up the wagon. Tonight we'll pull out to the edge of town and find a good place to park for the night."

"Ace, our wagon is almost full already. Pretty soon there won't be enough room left for the children!"

"Well, be sure you get enough supplies to last us. If we need to, we'll buy another wagon and a team of oxen to pull it. We can use the oxen to help clear our land when we get there."

Leaving Amaly busy buying supplies, Ace walked across the dusty street to the saloon. He started up the steps and noticed two rugged cowhunters sitting on the porch, whittling and chewing, talking to each other. Each wore a pistol on his hip and appeared strong enough to put in a good day's work.

Stopping on the top step, Ace introduced himself and told them, "I'm on my way west and south of here to claim a one-hundred-ninety-two-thousand-acre Spanish grant. I'm looking for two good men that know something about the Florida Territory, and who might be interested in helping to start up a new ranch. Would you know of anyone around here that might be interested?"

The two men exchanged questioning glances, and finally the older one answered. "I'm Lobo Savanne, and this-here is my pardner, Cotton Smith. We just left a cattle drive where no one knew what they was supposed to do. We ain't interested in playing nursemaid to a bunch of tenderfeet, but we'd like to hear more about what you think you're gonna do."

Lobo was lean and hard, and his sunburned skin was as rough as alligator hide. A flat, wide-brimmed hat covered most of his brown hair, but his clear green eyes projected honesty. Ace liked a man who looked you directly in the eyes when he talked to you. What's more, he and his clothes were fairly clean for having just left a cattle drive.

Ace turned his attention to the younger man. "Where do you come from, Cotton?"

Cotton stood well over six feet tall. His blond hair was undoubtedly the inspiration for his nickname. He had a ready smile on his face and a twinkle in his pale blue eyes. When he started to speak, Ace knew immediately that he had grown up in the South. "My folks had a cattle spread in Alabama," Cotton drawled, "but they got burnt out by Indians a few years ago. I been punching cows for other people for near-bout six years. I like the idea of starting something new, if I think it'll make a go of it."

The three men talked for several hours that afternoon, and the next morning, when the Dovers left town with their two filled wagons, Lobo Savanne and Cotton Smith went with them.

Life had been hard in their new home. While gathering cattle and building their log house near one of the many springs in the northern part of the Florida Territory, the Dovers and their men were forced more than once to fight rustlers and renegade Indians.

In addition to running the house, Amaly put a big priority on education and set aside part of each day to teach all of her children reading, writing, and numbers. She recognized the value that these skills could offer them in the years ahead. Standing on the threshold of this virgin frontier territory, she could visualize unlimited opportunities for those smart enough and strong enough to seize them, and she was determined to provide her children with those opportunities.

On the initial Spanish grant, there were three natural springs swelling the creeks and providing clear sweet water for people, cattle, and wildlife.

"Why don't we call it the Three Springs Ranch?" Amaly asked one day, and although additional springs were later found on properties the Dovers bought and added to their holdings, the original name remained through the years. Neighboring ranchers simply referred to it as the TSR.

In 1815, when the Dovers first claimed their land, pioneer cattlemen often established their herds by catching and branding the cattle that roamed the Territory. Deserted by former owners, these maverick cattle had run loose in the wilderness for many years and were wild and hard to catch. It had been difficult and dangerous work catching the cattle to mark and brand them. Cotton and Lobo were good cowhunters and had been a big help in getting the herd started.

Lobo was killed during an Indian raid just three years after starting the ranch, but twenty years later, Cotton had become a fixture with the TSR.

From the beginning, Ace had been careful not to put his brand on any Seminole cattle. "We have always enjoyed peaceful relations with the Seminoles," Ace liked to remind his men. "I aim to keep it that way."

Through the years, Ace managed to lay claim to another large ranch from a Spaniard to his north. Bit by bit, additional acreage was acquired from settlers who had either gone broke or left because of the hardships of life on this wild frontier.

Ace made certain that all transactions were registered at the courthouse in Tallahassee. He recognized the importance of establishing ownership before additional settlers moved into the territory, and he also registered his TSR brand and under-bit earmark.

In 1922, the town of Cow Ford became known as Jacksonville, in honor of Andy Jackson, but it still held a place in Ace and Amaly's memory as Cow Ford, where they hired their first two cowhands.

During the fifteen years since Ace and Amaly had

opened their home and their hearts to the two Ballowe brothers, their Three Springs Ranch had grown to 650,000 acres of good prairie and rolling hill land that produced excellent cattle for markets from Mobile to Savannah and as far south in the Florida Territory as Fort Brooke. Ace Dover and his four sons were recognized and respected as expert cowmen.

TSR was divided into four divisions. The Dovers had built their home on the original Spanish grant near one of the cool freshwater springs, so that they could have a springhouse for storing vegetables, milk, and meat. This area, known as the Central Division, was still the main headquarters for their extensive land holdings. The home had grown from a simple one-room, round-log cabin to the present square, hewn-log dog trot house with two rooms in a large attic and five rooms downstairs.

The Three Springs Ranch had become the largest ranch in the territory. Each son was the ramrod for one of the four divisions, and Marv filled in wherever she was needed. For the past six weeks, during Treff's absence, she had been running the largest division, the Leon, down near the Indian territory.

It always amazed Ace that anyone as beautiful as his only daughter could be such a competent cowgirl. Other women in the surrounding territory sometimes expressed disapproval at the way Marv straddled her horse and handled a gun, and she was often criticized for wearing dungarees, "just like a man!" But Ace was openly proud that his daughter could work a bunch of cattle and rough cowhunters as well as any of her brothers. Marvelous knew how to be hard-boiled all right, but seldom found it necessary because she substituted level-headed intelligence for angry outbursts. Ace had overheard cowhands puzzling over the almost constant smile that lit up her whole face. It made them wonder what she was up to. But whenever one of her men failed to do his job, he soon found out there was steel behind that smile.

In spite of all that, Ace thought as he watched his daughter enjoying her breakfast, Marv, like her mother, was a very charming, feminine Southern lady.

"Gramaly," Brad complained, using the name the twins called their grandmother, "I'm still hungry and Uncle Rusty said he ate the last biscuit!"

"No, Brad. There's plenty more in the kitchen. Don't pay any mind to your uncle's teasing. He just likes to worry his sister."

"I want some more, too," Curry piped up, not wanting to be outdone by his brother.

"Boys!" Cissy said. "Where are your manners? What kind of sons am I raising?" But she softened her words with a smile.

"You haven't even finished the ones on your plate," Ace gently admonished his grandsons. "Maybe you need more gravy on them."

Ace let his eyes circle the table. "Now that we're here together, I think we should discuss the rustling problem we're encountering recently." He turned his attention across the table to his youngest foster son, who managed the westernmost division of the TSR. "Ten, are you still having trouble with rustlers on the Fannin Division?"

"We don't lose many at one time, but we find small groups missing now and then," Ten explained. "Those wild cattle tend to stay in the same area all the time, so we can tell when some are gone. We trail them for a ways, but ain't never been able to . . . " Catching Amaly's look of disapproval, Ten corrected his grammar. "We *haven't* been able to find out where they go." Ten often let his speech slip into the vernacular of the men who worked beside him day in and day out, but he was careful not to let his tongue slip in the presence of Amaly Dover! He gave her a sheepish smile. "Sorry, Mama. Anyways, who-ever's stealing our cattle must be someone who knows how we operate and where we're working. There's two or three small ranches on our west border, but I don't think any of those people would steal cattle," Ten continued.

Jeremiah ramrodded Santa Fe, the division to the north of Central. "I hear rumors of a group of outlaws hid-ing in the freshwater coastal marsh, over around Fish Creek. Nobody I've talked to has seen them, but several small spreads along the edge of the marsh have reported losing cattle."

"There's a rumor that there may be another group of outlaws in the Gulf Hammock down south and east of the Leon," Marv told them.

"Ten," Ace asked, "have you hired any new hands?"

"Yes, sir," Ten replied. "In fact, we had to hire three cowhands when we did our last calf branding. We had one hand killed in a gunfight over near Hickstown, and another went back to South Carolina. Our calf crop was bigger this year, so it took more cowhunters to do the job. After we finished marking calves, we let two of the extra hands go, but one is still with us."

"During my last trip to Tallahassee, I heard that a

feller named Abe Zink had left Mississippi and was thought to be in the Florida Territory," Ace warned them. "Abe and several other gunhands work together, rustling cattle and robbing travelers. They're all top cowhands. They've rustled cattle in Texas, Alabama, Mississippi, and Georgia, but somehow they always manage to stay one step in front of the ranchers they hit."

Rusty, who managed Central, had been quiet during most of the talk, but now he spoke up. "I think one reason they haven't been caught is because they seem to plan so carefully. Sometimes one of them will work on a spread long enough to learn where the cattle are located and figure out the best way to steal some without being caught. I've heard they're so slick that some of the bigger outfits don't even know their cattle are gone until a month or two later."

"Where do they sell the cattle they steal?" Jeremiah asked.

"Apparently they work with a smuggler that sells the cattle in Cuba," Ace answered. "That way the cattle don't ever show up in Saint Augustine or down around Fort Brooke. They simply vanish from the Territory."

"Where would they meet the smuggler?" Jeremiah asked skeptically. "How could they keep the cattle hid while they're getting a group together?"

"Jeremiah, I don't know all the answers. Perhaps they load them on a boat near the mouth of the Suwannee River. Maybe they have another loading spot," Ace said. "There's no one that knows the woods in the Florida Territory better than Treff, and that's one of the reasons I sent for him to come back from Mobile, to see if he can find out what's going on."

"I keep a couple of cowhands in those two line shacks we have on the north end of the Santa Fe, and they haven't reported anything unusual happening there," Jeremiah said. "So far, the main problem we've heard about in the north has been with Indians coming out of Georgia and Alabama and killing cattle. They haven't bothered us, but some of the spreads to the west of us have reported cattle being killed."

Ace pushed his chair back from the table and moved his lean body to stand behind his wife. "Well, let's move on to more pleasant things. Today is for resting from the last six days of cowhunting. Amaly wants Marv and Cissy to help her with some things around the house today. Jeremiah, you and Rusty and Ten come with me, and we'll take a look at those cow ponies Cotton brought in from Georgia. You can each pick out some to use in your division, and we'll start breaking them. If we're forced to fight outlaws, we may need some extra horses."

"I'm going too," Brad declared, jumping up from his chair.

"Me, too!" Curry echoed, close behind him. "We're cowhunters, and we gotta go with the rest of the men."

Ace smiled at his grandsons. "Come on, boys. You can check out that new litter of pups old Linda Lou had."

As they put on their hats to leave, Amaly called after them, "Don't get so busy you forget to come to supper. It'll be ready about two hours before dark."

"Marv and Cissy," Amaly said when the three of them were alone, "I need your help today. Treff will be here for supper tonight, and I want to have a special meal for his homecoming."

"Mama, why didn't you tell us he was coming? When did you find out?"

Amaly could not answer Marv's question, because she didn't know herself. But somehow her maternal instinct always told her when one of her sons was returning after a long absence. She knew that Treff would arrive today, though she had told no one until now. "Something tells me he has had trouble on the way from Mobile," she said, "but I don't think it's too serious."

Marv had always known of Amaly's strange mystic power that gave her amazingly accurate glimpses into the future. She used to laugh when Amaly made this kind of prediction, but she learned long ago that she should never question Amaly's forecasts.

"Tell me what you want me to do," Marv said. She was happy to have this time with her mother and Cissy, and excited to think that Treff would soon be home.

While the three women worked in the house, Brad and Curry ran off to the barn to check on the new puppies, and the men walked down to the horse corral, where the cowhands were breaking a new bunch of ponies. In spite of the hard work involved, the men always enjoyed this break in their everyday routine. It gave them a chance to show off their riding skills and have a little fun.

Cotton Smith, seeing the Dover clan approaching, jumped down from his perch on the corral fence. A smile spread across his face. "How do y'all like these?" he asked, pointing toward the new group of horses.

Jeremiah gave the handsome horses a look of approval. "Where did you find these mangy-looking critters, Cotton?"

Ignoring the good-natured jibe, Cotton explained. "We heer'd about a group of horses for sale by a rancher in Georgia who wanted to move back up north. After we looked 'em over, we cut out eight that was too puny and didn't look like they could last workin' these palmetto woods. We made a good deal for the rest. They're larger than them cow ponies you find further south from here."

"They ain't too bad," Ten teased. "I reckon they'll do in a pinch, till you can get something better."

"By the way," Cotton said, without acknowledging Ten's words, "they're all up for grabs except that chestnut mustang in the corner. I've done put my name on that one."

"Aw, Cotton, I thought you knew horses better than that," Rusty said, "Why did you pick out such a ratty-looking, mean-eyed, funny-looking crow bait?"

"I tell you what," Ten offered, "just to keep you from being too embarrassed about riding a worn-out horse like that, I'll help you out and take it over to the Fannin. Maybe I can find an Indian who needs a some extra meat for his family."

Cotton just kept smiling. He knew he had found a horse to live with, and he was proud to know the other men thought so, too.

Several other ranch hands meandered over from the bunkhouse to watch the activity and lend a hand. After the horses had been divided into four groups, the real work began. Some of the horses needed shoes, and each of them needed to be marked with the TSR brand and ear under-bit. Most were not broken to ride and rebelled when saddles were placed on their backs.

There was much whooping and hollering as the horses bucked and twisted, trying to throw the persistent riders to the ground. Although it was a hot, dirty job, working with the horses turned into an afternoon of fun, providing a mental diversion from the growing concerns and unrest that seemed to be increasing throughout the Florida Territory.

7

WHEN THE SUPPER BELL RANG, work in the corral ceased.

"Time to wash up," Ace announced. "You boys give Cotton a hand here to get these ponies back in the holding pasture. I'll meet you up at the house."

Just as the cowhands released the last of the ponies into their holding pasture, a figure on horseback emerged from around a bay head in the west and approached the homestead through the Hazzard Prairie. As the rider drew closer, Ten was the first to recognize Treff and Rojo and breathed a sigh of relief that his brother had finally made it back from Mobile. In his eagerness to see him, Ten unhitched a pony and rode bareback across the pasture to meet him.

"Treff!" he called when he was within shouting range. "Man, am I glad to see you!"

"Ten, what's wrong? Is Mama okay? Sis? What's going on?"

"No, no, Treff. Nothing like that. Everybody here's okay." He turned his horse to ride alongside his brother. "How 'bout you, Treff? Are you all right?"

"Yeah, sure. I'm fine. But I got this letter from Ace that kinda worried me. What's eating him?"

"Well, we been having some trouble here at TSR, and Ace is convinced that you're the best man to handle it. But wait and let him tell you about it."

Cheers from the corral welcomed the traveler home as Treff rode toward the barn.

Jeremiah and Rusty greeted him with grins and shouts of welcome, visibly excited over their brother's return.

"So you finally decided to come home, did you?" one cowhand chided.

Another asked, "Did you enjoy that easy life while we were back here slavin'?"

Their easy banter left no doubt that the ranch hands were glad to have him back.

"It 'pears to me like you fellers are the ones who've been having a good time while I was away," Treff said, turning his gaze toward the pasture. "Those are some pretty nice ponies I saw you turn out. Where did you find them?"

"Cotton made a deal with some guy in south Georgia," Rusty explained. "Would you like to trade Rojo in on a good horse?" He grinned, knowing already the answer to his question.

"I reckon not, but they do look like a pretty strong group. Cotton did a good job when he found those." Treff slid out of his saddle and gave a nod of approval.

While he unsaddled Rojo and stored his gear, Treff pressed Ten for more information. "Ace never asked me to come home early before. What seems to be the problem?" He continued brushing Rojo while they talked.

"Things are getting pretty touchy around here lately. The Seminole Indians have killed some of the new settlers, fighting to protect their grazing rights," Ten explained.

"And that's why he sent for me to come home?" Treff asked.

"No, there's more. We think we've been losing some of our cattle from the Fannin and maybe the Santa Fe, and Ace thinks it's urgent for us to tighten security as much as we can."

"So where do I fit in?"

"I'm not exactly sure what kind of an idea he's cooking up, but you can bet your best pair of boots that he's got a plan, and I guess he means for you to be a big part of it."

Treff gave Rojo some hay and a scoop of grain. Then, picking up his saddlebags, rifle, and bedroll, he followed his brother to the house, making a great effort not to limp.

Ace, Amaly, and Marv met him at the door and welcomed him with hugs and laughter. Pulling himself out of their embrace, he grinned. "The best part of a trip is coming home," he declared. "We have a lot of friends all through the Territory, but it's just not the same as being with my own family. Yep, it sure is good to be here!" he confirmed, as Amaly and Marv grabbed him again and smothered him with affection.

Cissy tried to grab hold of the twins as they raced around the room shouting, "Yipee! Uncle Treff's home!"

After the men washed up, Ace ushered them toward the dining room, where Amaly and Marv and Cissy had arranged fresh flowers on the best tablecloth and covered it with enough food to feed an army.

As the family gathered around the supper table, everyone began to talk at the same time, loudly rejoicing to have their family circle complete once more. They paused while Ace said grace, but at the sound of his hearty "Amen," the cacophonous chatter began anew.

"Did you bring me a present, Uncle Treff?" Brad begged.

"Did you shoot any bad guys?" Curry wanted to know.

"Hush, boys," Cissy commanded. "Finish your supper and let your uncle eat in peace."

"It sure is good to see you, son," Ace said when he could get a word in edgewise. "We've been concerned about whether you got our message."

"Yes, sir. Lenny gave me your letter, and I left immediately the next morning, but it's been a slow trip back. I came through the woods instead of the mail route. There were a couple of delays along the way." Table conversation ceased, and all ears hung on Treff's words as he began to relate his experiences.

He saved the best for last. "I ran into He-with-One-Eye-of-an-Eagle." Treff's eyes turned to steel when he mentioned the name of his hated nemesis. "His band of outlaws are killing cattle brought in by some of the new settlers in the Territory. I'm happy to report that I left a bullet in him, but I'm mad as heck that he got away alive. I still hope to meet that rascal face-to-face, and I'm pret-

016875

ty sure I will before long. I sent him a challenge that will make him lose face if he doesn't do something. But now we'll *really* have to keep a sharp eye on things in the northern part of the ranch."

"Oh, Treff!" Amaly protested. "Let go of that hate, son. It's not worth getting yourself killed for!"

"Don't worry, Mama. That red man thinks he's the biggest toad in the puddle, but he's just a little ole tadpole to me, not even worth a cup of water to swim in."

"His bunch has been raiding south Georgia and the northern part of the Florida Territory for a long time," Jeremiah put in. "It seems near-bout impossible to catch 'em. I wonder where they have a hideout."

"I don't know," Treff replied, grinning sheepishly, "but there are three less in their gang today. We had a little meeting at the Gruber spread yesterday that left three of 'em dead. It's too bad their leader wasn't the fourth. That new rifle worked real good. Y'all are gonna like those. We need to be sure and carry them whenever we go out to work."

It was so good to be home, Treff thought again, as he feasted on Amaly's perfectly cooked deer tenderloin, collard greens, sweet potatoes, and beaten biscuits.

"Save room for dessert," Amaly warned them. "Marv made fresh blackberry cobbler, and Cissy made her brown-sugar apple pandowdy."

"I want pandowdy," Curry declared.

"I want some of both," Brad said, trying to out-do his brother.

"If you don't sit up and eat like gentlemen, you might not get either," Jeremiah threatened his sons, but his smile took the edge off his threat.

After supper the family drifted out onto the spacious porch that spanned three sides of the house, to continue their conversation over mugs of steaming hot coffee.

"You know," Ace mused, "most of our cattle tend to be clannish. A group will cluster up with a lead animal and pretty much stay in one area. They might wander a little when grass gets short or when the woods are burning, but our cowhunters are good about keeping up with them, and they pretty well know where to find them. Ten thinks we've lost part of two groups recently. He thinks we're missing about sixty head."

"Ten, are you sure those cattle haven't just wandered away to find better grazing?" Treff asked.

"Not likely, because we have eight or ten calves that have lost their mammies," Ten replied. "You know they would have followed the cows if they could. And we're missing a bunch of older steers that were about ready for market. A few of those steers might hide in a palmetto patch or swamp, but mostly they like to stay together."

"Do you have any idea what's happening to them?" Treff asked.

"Well, the way I figure it, our cattle are scattered over such a large area that if they're being stolen, it has to be by someone who knows where they are," Ten answered.

"What about the other divisions?" Treff asked.

"Jeremiah thinks he might have lost some steers," Ace said, "and some of our neighbors to the west have complained about losing grown cattle."

Rusty said, "We've been getting reports from some of the hands in Central that the Seminoles have been losing calves from the Payne's Prairie herds. It sounds like someone is swinging a pretty wide loop on the north and east sides of their herds during branding time."

"Last week I heard the Romeo Ranch south of us lost quite a few head, but I don't have any details," Marv added, "but we don't think we've lost any from Leon. Daddy, have you told Treff what you told us the other day about that outlaw from Mississippi?"

"What's that?" Treff asked, arching his eyebrows.

Ace repeated what he had told the others earlier in the week. "The last time I was in Tallahassee, I heard a rumor that Abe Zink had left Mississippi and was now in Florida. His group has been robbing and stealing all the way through Texas, Alabama, and Mississippi."

"I stopped by Chico Leon's on my way home," Treff said. "According to Chico, Zink was in the Pensacola area when we took the last group of steers to Mobile. Zink lost a couple of his gang there when some Pensacola cattlemen invited them to a necktie sociable. That was about six weeks ago," Treff said, "and, according to Chico, the out-laws were headed this way when the posse lost them. It's possible they could be doing some of the rustling, but there are some other outlaws in the coastal swamps west of us. And don't forget about that thieving Godwin family living in the swamp south of us. We've known for a long time that they swing wide loops."

"We had a visitor stop at Santa Fe on his way to Pensacola about a month ago," Jeremiah said." He told us about some rustlers in the south that had been loading cat-tle on board a boat and selling them in Cuba. Do you think something like that might be happening up here?"

"I wouldn't rule out the possibility," Ace said. "How did they know that was happening? Have they caught any of 'em yet?"

"This fellow told me Pablo Munez of the MP Ranch had caught one group and hung them on the spot. That seemed to put a stop to their problem, at least for now."

"Well, it hasn't stopped our problem here," Marv declared. "It's a real mystery. Hard as we try, we can't find any stolen TSR cattle, yet they continue to just disappear."

Ace pounded his fist on the porch railing and spoke emphatically: "We've got to find out what's going on, and put a stop to it before we have any more losses! We must find out who is rustling our cattle, and that's the reason I sent for Treff to come home. I want him to spend whatever time it takes to try to find some answers.

"Marv is doing a good job. She could continue managing the Leon. This would leave you free, Treff, to spend time in the woods and to visit with our neighbors. Times could get hard if the army and Seminoles begin to fight another major war. We need to protect ourselves the best we can."

"Ace, if I do that, I'd need Paul Billy to go with me," Treff said. "That Seminole is the best tracker I know." Turning to his sister, he asked, "Do you think you can get along at Leon without him, Marv? He is held in great respect among the tribes, and he would make my job a lot easier. Besides, it would be better to have two of us, in case we needed to send back a message to some of you."

"I'd have no problem with Billy going with you," Marv said. "Right now, we're at a time when work is slack. We may help the Moores do some calf branding in a couple of weeks, but that can be done without Paul Billy." Secretly, she felt relieved that her brother would not be traveling alone.

"Treff," Amaly spoke sharply, "did I see you limping as you walked up from the corral?"

Treff had hoped no one would notice. The wound was not greatly bothering him. Looking innocently at Amaly, he said, "Oh, Mama, I just got a little old scratch when I was fighting with the Indians at Grubers' place. It really doesn't amount to anything."

"How did you get that little old scratch, Treff?" Amaly knew Treff didn't want to discuss the matter further, but her piercing eyes demanded an answer.

Like a cornered jackrabbit, Treff finally had to admit that he had been shot with an arrow.

"Let me look at that right this minute," Amaly insisted, striding toward her son. His brothers whooped with laughter, seeing Treff obliged to obey the orders of the real boss of the Dover household! But a careful inspection revealed that Maud Gruber had done a proper job of cleaning and bandaging the cut. "It looks pretty good," Amaly admitted, "but you are not fixing to go back out in the woods until that wound is better healed. It will be at least a week before you can leave."

"Oh, Mama . . . " Treff started to protest, but Ace held up his hand.

"Treff, you know your mother makes those kinds of decisions in this house. I can't send you out until Amaly says it's time."

"That's all right," Treff agreed, though not out of choice. "I'll need a week to get ready, anyway. Rojo can use

a few days of rest and I want to check on a few things."
He turned his most winsome smile in Amaly's direction.
"But I would like to talk to Paul Billy tomorrow, if he can
be reached. I'll have some work for him to do before we
start."

"Leave that to me," Marv assured him. "I'll take care
of getting him here."

"Thanks, Sis." Treff stood and stretched. "You know,
folks, it sure is gonna be good to sleep in my own bed
tonight. The last two weeks have been mighty busy. I
believe I'm about ready to go inside. The mosquitoes are
beginning to bite out here."

Treff went in the house, walking slowly, trying hard
not to limp, and the rest of the family followed.

A long-time custom at the Dover Ranch was to
have a few moments of devotion every Sunday night
before blowing out the candles. Seated around the table,
they watched Ace lift the family Bible from the shelf and
listened as he read a passage of scripture. Every head was
bowed as Amaly said a short prayer, remembering to give
thanks for Treff's safe return. Afterwards, they all went
quietly to bed, realizing that the next morning would
begin another busy week.

Caleb nosed his ship gently against the weather-beaten
pilings in Mobile Bay and watched Juan secure the
anchor and lash the ship to the pilings. Leaving Juan to
stand guard, he lowered the dinghy into the bay and
rowed slowly toward the saloons that lined the waterfront.

His first stop was the Frog Eye Saloon, owned by his

old friend, Honey Black. Caleb never did know if that was her real name, but the two of them had been partners in the smuggling business for a long time. In fact, Honey was part owner of the boat he used to haul his stolen cattle to Cuba.

They also enjoyed each other's personal favors. Whenever Caleb was in Mobile, Honey's other boyfriends knew enough to sit on the sidelines and wait until he left. Caleb always eagerly anticipated spending a few days and nights enjoying the comforting companionship of his favorite girlfriend.

Caleb admired her long brown hair, the color of fresh-roasted coffee beans, and was totally unaware of the increasing efforts she had to put into maintaining that color. Almost six feet tall, Honey's once trim and youthful body was no longer slim, but she took great pride in dressing to accentuate her voluptuous curves and walked in a way that made sure they could not be overlooked. She was famous for the hickory club she always wore at her waist. Her dark brown eyes never missed anything going on in her place, and she didn't hesitate to use the club on anyone who got too rough.

Honey managed to know everything going on between Mobile and Pensacola. She and Caleb had profited from that knowledge more than once.

Her merry eyes lit up when Caleb came through the swinging doors of the saloon, and she hurried to embrace him. "Caleb!" she exclaimed. "I didn't expect to see you for several months. What brings you to Mobile at this time of the year?"

"I just couldn't stay away from my favorite gal," he said, pulling her close and smiling.

"Hah, I know that ain't so. You must need something other than my tender loving care."

"Tender loving care comes first, you beautiful thing," Caleb said, caressing her between the shoulder blades. "What time do you close?"

"Sugar, you know we don't hardly ever close, but Fat Sally can look after things. It ain't been very busy tonight, anyway. Let's go upstairs."

❖   ❖   ❖

Much later, propped against soft pillows in Honey's comfortable rooms over the saloon, Caleb enjoyed one of his favorite Havana cigars and a glass of her best bourbon that never reached the lips of the downstairs customers. Honey, still half asleep, slowly opened one eye and asked, "Are you ready to tell me the other reason you made the trip to Mobile so soon after your last visit?"

Gently caressing her soft shoulders with his callused hand, Caleb murmured, "We got big trouble, Honey. Hurley got hisself caught rustling cattle, and him and his three men was hung. Now we got no way to get any more steers. We need a new contact person. I thought I'd try to locate Abe Zink to see if we could make a deal, but I don't know where he's at. I figured you might know."

"The last thing anybody saw of Abe, he was heading east with a posse on his tail. He lost two men in the chase, but Abe and the others escaped when they got near the Blackwater River."

"Who could I talk with that might know how to put me in touch with him? Or maybe you know someone else for the job. We gotta find somebody right away to furnish us cattle for the Cuban trade. We need to make good use of that market while we still can."

Honey thought for a moment. "Abe would be the best, if you can find him. You might stop at Slim's Dugout in Apalachicola and talk with Gimpy Lysek. Then your next best bet might be Maceo Durango who has the Hideout Bar down at the Hittenhatchee River. One of them might could help you."

Honey snuggled against his chest and lay silent for a few moments before she ventured, "Caleb, have you ever thought about hooking up with one of the bigger cattle-men in the Florida Territory and doing this thing legal-like? You might not make as much money, but at least you wouldn't have to worry about having your neck stretched!"

"Aw, Honey, I don't think I'm ready to do something like that," Caleb replied.

Honey smiled to herself. She could tell by the way he dragged out his words that she had planted a new idea in his mind.

Caleb put his cigar in his empty whiskey glass, rolled over, and pulled her into his arms. "Those are all good ideas," he murmured in her ear, "but I got a better one."

The next morning Caleb rose at daybreak and left the upstairs comfort of Honey Black and the Frog Eye Saloon to cast course for Apalachicola.

Located at the mouth of the Apalachicola River, the

small fishing village had rapidly become a booming sea-port. Georgia cotton growers in increasing numbers were using the river to ship their product to New York garment mills. The river was heavily populated with boats that docked at the seaport, providing a lucrative business for the saloons and gambling halls that lined the streets of the waterfront. With no law officers in Apalachicola, outlaws felt safe to stop here for supplies. While purpose-ly appearing to relax and rest from their travels, they can-nily ferreted out gossip and rumors that told them where money or treasures might be available for theft.

Caleb eased his boat into the bay and dropped anchor. He used the dinghy to row to the docks and soon found his way to Slim's Dugout, where he introduced himself to Gimpy Lysek. Gimpy had obviously been a seaman at some time in his life. A large, elaborate model of a schooner held a prominent place in back of his bar and was reflected in the clear glass mirror. He wiped the bar with a greasy cloth. "What'll you have?"

Caleb ordered a shot of straight bourbon and a full bottle, and slung a couple of gold doubloons across the counter. "Keep the change." He sipped his drink and looked around to make sure no one else was within earshot. Then, lowering his voice, he said, "Honey Black, up Mobile way, said to see you. I'm trying to locate Abe Zink about a business deal. He's supposed to be in these-here parts, and she thought you could help me."

A skinny, mean-eyed, dried-up man, with a limp that had given him his name, Gimpy had seen too much of the dark side of the world to trust anyone. "Whatcha want to see him about?"

Caleb did not want to spread that word around, so he pretended not to hear the question. "Abe and I done a little business in the past, and I'd like to catch up with him. For old time's sake, you might say."

Gimpy caressed the gold doubloons in his palms and eyed his new customer thoughtfully. It never hurt to encourage the friendship of a man with deep pockets. "Abe and his men have been in a couple of times," he finally admitted, "but I haven't seen them for over a week."

"Do you know how to find 'em?"

"No," Gimpy replied. "Abe has lasted a long time by not telling people where he can be found."

"I'll be staying in town for three days. I'll come by to have a drink every evening about sundown. If Abe comes in, tell him Captain Caleb has a deal for him. If I find him, it will be worth his while, and yours, too."

Caleb needed to replenish his supplies and get more firewood for his boat. He spent the next three days making his purchases, stopping in every saloon and gambling hall in town, discreetly asking questions that might lead him to Abe Zink. He had almost given up the search for the outlaw when, on the night before he planned to leave for Hittenhatchee River and the Hideout Bar, he sauntered into Slim's Dugout. He approached the bar and purchased another bottle of bourbon.

Gimpy caught his eye and jerked his head in the direction of the back. "I got someone you need to meet," he growled.

Signaling Caleb to follow, Gimpy took him into the back room where a slender young cowhunter was seated at a table, obviously enjoying a robust meal piled on a tin plate.

"This is Tommy Gohn. He might know how to get in touch with the fella you want to see." Without further comment, Gimpy turned and left the two men to themselves.

Tommy cut his thick steak into small bites and chewed it slowly, studying the newcomer with dark, suspicious eyes. Caleb noticed that he ate awkwardly with his left hand, while his right hand was never far from the gun strapped to his hip.

After a few minutes, Tommy asked, "What did Gimpy say your name was?"

"My name is Caleb."

"What do you do?" the young man asked.

Caleb felt certain Tommy already knew the answer to that question, but he said, "I'm a steamboat captain. I haul produce here and there."

Tommy said nothing. He only chewed his meat and continued to stare at Caleb.

Caleb was fast running out of patience. "Look here, man. I'm trying to find Abe Zink. He and I done a little business in the past, and I think I have something he might be interested in."

"What kind of business?"

"That's between him and me; it is not your business," Caleb said. "Gimpy told me you might know how I could reach Abe. If you can't do that, I don't want to waste any more of my time." He started to rise from his chair.

"Hold on, don't be in such a hurry," Tommy said. "I

can reach Abe, but I don't know when. I don't know you, and I don't know if I should tell him you are looking for him. I gotta decide."

"I'll tell you this *once*," Caleb stated coldly. "I am going to weigh anchor in the morning and go to the Hittenhatchee River. I'll be at the Hideout Bar. If you see Abe, you tell him Captain Caleb is trying to see him and let him know where he can find me. It'll be a safe place for him to come. I'll wait a couple of weeks, and if he don't show up, I'll go on down to Fort Brooke and look for someone else. If you do see Abe, I suggest you decide to tell him I want to meet him. Abe don't like fellers inter-fering with his messages, and he might be very angry."

Without another word, Caleb picked up his bottle, stalked across the room and out the door, letting it slam behind him.

8

THE DAY WAS STILL NEW when Jeremiah loaded his family into their wagon to return to the Santa Fe on Monday morning. The twins hung out the back of the wagon, waving good-bye.

"Don't let the Injuns shoot you again, Uncle Treff," Brad shouted. "Gramaly might not let you come to see us anymore."

Treff laughed and waved to his nephews until they were out of sight.

Ten and Marv had already packed their saddlebags and ridden out before daylight to return to their divisions and begin the week's work.

Amaly sent generous parcels of food with each of her children and stood on the front porch to watch them ride away.

Treff was anxious to begin his search for clues that would shed light on the mysterious disappearance of cattle, but Amaly's unwavering ultimatum blocked his plans.

Instead, he cornered Rusty as he was leaving to check cattle on the western boundary of Central, hoping to learn more from him about the locations of the missing cattle.

Rusty stood slightly taller than Treff, and although the two were not blood related, they shared the same muscular build and clear blue eyes. Rusty was the prankster of the four boys, but when it came to cattle, he was all business!

"The big steers Ten lost were on the Boot Prairie, next to the Suwannee River," Rusty said. "His men saw the group about four weeks ago, but then, just two weeks later, his range riders couldn't find hide nor hair of them."

"What about the cows he lost?"

"They were in a brood herd about fifteen miles from the steers, in the northeast corner of the division. The cowhunters noticed some calves that had lost their mammies and looked around to see if they could find them. That's when they realized they were gone. There weren't any buzzards circling overhead, and they didn't find any dead cows, so it beats me where they could've got off to. The cows were grazing some of that good Wacacha Marsh grass. It's just not natural for them to wander away from that."

"Wasn't there anything that looked suspicious? Horse tracks, cattle hoofprints, or anything like that?" Treff pressed for even a small detail that might have been overlooked, that could shed some light on the mystery.

"I went over there myself and helped Ten search the area. We thought we found cattle prints of the big steers going into the Suwannee River, but we couldn't find anything on the other side to show they had come out."

Treff scratched his blond head thoughtfully. "Rusty, Ace told me that Ten hired three new cowhunters during the last couple of months."

"Yeah, Ten put on three new hands during calf-marking season. Two of the fellas moved on when we finished, but one is still with us. Why?"

"What's he doing now?"

"He's working on a dam we're building across Dubee Creek. He wanted a job with our range-riding crew, but we needed him worse where he is."

"When will the dam be finished?"

After calculating for a few moments, Rusty replied, "They should be through by next weekend. It's just a small dam to hold some water up for a group of cattle we want to keep in that area."

"Can you and Ten get along without him?"

"I'd need to check with Ten, but I think we could manage okay without him," Rusty said. "What are you getting at, Treff?"

"Just a hunch. How 'bout letting him go when they get through with the dam. If you want to, y'all can tell him we'd like to use him again when you have more cow work."

"Sure, I believe we can do that."

"When Paul Billy gets here, I'd like for y'all to ride by the dam so you can point out that new man to him. Be sure you don't let the new man see Billy, though, because I plan to have Billy follow him for a couple of days when he leaves, to find out where he goes."

"I dunno, Treff. I hadn't thought of that. Maybe you're on to something."

"Don't let any of the cowhands get wind of what we're doing," Treff suggested. "If the new man begins to suspect our plans, it could blow the whole deal."

Rusty picked up his rifle. "I better get going, Treff. I got a crew fixing to brand some new cattle in the Balboa pen. Come on out to the barn while I saddle up."

Glad for a chance to check on Rojo, Treff limped out to the barn with Rusty. While Rusty was saddling his horse, Treff gave Rojo a thorough brushing. When he bent to scoop up some grain, Rojo nuzzled his back in appreciation.

Treff checked his horse's feet and found them in good condition. He petted Rojo on the neck and rubbed him between his ears. "You sure get spoiled in a hurry, don't you? I want you to get rested up this week, 'cause we're fixing to have a couple of busy weeks after this." Rojo bobbed his head as though he understood.

Rusty, mounting his horse, cast a sympathetic eye at his brother's injured leg. "Don't worry about the new man, Treff. We'll take care of everything. You just take care of that leg and keep Mama happy."

After Rusty rode away, Treff hobbled back to the ranch house to find Ace and tell him about his newly made plans.

He went to his room to collect his two saddlebags before heading for the main office to give Ace the rest of the gold from the Mobile cattle sale.

Many cowmen just kept their gold wherever they could find a pot to hold it, but not Ace Dover! Ace had a secret safe hidden beneath the floorboards of his office where he cached his gold. Occasionally he put small amounts of it in a bank in Tallahassee, but he was not absolutely certain how far he trusted the man from Boston who owned the bank.

When Treff walked into the office, Ace looked up from his ledger, pleased to see him. "Come in, son. How's the leg?"

Treff shook his head. "It's real tough, Dad, just sitting around waiting for this thing to heal."

Ace was touched, and coughed to cover his emotion. Although their mutual affection was evident, Treff seldom called him "Dad." Calling Amaly "Mama" had rolled naturally and easily from the mouths of the two orphaned boys, but to ten-year-old Treff, his benefactor and guardian had remained simply "Ace" except in times of extreme stress and tension.

Ace could sympathize with his impatience. "I know you want to get started, Treff, but I've learned through the years to respect Amaly's decisions. Her hard ways are born out of love, and experience has taught me that it's usually best to listen to her."

"I know that," Treff agreed. "I'm trying to be patient."

"Have you had a chance yet to visit with Rusty?"

"Yes, we had a long talk this morning. I'm waiting for Paul Billy now. I want him to do some tracking this week that can best be done by one person. Rusty and Ten are going to let that new man go as soon as they get the Dubee Creek dam finished, and I want Billy to follow him for a day or two. It might be interesting to find out where he heads for."

Treff hoisted the two heavy saddlebags and let them fall on Ace's desk with a satisfying thud. "We had a good cattle drive to Mobile," he said. "We ran into a little trouble with some rustlers, but we took care of them. The cattle arrived in good condition, and everyone was satisfied. In fact, they said they want another herd right after the first of the year."

"You have any problems with Indians?" Ace asked.

"Not really, but I understand they are bothering some of the new settlers, and I heard they've been a problem to some herds being driven north to Alabama markets. The only Indians I saw were that bunch I tangled with at the Grubers' spread. I heard Cotton met up with a different group on his way home, but he got by with giving them some grub."

"Yeah, Cotton told me about that. It'll be interesting to see if anything comes out of this new idea of yours. What other plans do you have up your sleeve?"

"For one thing, I want to check on that rumor about Abe Zink being in the Territory. He could be involved in the problems Rusty and Jeremiah are having."

"Yeah, from what I hear of him, we don't need his kind around here."

"I'll see what I can find out about him."

"The thing that puzzles me most about this whole situation is what happens to the cattle after they're stolen," Ace said. "Jeremiah says they just seem to disappear. Last time I was in Tallahassee I heard about that rustling deal down south that Jeremiah was talking about yesterday. Stolen cattle are shipped to Cuba, and once the cattle are gone, there's never a trace of them. Maybe we need to look at that possibility."

"Another concern of mine," Treff said, "is the war

that seems to be breaking out again with the Seminoles. We've always worked well with the tribes in the past, and we need to do everything we can to preserve that fragile peace."

As father and son continued to discuss cattle problems, they gradually became aware of the distant beat of a horse's hooves. Treff walked to the window and pulled back the curtain in time to see the rapid approach of a horse and rider, trailed by a cloud of dust.

"That's Paul Billy," Treff said, and went outside to meet him.

Paul Billy had worked for the TSR for fifteen years, ever since the day Ace Dover helped him recover a bunch of cows stolen from his small herd.

Orphaned in infancy, Billy was never certain of his exact age, but his best guess was that he was forty-four. A quiet, slender Indian, he had spent his entire life in the wilderness of the central Florida Territory and understood the ways of the various Seminole tribes, as well as the animals and birds that flourished therein.

Billy knew the best and safest ways to get around in the forests and in the swamps and marshes that abounded in the land. He was recognized as the best tracker among all the Seminole tribes, and he had shared much of his knowledge and skills with his friend, Treff Ballowe. It was no wonder, then, that Treff sought Billy's help to carry out the mission that Ace had assigned to him.

Treff met him by the hitching rail. "Paul Billy! It's great to see you again!" Treff exclaimed, grabbing his friend's hand and slapping him on the shoulder. "Come in and we'll get some coffee to drink while we talk."

Sitting on the porch in rocking chairs, their feet propped up on the railing, the two friends talked.

"Your sister said you needed to see me," Billy began.

"Did she tell you the reason?" Treff asked.

"Not really. She said it had something to do with stolen cattle, and she said you needed my help."

Briefly, Treff summarized the recent problems that plagued the ranch and told Paul Billy why he had asked him to come.

Paul Billy listened intently. Finally he looked at Treff with somber eyes as black as coal and nodded his head. "I see you do have a big problem, but I still do not understand what it is you want me to do."

"Billy, I have an arrow wound in my leg, and Amaly won't let me leave until it's healed. I don't want to wait another week to start looking at things, so I need you to check on the situation around Boot Prairie. After that, drift down the west side of the Suwannee to the coast. Then work up the coast to the Hittenhatchee and then back to our west border."

"What should I be looking for that far away, except for cattle signs?" Billy asked.

"Look for any sign of cattle drives, any groups of cattle in unusual places. Keep an eye out for strangers, and as you travel along the coast, look for steamboats, either anchored or traveling along close enough for you to see. If you do see one, try to notice a name or anything that will help identify the boat."

"I can leave now and get started."

"First let's have some dinner. Then you need to go and see Rusty. He's branding in the Balboa pen. He'll take you by a group of men who are building a dam on Dubee Creek. Without anyone seeing you, he's going to point out a new cowhunter to you. The man's name is Slim Ritta. We're going to let the man go on Saturday afternoon. I want you to be close enough to headquarters to follow the man without letting him see you. Follow him for two or three days if you need to, to see where he goes."

"Do you want me to do anything with him?"

"No," Treff replied, "it's more important just to know where he goes, who he joins up with, or if he does anything out of the ordinary. That way, if it turns out he's a member of a gang, maybe we can catch the whole group instead of just one man. Of course, you may find he isn't going anywhere or meeting anyone. In that case, we'll know he's okay."

"When will I see you to tell you what I've found?"

"As soon as I can ride, I'm fixing to head for Wacacha Marsh and start looking for suspicious signs, but if Mama keeps me tied down, you'll need to come back here to see me before you follow Slim Ritta."

Paul Billy said, "When I come back here, if it is nighttime, I will signal with the call of the brown owl." He did not want to chance being mistaken for a stranger.

"That's good," Treff replied, "and I will answer with the same call."

Francesca stepped outside and clanged the bell that signaled dinnertime, and Treff and Paul Billy went inside to eat. On the way to the table, Treff said, "Be sure to pick up any supplies you need before you leave. Make certain you have enough food and ammunition. If you need anything, just see Ace."

After a meal of cornbread, turnip greens, and steak, followed by a cup of Amaly's good coffee, Paul Billy wiped his mouth and got up to leave. "That was mighty good grub, and I thank you."

Treff followed him to his horse. "I'll listen for your signal on Friday night, Paul Billy. That will give us time to talk about what you find before you leave on Saturday to follow Ritta."

"I will not forget." Paul Billy straddled his horse and rode away to find Rusty. Treff stood on the porch and watched him until he blended into the horizon.

The remainder of the week passed with the speed of a lazy land tortoise. Treff was bored senseless, but he could not shake Amaly from her mind-set. He spent time cutting some pine and oak wood for her kitchen stove, patched the barn and horse corral, and performed a few other jobs that were important for the ranch, but not at all what he wanted to be doing.

Friday night after dark, he sat on the front porch, rocking and talking with his parents. A gentle breeze from the north kept the mosquitoes at bay, and the air was pleasantly cool. The silence of the evening was broken only by the soft hoot of a brown owl. Treff paid no attention to the sound at first, but when it hooted twice again, he suddenly remembered the signal that Paul Billy planned to use! After his own call brought a response, he told Ace and Amaly, "Paul Billy is close by. He wants to see me, and I think I'll ride out to meet him. I'll be back soon."

Amaly frowned, but she did not try to restrain him.

Treff went to the horse corral and whistled for Rojo. The intelligent pony came to the gate immediately and lifted his head to receive his bridle. Treff led the horse to the barn for a blanket and saddle. Slipping his rifle into the offside scabbard, he stepped into the saddle and pointed his horse toward a cypress head where the brown owl called.

He had ridden only a short distance when he heard the brown owl call again. He gave his answering call and changed his course toward the sound. He rode for another half-mile before he heard the owl again, close by this time. He stopped and waited. Almost at once, as if dropped from a cloud, Paul Billy appeared by his side.

"Hello, my friend! Let's ride back to the barn. We can talk along the way."

"Treff, I have found many cattle signs among the palmettos and marshes to our west, but I have not seen any cattle. That is very strange. When I rode along the coast, I did see a steamboat anchored in Deadman's Bay close to the Hideout Bar on the Hittenhatchee River. There was no sign of any activity around the boat, but it looked like it could carry cattle. I wanted to let you know as soon as possible."

"That sounds very interesting, Billy. I may change my plans for going to the Wacacha Marsh and ride over to the Hittenhatchee instead. That new man, Slim Ritta, still hasn't seen you yet, has he?"

"No, Rusty and I were very careful about that. I have seen Ritta, but he has not seen me. Tomorrow is his last day, and I will follow him when he leaves."

"Good! Billy, did those cattle tracks seem to head in any particular direction? Did you find any horse tracks?"

"The cattle seemed to be drifting northwest, but they didn't look like they were being driven. We had a couple of rains that washed away some tracks. I didn't find any horse signs in the short time I was there. I could not follow the tracks very far, because I wanted to get back here before Saturday. But if anyone was working those cattle, they were going slow and easy and knew what they were doing."

"You've done a good job, Billy. Where do you think those cattle might be headed?"

"It would be hard to say for sure. They might be hidden in the wild country west and north of Warrior Swamp. In that swampland, it would be very difficult to find them. But if they are still in this part of the Territory, they could be holed up somewhere in the freshwater marsh. I guess the only way we can know for sure is to follow their tracks."

"Billy, I'm glad you'll be following Slim Ritta when he leaves. I'm hoping he may lead us to something. I'll go down and watch the Hideout Bar. I may take somebody with me. I'll have to think about who would be best suited for that."

Paul Billy started to pull away and then hesitated long enough to say, "Treff, you might take Patch Searcy with you. He is close-mouthed. He has worked for Ace a long time and is the best gun hand in any of the divisions. He would be good to have along if things got tight down on the coast."

"Thanks, Billy. I'll give some thought to your suggestion." As the two separated, Treff added a warning. "Be careful, Billy. If Slim is part of the Abe Zink crew, he will be dangerous if he catches you following him."

Paul Billy laughed. "A man cannot catch a brown owl, Treff." He turned his horse and disappeared into the blackness of the night. From far away, Treff caught the lonesome sound of a brown owl's cry as it floated on the night breeze.

When Treff returned to the ranch house, Ace still sat on the porch, waiting to hear about his meeting with Paul Billy. Amaly sat quietly beside him, the only sounds coming from the rhythmic squeak of her rocking chair.

Treff told them what Paul Billy had reported. Then he asked, "Ace, do you remember my telling you that when I crossed the Perdido River on my way back from Mobile, I had a short visit with Chico Leon?"

"Yes, you mentioned that Sunday. Do you think there's some kind of a connection to our problems?"

"Chico said a posse almost captured Abe Zink up near the Georgia line, but Abe and four of his men escaped."

"Are you saying you think Abe is rustling cattle in this area?"

"I don't know," Treff replied, "but if he is, and if we can find him, we need to move in on him now while he's short-handed. Paul Billy thinks I should take Patch Searcy with me when I go into the freshwater marsh."

"I think that's a good idea, Treff. In fact, you might ought to take Aldo Hagen along, too. Outfit each of them with one of those new rifles. That should be enough to handle Abe's group, if you do find them."

"Aldo would be good to have along if we encountered trouble, Ace. Now, if I can get a clean bill of health from that stubborn woman you're married to, I would get started."

Amaly just smiled sweetly. "You get a good night's sleep, Treff, and we'll take another look at that leg after the sun comes up."

9

ACE SAT WITH HIS HEAD bent over his office desk, his pen scratching figures into the black leather book that held his meticulously accurate records. His face crinkled with a satisfied smile. Despite the record cold temperatures of last winter, the year had been good. He closed his book and went to the kitchen to share this news with Amaly.

Autumn was his time for inventorying his holdings and calculating the accomplishments of the past twelve months. Calves had been marked and counted. Now it was time to make plans for the approaching winter months.

Autumn was an important time for others in the Dover family, as well. Amaly was busy making plans of her own. With the corn picked, sweet potatoes dug, sugarcane ground, and molasses made, it was time to plan a frolic. The springhouse was fairly bulging with fruit, vegetables, and smoked meat. The storeroom was filled with the winter supply of staples from Wanton's store. Wild turkeys, hogs, and deer roamed the woods in abundance, and the alligators that slid silently through the swampy marshes promised to provide good gator tail. It was time for the Dovers to share with their neighbors and have a bit of fun!

Amaly had to laugh when she referred to her "neighbors." The closest were a half day's ride away. Life in the Territory was vastly different from her life as a young girl in the city, where her best friends lived just across the street!

For the past ten years, the Dover open house had always taken place the second weekend in October, and people came from many miles away to take part in the gala celebration. Throughout the Territory, settlers came by horseback and by wagons, happily joining together for a three-day frolic, eating, dancing, singing, and visiting.

Each year there were new faces to meet as more settlers migrated south and babies were born, and sadly, other once-familiar faces were conspicuously absent as families moved to other parts or were diminished by death and hardships. But this annual reunion of neighbors drew the return of many friends who had been coming since the first Dover get-together back in 1826.

Amaly dried the last of the supper dishes and put them in her cupboard. "Come sit on the porch with me, honey," she coaxed her husband. "I've been thinking about plans for the frolic, and I need to get your ideas on a few things."

Ace needed no extra encouragement. He always looked forward to this time of the day when chores were finished and he could sit in the rocker and talk with his wife. He closed his book and put away his pen. "I'd prob'ly agree to that if you'd sweeten up your offer with a cup of coffee."

Amaly laughed. "With cream and sugar," she promised.

As the couple sat side by side in the cool purple twilight, their chairs squeaked in rhythm as they rocked and talked.

"Now, what was this idea you wanted to ask me about?"

"Well, I'm just a mite worried that a lot of our friends won't come this year. With all the unrest among the Seminoles, and the widespread rustling and robbing we've been hearing about, I'm not sure they'll feel easy about leaving their homesteads." Amaly knew that without law officers in the Territory, people had to use their own resources to protect their homes and possessions.

Ace rocked without answering until Amaly finally asked, "Do you have any idea how many people might come this year?"

"No," Ace replied. He drained his coffee cup and set it on the porch rail. "When I had the wagon over to Wanton's store the other day to pick up the supplies you ordered, I tacked up a notice to remind everyone to come. I asked Jeremiah to do the same thing when he was at the way-station on the mail route north of us."

"Last year there were fourteen families and a few cowhands from their ranches," Amaly said. "There must have been over a hundred people, not counting our own group. We surely had a good time!"

"It's hard to tell this year. There are three or four new families that have moved into the area. But a lot of rustling is going on to our north and west, and I know people will be worried about leaving their spreads unprotected."

"Then, of course, we lost two good neighbors when Maebelle and Will Crochet were killed by those renegade Indians last spring."

"It won't be the same without them," Amaly lamented.

"And we won't see Louis and Thelma Perkins this year, since they sold out and moved back north. The frontier has not been kind to some of its people!"

Ace knew how much the companionship of the other women meant to Amaly, and he hoped their neighbors would all make an effort to come.

He always made it a policy to allow each of his cowhands to join at least one night of the festivities. That would be more difficult this year, but somehow he would manage it.

He glanced at Amaly out of the corner of his eye before he eased in his next announcement. "When I was in Wanton's last week, I saw Zeke Mongol of the Brown Owl Ranch. I made a point of inviting him."

Amaly's nose wrinkled a bit. "I've always had a problem feeling easy around that man," she admitted.

"I know you have, and I can't fault you for that. A lot of people wonder where he came from. Some say he throws a wide loop when it comes time to mark and brand calves. And he doesn't have a wife to help you women with all the work you have to do." He reached over and patted her hand. "Anyway, I don't know if he will want to leave his place, what with all the problems he may have from the Seminoles. But I did invite him to bring three or four of his top people and come, if he could."

"It might give you a chance to learn more about his people and his ranch operation," Amaly admitted.

Glad to have the matter settled without a fuss, Ace hastened to change the subject. "We'll have the barn cleaned up by the first of next week. People might need a place to sleep, particularly if it rains. I'll get the crew to dig some cooking pits and chop up some oak and hickory wood. We'll set up tables under the oak trees. A couple of days before the festivities, I'll have the men go hunting for turkeys and hogs and a deer."

"Don't forget the gator tail," Amaly reminded him. "Folks around these parts look forward to that."

"You don't need to worry about that. We might get a few 'possums, too."

Amaly wrinkled her nose. "Not for me, thank you very much! The ladies that have been here before will bring cakes and pies. Someone always brings a croker sack full of collard greens. And we'll have the cooks make beaten biscuits every morning."

Ace smacked his lips just thinking about it. "That's always a favorite, particularly if we have some cane molasses or gravy to go on them."

"We'll ask Francesca to bring in some extra help for the weekend." Francesca had worked in the house for Amaly for the past nine years and always looked forward to helping with the open house celebration.

"We can depend on Johnny Coe to bring a couple of gallons of his homemade corn liquor," Ace added. "That always seems to liven things up, but we don't ever have enough to cause any real problems."

"Can you arrange for three or four fiddle players?" Amaly asked.

"Yes, that's already been done," Ace assured her. "We'll get the same ones we had last year, if that's all right with you."

"Do you think Treff will be here?"

Ace thought about that before answering. "I hope so, but I can't say for sure," he finally said. "We're starting to have some of those same rustling problems other people have been complaining about. Treff's return will depend on what happens during the next ten days."

"Where did he go? You never have told me!"

"He, Aldo, and Patch went into the freshwater marshes two days ago to look for cattle. I'm not certain how long they'll be gone, but don't talk about it in front of Francesca or any of the help. We don't want the crew to know anything about where they went or why they're gone," Ace cautioned.

Not wanting to worry Amaly, Ace said no more. But Amaly knew without being reminded that Patch and Aldo had both been top gunhands before coming to work for the TSR. She had no trouble figuring the reason they had been asked to go with Treff.

Zeke Mongol sat in his kitchen, hunkered over his second cup of coffee, brooding about his meeting with Ace Dover in Wanton's trading post. He had never socialized with any of the other settlers in the Territory, and he wondered why Ace had invited him to their open house.

Zeke seldom went to Wanton's, because it meant that he had to travel through areas grazed by Seminole cattle. His Brown Owl Ranch was having more trouble with the Seminoles this year, because Zeke's cattle kept drifting onto their pastures. He had already lost about eighty head that had been killed by Indians. Even though he swung a wide loop now and then, he couldn't afford to have that many of his cattle killed.

Zeke felt frustrated. He didn't want to go public with his problems. He much preferred to remain lost in the Florida Territory, taking care of his own problems by himself. The last ten years, since his coming to the Territory, had been good to him. Now he was afraid that publicity about his Indian problem might drift northward and fall onto the wrong ears. He didn't want his former business partners to discover where he went after he left Boston carrying quite a bit of their money with him.

Before coming to the Florida Territory, Zeke had managed a lucrative import-export business for a group of rich merchants in the New England colonies. There was great demand in Ireland and England for lumber from the new colonies, and there was also a good profit to be made on the return trip transporting convicts from England to the colonies. In addition, the company imported staples that could not be found in New England. His partners, who knew him as James R. Martine, were well satisfied with their manager's clever work.

Being an enterprising young man who had grown up on the crime-infested streets of London, James Martine dedicated his whole life to attaining wealth. He craved freedom from the squalor of his youth and felt no qualms about stealing from his partners to help reach his goal. For several years, he had systematically skimmed a small sum from each round trip the company ships made, depositing the money in a Savannah bank under the name of Zeke Mongol.

When his partners began to suspect that he was stealing their money, Martine had left Boston carrying most of their money in his valise. He told his friends he was taking a trip north to Maine. Instead, after leaving Boston, he turned west and then south, always careful to avoid contact with people.

In the Carolinas, using the name Zeke Mongol, he found a job with a farmer, where he worked for a year. To protect his identity, he grew a beard, wore farm clothes, and learned as much as he could about cattle. In 1826, he decided it was finally time to start his new life, and the isolated Florida Territory seemed the perfect place to begin.

His first few years were hard, but greed was the driving force that eventually made his dream of wealth a reality. He established his ranch on the east side of the rich Payne's Prairie which was owned by the Seminole Indians. He found it fairly easy to accumulate unmarked cattle from the wilderness of the Territory, and he and his cowhands never hesitated to swing a wide loop during marking and branding time.

As Zeke gulped down the muddy dregs from the bottom of his coffee cup, Cal Whitney, his northern division foreman, pulled up a chair and slung his legs over it.

"Mind if I join you for a cup?" Not waiting for an

answer, Cal filled his cup from the tin pot on the table.

"Cal, do you know any of the people at the TSR ranch?"

"Not really, boss," Cal replied. "We've got the Seminole Indians between us and them. I hear Ace Dover ain't had no problems with the Indians, but I sure can't figure a reason for that."

"Beats me, too," Zeke agreed. "I run into Ace at the trading post last week, and he invited us to a frolic at their ranch. It starts Friday of next week and goes on all weekend."

"Boss, I don't think we should go away and leave this place for three whole days. We might not have nothin' left by time we come back."

"You're right," Zeke agreed. "But I've never been on their spread, and I'm trying to decide if it might be smart to accept the invitation just to learn a little bit about them. I wouldn't want to stay but for one day, though."

"That might not be a bad idea, at that. We might need some help one of these days. The way the Indian problem is growing, the more people we know the better," Cal replied. "Besides, a frolic might be kinda fun for a change."

"Does that big guy still work in our southern division?"

"Drag? Yeah, he does," Luke replied. "Al tells me he's been doing a good job. He don't seem to fit the regular cowhunter description, but he does as good a job as anybody. He heads out for Jacksonville on the weekends quite a bit. He must have a girlfriend up there."

Zeke cracked his knuckles, a sure sign he had something important on his mind. "I think I'll go to the TSR frolic on Saturday. You and Al Green and Drag Johnson can go with me. That might give me a chance to learn a little more about Johnson. You and Al arrange to have your cowhands ride our boundaries all day Saturday while we're gone, especially on our western side near the Seminoles."

Zeke cracked his knuckles again and let his eyes drift out the window. He wondered just why Drag Johnson went to Jacksonville every weekend.

❖   ❖   ❖

Approximately eighty miles northwest of the Brown Owl Ranch, a group of cattle stirred lazily in the first light of day. They began to graze placidly on the lush green maidencane in the marshes north of Deadman's Bay.

Abe Zink and his band of outlaws had been furtively gathering cattle, a few here and a few there, until they had collected about three hundred head. Now they were just letting them fill their bellies on the good marsh grasses while Abe tried to make up his mind what he should do with them.

Since losing two of his best men to that posse near Pensacola, he had tried to be more careful. He only had four men left, and one of those, Tommy Gohn, had stayed behind in Apalachicola to prospect for other opportunities to line their pockets with gold.

Abe and his three men were just finishing up a cold breakfast when Tommy Gohn rode into camp.

"It's a good thing I ain't the law, or you all would

have been in deep trouble," Tommy said, scoffing at their lax security. "But don't worry; nobody saw me comin'."

"If you'da been the law, you'd be dead now," Abe growled. "How come you ain't back in Apalachicola where we left you?"

"This here steamboat captain come into the saloon lookin' for Abe Zink. Gimpy Lysek brought him over and I got to talkin' with him. He claims he's a friend of yours, and he wants to get in touch. He wouldn't tell me what he wanted."

"What did he look like?"

"I don't remember nothin' special about him; just like a ordinary steamboat captain. Anyway, he told me that if I happened to see you, to let you know he was gonna anchor in Deadman's Bay, near the Hideout Bar at the Hittenhatchee River. Said he'd wait for a couple of weeks to see if you happened to show up. If you didn't come, he was fixin' to head down toward Fort Brooke and look for someone else."

"Did this-here steamboat captain happen to tell you his name?" Abe asked.

"Yeah, he said his name was Captain Caleb. He acted like you knowed him."

Abe's eyes narrowed as an idea began to grow in his mind. This just might be a way to get rid of the cattle his men had stolen.

"Yeah, I know him. You fellas watch the cattle. Don't let anyone ride into camp the way Tommy did. I'm gonna go see what Captain Caleb has in mind. I should be back by dark or shortly after."

Abe thought he knew of a way to load his stolen

cattle on Caleb's boat. Having brains sure paid off in the long run. Maybe things were finally going to work themselves out.

10

DENSE HAMMOCKS, DEEP SWAMPS, and countless gator nests surrounding the Hideout Bar at the mouth of the Hittenhatchee River created natural protection from unwelcome guests, making it a popular place for outlaws. The Hittenhatchee, despite the several creeks that drained into it, contained waterfalls that made boat travel difficult, if not impossible. Any man who did not know his way around the tidewater swamp would be a fool to try to reach the coast by following this black-water river.

Small wonder then, that Abe Zink thought that this part of the Territory would be a perfect spot to load his stolen cattle onto Captain Caleb's steamer. In years past, Abe had spent many months in this area. He knew his way around, and he knew exactly how he would load the cattle. The only obstacle left to hurdle was cutting a satisfactory deal with Caleb.

As he plundered his way toward the obscure town of Hittenhatchee, Abe's fear of being recognized diminished, and as a result, he grew more careless.

With his thoughts totally focused on the most profitable way to present his deal to Caleb, Abe failed to detect the three horses hidden among the oaks near the mouth of the river.

Long days of patience were finally beginning to pay off for the trio from Three Springs Ranch.

"That's Abe Zink, all right!" Treff whispered. "That's the face we saw on the "Wanted" poster back at the stagecoach way station."

"Yeah, and we ain't gonna lose him this time," Patch declared, remembering how just last week Zink had slipped from sight as they stealthily followed him through a wet marsh.

From their stand in the dense copse of pine trees, they watched him disappear between the swinging doors of the Hideout Bar. Treff had to grab Patch by the arm to restrain him. "Not yet," he cautioned. "We'll just sit here and watch to see what happens. I'm interested to see if anyone comes in from that steamer anchored out in the bay."

Aldo slapped at a mosquito. "Damn!"

"What is that?" Treff asked.

"Just a dern gallnipper," Aldo said. "They're meaner 'n hornets!"

"No, I meant that flash of light reflection. Didn't you see it? Look! There it is again, coming from the steamer."

Three pairs of eyes focused on the steamboat and watched a ray of the sun bounce sporadically from its stern.

"That looks to be some kind of a signal," Patch murmured. "Look! They're lowerin' a skiff over the side."

A dinghy was dropped into the bay and inched toward shore. Even before it hit the bank, the saloon doors swung open, and Abe Zink emerged. Treff and his men kept their silent vigil as Abe hustled down to the water's edge and stepped into the waiting rowboat. He plunked himself down in the bow, and the dinghy moved out to the anchored paddlewheeler.

Patch had almost exhausted his patience. "Don't you think we ought to make our move now?"

"We need to stay out of sight," Treff reminded him. "If anyone in the bar spots us, we'll be in big trouble. We don't want Abe to know he's been followed. Let's just sit and wait."

When Abe reached the cattle boat, the first thing that caught his eye was the abundance of empty pens just waiting to be filled with his cattle. His leathery face broke into a broad grin. "Caleb, I never expected to see you up here. Last I heerd you was operatin' down south."

Caleb did not wish to appear too eager. "Well, I tell you how it is," he replied, "I got to thinking about you last month, and decided I would try to look you up. Things is going along pretty good down yonder, but I just got to wonderin' if it would be profitable to work up here in the north, too."

"How did you find me?"

"Didn't know if I would," Caleb hedged. "In fact, if

you hadn't come along in a day or two, I was going on back to Fort Brooke. I got me some sweet deals working down thataway."

"That still don't tell me how you found me."

"I didn't find you," Caleb said. "You found me. I run into Gimpy Lysek back in Apalachicola a while back, and I asked him if he knowd where you was at. He introduced me to some kid that knows you, and I told the kid where I'd be for a couple of weeks, just in case you wanted to look me up. But I told him I wasn't able to wait forever. It looks like he musta got word to you."

Abe nodded and waited to hear more.

"How about a glass of good Cuban rum?" Caleb asked.

"That sounds good to me. I ain't had no good rum in a long time. Is that what you wanted to see me about, smugglin' Cuban rum?" Abe asked.

"No, but that might not be a bad idea," Caleb replied. "We go to Cuba about once a month and come back empty. Maybe we oughta start bringin' back a few barrels of rum."

"What do you haul down to Cuba?" Abe asked, although he already knew the answer. Those pens weren't made to hold rum!"

"We been smuggling cattle into Cuba. A good steer delivered in to Havana is worth a couple o' Spanish doubloons. We work with men who can get us the cattle, no questions asked, and we haul them to Cuba and split fifty-fifty."

Caleb paused to refill Abe's glass before he continued. "It's been a good deal for everybody. The main danger be fer the feller gathering up the cattle and then holdin' 'em till we can get 'em loaded aboard ship. After they get loaded and we pull away from shore, the hard part is over, and the cattle ain't never found again."

"Loading the cattle wouldn't be no problem," Abe said. "I know where there's a natural loadin' place just north of Mud Swamp, about ten miles from here."

"Does that mean you'd like to try it?"

Abe appeared to be thinking about it. He didn't want to spoil his chances for a good deal by sounding too enthusiastic. "How about another glass of that rum?" he said.

While Caleb poured rum into his glass, Abe pretended to wrestle with his decision. "We might try to find a bunch of steers for you to haul one time. That would give us a better idea about how we liked your deal. How long did you say it took to make a round trip?"

"No more than four weeks from here. If everything works good, maybe three weeks. We could meet you right here with your share of the money."

"What kind of money? I don't want none of that-there Cuban paper trash."

"Gold!" Caleb assured him, rolling the word over his tongue. "Solid doubloons."

Abe nodded his satisfaction, fighting to keep the greedy sneer from his lips. "Do you know Gopher Landing?" he asked.

"Ain't that the point with the eagle nest in the top of that tall pine?"

"Yeah, that be the place. They's enough water there for your boat to operate, and we can load cattle from there. If you tie up there in four days, maybe we can come up with about three hundred cattle for you." Abe scowled to hide his pleasure at finding a way to market the cattle he had already rustled.

Caleb was equally pleased, but equally reluctant to show it. He noticed Abe's glass getting low. "How about getting you a bottle of that rum to take with you?" he asked.

"I reckon as how that'd be acceptable," Abe replied. "Then if I can get your man to row me back to the Hideout Bar, I best get started tryin' to find us some cattle."

"Don't bring me no scrawny ones. They gotta be good."

"You can count on that!"

Caleb reached up to the shelf above his head and pulled down another bottle of rum. He stuffed it in a leather pouch and pulled the drawstring tight around its neck. He handed it to Abe as a gesture of binding the deal they had just agreed on. Then he called to his first mate. "Juan, take Señor Zink back to the saloon. He has a lot of work to do."

Caleb stood on deck and watched the rowboat move toward shore. He twisted his clasped hands and smiled. He felt very good. Now he had a new pardner and in four days he would be on his way to Havana with another load of cattle.

Abe was also feeling good. As he sat in the Hideout Bar having one last drink, he thought about the deal he had just made with Captain Caleb. He could already smell the gold. Even if he only got one doubloon per head as his share, that was a hell of a lot better than holding up travelers on the Pensacola mail route. Yessiree! This had been a good day!

He needed to get started if he was going to make it back to camp tonight. He staggered out of the bar and lurched toward his horse, careful not to damage the bottle of good rum Caleb had given to him.

The ground beneath his feet seemed to rock in unsteady rhythm as he tried twice to climb on his horse's back. On the third try, he made it and started through the woods.

As his horse headed toward camp, Abe threw caution to the wind. Who would think of looking for him way out here in the middle of nowhere? Every once in awhile Abe would stop and watch his back trail just out of old habit. And as long as he was stopped, he might as well taste just a small nip of that good Cuban rum again. He felt neither aches nor pains. He felt good!

Yet, despite the fact that the rum had dulled his senses, his instincts warned him that something was not quite right. He couldn't explain why he felt that way. Probably he was just worrying about nothing. What could possibly be wrong when everything was going so right?

His horse seemed to know the way, as he sloughed through the murky swamps, weaving around cypress stands and jumping fallen trees.

Abe stopped once more to check his back trail. Finally, with the help of the rum, he pushed aside all thoughts of being followed and allowed his horse to carry him back toward camp.

From the shelter of the trees, Treff, Aldo, and Patch watched Abe slowly ride away. "We need to follow him," Treff whispered. "Be careful no one from that bar spies us, and stay far enough back so Abe can't see us."

Patch watched Abe for a few minutes and then chuckled softly. "I think the great leader of the pack is drunk. He can't hardly set on his horse."

"Maybe not," Treff responded, "but he's managed to keep from being caught for many years. We've come this close. We sure don't want to mess up and miss him now. But we need to catch the whole lot of them, so we have to be careful."

The quarter-moon did little to penetrate the darkness, and the dense canopy of cypress trees cast ghostly shadows that further diminished their vision. Deeper into the swamp, the three men followed Abe's lead, able to catch only occasional glimpses of him in the waning light.

Frogs chirped a noisy chorus, and somewhere an owl called through the otherwise still night.

"How much farther you reckon he's gonna take us?" Aldo asked, his eyes straining to keep Abe in his sight.

No sooner had he spoken when Abe Zink suddenly disappeared from view as though swallowed up by the dense palmettos. His followers were momentarily mystified.

If Treff and his men had not followed Abe from Hittenhatchee, they would probably never have found the outlaws' camp. Treff had to admire Abe's craftiness in selecting this remotely sequestered hideaway. Situated under a grove of massive, moss-laden oak trees that smothered campfire smoke, it was surrounded by tall, thick palmettos that completely hid the sight of fires and the movement of horses and men. It would be almost impossible for an outsider to creep up on the camp undetected.

To the north of their camp was a green marsh where their stolen cattle grazed. The marsh was filled with maidencane, so lush and verdant that the livestock had no reason to wander away.

Treff had watched Abe ride north of the camp before cutting back south through the marsh, apparently to let his men know who was coming. After entering the camp through a small opening in the north side of the palmettos, Abe was no longer visible to Treff and his men.

"They got a lookout just to the west of that openin' where Abe went in," Aldo said. "You can't see him too good. He's settin' on a log in the tall grass."

"You know," Treff said, "we're pretty lucky Abe didn't see us when he turned around and doubled back through the marsh. I reckon his love affair with that bottle of rum probably helped us out! Patch, can you slip around to the other side of those palmettos, and see if there's any other way to get in or out of that place?"

Patch tied his horse to a bush, took his rifle, and disappeared into the thick underbrush.

Waiting for Patch to return, Treff and Aldo remained motionless in the dense scrub about half a mile to the east of the camp. The sharp palmetto fronds felt like needles piercing through their cotton shirts, and the mosquitoes were as thick as fleas on a dog's back.

Patch returned as silently as he had left. "That clearin' is like a cave. They's well hidden, all right, but they's also penned in," he reported. "I don't see no way in or out of that camp except through the marsh."

"If they plan to move these cattle down to the coast, they're probably fixin' to start in the morning," Treff said. "Would it be better to ambush these guys during the night, or should we wait until they start moving cattle in the morning?"

"The moon ain't full, but they's enough light tonight fer us to see what we're doin'. We better wait till they go to sleep, though, and then take 'em," Aldo suggested.

"Yeah, I think that'd be the safest way," Patch agreed.

"You're right," Treff said. "Let's get some rest now, and we'll make our move after they're asleep."

The faint glow of the outlaws' fire grew dimmer and the murmur of their voices gradually decreased into silence. Treff watched as the man on guard stood, stretched, and went inside. After only a moment, the guard returned with a cup in his hand and sat down again. His movement helped the watchers adjust their eyes to the darkness.

"There is no other easy way out of their camp," Treff whispered, confirming what Patch had discovered. "If we can get rid of the lookout, we can control that hole. I'd really like to get their horses, but I don't see how we can do that."

"Treff, if you can take care of the guard, me and

Aldo can get inside the camp. We'll slip through the openin' and get on opposite sides of the circle. Between us on the inside and you on the outside, we should be able to take them rascals before they wake up and know what's happened."

"I can take care of the sentry without any trouble," Treff assured them, "but each one of those guys inside will be sleeping with his gun next to his head. They'll be quick to react."

"They can come quietly or die tryin' to find us in the dark," Patch replied. "The glow of the fire still gives a little light inside for us to see them, but they'll have a hard time seeing us along the dark outer edges."

"Wait until you see me take care of the guard, and then make your move. It will take me a while to do this without making a lot of noise." With that, Treff took his rifle and melted into the darkness.

Aldo and Patch strained to watch but could see not the slightest sign of movement anywhere. "I think our boss must be mostly Injun," Aldo whispered. "I ain't never seed no white man what could get around in these-here woods like him."

"Watch the guy on guard," Patch said. "We won't see nothin' of Treff before he takes him down."

In their cramped hiding place, the minutes crawled into what seemed like an hour. At last, they saw the guard rise to his feet and walk a few steps, peering forward into the darkness as though something had attracted his attention. He neither saw nor heard Treff rise from behind him. Suddenly sensing trouble, he whipped around. In the flash of an instant, before he had time to shout a warning to the sleeping men, something hard and heavy smashed over his head, and he slipped into unconsciousness. Treff caught his falling body and silently eased him to the ground. Putting the guard's gun in his own belt, Treff tied the man's feet and hands with some pigging string. He stuffed his mouth with a bandanna and left him facedown in the dirt.

Out of the corner of his eye, Treff caught a glimpse of Patch and Aldo creeping toward the palmettos. He watched them move inside the camp before he turned back toward the marsh to see and stop anyone who might try to escape through the opening of the palmettos.

In the glow of the embers, Treff saw Patch throw a log on the smoldering fire. A spray of sparks spiraled and momentarily illuminated the sleeping outlaws. Aldo's voice sounded loud and stern through the midnight silence. "Keep your hands off your guns and reach for an oak limb." He took a quick step to one side, pivoting away from the sound of his own voice.

The spontaneous reaction of the outlaws was born of many years of lawless living. In an instant, every man rolled over and began firing toward the sound of Aldo's voice, and the result was a mass of confusion!

When Patch shot from the opposite side of the opening, the outlaws realized they had more than one attacker to contend with. Aldo's bullet found its target, and a giant of a man slumped to the ground, wounded but very much alive. Patch threw himself to the left as the downed man kept firing wildly, trying to locate his attackers.

In the midst of the confusion, one horse raced for

the opening in the palmettos, its rider blazing relentlessly with his pistol. Apparently the animal had been saddled and ready to facilitate an escape in case of emergency. Patch fired at the rider, but missed. The horse and rider reached the opening and were halfway through when the thundering blast of a gun flashed from the marsh, lifting the man out of the saddle and propelling him through the air. His body hit the ground with a thud and did not move. Eerily visible in the pale moonlight, his shirt turned an intensifying shade of bright crimson.

"Anybody else want to try that?" Aldo asked.

"Don't shoot," a voice pleaded.

"Then do as I said, and reach for those oak limbs," Aldo repeated. "You on the ground, if you can't stand, throw your gun away, and put your hands over your head."

Realizing the futility of their situation, the outlaws raised their hands in defeat.

Patch and Aldo emerged from the darkness. While Aldo kept his gun drawn on the rustlers, Patch gathered their guns into a pile and tied their hands behind their backs. Two wounded men lay motionless on the ground, staring silently at their captors with hatred in their eyes.

Patch went outside and dragged the guard inside the camp, where he removed his gag and dumped him beside his buddies.

Outside the confines of the camp, Treff remained hidden and silent, shielded by the tall marsh grasses and palmettos. He watched to detect any slight movement in the body of the outlaw he had just shot. Was he dead or only pretending, waiting for Treff to reveal himself?

Treff did not enjoy killing. It was never a sport with

him as it was with some men. Even wild animals he only killed when there was a purpose. But tonight he had a purpose.

He approached his victim cautiously, his rifle in a ready position. The outlaw was lying facedown, apparently unconscious. Treff bent over the still figure and, grabbing him by one arm, flipped him over. "*Good gosh amighty!*" he exclaimed. "*It's Abe Zink himself!*" He felt for a pulse but discerned not even the faintest flutter. Abe Zink was dead.

"What are we gonna to do with these other four fellas?" Patch asked. "Maybe we just oughta string 'em up right here on these-here oak trees and be done with it."

"Make sure they don't have any guns or knives on them," Treff said. "Take off their boots and throw them in the swamp. Tie their hands and feet. I have some more pigging string in my saddlebags if you need it."

"I'll get it," Patch volunteered.

"Aldo, why don't you get our horses while I add more wood on the fire and make sure their horses are tied. We'll wait until daylight to decide what we'll do."

After checking the prisoners' horses, Treff threw on some branches and a small log to stoke up the fire and made a kettle of coffee. Aldo went to fetch their horses, and when he returned, the three men sat on the ground to rest and drink coffee. Then each took a turn guarding the camp while the other two slept.

At the first light of day, Aldo stood guard while Treff and

Patch wove their horses among the cattle, checking their brands. They recognized several familiar brands in the herd, including some from the TSR.

"I don't see none I ain't seen before," Patch declared, "except for that strange HO-over-Bar. Where do you reckon them cows come from?"

Treff shook his head without answering.

When they had completed their examination of the herd, they reentered the confines of the camp where Aldo stood guard over the prisoners. "Aldo," Treff said, "ride to headquarters and tell Ace where we are and what we've done. Find out what he wants us to do with these four rustlers, and bring back five or six cowhands to move these cattle to a corral where we can separate the different brands."

Patch added a word of caution: "Aldo, be careful goin' back to the TSR. We still have them bands of Injuns from south Georgia to deal with."

After Aldo rode away, Treff and Patch tried to talk with the rustlers but without much success.

"Ain't you gonna give us any food or water?" one whined.

Ignoring the question, Treff asked, "Where were y'all planning to take the cattle?"

His only answers were angry stares.

"Patch, would you like some more coffee and some jerky? It sure does taste good!"

"Man, this stuff is plum delicious!" Patch agreed, smacking his lips and making a great show of enjoying the food. "It shore would be nice to know where they was fixin' to load these-here cattle, wouldn't it?"

"I think they were going to be loaded on that paddlewheeler we saw down in Deadman's Bay, but I sure didn't see any place there to load from."

There was no response from any of the rustlers except groans of pain from the two who lay wounded on the ground.

"What are we going to do with Abe?" Treff asked.

"We could bring him inside here and start us a hangin' tree. Then these other four rustlers could join him when the crowd gets back," Patch replied.

"That's a good idea! If I can find his horse, I'll just load him up and bring him back inside." Without looking at the rustlers, Treff strode through the opening and outside the concealing ring of palmettos. When he returned, Abe hung limp and lifeless, draped over the saddle of his pony. Leading the horse to the back of the camp, Treff tethered him in full view of the four outlaws. "I think I'll leave him there for now," Treff stated. "We can decide what to do with him later."

Only then did Treff turn to look the rustlers straight in their eyes. "Now, does anyone want to tell us where Abe was planning to take these cattle?"

But still there was no response.

Next morning in the early daylight hours, Aldo returned to the outlaw camp with six additional cowhands. Seeing Treff, he broke into a wide grin. "Yore Pa was mighty tickled when I told him what you done! Since there ain't no law south of Georgia, and no jails, we gotta decide what the penalty for rustlin' cattle should be. Ace, he thought on it fer a spell, and then he allowed we should hang them rustlers and leave 'em right here. He wants us to take the cattle to the Latigo corral. He said that'd be the easiest place fer t'others to pick up their cattle."

Treff grimaced. He had no problem fighting outlaws, but he was not good at hanging people. However, he knew it had to be done if law and order were to come to the Florida Territory. And he figured if the cowhands did the hanging, word would soon spread that it was not smart to rustle cattle in the TSR area.

"You and Patch and the others take care of that hanging chore. Soon as that's done, we'll collect their horses and start for home. Save their saddles and gear, and we'll keep all their guns, of course."

A week later, Caleb was still anchored at Gopher Landing waiting for his cattle. He finally decided they had waited long enough. "I guess they ain't a-coming, Juan. I reckon they must not've been able to find us any cattle."

Juan pulled up the anchor, and the new pardnership came to an end almost before it began.

"Captain Caleb," Juan ventured, "perhaps misfortune has fallen on Señor Zink."

"That is possible, Juan." The Captain looked down into the murky waters of Deadman's Bay and let his thoughts drift with the tide, to Fort Brooke and then to Mobile and Honey Black, and all the years that stretched ahead of him. He had often stated that a man should know when to let go of an opportunity and turn his talents in a different direction. Perhaps now was that time. Perhaps he could find a large cattle operation and a cattleman who would be willing to send his own cattle to the Cuban market. That would be a safe business, and if he had to settle for a few less doubloons, at least he could sleep without a gun in his hand. He guided his boat along the west coast of the Territory and wondered what Honey Black would say when she heard about his new plans!

11

THE CRACKING SOUND of blacksnake whips split the silence of dawn, and cattle responded lazily by pushing themselves up from their resting places, lowing to register their mild protest. After grazing good marsh grasses for the past weeks, their full bellies rendered them docile and surprisingly easy to round up.

With the extra cowhunters from the TSR and the help of their cow dogs, they soon had the cattle heading east, winding their way around clumps of palmettos, swamps, and marshy bay heads.

Treff tried to fill the recesses of his mind with the sights and sounds of the animals in an effort to push out the ugly picture of five men dangling side by side from the limb of that oak tree.

"Patch," Treff said, "Ace sent word he wants us to take these cattle to the Latigo pens. There's enough grass there for a few days, and plenty of fresh water, and the pens are big enough to handle all these cattle. That place is fairly close to the ranchers who have cattle in the group, so it shouldn't be too troublesome to get them back to their rightful owners."

"Aldo and I seen five different brands besides the TSR brand. We recognize four of the brands, but we ain't never seen that HO-over-bar brand before." Patch looked to Treff for an answer.

Treff shook his head without answering. He was certain he had seen that brand. Why couldn't he remember where?

Traveling at grazing speed seemed to maintain a calming effect on the cattle as they ambled along through the thick brush. Occasionally the crack of a blacksnake whip echoed through the woods, driving a wayward steer or cow back into the herd, but on the whole, the drive moved along easily.

"Aldo, why don't you drift away from the herd and let those four outfits know we found some of their cattle?" Treff suggested. "We can be in the Latigo pens day after tomorrow by late afternoon. If each ranch will send some men to help us work the cattle, we can get them separated, and everybody can take their own cattle back home before the weekend."

"And while you're at it," Patch added, "you could mention that HO-over-bar brand. Somebody ought to know the outfit."

"That's a good idea," Treff agreed. "We'll meet you at the Latigo pens, Aldo. Be careful, and watch your back. Just because we put a stop to Abe Zink and his band of scalawags, we still can't afford to grow careless."

As Treff watched Aldo ride away, he continued to

puzzle over that unfamiliar <u>HO</u> brand. He was absolutely sure he had seen that mark before, but for the life of him, he could not remember where.

❖   ❖   ❖

Just before dusk of the third day, the herd drifted into the Latigo pens and began at once to graze the sparse grass and slake their thirst from the cool waters of a flowing well. Many of the neighboring ranchers had already reached the pens and waited in eager anticipation. As soon as they caught sight of the dirty, weary drivers returning with their herd, they gave them a helping hand, opening the gates to the pens and closing them after all the cattle were inside. Smiles spread across their faces as they began to recognize cattle wearing their own brands.

"Man, that is one purty sight!"

"Look yonder! There's some of mine!"

"I never thought to see them cows again!"

"You done a fine thing, son!"

Treff accepted their enthusiastic words of appreciation with a modest smile. "Do you want to start separating the cattle now, or would it be better to start at daylight in the morning?"

After discussing it among themselves, Tom Pickens of the Double-O spoke up. "We think we'd be better off to wait till tomorrow."

"That'll give us more daylight to move the cattle back to our own spreads," another man pointed out, and the others readily agreed.

"Why don't you camp here tonight, where you can

161

keep an eye on the cattle?" Treff offered. "I'll send our cook up with some grub. I can't stay here with you, because I have another meeting set up, but Patch and Aldo can stay, and I'll leave two other men to help you. The rest of our cowhands better head back to the Central Division. Ace needs them to help with some work he has going. Feel free to use our line shack on the west end of the pens."

Treff had difficulty getting away. Every man wanted to shake his hand and thank him personally. He wanted to wind up his business here and leave. He was anxious to meet with Paul Billy, but first he must send some men to ride the northern and western borders of the Fannin. He couldn't chance losing any more cattle from that division.

He instructed his cowhands to gather the outlaws' horses to deliver to the corral at TSR headquarters. They could swing by and drop them off on their way to the Fannin Division. Ace could always use extra horses, and it was a sure bet that Abe Zink and his men wouldn't be riding them anymore!

After Treff sent his men on their way, he turned to Aldo. "As soon as all the cattle are separated, you and one man take the big steers, and Patch and the other hand can take the female stock to the Fannin Division. Try to put the cows back in the area with their calves."

"You know how cantankerous them cows can be, Treff," Aldo reminded him. "They might not claim their calves after being away so long."

"And what about the unclaimed cattle?" Patch asked. "Them with that brand we don't recognize. What do we do with them?"

"Leave them in the pens, and we'll decide about them later. They'll have plenty of water and enough grass for a week or two."

Before mounting his horse to leave, Treff gathered all the ranchers around for a final word. "I sure hope y'all can be with us next week for our open house at the TSR. I know this is a busy time, but please come if you can. I'm real sorry I have to leave you this evening, but I have some important business to take care of, and unfortunately it can't wait any longer."

Mike Stanley, of the Crazy S Ranch, spoke for the group when he said, "Treff, we can't thank you enough for what you've done. We know you've been away a long time, and we understand you need to go. We'll see you next week, and talk about this some more."

❖　　　　❖　　　　❖

As he rode south toward Central headquarters, Treff cupped his hands around his mouth and gave a soft hoot. The sound drifted through the pines and echoed back to him so realistically that he was not sure whether he heard the answer of a real live owl or a signal from his friend. But in minutes, Paul Billy appeared at his side, erasing any doubt.

"Boss, I followed Ritta like you asked," Billy said, a proud grin spreading over his rusty face.

"I never doubted that you would," Treff assured him. "What did you find out?"

"Not as much as I wanted to. He rode to Jacksonville and seemed uncertain, like he was trying to decide what to do. He went to a saloon and had a few drinks, and then he got into a card game, and that was about all. Then last Sunday, I was about to give up on finding out anything when he met a fat feller, and they talked a long time. Pretty soon they were joined by a tall, light-haired man. I didn't know either of those men. Never saw either of them before."

"Billy, could you hear what they said?"

"No, I had to keep hidden from them, so I never could get close enough to hear their words."

"What happened next?"

"After about an hour, the light-haired man left and rode south on the Alachua Trail. Slim Ritta and the fat man rode northwest from Jacksonville. I followed them until they went into the Okefinokee Swamp. The fat feller appeared to know where he was headed. I thought I should come on back to talk with you."

"Well, it's good to know that Ritta was not one of the Abe Zink gang. Maybe he was lucky enough to find another job," Treff said. "I sure don't want to suspect an innocent man."

"There are not many cattle in the Okefinokee," Billy replied skeptically, "but maybe he did find something."

As they continued their ride toward headquarters, Treff said, "Billy, I'm sure you've already heard that we found a big group of rustled cattle west of here."

"I would like to hear about it from you."

Treff proceeded to fill in all the details to let Billy know everything that had happened.

In the distance, they could hear laughing and hammering and boards being slammed together. "Ace has some of the men making tables and digging pits for roasting meat," Treff explained. "The Dover celebration is just a few days away. Billy, let's don't go looking for any more cattle until after our open house. Don't you need to go home and check on your own cattle?"

"It would be good if I could," Billy replied.

"Then do it, Billy. Before you go, you might check with Amaly or Ace to see if they want you to bring any game when you return. You could get some turkeys or a deer on the way back from your spread."

As Billy turned his pony, Treff added, "If Marv can spare you, I'd like for you to stick around here all three days of the open house to help out. That will give you an excuse to see everyone who visits."

❖   ❖   ❖

On Friday, the squeak of wagon wheels announced the early arrival of friends and neighbors as they began pulling into the Dover yard for the open house. Spirits were unusually high, not only because of the recovered cattle, but also from widespread relief over the news that Abe Zink and his men would no longer be a threat. Word had spread rapidly throughout all of the Florida Territory. But in spite of that, just as Ace had predicted, all of the guests had left people at home to protect their property.

An aura of merriment filled the air as old acquaintances were rekindled and new friendships begun. The gift of three days to share experiences and visit with friends was a rare luxury, one that would be talked about and remembered for years to come.

The women clustered in groups to help Amaly and Cissy prepare and assemble the food. Young brides and new mothers listened as older women freely offered their advice learned from experience. Small babies were passed around, so that each woman could cuddle and admire the newest additions to the Territory. Words piled on top of words, and everyone seemed to talk at once, but the busy hands never stopped working, and the laughter that permeated the air was proof positive that this was a happy day.

The menfolk, busy turning a variety of meats over the hot coals in the pits, centered their conversation on cattle and horses. They all wanted to learn more about how Treff found the rustled cattle, and how he managed to get the best of Abe Zink. "That outlaw eluded us all for longer than I care to admit," one man declared. Treff just smiled a secret smile. He continued to turn the spit that skewered a big wild hog, one that Ace had fattened especially for this occasion.

Small children raced shrieking through the yard, playing tag and hide-and-seek with Brad and Curry in the lead. Others gathered in groups, squatting on the ground to play marbles or mumblety-peg. Little girls cradled corncob dolls in their arms, comparing their "children" in much the same way that their mothers were doing.

A year had gone by since some of the families had seen each other, and everyone seemed hungry for news and fellowship.

Treff enjoyed helping to cook pork and beef over the oak wood coals, but he left the pits to wander across the grounds and visit with some friends he had not seen since last year's frolic, and he especially wanted to meet some of the new settlers in the Territory. He was grateful for this annual respite which gave him a chance to forget about business for a few days. But his insistent thoughts kept drifting back to his meeting three days ago, when Paul Billy returned after following Slim Ritta to Jacksonville.

Since that meeting with Billy, business had been pushed aside while attention focused on preparations for the frolic. Now, as Treff mingled among his friends and neighbors, shaking hands and welcoming them, he used his ready smile to mask his concerns.

All day Friday, people continued to arrive. As Ace had predicted, Johnny Coe brought several jugs of his corn liquor, and Paul Billy arrived with a generous supply of venison and two large turkeys. Cakes and pies multiplied on the long tables as if by magic. Steam from open kettles of swamp cabbage mingled with the tantalizing aroma of meat roasting in the pits and drifted upward through the trees. Three of the four fiddlers arrived early and could already be heard playing their lively tunes in the barn.

At last it was time to gather for the meal. Ace banged on his dinner bell to capture the crowd's attention. "We would like to give thanks for each of you being here with us today and for all the many blessings the good Lord has bestowed on us this past year, so let's all bow our heads."

Silence fell over the group as Ace raised his hearty voice in prayer. "Our Heavenly Father," he began, and even the smallest children stood motionless, eyes closed and heads bowed. At the final "Amen," the noise revived as though it had never stopped, and everyone circled the tables, heaping their plates to overflowing.

"Land sakes," one woman declared, "I want to try some of everything, but I'd have to stay here a week to do that."

"Ace, you and Amaly outdone yourselves this year!"

Music from the barn soon set feet to tapping, and some of the young people drifted in that direction. Treff, with his plate in his hands, stood just outside the barn to watch the couples whirl around in time to the lively tunes. He was pleased to see that their guests were having so much fun.

Most of the people had traveled a long distance to reach the TSR. Now, with their appetites satiated, they were tired and ready to relax. The fiddlers came outside to fill plates from the ample supply of food remaining on the tables, but after only a brief break, their music continued. Their melodies now were slow and soothing, in keeping with the mood of the crowd.

Children began to yawn, and soon people began to disappear in the darkness to find a place to sleep. Everyone wanted to be well rested for the main day on Saturday!

Some had wagons to sleep in or under. Others found places in the four corners of the barn or on the porch of the Dover house, where they could listen to the music as they drifted off to sleep. The music in the barn lasted for another hour, and then all was quiet except for the songs of whippoorwills and other night birds—and an occasional snore.

❖ ❖ ❖

Much to her distress, business at the Leon Division had prevented Marv from coming home on Friday, but when she rode into the horse corral on Saturday, her presence caused an immediate stir. Young men suddenly began to show off in whatever way they could think of to attract the attention of the pretty girl with the flaming hair.

If Marv noticed their antics, she showed no evidence of it beyond a friendly smile and a wave. After storing her saddle and gear and turning her horse loose into the corral, she went into the house to clean up and change clothes.

As soon as she walked through the door, the women in the kitchen clustered around her. "My, she gets prettier every year," one of the women told Amaly.

"You're plum growed up, honey," another exclaimed. "Reckon you'll be gettin' yourself married before long."

Marv's cheeks matched her hair. "No time soon," she replied, and hurried off to her room.

Her would-be suitors stood just outside the kitchen door, awaiting her return.

"She shore is pretty," Hardy Jones said.

"Yeah, and she can ride a horse and shoot a gun!" Will Wade added.

"You reckon she can cook?" Hardy wondered.

"As pretty as she is, who would worry about cooking," several young men said at the same time.

After Marv changed clothes, she found her parents on the porch and gave them each a kiss. They were talking with some people who were new to the Territory. "This is our daughter," Amaly said, proudly introducing her to several people at once.

"Marv," Ace said, "I'd like you to meet Zeke Mongol, owner of the Brown Owl Ranch east of Payne's Prairie. And this here is Al Green and Cal Whitney, two of his foremen. And I want you to meet Drag Johnson, a new employee of the BOR outfit."

As Marv shook hands with her new acquaintances, she smiled politely at each one, her thoughts wandering over the frolic and all the fun ahead, until she looked into the deep brown eyes of Drag Johnson. She tried to look away, but an unfamiliar stirring, a feeling she could not explain, held her attention on this imposing newcomer, and she knew at once that she wanted to learn more about him.

"Welcome to our home." She turned to Zeke Mongol. "We've heard a lot about your ranch, and we're just real happy you could be with us this year," she said, smiling widely to conceal the unsettling effect of Drag's presence.

"Thank you, ma'am," Zeke said. "It's too bad our spreads are so far apart. We can't stay but for the day, but we sure do appreciate the chance to get better acquainted with y'all."

Amaly was aware of the subtle change that occurred when Marv shook hands with Drag Johnson, and she made a mental note to be careful in expressing her reservations about the Brown Owl Ranch. "Ace, why don't you introduce Zeke and his men to the others, while Marv, Cissy, and I help the other women finish getting dinner ready?" With that, she grabbed Marv by the arm and gently pulled her into the kitchen.

❖ ❖ ❖

Drag Johnson's experience with women was limited to dance hall girls and a couple of country belles in the backwaters of Mississippi. Within those limits, he had experienced a great deal of success. Convinced that women could not resist his charm, Drag knew he was going to see more of the beautiful daughter of Ace Dover! Yessirree, things were working out just like he planned! He could hardly believe his good fortune! Right here in front of him was the woman who would help him reach his goal, and very soon now he would be a big, important cattle owner in the Territory. He just needed to play his cards right! He found it almost impossible to keep his mind on business as he was introduced to other people. All he could think about was Marv Dover and the unbelievable progress of his plans.

As soon as the noon meal was over, the women cleared the tables and put the food away, while the men began setting things up for the big barn dance scheduled for that evening. Saturday night was always the most fun for everyone, and excitement ran high all afternoon.

Late in the afternoon, Zeke Mongol gathered his group of men around and told them, "We best be making our regrets with the Dovers, so we can get back through the Seminole land before dark."

Drag hung back and waited for a chance to speak to Zeke alone. "Boss, would it be all right with you if I waited till morning to start back? It's been a long time since I've been to a barn dance, and I shore would like stay for that, if you don't have any objection."

"It's fine with me, if our host don't care," Zeke replied. He smirked knowingly. "You're probably wasting your energy if you think you can make time with the Dover girl, though."

"Boss, I ain't never seen a gal I couldn't make time with. Anyway, it'll be mighty nice to spend the night here and come back to the Brown Owl tomorrow."

During the afternoon, Treff sought out Patch to ask him about the cattle in the Latigo pens.

"Did you get all of the cattle to their rightful owners?"

"Yeah, we think we did," Patch answered. "The only unclaimed cattle are them eighteen head with the HO-over-bar brand. They're still in the pens. There's enough grass for a couple of weeks, and the flowing well provides plenty of water.

Like the sun coming out from behind a cloud, Treff suddenly realized where he had seen that <u>HO</u> brand! He had seen it on the spread of Hank O'Mara over by the Yellow River near Pensacola. The HO-Bar Ranch! He would send a rider out there next week.

"Patch, I know now who that brand belongs to. I saw it on the way home from Mobile this last time." He told Patch the whole story of finding Hank O'Mara wounded and robbed by outlaws, and drew a map in the sand to show Patch the location of Hank's spread.

"Monday I want you to ride over there and let him know we have eighteen head of his cattle. Invite him to come down here and get them. I'd like for our family to meet him. But if he's too busy to come, or if he would rather just sell them, you can go ahead and make a deal with him. Tell him we'll pay him nine dollars a head; that's a fair price. And be sure to get a Bill of Sale. Take enough money with you in case he decides he wants to sell, but try to get him to visit us anyway, whether he wants his cattle or not."

"I'll leave before sun-up on Monday," Patch promised.

"The trip will give you a chance to get the latest reports about the renegade Indians from Georgia and Alabama. See if you can find out what's going on."

After supper Saturday evening, the fiddlers played with renewed energy. Their tunes were so spirited that some people suspected they had found one of Johnny Coe's jugs, but the musicians denied the accusations. Square dancing began with a frenzy. Almost everyone joined in as they circled right and then left; young, old, and in-between all shared in the merriment.

"Swing yor pardner, do-si-do!" Grampa Stevens was the same caller they had used for all the years Treff could remember. Nobody knew the old cowhand's age or where he came from, but he sure could call a good square dance. He knew just how to persuade everyone to take part. Many

HERB & MUNCY CHAPMAN

a youngster had learned to square dance under the old man's patient direction.

Treff stood by the barn door, absorbed in watching the dancers. As the fiddlers paused between tunes, Treff heard a soft call of the brown owl and knew that Paul Billy was beckoning him outside to speak with him. He made sure that no one noticed when he casually ambled outside.

Standing in the shadow of the barn, they spoke in whispers. "Treff, that tall, light-haired man dancing with Marv is the same man I saw meet with Slim Ritta and the fat feller in Jacksonville."

Treff was amazed at this shocking bit of information. "Are you sure?" he asked, knowing the answer already, and Paul Billy nodded to confirm it.

If Treff had wondered about the man dancing with his sister, his interest now immediately increased. Just who was this man, Drag Johnson? Where did he come from, and what was his connection with Slim Ritta? It seemed highly unlikely that those two even knew each other. And who was the fat man? Were they all involved with the BOR Ranch?

"Paul Billy, I want to know more about Drag Johnson. I want you to follow him when he leaves. Don't let him see you, but don't let him out of your sight. If he goes to Jacksonville, follow him to see what he does. If he goes straight to the BOR, you might just as well come on back here till the end of the week, but I still want you to go to Jacksonville next weekend to see if he meets with the same people. And while you're there, see if you can get a name for the fat man."

Paul Billy knew that the BOR people were suspected of throwing a wide loop, even though they had never been caught in the act. He understood why Treff wanted to know Drag Johnson's connection, especially now that Marv might be innocently involved.

After their talk, Paul Billy disappeared into the quiet darkness of the night and Treff slipped back into the barn to join the dancers.

The young ladies were dressed in their fanciest clothes, and their ruffled skirts whirled around their ankles as the young men spun them around the floor. The young men tried to out-do each other with their fancy steps, each hoping to attract the attention of a special girl.

Having made his arrangements to stay over the night, Drag Johnson entered into the dancing with an expertise obtained in saloons of the bayou country of Louisiana and Mississippi. He was one of the best dancers on the floor and drew discreet glances from many of the pretty young girls. Marv Dover was no exception. She watched him out of the corner of her eye, still trying to understand the unsettling effect his handshake had caused.

She could feel the color rising in her cheeks when she saw him coming toward her. He was indeed different from any man she had ever met. His appearance and manners were quite distinguished. She felt confused and unable to think of the right words to say when he asked her to dance. That was not at all like Marv Dover, who managed cowhands every day and considered herself a capable, self-reliant woman.

As he spun her around the floor, Drag looked into her eyes. "You dance very well. I'm happy your father invited me to spend the night, and I'm glad Mister Mongol was able let me get back to work a day late."

"What do you do for Mister Mongol?"

"Oh, he had some problems and I just agreed to help him out a while. I was on my way down to Fort Brooke when I stopped at the Brown Owl Ranch. Mister Mongol had lost a cowhand and was looking for someone to fill in. One thing led to another, and I said I'd stay and help him through the marking and branding season, just as a kind of favor, you know. I need to be on my way to Fort Brooke, so I am happy the season is about over."

"I—that is, we are glad you could come and join us this year. I guess if you are going on to Fort Brooke we may not have that privilege again." Marv felt a strange combination of disappointment and relief when she thought of the possibility that Drag would soon pass out of her life. She did not understand her own emotions at all!

Drag was quick to make it clear that he had no such intentions! "Now that I've found you, I assure you I'll be back. That is, of course, if you'll permit me." Without seeming too forward, he wanted to impress her with his interest in returning, and he did not have a lot of time.

A young man tapped Drag on the shoulder to claim Marv for the next dance. Marv tried to hide her disappointment as Drag released her to the arms of Hardy Jones. As he whirled her away, she called over her shoulder, "We would welcome you anytime."

Almost every young man present lined up for a turn

to swing Marv Dover around the room and impress her with his talents on the dance floor. But although she spent the rest of the evening gaily dancing to every tune, she was never able to completely erase the tall, fair-haired man from her thoughts.

12

AFTER DINNER ON SUNDAY, the Dovers' friends began gathering their belongings and making preparations to start back to their own homesteads. Handshakes and hugs and even a few tears made it evident that everyone hated to leave. Because the recent increase in outlaw activities had heightened anxiety about personal safety as well as the protection of property, those who could do so hoped to reach home before dark.

"I swan, I do believe this-un's been the best yet," an elderly neighbor declared, putting her plump arms around Amaly's shoulders. "You and Ace done yourselves right proud, and I just hope I live to come back ag'in next year!"

"Livie, we're counting on it," Amaly assured her. "And from the looks of things, you'll have another grand-youngun by then to bring along with you."

One by one, the families came forward to express their appreciation for the warm hospitality and their genuine affection for the family who made it all possible. For many, the fun and fellowship of this memorable weekend would be the last social event for a full year.

Drag Johnson had paid his respects to the Dovers on Saturday night. "I'll be leaving before daybreak tomorrow, so I want to thank you now for inviting me. It's been a mighty pleasurable weekend." Then, pulling Marv aside into the shadows, he spoke to her in lowered tones. "If it's all right with you, I'd like to visit here again in three weeks."

Marv wondered if he could hear the loud hammering of her heart. She tried to control the quaver in her voice. "I—that is, we—we'd all be happy to see you." She made a mental note to tell her parents, so that if he did return, they would not embarrass her by acting surprised. Seldom at a loss for words, Marv floundered for an appropriate phrase now, one that would be polite without sounding forward. "We were glad Mister Mongol and the rest of your group were able to be with us this year, even though it was a short visit." She smiled and edged her way back into the light.

Drag had already decided to leave as early as possible the next morning. The quicker he returned to the BOR, the quicker he could move ahead with his plans. He knew that he would have to go to Jacksonville for the next couple of weekends, but maybe in three weeks he would stop here again and sample the sweet nectar of Marvelous Dover's charms before traveling on down to Fort Brooke and another step closer to success.

When he rode out at dawn on Sunday, he wore a wide smile of satisfaction on his face. He congratulated himself on the fine way all his plans were falling into place. He was so absorbed in his plans for the future that he had not even the slightest suspicion that the keen, dark eyes of Paul Billy were watching his every move.

After the last of their guests had ridden away, the Dover family congregated on the front porch to discuss the weekend activities. Amaly collapsed into the nearest rocking chair, and Ace claimed the one beside her.

Cissy herded her two sons inside for a nap. "Aw, Mom, we ain't even sleepy," Brad protested.

"We *aren't* sleepy," Cissy corrected, pushing them ahead of her toward the door.

"Shucks, Mom," Brad persisted, "me and Curry are cowhunters, and cowhunters don't take naps!"

"Well, I know at least two who do," Cissy told them, following them into the house.

"Come on, Ten. I reckon we better help with the clean-up," Rusty said, watching several of the hands busily working to return the yard and the barn to normalcy.

"I'll help for a while," Ten agreed, following Rusty down the steps, "but I need to get back to the Fannin before dark."

"And I better go get our wagon and bring it around here to the front so me and Cissy can get loaded up while the boys are asleep," Jeremiah said. "Can't get much done with those two underfoot."

Marv sat on the top step, and Treff stood leaning against the porch rail. "I've been wanting to tell y'all, but

I just haven't had the chance. I finally remembered where it was I'd seen that HO-over-bar brand. It belongs to the young man I told you about that I found wounded in the woods on the way back from Mobile, name of Hank O'Mara. He has the HO-Bar Ranch over by the Yellow River. I already talked to Patch about going over to see him tomorrow."

"That's great!" Ace replied. "He'll sure be surprised. Bet Mister O'Mara never thought to see those steers again. They're a decent-looking bunch, too. Maybe he'd like to sell them to us."

"I told Patch we could offer him nine dollars a head and see if he was interested," Treff said.

Ace thought about this for only a moment. "Yep," he agreed, "that sounds fair enough."

"I told Patch to invite O'Mara to come and visit with us, regardless of what he decides to do with his cattle."

"I hope he'll come, then," Ace said. "I'd like to meet the feller."

Treff had another thought to present to Ace. "I'd really like to be free the next three or four weeks to continue working on our security needs. I think Paul Billy and I may be on to something, but we need more time. So is it all right if Marv stays on to manage the Leon Division?"

"That's fine with me," Marv said quickly, trying to conceal her eagerness. She enjoyed working outdoors, and she loved the feeling of independence that came with managing a division of her family's ranch. She wished she could do it all year long. It sure beat cooking and cleaning house and sewing! Men got all the good breaks!

"Son, I'm proud to hear you're making headway. Want to tell me about it?"

"Not yet, Ace, but if you'll let Marv continue at the Leon, I hope to have something to tell you before long."

"It's important for all of us to put a stop to the rustling and the Indian raids from the north," Ace admitted. "Your Mama and I worry a bit about Marv being out in the woods, but I have to admit she's managing that division as good as any man could, and I know she's happy doing it."

Amaly's brow creased, and her rocking chair picked up speed, but she wisely maintained her silence.

"I'd best get my gear together and start back to the Leon headquarters," Marv said, jumping up from the steps before her father could change his mind. "I need to be there at daylight in the morning." She hurried inside to pack her saddlebags.

When Treff was at last alone on the porch with his parents, he spoke to them in confidence. "There's something else I want you both to know. I feel bad about not telling Marv everything I'm doing, but you need to know that I have Paul Billy trailing that fellow that calls himself Drag Johnson. Paul Billy's going to keep a close eye on him for the next couple of weeks. I found out that he met Slim Ritta and another fellow in Jacksonville, and I want to know more about him. I couldn't help but notice that Marv seemed more than a little attracted to our guest, and I want to be careful not to hurt her feelings or to have her think I'm being overprotective of her."

A satisfied smile erased the creases from Amaly's

brow. "Ace knows I have had a difficult time feeling comfortable about Zeke Mongol. There is just something about that man that makes me uneasy."

"Now, Amaly, we've never been ones to judge people by gossip. There's been a lot of rumors about the Brown Owl Ranch, but nothing has ever been proved."

"I know, I know." Amaly admitted. "Still, I'll be more than happy if Treff can find out something about Zeke Mongol and his gang, and especially that Johnson fellow that seems to be sweet on Marvelous."

Ace nodded. "I hope you're able to find out more about him, Treff. It's time to put those rumors to rest if they're false, but if they're true . . ." He let his unfinished sentence hang in the air.

"Marv told me that Mister Johnson has asked permission to visit here in three weeks," Amaly told Treff. "If you could learn something about him, I'd feel a lot more comfortable."

Their conversation ended as Marv bounced out of the house carrying her saddlebags, and Jeremiah pulled his wagon up to the front porch.

"Land sakes! All our children are going to be leaving us at once, Ace! Let me get up from here and pack up some of those vittles for them to take back with them. We have enough left over to feed us all for a month!"

Ace descended the steps to help Jeremiah load his wagon. On the porch alone with Treff, Marv took advantage of an opportunity for a private word with him.

"Treff, there is something I've been wanting to tell you, but I don't want Mama or Daddy to hear me. I don't want them to change their minds about letting me go."

"What is it, Marv? Some kind of trouble?"

"Probably not, but I think you should know. Last week, Cotton reported seeing a couple of the Godwin boys looking at a herd of our cattle in the Peoples Pasture down at the Leon. The Godwins high-tailed it when they saw our TSR rider coming their way. We don't know what they were doing, but they had no business being there at all."

"I'm glad you shared this with me, Marv. Just have the fellows keep an eye out on our southern border. Next time I'm down that way, I'll get over to Grandma Godwin's and warn her to keep her sons off our property."

Monday morning skies were clear and blue, randomly dotted with cotton-white clouds. A bald eagle soared silently above the treetops in search of his morning meal. Mockingbirds and a meadowlark warbled their songs, and to Treff, as he stood on the porch of the Dover house waiting for his Indian friend, it seemed a beautiful start to a new week.

He listened for the call of the brown owl as his eyes scanned the surrounding woods, anxious to spot Paul Billy and hear what he had learned by following Drag Johnson Sunday morning.

"Good morning, my friend!"

"Paul Billy! You never cease to amaze me! I was looking for you in the wrong direction." Treff shook his head, laughing. "You have an uncanny ability to remain invisible until you choose to be seen!" He watched Billy tie his pony to the hitching rail. "I'll go inside and get us some coffee, and we can sit out here and talk."

When Treff returned to the porch, he was carrying two large enameled mugs filled with steaming coffee. "Isn't this a beautiful Monday morning, Paul Billy?"

"Yes, it is. But the winds are gently whispering among the palmettos this morning, telling us to be careful. They say there is trouble before another moon passes."

Treff had learned long ago to pay attention to Billy's warnings. He didn't understand how the Indian was able to forecast the future so accurately, but past experiences had taught him to listen.

"What does the wind talk about, Paul Billy?"

"It doesn't tell me; it only says 'be careful.'"

"What did you find out about the tall, fair-haired man?" Treff asked.

"He went directly to the BOR headquarters. Then he went south and rode the border of the property with another cowhand. I saw nothing unusual."

"Was anything wrong when you checked your own cattle last week?"

"No," Paul Billy assured him. "Everything was in good shape. Paulito watches things good. He will continue to do a good job."

"I'm glad to hear you say that, because you and I need to spend a few days north and west of the Santa Fe Division looking for signs of strangers and possible trespassers. That will put you closer to Jacksonville next weekend when you go back to see what you can find out about the fat man and anyone else you think might be connected to Johnson."

"When do you want to start?"

"I know you've been going pretty strong and steady. You need to catch a little rest, and your horse could use a break, too. We'll leave at daylight tomorrow. If you want, get one of the new rifles and some ammunition to take with you."

❖   ❖   ❖

Next morning the two of them rode north from the Central Division headquarters. The sure-footed ponies worked their way through the thick scrub, dodging gopher holes as though they had eyes in their hooves. The air became cooler as they approached the Santa Fe River.

"Let's cross here," Treff suggested, pointing to a bend where the river narrowed and the horses could step easily through the rocky shallows.

The two men followed the river's winding north-westerly course, keeping their eyes focused on the ground for signs of strange horse tracks, but all they saw were ordinary deer and hog tracks, along with the tracks of birds and small wild animals.

"There's a watering place around this next bend," Paul Billy said. "Let's stop a minute and give our ponies a chance to drink."

Climbing out of his saddle, Treff bent close to the ground. "What kind of track is this, Paul Billy?"

"Those big ones are bear tracks, and those smaller ones are the mark of a panther. This is a popular watering spot for the animals, but I don't see any horse tracks."

The men stooped to splash the cool water on their faces, and Paul Billy cupped his hands to smell the water. "This is sweet water, good to drink," he said, lifting his hands to his lips and drinking his fill. Treff, following his lead, did likewise.

Both men and horses felt refreshed as they continued their journey along the riverbank until the river turned to the southwest. Pulling Rojo to a stop, Treff said, "Lets drift on west toward those springs near John Whit's place."

"Isn't his place just this side of the Suwannee River?"

"Yes. We can cross the Suwannee there and follow it up to Suwanoochee Creek. After that, if we still haven't found anything unusual, let's drift around the part of the Okefinokee that tries to come into the Florida Territory. When we reach the southern part of that, it will be time for you to head into Jacksonville."

"What will you do then?"

"I think I'll drop down the south branch of St. Marys River on my way back home."

"Treff, why don't you follow a westerly track from here, while I make a big circle to the east and north around the Itchetucknee River? We can meet at the springs by Mister Whit's spread."

"That's a good idea, Paul Billy. If either one of us gets there after dark, we can use the brown owl signal to find each other. Some of that forest you will be traveling through is mighty thick. It may take you longer than me to reach the springs."

"You're right about that forest being thick, Treff. It's

the perfect place for outlaws to hide out. That is the reason I want to ride through the edge of it. But if I find any sign of a hideout, I won't do anything until I talk with you."

"I like your idea, Billy. That gives me a little extra time to stop by the way-station on the postal route and visit with that nice old couple who lives there. I'll find out if they've had any trouble with outlaws, and I'll see you this evening."

The two men parted, and Treff cut north through the woods. Traveling alone, he had only his horse to talk to. He watched the ground for signs of unshod pony tracks. "Doesn't look like Indian ponies have ridden through here recently," he decided. "At least, not since the last rain." Rojo responded with a slight nod that seemed to indicate his understanding.

Treff searched without success for signs of unusually heavy cattle movement. Occasionally he spotted cattle grazing between clumps of palmettos, but they quickly scattered out of sight as soon as they saw him. By mid-afternoon, Treff welcomed a reprieve from the unseasonable heat and allowed his horse to slacken his pace. They traveled easily through the peaceful green meadows that dotted the northern part of the Territory and watched herds of deer graze along the edges. The air was filled with the sounds of birds, giving no indication of any disturbances or intruders in the area. Everything seemed perfectly normal. Even Rojo's ears remained relaxed, and in spite of the seriousness of his mission, Treff found himself enjoying his ride.

When he reached the postal route, he turned east

toward the way-station. He had not seen Zeb and Ethel Sorenson in over a year, so he looked forward to stopping for a short visit. As he dropped his reins to the ground, Zeb came shuffling out the door to see who had just arrived.

"Well, lookee what the cat drug in! Ethel, put the coffee pot on. We got us a stranger among our midst. We-uns thought you had done forgot where we was, young man," Zeb exclaimed excitedly.

"I could never forget y'all," Treff said. "Your wife's cooking is too good to forget. She's famous from Jacksonville to Pensacola for her meals."

By this time, Ethel had come out the door. Hugging Treff around the neck, she blushed from his praise. "Just because of them good words, you have to come in and have a piece of my apple pie with your coffee." She took Treff by the arm and pulled him into their small hut. The air was fragrant with the spicy aroma of cinnamon and fresh-baked apples.

"Zeb, now I know why you always look so healthy around the middle," Treff declared, lifting a hefty forkful of warm apple pie to his lips. "I never could understand how you ever convinced this pretty lady to come all the way out here in the woods to cook like this. That was sure your lucky day!"

"Treff, you be just as full of blarney as ever," Ethel exclaimed, "but don't stop. I love it!"

"Seriously, as well-known as you are, you should consider moving into Jacksonville or Tallahassee and opening an eatery," Treff said. "Everyone would eat there. There just ain't enough places to get a good meal in this territory." Without Amaly near to correct him, Treff slipped into the easy vernacular of a Cracker cowhunter.

"We done talked about that some," Zeb admitted, "but me and Ethel be pretty happy where we're at. We don't rightly know how we would manage to start a place like that, no-way."

"Whenever you decide you want to make such a step, I'll be glad to help you," Treff volunteered. He realized that their major problem was a lack of money. In addition to an act of kindness, he knew that it would be good, sound business to help them get started.

"What are you up to?" asked Ethel, deliberately changing the subject. "What brings you this way?"

"I'd like to tell you it was to get a piece of your apple pie, but I am really checking to see if I can pick up on any signs of strangers or Indians being in the area."

"They's been new people coming in from the Carolinas and Georgia," Zeb said. "I heerd about some west of us that's had some of their cattle kilt by Injuns. They ain't been no trouble right here, but last week I did hear that Ito Bensen lost about fifty head of cattle to rustlers, east of here."

"Was he able to find where they went?"

"No, Treff, he weren't. They headed north toward Georgia, but then they was a heavy rain that washed out their tracks."

"Have you heard anything about He-with-One-Eye-of-an-Eagle?" Treff asked.

"People round about think his men been killing them settlers' cattle, but no one has seed him with 'em. The rumor we hear is that you done sent word to him that he was a coward, and someday you would wear the feather from his hair," Zeb said. "Them's dangerous words, son!"

Treff smiled. News sure did find a way to travel fast! Then his smile vanished and his eyes turned to cold, hard steel. "That's true, Zeb. He is carrying one of my bullets today, but unfortunately he is still alive and continuing to cause problems. I look forward to finding him. I've got some unfinished business to settle with that savage."

Ethel's face clouded with worry. "Treff, be careful, darlin'. No one has ever been able to catch up with that Injun. He be smart as a fox and mean as a rattlesnake. But even a rattler will give a man a fair warnin'. That one will kill you from ambush if he can."

"I sent word to him that ambush was the only way he would ever try to get me," Treff said. "I told him he was afraid to face me. He is filled with vengeance and pride, and I hope my message will bait him to save face by meeting me in the open."

Finishing his second cup of coffee, Treff pushed himself up from the table. "Ethel, that piece of pie was just outstanding! If I ever find a woman who can cook like you, I might consider marriage myself. I thank you both for your hospitality. It would be a pleasure to stay longer, but I'm due to meet a man, and I need to be on my way." He put his arms around Ethel and gave her a warm hug before he shook hands with Zeb. "Take care, you two. I'll stop in again when you least expect me."

The couple stood in the doorway and waved to him until he was out of sight.

Treff threaded his way through the oaks and pines

and palmettos toward the springs where he was to meet Paul Billy. He kept thinking about the cattle lost by Ito Bensen. They were not among the herds they had recovered from Abe Zink. There must be another group of rustlers working this part of the Territory. He should get word to Jeremiah to let him know as soon as possible. The Santa Fe Division might conceivably be close enough to have cattle rustled by that same group of outlaws.

When he heard a distant sound of running water, Treff knew that he and Rojo were near the springs where they were to meet Paul Billy. Following that sound, he soon came upon the clear, bubbling pool of fresh water.

Treff swung himself out of the saddle and searched the area for tracks, at the same time picking up small pieces of dry wood. On the south side of a thick stand of oak trees, he built a small fire in a sheltered spot west of the springs. If the fire produced any smoke, the thick canopy of oak tree limbs would prevent it from being seen. After putting a tin of water on the fire, he unsaddled Rojo, gave him a good brushing, and turned him loose to graze. He knew that he and Billy would not sleep by the fire, so he might as well wait until later to tether the pony, after they chose a spot where they would sleep.

In the blue haze of early evening, he heard the call of a brown owl and knew that Paul Billy was nearby. He waited until he heard the call once more before he answered. He gave his soft reply, and, quite as he expected, Billy immediately emerged without a sound, out of the dusky shadows.

"You made good time, Paul Billy. I've only been here long enough to make some coffee. I did spend some time with the Sorensons over at the way-station, and that held me up awhile."

Billy unsaddled his horse, listening quietly as Treff related everything he had learned from his friends at the way-station. Billy shook his head. "Just as we feared, it looks like we have another gang of rustlers in this area."

"That's the way it looks," Treff agreed. "Now tell me what you found. Did you see anything suspicious on your way here?"

"I saw enough unshod pony tracks going south in the woods to know you need to be very careful on your way home," Paul Billy said. "My guess is that they came from the Georgia border. About fifteen or twenty ponies went into the woods just east of Becker's Point, and they didn't come back out that same way. Of course, they could have come out somewhere else, but I didn't try to follow the tracks for fear of alerting them that someone was around. If they don't see my tracks, they won't know I was there."

"Did you see anything else?

"As I came northwest from the heavy woods, I saw an occasional set of tracks of one, and sometimes two, unshod ponies traveling towards the southeast. It looked to me as if a band might be gathering to make a raid someplace. Other than that, I didn't see anything unusual."

"It begins to look as if we did the right thing in making this trip, Paul Billy. I don't know what we can do, but at least we will be better prepared."

❖   ❖   ❖

During the next two days, the men rode north a short way into Georgia before turning south along the western border of the Okefinokee Swamp. Although they kept a keen watch for any visible signs of horse or cattle tracks, they were unable to turn up any new information.

"Paul Billy, didn't you live in the swamp at one time?"

"When I was a small boy, my family lived in the swamp. The Okefinokee covers a very large area, and in it there are many islands. There are not many Seminoles left on the islands. Now it is mostly outlaws who live there, or people making moonshine, and a few settlers that are trying to make a living in the swamp."

"Have you been back to the swamp since your family moved south?" Treff asked.

"Once or twice with my father, but not enough to be able to find my way easily. A man can easily get lost in the swamp if he is not careful," Paul Billy replied. "Many have disappeared in there and were never heard from again."

Although the two men did not travel deep into the swamp, Treff was happy to be in the company of one who knew more about this area than most. He doubted that Paul Billy would remain lost for very long, no matter where he was.

When they reached the southern end of the swamp, the two friends said their good-byes and prepared to separate. Paul Billy again reminded Treff, "Don't forget what the whispering winds told me earlier this week. Be very careful as you ride along the south branch of the Santa Fe River and around that lake it runs through."

"I won't forget, my friend."

With a wave of his hand, Treff turned his pony and headed south toward the Santa Fe to see Jeremiah, and Paul Billy rode east toward Jacksonville.

Heeding Paul Billy's warning about the whispering winds, Treff used extreme caution as he worked his way south. He did not see or hear anything that aroused his suspicions until he approached the lake which Indians called the Lake of Blue Water. Suddenly Rojo's head came up and his ears twitched nervously, as he looked straight ahead. At the same time, Treff spotted the tracks of a large number of unshod ponies, all leading toward the lake.

Sensing danger, Treff felt his heart hammer and his pulse race through his veins. Placing his hand on Rojo's neck to keep him quiet, he eased his horse around in a westerly direction toward the Santa Fe Division. He did not want to meet fifteen or twenty renegade Indians by himself. He was not certain that they were unfriendly Indians, but he suspected they might be, because of the secretive way they had come to this meeting place. He could not afford to take a chance.

There was a good chance they were gathering to raid someone, and their target might very well be the northern division of the TSR! He had to alert Jeremiah at once, so that they could make preparations to be ready in case they were attacked.

He eased Rojo back from the lake shore, deeper into

the concealing shelter of the woods, and held his breath until he was certain his presence had not been detected. As soon as he had a comfortable margin of large live oak trees between him and the lake, he pressed Rojo into a ground-covering trot, heading for the Santa Fe to find Jeremiah.

13

TREFF REACHED SANTA FE headquarters only to find that Jeremiah had ridden out to the western part of the division. "He done left before daylight," the cook told him. "Said he needed to look at some steers that was about ready to go to market."

Treff hesitated only briefly before turning his horse to the west and riding off to find his brother. Fortunately, Jeremiah had already started home and was not far from headquarters when the two brothers met.

Even before Treff spoke a word, Jeremiah could read the urgency on his brother's face. He reined in his horse. "What's the trouble, Treff?"

"Jeremiah, I just came up on a band of Indians organizing on the western edge of the Lake of Blue Water. Sure as shootin', they're fixin' to raid somebody—us, more'n likely. I'm pretty sure they weren't Seminoles."

"How do you figure that?"

"Paul Billy and I have seen the tracks of unshod

ponies coming down out of south Georgia. They come sneaking in like panthers, in groups of twos and threes. I think the ones I saw by the lake are probably some of that bunch." Treff explained briefly what he and Paul Billy had been doing this week and about the warning Billy had given him from the whispering winds.

"How many Indians were in that group by the lake?" Jeremiah asked.

"I'm not certain, but judging from their tracks, I would guess there were around fifteen; possibly twenty. Paul Billy warned me that they might be working up a war party, and I didn't wait to stand around counting. I just high-tailed it out of there!"

"Do you think we should get a posse together and catch them in their camp?"

"No, I don't think that would be wise, Jeremiah. With war about to break out between the army and the Seminoles, I don't favor attacking a band of Indians like that when we aren't certain of their intent. So far, we've been able to keep good relations with the Seminoles, and I wouldn't want to make the mistake of attacking friendly Indians. 'Course, it goes without saying, I'd have no trouble defending our property if we are attacked by Indians, no matter what tribe they come from. But if we plan in advance, we ought to be able to take care of that group without too much trouble, if they do turn out to be a bunch of outlaws."

"Yeah, you're probably right," Jeremiah agreed. "We'll keep our men scattered on the east side of the spread for a few days, under cover where they won't be seen."

"And don't forget to keep someone on guard during

the night, in case the Indians decide on a night raid. I'll go down to the Central Division right away to alert Rusty. If we all work together maybe we can put a stop to the bunch of savages that have been killing cattle to our west."

"I sure hope so. I'm going up to the house to warn Cissy to keep the boys inside. I don't want to take any chances where my family is concerned."

"Jeremiah, I think I need to warn you about the bunch that follow He-with-One-Eye-of-an-Eagle. A while back, I sent him a challenge that's sure to have infuriated him, and he may be planning an attack to prove to me that he is not a coward."

"I heard about that. Treff, I know you and Ten have a special reason for the grudge you carry against that red devil, and I hope some day you get a chance to send him off to his happy hunting ground. Just be careful it's not the other way around. I don't believe he's a coward, and he's very smart, but he sure is a ruthless scalawag."

As Treff turned to go, he called a last warning over his shoulder: "Tomorrow is Sunday and the Indians might decide that's a good time to plunder. They might figure on us being shorthanded with some of our men off for the day."

"Don't worry about us here, Treff," Jeremiah assured him. "You just hurry on down to Central so Dad and Rusty don't get caught with their pants down."

Pushing Rojo to a fast canter, Treff arrived back at the Central Division just as the supper bell rang, but in his present state of agitation, he had little appetite for food.

Ace and Rusty, recognizing the swift approach of

hoofbeats, met Treff on the front porch. Treff gave them a quick summary of his urgent mission, and the three men sat down in the cane rockers to consider their options.

Finally, Ace made a decision. "We must organize a security network on the east side of this division. That might very well be the area the Indians plan to attack."

"I'll get started on that right away," Rusty said.

"Where is Paul Billy?" Ace asked Treff.

"He's gone to Jacksonville to check on Slim Ritta and those guys he's been meeting every week. Billy probably won't be back before Sunday night or maybe even Monday morning."

"We could sure use his help with this," Rusty said.

"I think I'd better travel down to the Leon Division tonight and alert Marv," Treff said. "She's probably far enough south to be safe from this group, but I want her to have her men armed and prepared, just in case the Indians do decide to attack that far south."

"Why don't you stay with her for a couple of days?" Ace suggested. "Your mother and I can't help but worry about her, and we'd feel a lot better about her if you were there. Rusty and Jeremiah and I have enough men to look after this end of things. We can send for Ten and his crew if we need more help."

Treff had mixed emotions about Ace's request. He wanted to be in two places at once. He did not want to leave and miss a possible chance to meet He-with-One-Eye-of-an-Eagle face to face. His heart pumped faster just imagining the opportunity he had craved for so long! But when he thought of Marv down at the Leon Division, there was no question about which of his priorities was most important, and he realized that Ace's plan made sense. "That's a good idea, Ace," he finally admitted. "If Paul Billy comes back before anything breaks loose, you might get him to scout the area to find out what that group of Indians is up to."

Ace had fought Indians for many years when he first came to the Florida Territory, and he was confident that he and his men could handle things. Nevertheless, he held a high respect for the uncanny intuition and skills of Paul Billy and knew that he could be a big help to them in times like this. "As soon as he gets back from Jacksonville, I'll have him scout the Indians, and then I'll send him down to the Leon Division."

"Treff," Rusty added, "I'll send Lucky Rollins to alert Ten to what is going on. He needs to know, even though his division is probably not in any danger from this bunch,"

"I'll stay at the Leon headquarters until Paul Billy comes to see me," Treff said. "And Ace, don't you and Mama worry about Marv. You know I would never let anything happen to her."

Amaly stuck her head out the front door. "Didn't you men hear the supper bell? The food is getting cold while you're out here socializing!"

"We're coming," Ace promised, and the three men filed into the dining room. Treff took his place at the table and tried to eat, although his mind was on other things, and his stomach rebelled at the thought of food. Still, he thought, it was easier to eat than to face an interrogation from Mama, especially one that might put a damper on some of his plans.

As soon as he could politely do so, Treff asked to be

excused from the table and went to the barn to saddle his horse. He checked his saddlebags, making sure he had a good supply of ammunition, and headed south to the Leon Division.

Dawn streaked the horizon with shards of silver as Treff approached the headquarters of the Leon. Early morning was his favorite time of day. Dew glistened on the wiregrass like tiny diamonds, and a chorus of birds filled the air with music to announce the beginning of a bright new day. To his right, through the haze over a small pond, Treff watched ibis and egrets forage in the shallow water for food, while in the distance, three deer grazed contentedly. In this peaceful setting, it was hard to imagine that the Seminoles were in a fight for their very existence, and that not far from the Santa Fe, at this very minute a war party of outlaw Indians might be gathering to plan a deadly attack.

As he rode into Leon headquarters, he saw the cook come out the back door carrying a bucket toward the water pump. Treff raised his hand in silent greeting to let the man know of his arrival. Without stopping to talk, Treff guided Rojo on toward the stables and dismounted. "You've put in a lot of miles in the last twenty-four hours, Rojo. What you need now is food and water and a good rest." Treff brushed the horse's coat to a glossy sheen. "I have to take good care of you, Rojo. I wouldn't know how to get along without you!"

Placing the horse in a stable stall, he gave him a generous scoop of grain, a double handful of hay, and a lump of sugar. "That should take care of you for a while," he said, patting the horse's damp flanks, and Rojo nuzzled his neck in appreciation. Treff picked up his rifle, slung his saddlebags over his shoulders, and trudged up to the main building.

The headquarters buildings of the Santa Fe, Fannin, and Leon all shared an identical layout. The east end of the log building contained a small but comfortable office, furnished with a table and three or four benches. The manager's living quarters on the west end consisted of two bedrooms and a small room for reading.

Even though her children were now grown, Amaly encouraged them all to continue to read as many books and newspapers as their busy schedules would permit.

In the center of the building was a large mess hall where everyone congregated for meals unless they were in the woods working cattle. Next to this, a kitchen extended to the north.

Each room contained at least two slots in the walls, through which rifles could be fired in case of attack. A wide, comfortable porch bordered the south and east sides of the building and was a favorite gathering place in warm weather.

Several yards from the main building, a bunkhouse was attached to one end of the stables, although cowhunters often slept on the ground when they were checking cattle in the woods. On Sundays, most cowhands could usually be found at headquarters.

To keep from disturbing Marv at this early hour, Treff quietly placed his rifle and saddlebags on the floor inside of the front door of the office and sat down at one of the long wooden tables to have breakfast.

Hank Tomlinson had been cooking for the Leon ever since he broke his hip and three ribs when his horse stepped in a gopher hole and fell on top of him. Hank had limped ever since, and riding was so painful that he could only tolerate the suffering for very short distances. Making him a cook had been an act of mercy in the beginning, but he had surprised them all by proving to be a more-than-decent cook, even though the cow crew constantly made a point of telling him otherwise.

"Good morning, Hank. I've sure been looking forward to some of your biscuits and gravy, especially if you throw in about three eggs and a cup of coffee."

"That's easy to do, Treff. Better than that, I have a hot pork chop sitting here just waiting for you to come home."

"Outstanding, Hank! I sure do miss your cooking when I'm away from here."

While Hank cooked his eggs, Treff continued to talk. "How are things going with your aching bones, Hank?"

"We be getting along tolerable well, Treff. Some days are worse than others, but most of the time we manage."

The sound of Treff's voice woke Marv from a deep sleep. Could it really be Treff, or was she just dreaming? Quickly, she pulled on her clothes and splashed cold water on her face. Without pausing to brush her mass of tangled red hair, she rushed out to see her brother. She grabbed him around the neck and hugged him, almost knocking him out of his chair. "Oh, Treff, it is you! What a nice surprise!" Then suddenly realizing the unlikely occurrence of such an early morning visit, her face clouded over with worry. "Is everything all right with the folks?"

"They're fine," Treff hastily assured her. "I came to warn you that I've spotted some Indians gathering near the Lake of Blue Water. We have reason to believe that they are some of the outlaws from Georgia and Alabama. During the past twenty-four hours, I've been to each division, just to alert everyone. This is my last stop, and I plan to stay here until Paul Billy comes to get me."

"Oh, Treff! Do you really think they will come this far south?"

"No, I don't think they'll want to get this far from the country they're most familiar with," Treff predicted. "They must know the army and the Seminoles are fighting, and they won't want to get mixed up in that. But of course we can't be certain, and I think we should be prepared."

Marv sat across from Treff, and Hank brought out a cup of black coffee and placed it in front of her.

"I suppose you've heard about my challenge to He-with-One-Eye-of-an-Eagle? Word seems to have gotten around." Treff chuckled.

"It's nothing to laugh at, Treff. You know he's out looking for you, and he'll stop at nothing to get his hands on you." Her big green eyes clouded with concern. "We'll need to keep at least a small crew riding our southern boundaries, but I think we should have most of the men patrol our east borders for the next couple of days."

"I agree with you, Marv. Remind them that if we have to make a stand, the headquarters building is the best place."

"I will. You look exhausted, Treff. When is the last time you slept?"

"I don't know, but I'm going now to catch a few winks. Wake me up when it's time for dinner." Treff pushed himself away from the table and reclaimed his rifle and saddlebags. "Don't worry about being quiet, Marv. I feel like I'll be able to sleep through anything."

Treff went to his room and sat on the edge of his familiar bed to pull off his boots. He didn't even bother to take off his work clothes before he sprawled across his comfortable feather tick, and almost immediately he was snoring like a logger.

As the cowhands sauntered in for breakfast, Marv related all the things that Treff had told her. She concluded by saying, "Don't forget to take along plenty of ammunition for your rifles. If you find yourself in any kind of trouble, fire a couple of shots, and someone will come to help you. Come back in for dinner, and we'll talk about what else we should do during the next couple of days."

On Sunday morning, as Paul Billy waited across the street from the Cowhunters Saloon, he began to wonder if his trip to Jacksonville this weekend had been for nothing. He had not seen a trace of the three people he came looking for, and he was beginning to feel discouraged. He was about to go down the street for a plate of beans when he heard the sound of horses approaching from the northwest. Looking back, he gave a smile of satisfaction as he saw Slim Ritta and the fat man riding into town.

He waited until they had hitched their ponies and entered the Cowhunters Saloon. Then he drifted down the street and leaned against the wall of the General Store to watch. Because the Seminole conflict was starting to become more widespread, Paul Billy did not want to call attention to his presence in the town.

In about an hour, he was rewarded by the sight of Drag Johnson swaggering up the street from the other direction. When Drag was even with the Cowhunters Saloon, he looked furtively both ways before disappearing through the doors.

As casually as he could, Billy strolled across the street to peer through the doors of the saloon. He could see the three men huddled over a table at the back of the room, completely absorbed in conversation. If only he could get close enough to hear what they were saying! But Billy knew that this was impossible without revealing his identity, so he returned to his earlier lookout spot and waited for them to come out. It was two full hours before the three men emerged through the swinging doors, mounted their ponies, and left town the way they had come.

As soon as the men were out of sight, Paul Billy returned to his horse and headed southwest toward the Central Division. The words from the whispering winds kept echoing in his mind, and he urged his horse to a speed that left clouds of leaves and dust whirling up behind him. Something dark and dangerous was looming ahead; he could hear it in the wind. It bothered him that he still could not get a clear picture of the danger, but he was certain that somehow it involved the Dovers.

Billy's southwest route pointed him around the lower edge of the Lake of Blue Water, so he missed the pony tracks that led to the lake from the north. While he was still a great distance from the lake, his sensitive nostrils caught a whiff of smoke, even before he observed the gray puffs rising above the trees. He paused to listen and heard the faint sound of Indian chants echoing through the forest.

He did not linger to determine what it meant, but instead hurried faster, hoping to reach the ranch by dark.

The horse began to show the strain of his rider's urgency. His coat glistened with perspiration, and his pace slackened noticeably. Although he was anxious to get to the TSR, Billy knew that his faithful animal had been ridden hard and needed to rest. After they crossed the Santa Fe River, Billy turned his horse toward a nearby spring and stopped to claim an hour of rest for them both.

They were about six miles east of Santa Fe headquarters, and about the same distance north of Central. Even though darkness was beginning to fall, Billy knew that without rest, his horse would not be able to make it to either place. He led him to the spring and let him drink his fill of the cold, bubbling water before tethering him where grass was available. Satisfied that his horse was well-situated, Paul Billy leaned back against the bark of a spreading live oak tree and went to sleep.

He was dozing when he began to feel the vibration of the ground beneath him, barely perceptible at first, but growing stronger by the second. Instantly awake, he mounted his pony and peered through the dusk to discover the cause of the earth's tremor. In the distance he was barely able to see a group of Indians swiftly riding directly toward him. Swift as a streak of lightning, he slipped back out of sight among the heavy oak trees. Had they spotted him? He was almost certain they had not. He must get to the Santa Fe Division at once, to alert Jeremiah and his men. He figured the Indians would stop at the river long enough to water their horses, and that would give him a head start. He turned his horse in the direction of Santa Fe headquarters and gave him full rein. The intelligent horse seemed to sense his rider's urgency and bolted through the thickets as though he had been resting all day.

When he neared the ranch, Paul Billy signaled with the brown owl call and waited to receive an answer. Galloping up to the ranch in the dark unannounced could be dangerous, and he did not want to end this jour-ney with a bullet in his chest. When he heard the soft brown owl echo, it was a mighty welcome sound! Following the call of the owl, he was soon able to locate one of Jeremiah's cowhunters, Whitey Govern.

"I knowd that was you as soon as I heard you, Paul Billy, cause we ain't had no brown owls around here of late."

"I was very relieved when you answered my call," Billy admitted. "Listen, Whitey, there's no time to waste. There's a big group of Indians headed this way. By now, they're probably already west of the Santa Fe River."

Alarm sounded in Whitey's voice as he began to bark orders. "You go on to headquarters and let Jeremiah know, while I get word to the riders up here. Be sure you use that same signal when you get near the buildings, Paul Billy, because Treff has done told us that something like this might happen. Everyone is on the lookout, and they've all got guns. Tell Jeremiah if we have any trouble, I'll fire my pistol twice to let others know, and for them to do the same."

As he neared the buildings, Paul Billy once again used the brown owl signal until he obtained a response. Jeremiah's response was almost instantaneous, and Billy rode forward without fear.

"What is it, Paul Billy? What's happened?" Jeremiah knew this was no ordinary social visit.

As concisely as he could, Paul Billy told Jeremiah everything he had seen by the lake and of his conversation in the woods with Whitey Govern. "Are you sure you have enough men to handle an attack if it should come down to that?"

"Based on what you've told me, I think we'll be okay. We've already been making our plans. I hope we're ready."

"Then I need to get on down to Central to alert Ace and Rusty. Could you let me have a fresh horse? I've been pushing mine pretty hard, and I don't know how much farther he could go."

"Hey, that's no problem," Jeremiah responded. "There's a bunch in the corral. Take your choice. Put yours in the barn and give him some grain and hay."

After Paul Billy took care of his horse and settled him in the barn, he chose a fresh young pony from the corral. Jeremiah helped him saddle up. "I can't thank you enough for your warning, Paul Billy. Tell Dad to be careful and not to worry about us over here. We'll be fine."

"Jeremiah, I think the Indians will probably wait until dawn before they try to do anything. After I talk to Ace, I will try to scout out where the group is camped. That will give us a better idea where they might attack."

Billy rode into the night as quietly as he had come,

but now he knew at last what the whispering winds had been trying all week to tell him.

Paul Billy chose little-known paths to take him into the Central Division, west of headquarters, escaping the eyes of the riders Ace and Rusty had positioned to guard the eastern border. He felt safe traveling this route and did not find it necessary to send his signal until he reached a cypress head west of the main building. Here he would remain safely concealed until he was recognized.

He called twice before he received an answer. He repeated the call, then pulled out from the shelter of the trees and rode toward the building.

Ace and Rusty met him as he cut across the pasture. "We sure are glad to see you, Paul Billy!" Ace greeted him with an outstretched hand. "We hoped you might get back tonight, but we weren't sure you would."

Paul Billy, though always polite, did not waste time on pleasantries. "Mister Dover, you have Indians camped somewhere between the Santa Fe River and the ranch. I have just come from Jeremiah, and he wants you to know he and his men are ready to defend against attack. I hurried as fast as I could to tell you about these Indians, because I don't know exactly who they are or what they plan to do."

"Where did you see them, Paul Billy?"

"I was resting at the springs, about six miles east of Jeremiah, when I saw them riding directly at me."

"Did they see you?"

"No, I don't think so."

"Billy, could you tell how many there were?"

"It was almost dark, and I was not able to get a good

count. It looked like about eighteen or twenty in the group."

"If we knew what they planned, we could easily handle a group that size," Rusty said.

"I don't figure they will do anything before dawn," Billy said. "If I could get a couple hours' sleep before then, I would scout around and try to find out where they are. Then I could follow them and maybe warn you or Jeremiah."

"That's a good idea, Paul Billy. Find you a spot in the bunkhouse, and we'll wake you in a couple of hours if you don't get up on your own."

"Don't worry about your horse," Rusty added. "We'll take care of him and see that you have a fresh one when you leave."

After Jeremiah had watched Paul Billy ride away from Santa Fe, he gathered his cowhands together to tell them what he had learned. "Paul Billy doesn't think the Indians will attack before daybreak, but we can't take any chances."

Rio Penta, a foreman and one of the older, more experienced hands, had an idea. "Why don't we set a trap?"

"What do you mean?" Jeremiah asked. "Tell me what you have in mind."

"Well, why don't we move that herd of steers from the Bodie pasture to the Egret Marsh on the eastern border? We could do that tonight if we was careful. Then we can set about half of our crew amongst the palmettos northeast of the marsh and the other half in the woods just to the southeast of the marsh. If the Injuns see them nice, fat cattle, they might take the bait and raid the herd. If they do, we would have 'em in a crossfire."

Jeremiah thought about Rio's idea. He looked up into a clear, starry sky, with barely enough moonlight to work by. The cattle might move if they didn't spook. If the plan didn't work, the cattle could be left in the marsh to graze on the good maidencane, and no harm would come of it.

Finally he agreed. "All right, let's try it. Rio, you take about eight cowhunters and see if you can get the herd to move. If the cattle spook, just let them go and we'll collect them tomorrow. If they go to the marsh, just let them do what they want. Put your men in the palmettos north of the marsh before daylight, about twenty feet apart. All of you take your rifles and plenty of ammunition. Get some sleep if you can, but keep somebody on watch all the time."

Rio selected the eight men he wanted. "Each of you fellers better take some water and jerky. When we settle down in them palmettos, we won't be coming out for no breakfast," he said.

Jeremiah told them all, "I'm going to send Les Wingate down to tell Ace and Rusty what we're doing. They'll be making their own plans, and they need to know about ours. The rest of us will get something to eat and some water, and then we'll spread out in the woods just southeast of Egret Marsh and wait for daylight. I'll take my telescope; it might help me to see what's coming.

The woods are mighty thick east of our ranch, and the Indians could be pretty close before we see them."

Later that night, in the darkness that is blackest just before dawn, Les Wingate cupped his hands around his mouth and aimed his signaling call toward Central Division headquarters. After several tries, he finally got a response that told him it was safe to approach the building.

Ace and Rusty stood in the yard, surrounded by a group of cowhunters who appeared to be mapping out their plans and assigning responsibilities. Every eye in the group focused on Les, wondering what news he came to bring them.

Les began to unfold the details of Jeremiah's plan to set a trap on Egret Marsh.

Both Ace and Rusty seemed pleased and excited about the plan, and if they were apprehensive about the danger surrounding Jeremiah and his family, they both made a great effort to conceal it.

"Grab something to eat, Les, and then you might as well stay here and join our men for the rest of the day," Rusty said. "We'll have to go ahead with our own plans as if we didn't know anything about what Jeremiah is doing. We don't know what the Indians are planning, and we can't take a chance by leaving this division unprotected. The only change we'll make in our plans is to send four men up to the northeast corner of this division to hide in the woods, in case the Indians try to come in our back door. Les, as soon as you get something to eat, you can go with that group."

"Just grab some grub and take it with you," Ace prodded impatiently. "You four men need to get started as soon as you can. You ought to be hidden before daylight, but if you don't get a move on, that may not be possible. Be careful to stay concealed in the thick trees if you move in there after daylight."

"Right, Dad," Rusty agreed. "I'm going to divide the rest of you men into groups of three, and I want you to scatter out about a mile apart along our eastern border."

A nervous rumble sounded through the crowd, followed by silence as they waited for their assignments. "If you get into trouble, just remember that gunfire will draw the other groups to help you," Rusty assured them.

"We may not see any Indians today," Ace said, "but I think we should keep one man here with you and me and Amaly to protect headquarters, just in case we do."

"Let's keep Jose Lee here with us. He can help Francesca with the cooking and chores. If we get any wounded men, Mama is going to be so busy doctoring, she'll need all the help she can get."

"I don't even like to think about that," Ace admitted, "but you're right. Your mama's a fair hand at doctoring, and she even knows how to handle a rifle if she has to."

"Mama? A rifle?" Rusty just learned something new.

"Get on with you now," Ace admonished, flustered that he'd said more than he meant to. "Go wake up Paul Billy so he can get a bite to eat before he heads out toward Payne's Prairie. Be sure he knows what's going on over at the Santa Fe Division. Tell him to signal us if the group heads this way instead of going into Jeremiah's trap."

Rio Penta had selected his cowhunters wisely, and they had no trouble moving the steers to Egret Marsh before daylight on Monday. The cattle welcomed the maiden-cane in the marsh and grazed happily for an hour before they lay down on the sodden ground to wait for morning.

Rio congratulated his men. "That was a job well done. It ain't even daylight. Find yourself a place to settle. I'll stand the first watch."

Each man selected a hiding place. After carefully checking his ambush spot for rattlesnakes, each cowhunter tied his pony behind a bush, picked up his water and jerky, and pulled a rifle from his saddle before hunkering down in the brush to wait for daylight.

At the same time, about three-quarters of a mile south, Jeremiah and his men were busy selecting spots in the thick underbrush that would give them a good view of the marsh. Then they too settled in to wait for daylight.

Just six miles north of Central Division, an Indian sat proud and erect on his pony, scanning the area with his one good eye. He chose a high spot near the edge of a dense forest, about two miles east of Santa Fe. His men waited in the woods while he scouted the area, but they were growing restless and impatient, anxious to begin the attack. As their mighty leader, he alone must choose the proper moment to move ahead with his plans.

He was confident that the tall marsh grass and palmettos would provide adequate cover to allow him to move slowly from place to place without being seen. His sense of security might have weakened if he had realized that at that very moment, Jeremiah Dover was perched high in an oak tree on the edge of the ranch, searching for him through the lens of his telescope.

For a long time, the Indian and his horse stood motionless on the gentle rise of earth. The first faint light of day filtered through the green, leafy canopy above his head, reflecting shadows on the patch he wore over one eye. After several minutes, he moved to another place and again stood studying the land in front of him, trying decide the best and safest way to attack.

He had been called a coward! He would soon prove which of them was the coward! He must do as much damage as possible to the ranch of the Utinara Kid! Then he would cut out his tongue before he dared to call him a coward again!

His one keen eye focused on the scene of cattle rising to their feet to graze in the tall grass of the marsh. He kept watch for a long time before he finally satisfied himself that there was no one around to guard the cattle. Finally he raised one arm in a signal that called the rest of his men to him. Dividing them into two groups, he sent one group into the south side of the marsh, and he led a group to the north side. As they moved forward, their excitement mounted! This was going to be a great day for the War God! Many cattle would soon be dead!

As the Indians wove their way in and around the dense palmettos, each step took them closer to Egret Marsh. Jeremiah, from his high perch, caught a flicker of movement, and a surge of excitement coursed through his body. He slithered down the trunk of the tree, unmindful of the rough bark that cut into his callused hands like bits of ground glass. His words came out in a hoarse whisper. "There are eight Indians coming right toward us and ten more heading north of the marsh. They must be heading for the cattle. They haven't seen us, so hold your fire until they get all the way past us. Make each shot count; we don't want a single one of them to escape."

Lying on his belly beneath a bush, Jeremiah propped his rifle on a log and waited for the Indians. He held his breath as the hoofbeats sounded closer and closer.

At a signal from their chief, the two groups of Indians charged toward the marsh, their excitement resounding in their whooping voices. The early dawn reflected ominously on their brightly painted skin as they thundered into the marsh, their guns blazing and their victorious war cries rising in the air. Startled cattle began to drop to the ground.

As suddenly as a bolt of lightning, deadly gunfire erupted from the palmettos on the north side of the marsh and from the thick brush on the south.

One by one, Indians began to fall from their ponies, terror and amazement registering on their faces. In vain they tried to return fire, but their rifles were empty, their ammunition spent by firing at the cattle, and they were defenseless. Too late, He-with-One-Eye-of-an-Eagle realized that he had led his men into a trap, and he screamed at them to get away. Midst the gunfire from two directions, and their brave chief shouting at them to retreat, the Indians were greatly confused, and the result was pandemonium. As the noise of rifle and pistol fire escalated, Indians continued to drop to the ground. In their confusion, some were slow to react, but others turned and raced back to the safety of the woods. Through the trees, they watched in shock as their mighty leader turned to make his escape.

Before his horse could reach the sheltering trees, the chief felt a sharp blow to his right shoulder. He was struggling to stay on his horse when he felt the final blow to his head that caused him to lose control. His horse reeled, and the Indian catapulted to the ground before his whole world turned black and silent. Drifting in and out of the cloud of darkness, he tried to move but his body refused to respond.

As suddenly as it had begun, the gunfire ceased. Several warriors had managed to get away. Others were scattered among the tall maidencane, where they had landed as they fell from their horses. The morning air hung silent until birds, deciding the melee was ended, gradually began to lift their voices in song. Several Indian ponies began to graze the marsh grass, unaware that their masters would never ride them again.

Jeremiah cautiously pushed his head above a mound of palmettos. "Don't be in too big a hurry to come out from your cover," he warned his men. "There may still be live Indians hiding in the grass." After a wait of several minutes, the cowhunters began to cautiously emerge from their hiding places.

"Rio, have some of your men collect the dead and wounded Indians and bring them under these oak trees," Jeremiah said. "Whitey, you take three men and catch the Indian ponies and bring them to the trees. We'll take a count and see if we come out even."

Rio and his men found eleven dead Indians scattered around the marsh. As they were bringing them to the oak trees, Whitey came in with the same number of Indian ponies.

"It looks like we found everyone," Rio said. "I counted seven dead steers that I could see. The herd is pretty well scattered after that raid."

"Look at this!" Whitey exclaimed. "This-here Indian is wearing a patch over one eye. Do you reckon this-here is the one they say has the eye of an eagle?"

Jeremiah found it hard to believe that they had actually trapped the famous outlaw chief. He knew that Treff would be mighty disappointed not to have been a part of this. He felt quite sure that this was the Indian Treff and Ten had spent so many years searching for. That patch on his eye said it all. He was dead, all right. Mama could quit worrying about that one!

"Load an Indian on each pony, and tie his hands and feet together under his pony so he won't fall off," Jeremiah directed. "We'll take them all down to Central Headquarters."

"You want us to try and catch them Injuns what escaped?" one of the cowhunters asked hopefully. The success of the morning had stimulated the enthusiasm of the entire group.

"No, let's don't worry about them right now.

Alonzo, you and Pete and Shorty come help me take these eleven ponies down to the Central Division so we can show the dead men to Ace and Rusty. Rio, you and your crew better stay here to guard the eastern boundary in case the Indians return," Jeremiah said. "They just might come back here looking for their chief. In a day or two we'll try to pick up some of their tracks to see where they lead.

"And Rio, you better get some men out here quick to butcher these dead steers and try to salvage the meat and hides. It'll soon be too late when the sun gets up much higher."

"I'll get some fellers on that right away," Rio assured him.

"One other thing, Rio. I'd appreciate it if you'd send one of your men up to my place to let my wife know we're all right. Tell her all of our men are safe, and I'll be home soon to tell her about it."

As the group led the Indian ponies southward, He-with-One-Eye-of-an-Eagle was beginning what was to be his last journey on earth.

14

"PA, COME QUICK! LOOK A-YONDER!"

Rusty's shouts carried across the TSR pasture and brought Ace and Amaly both running to the front porch. "What is it, Rusty? What's the matter?"

Using their hands to shield the sun from their eyes, the two of them stood on the porch staring in amazement toward the direction Rusty pointed. A strange sight met their eyes. Coming out of the woods into the clearing, Jeremiah and three of his men rode slowly toward headquarters, leading a peculiar procession of horses and Indians.

Amaly, sizing up the situation immediately, turned and went back into the house. The riders were halfway across the pasture before Ace realized that every one of the Indians was dead, and he broke out in a run to meet his son.

"Good gosh amighty, Jeremiah! What have you gone and done?" But Ace's broad smile assured Jeremiah that his father was well pleased.

There was much excitement as family and hands crowded around to listen while Jeremiah told them about the Indian attack, and how Rio Penta's plan had trapped the Indians in a lethal crossfire by Santa Fe cowhands.

Ace slapped Jeremiah's shoulder. "Son, you sure put an end to at least some of our problems!"

The cowhands untied the Indians and laid them side by side on the ground. Ace looked noncommittally into each rust-colored face until he came to the one with a patch over one eye. He stopped in his tracks and gasped audibly. "This one here, you reckon he's the one Treff's been itching to get put his bullet in?"

"Yep, Pa, I think that's the one who killed his parents," Jeremiah confirmed.

"Rusty, you better send a couple of riders to the Fannin and the Leon Divisions, and tell Ten and Treff to come here to headquarters. We're going to need their help to identify this man."

"My brother is not going to be happy about this," Jeremiah predicted.

"Why not? I think he should be *very* happy. The man's dead, isn't he?"

"Deader'n a fish that's been out of water all day. But Treff was aiming to be the one to finish him off."

"Well, we can't do anything about that now. And we can't stand out here in the sun jawing about it all day, either. We better get these Indians in the ground before the whole place starts smelling."

"What should we do with the ponies?" Jeremiah asked.

"Turn them into the corral," Rusty suggested. "They look like pretty decent ponies. We can probably break them to the saddle, put some shoes on their feet, and have some good cow ponies."

Les Wingate came out of the barn leading a crew of cowhunters, each with a shovel in his hands. "Where do you want them Injuns buried?"

"Put the Indian with the eye-patch in one of the stables until my two brothers get here, Les," Rusty said, "and then load the others in a wagon and take them out to the edge of the prairie and bury them. Be sure to have them a long way off from our property."

"If we're sure this one-eyed man is the person Treff and Ten have been searching for, we'll bury him away from his men in a place where no other Indians can find him," Ace said. "That way his spirit will wander forever and never reach the happy hunting ground."

Jeremiah chuckled. "Hey, Dad! I thought Treff was the one carrying that grudge!"

Ace only smiled and turned back to the house to find Amaly and tell her all that had happened.

Treff and Ten both arrived before daylight Tuesday morning.

"I'm not sure I want to look at him," Ten admitted. "It's not going to be a pretty sight."

"Depends on how you look at it, little brother." But Treff had mixed emotions himself. Part of him hoped that the dead Indian in the stable would indeed be the coward

We want him to disappear from sight forever."

"Want us to keep his horse?" Les asked.

"Yes, we might as well. He's a fine animal. After you bury the Indian, turn his horse in with ours for now. We'll break him to saddle later. Let Cissy know I'll be back home in the morning, and tell Rio to be sure and keep the guard up tonight."

"What about them Injuns that got away?" one of the cowhunters asked. "Do you want somebody to follow their tracks to see where they went?"

"I've been thinking about that. Jose Lee is a good tracker. Tell Rio to send Jose and one other man to follow their tracks. If they can pick up a lead, I'd like to find out whether they're still in the area, or if they've gone back up to Georgia."

❖   ❖   ❖

By midmorning on Tuesday, things were beginning to return to normalcy, although everyone was still talking about the success of the clever eagle trap!

Before returning to their own operations, the four brothers sat down to a late breakfast with their parents. This was an unusual occurrence for the middle of the week, and Amaly was beaming with maternal pleasure. "Francesca, bring out another pan of those biscuits and another jar of my guava jam; some more of that venison sausage, too."

Treff piled scrambled eggs on his plate and reached for a hot biscuit. "You know, Mama, it seems like a big weight was lifted from my shoulders yesterday. I didn't realize how much I was burdened down by wanting to get even with that Indian."

Amaly smiled. "I think it is a big load off all our shoulders, Treff. We understood how you and Ten felt. But you will never know how thankful I have been through the years that Ace found the two of you and brought you home to me after your parents were killed." Her eyes misted as she looked at Ten and Treff. "Ace and I are proud to be the parents of four very fine sons."

Ace pulled a handkerchief from his pocket and blew his nose, then changed the subject abruptly to avoid showing his own emotion. "We expect Patch Searcy back before long, probably the end of this week or the first of next. We're hoping he'll bring the owner of those HO-Bar cattle back with him. We want all of you to come here to the headquarters next weekend to help make him feel at home. Treff, tell Marv we want her to come; and Jeremiah, don't you dare to come down without Cissy and my two grandsons."

The big family breakfast was like a holiday, and no one wanted to be the first to break it up, but finally Ten pushed his chair from the table. "The sun is up, and we have lot of work to do in the Fannin before we can come back here to meet our visitor from Yellow River. I sure enjoyed that breakfast, Mama. There is no other place on earth where the food is this good."

"That goes for me, too," Treff agreed. "I hate to eat and run, but if I can be excused, I do need to get back to work."

"You are all excused," Amaly said. "Thank you so much for staying over." As her sons rose from the table,

Amaly remained seated, and each son in turn bent to kiss her on the cheek before returning to work.

Treff and Paul Billy rode south to the Leon in silence. Billy made no comment about the new white feather stuck in the band of Treff's hat, but he was perceptive to Treff's churning emotions. He knew that his friend needed time to sort out his thoughts about the death of the great Indian chief.

They were almost at the edge of the Leon before Treff finally broke the silence. "Did you manage to see those men when you were in Jacksonville over the weekend?"

"Yes, I saw all three of them, but I still could not hear what they talk about, and I haven't been able to find out a name for the fat man. I wanted very badly to get closer so I could hear what they were saying, but I didn't think I should go into the saloon, what with some of the Seminole tribes at war with some of the settlers."

"That was a smart decision, Paul Billy. Next time you go, we need to send somebody with you; somebody that can go into the saloon without being recognized by either Drag Johnson or Slim Ritta."

"Maybe there's a cowhunter from the Fannin that they haven't ever seen, Treff."

"I can't think of anyone right off, but let me think about that for a day or two. But don't worry; we'll find somebody to send along with you when you go to Jacksonville this coming weekend.

"Paul Billy, let's swing by headquarters to let Marv know what happened up at the Santa Fe. I left her with a lot of baggage to carry. And I want her to know what we plan to do this week."

"Good. That will give me a chance to get a fresh horse from the corral."

"It's been awhile since I've ridden the entire border of the Leon," Treff said. "I'll visit with Marv while you switch ponies. Then I'd like to spend the rest of the week going around the whole spread. We can start at the northwest corner and go clear around the division, ending back on the north side by Friday. That'll put us close to Central. My folks are having some kind of a get-together, and I'm supposed to be there in time to eat supper Friday evening."

"That will work out well for me, too. It will let me get an early start to Jacksonville."

"Paul Billy, I may send Aldo Hagen to Jacksonville with you. I'll think about it during the next couple of days. I don't believe Drag Johnson would know Aldo, and he's a good gun hand, if it comes down to that."

At Leon headquarters, Treff saw Marv's horse hitched to a post by the front porch. "Looks like she's here," he said, dismounting and handing his reins to his Indian friend. "Paul Billy, would you take Rojo down to the barn and give him some water and grain while I visit with Marv? Get yourself another horse and whatever supplies you think you'll need for the next three days, and let's plan to leave in two hours."

Marv, inside the office working on records, heard her brother's voice and ran to the porch to meet him.

"Treff! Oh, I'm so relieved to see you. I've been worried ever since you left in such a hurry. Is everything all right with Mama and Daddy?"

"Everyone is fine," Treff assured her. "Let's go inside where we can talk, and I'll tell you all about it."

Treff followed his sister into the office and told her about the Indian attack at the Sante Fe Division. Seeing her eyes widen with alarm, he hastened to reassure her. "Jeremiah is fine. In fact, none of our men was even injured."

"But you left in such a rush, I was afraid something was terribly wrong."

"No, Marv. The reason I rushed out of here was because Ace called Ten and me to the Central Division to look at one of the Indians Jeremiah and his men had killed."

"What was so special about a dead Indian?"

"This Indian wore a patch over one eye," Treff replied tersely. "Ace wanted Ten and me to see if he was the one who killed our parents."

Marv did not need to ask the obvious question; she could read the pain in his eyes. Tactfully, she left him alone for a few minutes. "I'm going to the kitchen to get us some coffee. I'll be right back."

While the two of them sipped steaming coffee from giant tin mugs, Treff went into great detail telling Marv all that had happened over the weekend, but he was very careful not to mention the trips to Jacksonville.

"It will certainly be a relief if this group of Indians turns out to be the ones responsible for all that cattle slaughtering along the Georgia border. I'd have to guess that there are several groups, but this one was especially important to me because it's the group that killed my parents," Treff said.

Marv covered one of his big, rough hands with both of her own. "I know, Treff. I'm glad it's over."

"By the way," Treff continued, "Paul Billy and I are going to ride the borders of the Leon for the rest of the week. We'll be sleeping in the woods the next couple of nights. We plan to be at the red clay gully on the north border by noon Friday, so that we can get back to Central in time for supper. Mama and Ace want you to be there, too. Why don't you meet us at the gully and ride home with us?"

"Sure, I'd like that. It'll be great to sleep in my own bed for a couple of nights. Since you're here, would you like something to eat before you leave?"

"That sounds good, Marv. And how about asking cook to give Paul Billy some grub, too."

After lunch, Treff found Billy waiting for him by the hitching post. He had already saddled the horses, tied on saddlebags, and slipped their rifles into their off-side scabbards.

The two men swung themselves into the saddles and headed northwest. Their ponies splashed around dense stands of cypress and through bristly clumps of weeds turned brown in their late-bloom stage.

"You know, Paul Billy, our cattle sure are lucky having all this marshy area in our Leon pastures. Just look at the variety of grasses available to them all year long. With maidencane, savannah grass, and all these other grasses that thrive in wet areas, our cattle don't have to work very hard to find their food. It sure makes it easier for our crews to follow the movement of the cattle."

Many years ago, Indians had cleared much of the higher land for farming and housing. Undisturbed land areas were overgrown by wiregrass, which the Indians had learned to set afire in the spring of each year. Burning the old, tough grass allowed its replacement by young, green grass, providing cattle with good grazing in late winter and early spring and allowing other native grasses to grow when the cattle were moved elsewhere.

Wiregrass was everywhere throughout these dry land areas. North and central parts of the Florida Territory were indeed wiregrass country. The settlers from the north wisely followed the example set by the Indians, and each year the wiregrass was burned to provide young, tender grass for cattle.

Paul Billy looked up into the sky and observed a few dark clouds gathering to the west. "Treff," he suggested, "why don't we stay in that line shack in the northwest corner tonight? It's not fancy, but it will at least be dry if it rains."

"Not a bad idea at that. We could both do with a good rest after the last few days."

As Paul Billy and Treff guided their horses through the fertile marshes, curious cattle lifted their heads to look at them and then placidly returned to their grazing. Occasionally a few wild, nervous cattle skittered to hide in the tall grass or in the middle of thick oak trees or palmettos, but most of the animals were unconcerned, accustomed to cowhunters working around them.

Paul Billy seemed to know every animal. As they

passed one clump of oak trees, he pointed to the right. "Treff, that old whiskers steer is still hiding among that bunch of trees. He must be at least eight years old. We've tried every way we know to bring him in, but that danged steer is as stubborn as an old woman! Last year one of the cowhands was able to get rope on him, but he broke loose and got away."

"Paul Billy, why don't you shoot the animal next time we need some meat for the crew?"

"We have talked about doing that. The steer is getting a tremendous set of horns."

"I have my eye on those. They'd look mighty impressive hanging over the brick fireplace in Central headquarters. I know Ace would be proud to see them there."

Billy chuckled. "Well, do you and Mister Dover feel brave enough to come out here and try to get them?"

Treff let his eyes linger on the animal, sizing him up. "A couple of good dogs should be able to get that steer out of those woods where the cowhunters could get him."

"Treff, we already lost two of our best dogs trying to do just that."

By late afternoon the next day, the two men reached the south end of the ranch's western border, their eyes alert for signs of trespassers. They saw many sets of deer tracks and large flocks of turkeys in the woods. Occasionally they spotted a panther's tracks, but they saw nothing that would indicate unwelcome visitors.

As they approached the southern boundary, Treff had an idea. "We've still got several hours before dark. I'd like to check on that herd of females in the Olivita marsh. I haven't seen them in some time, but Marv seems to think mighty highly of them."

"You will like those cattle, Treff. Marv had us group the wet cows together and give them the best pasture. There are still a lot of young calves in the marsh."

"Why don't we camp here tonight," said Treff, "and then in the morning we can swing on down and the see the Godwin family. Rumor has it that those boys of old Grandma Godwin are stealing cattle from some of the people down south of us. Cotton saw a couple of her sons looking at our cattle in the Peoples Pasture last week. They have no business on our land. It might be good to let the Godwins know we get out and around in these woods. I'd like to brag about our new rifles and let them know how far they can reach."

"That's a good idea, Treff. They need to know we are watching them."

Next morning the two men cleaned up their camp-site and set out for the Godwin camp. As Paul Billy led them into the swamp, he asked, "Is that oldest Godwin boy out of the Fort Brooke stockade yet?"

"I heard he was out, and as far as I know, he is back home now. That sheriff down in Fort Brooke didn't have enough evidence to convict him of killing that man, even though everyone knows he did it. Fact is, I heard he was bragging about it in a saloon one night."

"He sure is mean," Paul Billy declared, as he led the way deeper into Gulf Hammock. This wild region was a mixture of swamp and sinkholes, interspersed with upland areas where outlaws were known to make their hideouts.

Treff followed him through the water-soaked area

where the trees were so tall and dense that the sun seldom reached the ground. Soon they came to a small clearing, in the center of which was a lean-to and a few benches.

Propped against a tall bay gum tree, a shabby old woman was busy skinning a rabbit. Her wild, white hair spiked around her head, and a lump of snuff caused a wide protrusion beneath her lower lip. Dirt permeated her skin and clothes, rendering them both colorless beyond a dismal gray. "Git down and stay awhile. There ain't no one here but me. Everybody has done gone to work and left me by myse'f. I be glad fer a body to talk to."

Treff knew better than to ask what kind of work her four thieving sons or her grandson were doing. "Where's your daughter?"

"Sulee Mae, she be out tryin' to catch herse'f a squirrel. She better be gittin' herse'f back here to he'p me afore I skin her 'stead of this-here rabbit."

Treff just smiled pleasantly. "Granny, it is mighty good to see you. You look just as young as ever."

The disheveled old lady, who looked as if she had never had a bath, peered at Treff with her beady black eyes. "Treff Ballowe, you be welcome to set a spell, but don't start tellin' me no tall tales about my beauty."

"Granny, you know Paul Billy, don't you?"

"Yup, I be knowin' him." She said no more.

"What are you doing?" Treff asked. "Why didn't you go along with your boys?"

"They figger I'm gittin' too old and would just be in the way. You know, it's hell when you git old. I ain't good for nothin' no more. Nobody listens to me. They just bring me a rabbit to skin now and then, so they kin have some stew when they git back."

Treff knew the old lady was blowing smoke. She was smarter than any of her sons, and she ruled the family with an iron fist. She taught each son, and even a grandson, how to steal as soon as he could walk. One by one, they all graduated from stealing candy at the nearest store in Fort Dade up to rustling cattle by the time they were half-grown. As long as they followed her instructions, the boys seldom got caught, but when they failed to heed her advice, they usually ended up in trouble.

"Granny, we're just out here fooling around in the woods like we do from time to time. It's too bad we can't get to see you on a regular basis. By the way, last week two of your sons were seen riding through our cattle in the Peoples Pasture. They really shouldn't be there, you know, and we'd hate to see one of them get accidentally hurt. You might want to give them a word of caution."

When Grandma made no comment, Treff pulled the rifle from his scabbard and ran his hand over its surface. "Last time I was in Mobile, I bought new rifles for our men, and I wanted to try one of them out."

Working hard to conceal her interest, the old lady focused her eyes on the rabbit in her bloody hands. "What kinda guns did you git?"

"They're breech-loading guns from Europe. They seem to be pretty accurate for about half a mile. Our men up north of here found they worked pretty well when they were attacked by a bunch of outlaw Indians earlier this week."

Treff could see the furtive glances aimed his way as he turned the rifle over in his hands.

"Well, Granny, we sure hate to leave you, but we

need to be riding on. It sure was good to see you! Tell your boys and Sulee Mae we're sorry we missed them. We'll be back to see you again, and next time maybe we'll bring you a deer to skin."

Granny's eyes lit up. "Don't wait too long! I shore would be proud to surprise them no-good younguns with a pot of venison stew!"

As Treff and Paul Billy mounted their ponies and rode out of Gulf Hammock, they could still hear the echo of the old crone's cackling laughter.

After leaving the Godwin camp, they rode along the southern and eastern sides of the Leon Division, continuing their search for evidence of unusual cattle movement or poaching, or unfamiliar horse tracks. All along the way, they witnessed a great abundance of birds and wild game and healthy, contented cattle, but no strange horse tracks. They did see an occasional human footprint, evidence that someone may have been hunting on the south end of the ranch.

Except for that one observation, Treff was well satisfied. "Things sure do look good, Paul Billy. We haven't seen anything worrisome during this trip. I'm glad we got over to see Granny Godwin. Did you notice how interested she seemed in everything we said? We need to keep a close watch on those cows and calves in the Olivita marsh to be sure we don't lose any calves."

"Treff, I think it was good you let her know we spend time in the south. Maybe that will discourage her gang from bothering us. But right now, I think you should be more concerned about the eastern side of this division. Some of the Seminole tribes have declared war on the new settlers that are moving in, and although I don't think they will cause us any trouble, you can never be sure."

"I sure hope you're right, Paul Billy. You know how my family values the good relationship we have always had with the Seminoles."

"Yes, and I believe that they respect that. But I have a feeling that Zeke Mongol might have trouble. The Seminoles believe he has been stealing some of their calves. They won't let him get away with that. He has already lost about seventy or eighty head of cows."

"My dad always said you generally reap what you sow, Paul Billy. We will continue to treat the Seminoles fairly and hope they will do the same for us."

The day was fast drawing to a close. Paul Billy said, "We aren't too far from that line shack on our eastern border, Treff. Let's stay there tonight, and it will be an easy ride tomorrow to the gully where we are to meet Marv."

"I like that idea. Maybe there will be a cowhunter or two stopping over at the shack. I always enjoy a chance to visit with some of our men, and they may have some recent news on what's happening with the Seminoles, and with the Godwin gang, too."

15

LATE SATURDAY AFTERNOON, Paul Billy and Aldo Hagen rode into Jacksonville. The sun at their backs gave them a clear view of the entire length of the dusty street, and they were relieved to see cow ponies crowded onto each hitching rack. In a town swarming with cowhunters for the weekend, two strangers riding into town would hardly be noticed. Gray dust drifted slowly upward around their horses' feet as they approached the busy main street.

"Where do these fellers usually meet, Billy?"

"They usually sit at a table in the back of the Cowhunters Saloon. I have not gone inside the saloon. I have only looked through the doors. They usually sit way back in the right-hand corner."

"You reckon they're here yet?"

Billy took a quick inventory of the horses tied in front of the saloon. "That red buckskin belongs to the fat man from the Okefinokee, but I don't see the horse that Johnson fellow rides."

"What does the Johnson feller look like?" Aldo asked.

"Tall and slim, with stringy blond hair. Walks with a swagger, like he thinks he's something special."

"You sure you don't want to go inside the saloon with me?"

"No, Aldo, I don't want to start a Seminole war in the Cowhunters Saloon. Some of those cowhunters ride into town just hoping for a fight to liven up their weekend, and I might give them just the excuse they're looking for." Paul Billy's white teeth gleamed when he grinned, and his dark eyes sparkled.

"I see what you mean, Billy. Why don't you go and get some grub in your belly while I go inside the saloon and mosey around? From your description I ain't likely to have no trouble figgerin' which one is the fat man. I'll meander up to the bar and see if I can learn somethin'. Then directly I'll come up to that café. We ain't had nothing to eat since daylight this morning, and I shore am hongry."

As the bat-wing doors swung closed behind him, Aldo worked his way through the crowded room to the bar and ordered a whiskey. Slapping the dust from his clothes, he paid for his drink and stood watching the noisy mob. Dance hall girls with their yellow hair, slicked-up dudes, and drunken winos—he'd seen them all in a hundred other saloons around the country. Finally, he allowed his glance to drift to the right back corner, and sure enough, there they were! Four cowhunters playing poker, one so fat his dirty shirt was straining against its buttons. Aldo was sure that must be the man from the big swamp.

Leaning against the bar, he finished his drink and felt his head swirl. "Where's a good place to get something to eat around this town?" he asked the bartender.

"You might try the Four Amigos Café down on the corner," the man answered.

"I'm so hungry I could eat leather. I'll meander that way and get me some grub. Then I'll be back."

The bartender swabbed the bar with a greasy cloth, not bothering to respond.

Leaving his horse in front of the saloon, Aldo walked down the crowded street, his eyes searching for Paul Billy. He reached the café before he found him, already seated at a table chowing down on a thick steak and three big ears of yellow corn.

"Paul Billy, I think I seen that fat man you been tellin' me about. He's so fat he was almost poppin' the buttons off the front of his shirt. And he was real dirty."

"That describes him pretty well, Aldo. Was Johnson with him?"

"I didn't see nobody that fit his description, but they was sittin' at the table, and it was kinda hard to tell."

"I just can't figure out why Drag Johnson comes all the way to Jacksonville to play cards with that dirty old man. If it's just for a game of cards, I'm sure he could find someone more desirable than that back at the Brown Owl Ranch."

Aldo ordered a plate of beans and a steak. "Make sure it's just as big as his'n," he told the waitress, pointing to Paul Billy's plate.

"Billy, it's gettin' late. After you're done eatin', go find you some place across the street from the saloon where you can see inside. I'll go back and try to get up close to the old Georgia boy and his buddies. Maybe I can pick up on what they're sayin'."

Billy finished his coffee and left four bits on the table. Drifting back along the street, he was careful to avoid attention. He spied a barrel directly across from the doors of the Cowhunters Saloon. He hoisted himself on the barrel and, pulling his hat down to partially cover his eyes, sat with his arms folded across his chest. To a casual observer, he would appear to be asleep.

Aldo finished his steak and beans, using a piece of cornbread to mop up the last few drops of lip-smacking juice. He drank two cups of coffee and signaled for the waitress.

She sauntered over to his table and eyed his empty plate, wondering what his complaint would be. "I reckon you liked everything okay. Your plate's as clean as a sow's tit!"

Aldo, unaccustomed to such straightforward talk from a woman, blinked. "Uh, yeah. The vittles was fine. I just wanted to ask you was there some place to get a room for the night."

She eyed him suspiciously, uncertain of his intentions. "Well, there's the Widow Perkins' rooming house next door. That's the best place in town, but mind you, she don't put up with no hanky-panky."

"No, ma'am," Aldo assured her. "I just want to rent a couple of rooms for next weekend."

"Well, Miz Perkins stays pretty full, but this far ahead, she might could fix you up."

Armed with that information, Aldo paid his bill and went to find the Widow Perkins.

After checking her records, Mrs. Perkins said, "I have only two left. If you give me a dollar on each one, I will hold them for you."

With that business accomplished, Aldo walked up the boardwalk toward the Cowhunters Saloon. He caught a glimpse of Paul Billy, and couldn't refrain from smiling when he saw his sidekick pretending to be asleep. He did not want Paul Billy to know how concerned he felt for him this weekend. Aldo knew that his own presence in this riotous town would draw little attention, but these days, a strange Indian was a horse of a different color!

For the second time that day, Aldo sidled through the swinging doors of the Cowhunters Saloon. He could see that the fat man was still seated at the same table, along with two other men. They were no longer playing cards but kept casting their eyes toward the doors as though they were expecting someone.

Aldo edged his way across the crowded floor to the bar and ordered a drink. He took his time to idly scan his surroundings. He could not afford to appear hurried.

A poker game was in progress at the table next to the one occupied by the fat man and his friends. Aldo could tell that the poker game was growing heated, and suddenly one of the players threw his cards down on the table in disgust. "That's all for me! I'll see you guys next month." With that, the disgruntled cowhunter pushed his chair back and stormed out of the saloon.

Aldo was excited. This might be the very chance he had been waiting for! As casually as he could, Aldo sauntered over to the game and asked, "Mind if I sit in?"

"If you got the money, the seat is yours," the dealer said. "What did you say your name was?"

"I didn't say, but you can call me Max." Aldo never used his middle name; no one could possibly connect him with it. "I'm just passing through on my way south, and thought I'd spend the night in town. I don't need to chase women, and I just thought I'd like to play a little poker to relax."

The dealer made hurried introductions as he passed out the cards. "My name is John, the sandy-haired youngster is Jake, and the other man is Tiger."

Aldo sat with his back to the fat man, an ideal arrangement that allowed him to listen without showing interest and without revealing a view of his face. It also let him see the front door, in case Paul Billy should need him.

After playing cards for about an hour, Aldo was pleased to calculate that he was just about breaking even. Pretending to use his roving eyes to ogle the girls, Aldo kept a close watch on the entrance. As the evening wore on, more and more cowhands streamed through the doors, many apparently carrying a month's pay in their pockets which the flamboyant dance hall girls were ready and willing to help them spend. A piano player in one corner pounded the keys with fury in order to be heard above the din of the growing crowd of merrymakers. With each passing minute, the noise intensified so that the men seated at the table had to shout in order to be heard.

"What do you do for a living?" Jake asked, eyeing Aldo over the top of his cards.

"A little of this and that. Right now I'm headin' down toward Fort Brooke, looking for cattle to buy."

"Why go all the way to Fort Brooke when you could maybe find all the cattle you want right here? What kinda cattle you be lookin' fer?"

Aldo pretended to study his cards while he thought about the question. "I know a feller who's in need of three or four hundred five-year-old steers." He feigned a look of boredom.

"What's he gonna do with 'em?" Jake seemed suddenly eager to learn more about this poker-playing cowhunter.

"That's his business," Aldo growled. "It ain't none of mine, and it shore ain't none of yorn. I just look for the cattle, and I don't ask no questions." He continued to focus his attention to his cards.

Out of the corner of his eye, Aldo saw a tall man come through the swinging doors and work his way to the bar—a tall, slim man whose stringy hair was blond, and who walked with an arrogant swagger! As soon as the man got his drink, he wove his way through the crowd and seemed to be heading right toward Aldo and his new acquaintances. But instead of stopping, he circled their table and stood just behind Aldo's back, over the table where the fat man sat. Aldo could hear every word with clarity.

"Evenin', fellers. Mind if I sit in a few hands of poker?"

"Howdy, Johnson. Pull up a chair. We was just wonderin' if you was gonna show tonight."

Aldo could hear a chair scrape the floor as the newcomer joined the table behind him. "Toke, don't you never worry about that. When I tell a man I'm gonna do somethin', it's as good as done."

"Snake, deal Johnson in. We need another feller to make this game more excitin'. You and Pasco don't have enough sense to keep up my interest." This comment was met with a spate of laughter.

Aldo did not dare to swivel his head to see which man claimed each name, but he imbedded them all in his mind for future use. Now he had to be careful to keep up with his own game while listening to what went on behind his back.

After they played a few hands of stud poker, Aldo heard Johnson say something about things looking pretty good.

What things? Aldo wondered, and then almost as if in answer to his thoughts, he heard Johnson say, "Toke, I got some cattle lined up that I think you might ought to look at; round about three hundred head."

A little later, Aldo heard Toke's reply. "We been gathering up some ourselves since the last time we seen you; maybe two hundred head. Added to them you found, we could put together a nice little number. Wanna go take a look at 'em?"

"I guess so, if they ain't too far away. Are they pretty good cattle?"

"Not too bad. Let's ride out and take a look at 'em. If we leave now, we could see 'em at daylight."

"That'd work out good for me," Johnson said. "That would give me time to get back to work tomorrow."

Aldo dropped a coin so that, in picking it up, he could steal a better look at the men behind him. He was beginning to separate and distinguish their voices. After another round of poker, Aldo heard the heavy scrape of a chair as the fat man pushed himself up from the table. "Well, let's go take a look."

Snake complained, "Just as soon as I win a little bit, you want to quit. Couldn't we play a few more hands?" he whined.

Toke growled, "Snake Leggitt, quit your bitching. Me and this gentleman got things to take care of that's a lot more important than this-here card game, and the stakes ain't no penny ante, neither."

There was a great shuffling of chairs from behind him, and Aldo stretched his arms and yawned. "You fellers have taken all I can afford to lose tonight. I need to catch me a little shut-eye before I head for Fort Brooke. I thank you for lettin' me sit in on your game tonight. I hope we'll meet again real soon."

The sandy-haired cowhunter looked panicky. "Wait a minute, Max. Where can I get in touch with you, in case I find somebody with steers like the kind you be looking for?"

"I plan on comin' back through here next weekend on my way back to Georgia. I'll be stayin' at Widow Perkins' roomin' house next Saturday night. If you want to meet me, just leave word with her, tellin' me where you'll be." With a slight nod of his head, Aldo left them at the table and went to look for Paul Billy.

He did not have to look far. Billy, hunched on the barrel, did not look as though he had moved a muscle during all the time Aldo had spent in the saloon. "Billy, I think we done hit pay dirt. I found out they call that fat man 'Toke.' Him and that tall feller named Johnson are fixin' to leave the saloon. You got any idea which way they'll go?"

"I'm pretty sure I can guess. I have followed them before. They always head for the Okefinokee Swamp."

"Well, what are we waitin' fer? Let's get our horses and head out that way to see if we can follow 'em."

❖   ❖   ❖

A three-quarter moon was rising over the river as the two men sat on their horses waiting for Toke and his group. On the outskirts of Jacksonville, a cluster of large oak trees sheltered them from view.

"Looks like we're in luck tonight," Aldo noted. "With that big moon up yonder, we shouldn't have no trouble seein' where we ride tonight, Billy."

"You won't think it's so lucky if they see us," Paul Billy reminded him. "For my part, I'd just as soon it wasn't quite so bright!"

"Will we be able to follow 'em into the swamp, Paul Billy?"

"It depends on where they go. We can't let them know they're being followed. I'm pretty sure the fat fellow has him a camp on one of the islands, and it may not be easy for us to go all the way."

"I thought they'd be here by now," Aldo said impatiently. "I hope we ain't missed 'em." He slapped at a mosquito on his neck.

In the shadow of the oak trees, Paul Billy pointed to a path that seemed to lead from the moonlit river into a forest of endless blackness. "We haven't missed them. That is the way they go each time I have followed them."

The brightness of the night would make it easy to see

and identify the men when they came this way, but once they rode into the dark, marshy woods, Aldo knew he would have to rely on Paul Billy's Indian instincts to guide them. He shifted uneasily in his saddle. "Billy, don't get separated from me and leave me stranded out in that swamp, you hear?"

Billy smiled, but did not have time to reassure him. The sound of approaching horses carried through the trees just minutes before a group of five riders filed by their hiding place. It was easy to identify the fat man they now knew as Toke and the tall man called Johnson. "That's them," Aldo confirmed in a whisper. Then he drew in a sharp intake of breath, and his eyes widened in surprise. "Billy! That second rider from the back is the young feller I played poker with tonight. His name is Jake."

"They must all be part of the same group, Aldo. Let's see where they go."

"When I played cards with Jake I told him I was tryin' to buy cattle for someone, and that sure grabbed his attention. He said he might know where I could locate some without goin' all the way to Fort Brooke. This whole thing is beginnin' to look mighty interestin'!"

When Toke and his buddies were a safe distance ahead, Paul Billy and Aldo rode out from the shelter of the oak trees and followed. Careful not to alert Toke and his group that they were being followed, they rode in silence. Even their ponies seemed to recognize the importance of traveling quietly.

Northwest from Jacksonville, they crossed a shallow river and managed to keep all five of Toke's group within their view until they entered the southeast corner of the big swamp. At that point, Billy and Aldo realized there was no way the two of them could continue to follow without being seen.

They reined their ponies to a stop to decide on their next move. "It'll soon be daylight," Aldo said. "I think we'd best head on south, back to the TSR. We sure don't want these fellers to see either one of us. I told that young feller called Jake that I'd be stayin' at the Widow Perkins' place next Saturday. I'm hopin' he'll rise to the bait if we don't scare 'em away. I have a feelin' I'm gonna see him again."

Paul Billy nodded his approval, and the two men turned south toward home.

By the time Paul Billy and Aldo reached the TSR on Sunday night, it was far too late to talk to anyone. The house was dark and quiet. The two men were so exhausted that they were happy to save their report until morning, and headed for the bunkhouse to claim a few hours' sleep.

Monday morning at the breakfast table, Ace extracted a full report from Aldo and Paul Billy, with Treff and Rusty helping him draw out every detail. Marv and her other brothers had returned to their own headquarters late Sunday afternoon.

After hearing of Aldo's visit to the Cowhunters Saloon, Treff said, "We definitely want you two to return to Jacksonville next weekend, but I think we need to find another man to go with you. Let me think about it."

Ace rubbed his chin in the gesture he used whenever he was in deep thought. "Do you reckon Drag Johnson is working with a gang of rustlers?"

"I don't know what to think yet. Everything sure looks funny, doesn't it? There may be a logical explanation for all of this, but I tend to agree with Mama that there is something not right about Zeke Mongol and Drag. Maybe we can find some answers next week when Aldo talks with his young poker-playing friend."

Treff looked across the table at the two men who had just returned from their assignment and felt well pleased at what they had accomplished. "Paul Billy, I know that you need to go check on your own place and catch up on some sleep. Afterwards, ride over and see what Marv needs, but come back here Friday afternoon. I might have a plan worked out by then. Ask Marv to come with you, and try to get here by the middle of the afternoon." Then, turning his attention to Aldo, he said, "You need to get some rest, too, and so does your horse. Then you can spend the rest of the week with Rusty, but be sure to come and see me Friday evening. I'll visit with Ace this week, and we'll work out some plans. I'll go over them with you and Paul Billy when you come back."

❖　　　　　　❖　　　　　　❖

Serenity reigned over the ranch as Treff sat on the front porch Wednesday morning, sipping coffee and watching the rising sun gild the eastern horizon. An azure sky, sparsely dotted with puffs of white clouds, carried the harmonious concert of birds, and Treff took time to reflect on the beauty of this final week of October.

In the distance, he watched the graceful flight of two bald eagles in search of a meal, soaring above the red-tailed hawk that was perched high in the top of a long-leafed pine, and somewhere in the distance, a whippoorwill called.

Interrupting his reverie, Treff glanced up and was surprised to see Patch Searcy emerge from the bunkhouse, followed by his friend Hank O'Mara. Treff almost spilled his coffee in his hurry to meet them.

"Hey, I didn't know you two were here. When did you get in?"

Patch said, "We got in sometime during the middle of the night. We ran into a couple of night riders north of here, and they told us there were some empty bunks. We crept in quiet-like and went to sleep. It's been a long trip. The bunks sure did feel good."

"Hank, it sure is good to see you again!" Treff exclaimed, vigorously shaking hands with the cattleman from Yellow River. "You look a darn sight better than the last time I saw you, with a broken arm and a couple of bullet wounds. Let's go inside and get some breakfast."

Treff called Francesca to let her know she had two more men to feed. Seated at the table, waiting for their breakfast, Treff pressed them for details. "Tell me about your trip. Did you have any problems?"

"Patch here tells me you've caught some rustlers and outlaw Indians since you left me in the bed with a broken arm," Hank began. "With that in mind, we decided to travel by the mail route much of the way, to have a quicker trip. We didn't have any serious problems. I hate to tell you, though, that there's still a lot of rustling going on to the west of here. Outlaws are still robbing travelers. Maybe you ought to come out our way and help put a stop to it, Treff."

Even though Treff did not take Hank seriously, it was nonetheless flattering to hear him express such confidence. "Hank, would you be able to stay and spend a few days with us? I'd like to show you some of the TSR. Our family will all be here this coming weekend, and I want them all to meet you."

"That's mighty kind of you, Treff. I'd like to see your spread and meet your family, but I'd have to plan to leave the first part of next week. I can't chance being away from home too long."

"Do you reckon you could ride a little more today?"

"That's not a problem for me, but maybe I ought to borrow a fresh pony so mine could rest."

"Patch needs to do the same," Treff agreed. "Patch, I'd like for you to take Hank up to the Santa Fe and introduce him to Jeremiah. Then show him those steers we think belong to him. You might just as well spend the night there and then swing through the northern part of the Fannin on your way back tomorrow. But be sure you're back by supper-time tomorrow, and tell Jeremiah and Ten to spend Friday night with us."

"Want us to take a couple of those new horses we got from Georgia?"

"You and Hank can pick out whatever you like. Give your horses some grain and hay before you leave, and we'll look after them while you're gone."

"Treff, I've sure been wanting to get over here to see

your spread. Patch has been telling me about it all the way from Yellow River. I've been giving serious thought to moving this way myself."

Francesca came to the table with two large platters in her hands. "Breakfast," she announced, and returned to the kitchen to bring out more food.

"You two go ahead and eat," Treff said. "I need to find Ace to discuss something with him. Patch, why don't the two of you take a couple of those new rifles with you when you go, and plenty of ammunition. You probably won't need them, but if you do, they'll be good to have."

Treff left Patch and Hank piling their plates with Francesca's hearty breakfast fare, while he hurried outside to look for Ace. He was suddenly eager to talk to him. During his conversation with Patch and Hank just now, a new idea had taken shape in his mind, an idea that just might shed some light on Drag Johnson's activities and answer some of the questions that had puzzled them all for months.

16

DRAG JOHNSON SMILED to himself as he guided his horse along the western boundary of the Brown Owl Ranch. And why shouldn't he smile? He had plenty to smile about!

First, there was that good-lookin' redhead over at the Three Springs Ranch who was crazy about him. He could read it in her eyes the first time they met. It was a comfort to confirm that the years he had spent in prison had done nothing to diminish the old Johnson charm. That part of his plan was going to be easy!

And the cattle deal was moving along better than he had even dared to hope. Last Sunday morning, during his meeting with Toke Bannon and his boys in the Okefinokee Swamp, Drag had listened with interest to the words of the cowhunter they called Jake. "Did you fellers see that yeller-haired dude I played cards with last night?"

"Yeah, we seen him. What about him?"

"He said he was going down to Fort Brooke to look for three or four hundred steers to buy. I told him maybe I could help fix him up with some cattle so he wouldn't have to travel so far."

"What's the feller's name?"

"He said it was Max. I never seen him before, but he's plannin' to be back in Jacksonville next Saturday night. He said he had a room at Widow Perkins."

"Where's he from?" growled Snake.

"He said he was from Georgia, but I don't know exactly where. He didn't have nobody with him."

Jake was obviously excited about the prospects of stealing some cattle to sell to the stranger, but Toke demanded to know more about this man named Max. "How do you know he ain't the law? I already got one marshal lookin' to stretch my neck."

"Well, he'll be back in town next Saturday night. We can all meet him and see how he sounds. If he turns out to be the law, we know how to handle him. We can bring him back here and feed him to the alligators in Dead Man's Slough, and he won't be the first one. On the other hand, if he's on the up-and-up like us, we don't want to turn our backs on a chance to pick up a big stake, do we?"

"He may not even come back to Jacksonville," Toke said, "but if he does, we'll see what he talks like. After that I can decide what to do."

As Drag recalled that conversation, greed began to take root and grow in his mind. He wanted to go back to Payne's Prairie once more to check on that herd of steers he had found a couple of weeks ago. If they were still in that same location, he would try to talk Toke Bannon into rustling the herd. There were at least two hundred nice, fat steers in the group. Mixed with the two hundred Toke had stashed away on the edge of the Okefinokee Swamp, they would make up a choice group of cattle to sell to Jake's new friend from Georgia. That should turn a tidy profit!

Sweat dripped from Drag's forehead as he slouched along thinking about what he might do with a few thousand dollars. Still, he was reluctant to ride back into Payne's Prairie. He stopped under an oak tree and wiped his face with his neckerchief. It sure was hot for the last week in October! He took off his hat to let a slight breeze riffle through his hair while he tried to decide about having another look at those steers.

Tension between new settlers and the Seminoles was getting hotter by the minute. Every day he heard new tales of settlers who were killed and scalped as they tried to move onto Seminole land. Drag had no desire to lose his scalp! Finally, greed overcame caution as he left the shade of the oak trees and turned his horse toward Payne's Prairie.

He had first seen the enticing herd of steers about two weeks ago, as they grazed placidly along the eastern side of the prairie. Every few days since, he had ridden in their direction to see if anyone rode herd on the cattle, and each time, he had seen no one. Their pasture grass was so good and plentiful that the steers never had cause to wander far from the spot where he had first seen them. Drag was convinced that an experienced group of cowhunters could slip in at night and steal them. With the benefit of an almost full moon, it should be easy.

When he drew near to the prairie, he could see the steers belly-deep in grass, as though they had not moved since his last visit. White egrets rose into the air as he approached the cattle, so he stopped under a cabbage palm about a half a mile away to avoid giving further signals of his presence. He scanned his surroundings in every direction, but there was not a sign of an Indian guarding these cattle. It looked inviting; almost too easy.

Drag turned his horse back toward the Brown Owl Ranch, completely convinced now that this was a herd Toke should take. He could hardly wait for the weekend and the chance to see his friend from the Okefinokee!

Over at the TSR, at the same time Drag was salivating over Seminole cattle, Treff was laying out his new idea to Ace Dover. "We need to find out if Drag Johnson and Zeke Mongol are in cahoots with those guys from the Okefinokee Swamp. Why does Johnson meet with them in Jacksonville every week? Where are they planning to find cattle to sell to Aldo?"

"Treff, Jeremiah calculates he's lost about twenty-five head of steers from the Santa Fe. All of this is beginning to come together in a very intriguing manner. What's this new plan you say you've worked out?"

"I figure we must find a way to get a look at those steers they have for sale, Ace. I've been thinking that we need to send someone to look at those cattle; someone who knows cattle; somebody who looks rich and important."

"What are you thinking of, Treff?"

"I'd like to ask Hank O'Mara to go to Jacksonville next weekend, to pose as the man Aldo is buying cattle for. He looks impressive. No one will know him. Maybe he could find out if all these fellows are working together, and it would not seem unreasonable for him to ask to see their cattle."

"Hank is our guest, Treff. It wouldn't be hospitable to ask him to do a thing like this."

"I'll admit that bothers me a little, Ace. But I did save his life during my last trip back from Mobile, and I know he'd be willing to help us. Besides, he hopes to move into this part of the Territory. He might as well start getting acquainted with some of the problems we have."

"Well, Treff, when Hank and Patch get back tomorrow, why don't we share what's been happening around here lately and see what he says? He might have some ideas of his own."

It was late afternoon by the time Patch and Hank reached the Latigo pens where the HO-Bar cattle were held, but Hank had enjoyed the entire day. He had never been on a more impressive spread than the TSR. Wildlife abounded everywhere. A variety of pasture grasses provided feed the year around, and all the cattle appeared to be in excellent condition to go through the coming winter months. Approaching the pens, Hank began to see steers marked with his familiar brand, and a broad smile spread across his face.

"These HO-Bar cattle sure are a long ways from home, aren't they? It probably wouldn't do to know where they've been since they were stolen. I wonder if the cowhunters who took my steers are the same ones who shot me and left me for dead."

"I can't say about that," Patch said, "but if they were, you won't be bothered by them no more. They are all restin' in peace about a day's ride northwest of here."

"How many steers did you find with this brand?"

"You need to check with Jeremiah when we see him this evening. Just a rough guess, I'd say they was about twenty head."

"They're sure in a lot better condition than they would have been if they had been up by the Yellow River all of this time! It makes me more convinced than ever that I should sell my place near Pensacola and move this way."

Hank spent half an hour inspecting the cattle that he had long ago written off as a loss. Finally Patch looked toward the horizon and advised, "We need to get back down to the Santa Fe headquarters before dark, so we best get started in that direction. That'll give you a chance to talk with Jeremiah about your steers. He can answer your questions better than I can."

Patch and Hank reached the Santa Fe headquarters at dusk and found Jeremiah giving instructions to a couple of his cowhunters about the next day's work. He looked up when he saw them riding in.

"Howdy, Patch, what brings you this way?"

"This here be Hank O'Mara, from out near Pensacola way, Jeremiah. We've been up looking at those steers carryin' his HO-Bar brand."

Jeremiah brushed the dust from his hands on his britches, and then eagerly shook hands with the young man from the western part of the Territory. "Hank, I'm glad to finally meet you, after hearing so much about you from Treff. Get down off your horse and stay the night with us so we can get better acquainted."

Hank slid out of the saddle and hitched his pony to the rail, but Patch stayed on his mount. "Jeremiah," he began hesitantly, "Uh, if it be all right with you, er, uh, I'm gonna leave you two together 'cause I got a little, uh, business to take care of while I'm up this way."

Jeremiah turned away to hide his grin. "That's fine, Patch. That will give me some time to visit with Hank."

"Ace wants us to be back to his place by tomorrow evenin'," Patch remembered to tell him. "He wants you and your family to come fer supper. He wants to get the whole family together while Hank is here."

Patch had never told Jeremiah about the pretty girl he was courtin', the young daughter of a neighboring rancher, but word spread fast in this part of the country, where neighbors hungered for news of each other, especially when romance was involved.

Jeremiah winked at Hank before he said, "Patch, this *business* you're going to take care of, why don't I send one of my men along to help you?"

"I reckon I can handle it all right alone, Jeremiah, but thanks anyway." Patch began to edge his horse away from the house, obviously anxious to head for the open stretch, but trying to maintain his courteous composure.

"All right, then, Patch, if you're sure you don't need

help. Hank and I will visit tonight, and he will be ready to go back to Central with you when you get back in the morning. You can tell Mama and Daddy that Cissy and the boys and I will all be there in time for supper Friday."

As Patch rode away, Jeremiah could not resist one last dig. "Patch," he called. When the good-natured cowhand slowed and looked back, Jeremiah yelled, "Watch out you don't let Nelly Ann slip a noose around your neck."

Patch grinned and spurred his horse into a full-speed gallop so that all Hank and Jeremiah could see was a cloud of gray dust.

"Patch is an interesting fellow," Hank observed. "I was surprised when he came clear out to my spread to tell me you had some of my steers this far from home. I had marked those cattle off as being lost forever. Y'all were certainly neighborly to send someone all the way out there to tell me about them."

"We were just glad that Treff was able to recognize your brand," Jeremiah assured him, as he helped Hank settle his horse in the barn. "Come on, Hank. Let's go up to the house so you can meet the rest of my family. Cissy has already set an extra place at the table. We didn't know just when you would arrive, but we've all been looking forward to your visit."

As the two men strolled toward the house, they were nearly knocked over by two tiny cowhunters in pursuit of an invisible enemy. "Wahoo!" they shouted, as they beat their hands against their hips to simulate the sound of galloping horses.

"Meet my twins," Jeremiah said, catching one boy

under each arm. "This one is Curry and this one is Brad. Life at the Santa Fe never gets dull with these two around. Every day they find something new to check out. We are going to have to put them to work one of these days."

Coming out of the front door just in time to hear the last comment, Cissy Dover put her hands on her hips and said, "We will have to discuss that later. The boys should learn reading, writing, and numbers before they go tearing off into the woods chasing cows." Her voice was stern, but her dimpled smile revealed her congenial nature. Then, seeing the stranger with her husband, she wiped her hands on her apron. "You must be Hank O'Mara," she said, offering him her hand. "We've been hoping you'd get here in time for supper. We're certainly happy to have you with us."

"Thank you, ma'am. It's a great pleasure to be here."

Cissy held the front door open. "Take your saddle-bags into the last bedroom on the left and then sit on the porch with Jeremiah and the boys while I finish getting supper on the table." With that, Cissy hurried to the kitchen to put the finishing touches on the evening meal.

Hank, Jeremiah, and the twins relaxed on the wide porch as darkness crept across the land and the night music began. Whippoorwills called, one to another, and from the edge of the springs, echoes of frogs filled the night. Occasionally the hoot of a brown owl joined the serenade of night sounds, and the grunt of a bull alligator could be heard in the distance.

"You all certainly have a nice place, Jeremiah," Hank said, leaning back in his chair and propping his feet on the porch rail. He was favorably impressed with everything he had seen and heard in this eastern part of the Florida Territory.

"We're very fortunate to have a large family that works so closely together," Jeremiah agreed. "Most of the credit for that goes to my parents. Dad provides the iron hand and business experience, while Mama manages to keep the family on a level keel and close together. And we were really blessed the day they took in Treff and Ten Ballowe."

"I wondered why they had different last names, but I didn't want to pry."

"They were new to the Territory when Indians raided their place and killed both their parents. I'll never forget the day Dad brought those poor, distraught boys to our home. They were both in a state of shock, but I must say that those two have turned out to be true members of this family."

"That was a very generous thing for your family to do."

"Actually, we're no different from many of the pioneer families in the Florida Territory. I'm sure I don't have to tell you how everyone down here works together to help his neighbors. We Dovers know that we've been more fortunate than some, though," Jeremiah admitted, "and Dad has never been reluctant to share our good fortune with others."

"I see a lot of opportunities in this area. In fact, I've been thinking strongly about moving east from Pensacola."

"Are you married, Hank?"

"No, I haven't found a young lady who would put up with me, nor one who'd be willing to settle down a long way from town. You are lucky indeed, Jeremiah. All the girls I've met like the social life in Pensacola too much to settle for ranch life, and they don't know the front end of a steer from the back end."

"So far, I am the only one of the Dover kids that's gotten married, but a couple of my brothers like to keep time with the girls. They both have roving eyes, but you never can tell when they might find the ones who'll settle them down. But personally, I'd be the first to tell you that it's really wonderful to have a partner who works beside you and shares your goals. And these two guys here on the porch with us are our special blessing!" His voice grew husky as he let his eyes linger on his two young sons. Abruptly he changed the subject. "Tomorrow Patch will come and take you through the Fannin."

"I'm looking forward to that. I hope to meet Ten while we're there."

"If you miss him tomorrow, you'll see him this week-end."

"I need to reach some kind of a decision on those steers you've been saving for me, Jeremiah. I'm mighty beholden to you and your family for that."

"What do you plan to do with them, Hank?"

"Probably the only sensible thing would be to sell them. It's a long way back to Pensacola. The other option might be to find someone to take care of them for me until I move closer. It seems to me the best solution would be just to sell them."

"My family would be interested in buying them if we

could get together on a price," Jeremiah told him. "They would fit in well with a group of steers we're getting ready to send to Mobile after the first of the year."

"You all have taken care of them for so long that I am agreeable to whatever price you feel is fair, Jeremiah. I normally don't sell that easily, but I'm deeply indebted to you all for everything that you've done for me. First, Treff saved my life when I was shot, and then he recovered all those stolen steers."

Cissy called from the kitchen, interrupting their conversation. "Supper is almost on the table, fellows. Brad, you and Curry go clean up. Wash your hands real good." Then, as an afterthought, she added, "With soap and water."

❖   ❖   ❖

The next day had scarcely begun when Patch returned, a wide smile splitting his face. Jeremiah gave him a knowing wink. "Well, my friend, it looks like you were able to take care of your business in a satisfactory manner."

Patch twisted his hat in his hands and shuffled his feet. His face turned a tell-tale pink. "Yep. Things went tolerable well."

"Come on in and have some biscuits and coffee before you and Hank head out for the Fannin."

Patch didn't need a second invitation; he was mighty fond of Cissy's buttermilk biscuits. He sure hoped Nelly Ann could cook like Jeremiah's wife.

"Patch, take Hank by Crystal Lake today and show him that bunch of female stock. I think he'd like to see them."

"I'll do that. We'll swing down through the middle of the Fannin Division on our way back to Central." Patch helped himself to another biscuit. "By the way, Jeremiah, I been meanin' to ask you; can you tell for sure if you've lost any steers here at the Santa Fe?"

"We're pretty certain we've lost thirty or forty head from the northeastern sections, but truthfully, I haven't had the opportunity to look everywhere. It's possible they may turn up around some of those bay heads in the marshes, but we suspect that someone has skimmed a little cream off the top, hoping we wouldn't notice," Jeremiah said.

"As soon as I can, I'll get back over this way and help you check everywhere. But I reckon Hank and I need to git going now, if we're aimin' to be back like Ace asked."

Hank was disappointed to leave Jeremiah and his family, but he knew they had a full day ahead. "Cissy, that was as good cooking as I have ever had. I sure do thank you for inviting me to stay."

"We hope to see more of you, Hank."

"Well, Jeremiah agreed to buy those HO-Bar steers he's been holding, but I've made up my mind I'm going back to Pensacola and sell everything I own so I can move this way. When that happens, I promise you'll see plenty of me."

One of the cowhands brought Hank's horse from the barn, already fed and brushed and saddled. Patch untied his horse from the hitching rail, and the two men rode southwest toward Crystal Lake. Hank turned back for a final look at Jeremiah and his family standing on the front porch waving to him. In a million years, he could not have guessed the hand of cards fate was preparing to deal to him.

❖   ❖   ❖

The ride back through the Fannin Division was quiet and uneventful, as Hank and Patch each became absorbed in his own thoughts. Following the trail around Crystal Lake, they came upon two cowhunters from the Fannin. "Howdy, Tom," Patch greeted the one he recognized.

Tom Phipps was tall and skinny, with a beard that hung six inches below his chin. He had been working for the Dovers for the last eight years, and was now a foreman in charge of cows and calves. He was always willing to talk to anyone who would listen, and was obviously delighted to see Patch.

"Patch, did ya notice that old long-horned brindle cow up on the north end of the lake? That old cow is eighteen years old and still having calves."

"Tom, this is Hank O'Mara, from Pensacola. He owns the HO-Bar brand, and he came down to see his steers we found a few weeks ago."

"Hah! Yore steers was shore a long way from home, wasn't they? It ain't no wonder people can't find their cattle when they git stolen."

Hank shook hands with the talkative cowhunter. "I'm sure pleased to meet you, Tom. We'd just been talking about that mossy-horned old brindle cow with the fine calf beside her. You must take good care of her."

"Me and her been together quite a few years. I wish

we had a lot more like her." Tom seemed to swell with pride when he talked about his female stock. He had a reputation for being one of the best cowhunters in the Territory when it came to producing good calves.

"Tom, have you all had any rustlin' or cattle killed during the past few weeks?" Patch always tried to stay on top of any new information about Indians or rustlers.

"So far we've had good luck, 'cept for that one time. And we got our steers back then. But Jeremiah thinks he may have lost a few head from the Santa Fe."

"Is Ten around here, Tom? I want him to meet Hank."

"No, Ten done took a crew over to the western side to work a bunch of cattle over yonder."

"Tom, could we get you to do us a favor?" Patch asked.

"Why, shore. What can I do fer ya?"

"We need to move on toward Central, 'cause Ace wants us back afore dark. Could you tell Ten he needs to come down to see Ace tomorrow afternoon? It would be a big help if you can do that."

"Don't worry about it. I'll see Ten at dark tonight, and I'll be shore to let him know."

"Thanks for your help, Tom." Patch and Hank waved as they rode on toward the Central Division.

When they rode into Central later that evening, Patch recognized Marv's horse in the barn. "Have you met the boss's daughter?" he asked.

"No," Hank said. "I haven't seen her. Where has she been?"

"Well, she runs the Leon Division whenever Treff is

who had killed his parents and destroyed his home. But another part of him hoped that the red devil still lived so that he could personally put an end to his evil life. "Come on, Ten. We might as well get this over with."

Ace led the two brothers to the stable. "You boys all right to do this?" he asked, noticing Ten's green pallor. He knew that the sight of He-with-One-Eye-of-an-Eagle would conjure up painful memories of the darkest day of their lives, but this had to be done.

"We're fine," Treff assured him. "Just pull that blanket down off his face, and let's have a look at him."

Ace watched his two sons closely. They stood together in the early dawn, grimly looking down into the face of the man who had destroyed their home and family. For a long time, they stood in silence, but their expressions provided the only identification Ace needed to confirm his earlier suspicions. "Let's go, boys. I'll get somebody to bury him."

"Take his eye-patch and that headband with the eagle feather, and store them in the springhouse as proof the man is dead," Treff said. "Let me decide what to do with those two things later."

Treff and Ten turned and walked out of the stables, and Ace, after replacing the blanket over the Indian's face, followed them.

"You and Jose Lee and those other three cowhunters go on back to the Santa Fe," Jeremiah told Les Wingate. "Put that Indian chief across his horse and take him deep in the woods. Bury him to the west of the Latigo Pens. Don't forget to take a shovel with you. After you bury him, scatter leaves over the ground so no one can ever find him.

busy doin' things for Ace. She's quite a cowgirl. She does a mighty good job, and . . . " Patch started to add that she was good lookin', too, but he decided to let Hank wait to find that out for himself. He chuckled as he imagined the picture forming in Hank's mind of an oversized, rough, tough woman, able to manage a bunch of cowhunters with a pistol in one hand and a whip in the other while she cussed like a man and spit tobacco juice.

"What's the joke?" Hank asked.

"Never mind. You'll find out soon enough."

They put their horses in the barn and treated them to generous portions of grain. Hank thanked Patch for his help. "You're a great guide, Patch. You made the trip mighty interesting. I won't ever forget it."

He hung his saddle and blanket in the barn and dusted off his clothes before he walked across the yard to the Dovers' house. He was tired, but good manners demanded that he go in and pay his respects to the family. As he trudged up the steps, he lifted his eyes to the door and thought for a moment that he must be seeing a vision. A beautiful green-eyed lady stood in the doorway, a profusion of wavy red hair floating around her slender shoulders.

"Hello! I'm Marv Dover. You must be the Hank O'Mara I've been hearing so much about."

Hank was momentarily speechless. He tried desperately to conceal the effect she was having on him. Taking off his hat and bowing slightly, he said, "Yes, ma'am, I plead guilty." His black curly hair fell down over his forehead and he made a futile attempt to smooth it. His brown eyes twinkled as he clasped the hand she offered, and he continued to hold it much longer than necessary. Her hand felt smooth and cool, at once strong yet gentle. He had never encountered such a beautiful woman!

Marv was coping with her own emotions! When Treff had told them about Hank O'Mara, he had neglected to mention that he was young and handsome, and that he was a trim but muscular six feet tall! And, oh, my, those eyes! Marv felt an immediate desire to know more about this attractive owner of the HO-Bar brand.

Ace and Amaly watched with amusement as the handshake between the two young people seemed to go on and on as though it would never end. Finally Ace stepped forward with his right hand extended.

"Hank, I'm Ace Dover, and this is my wife, Amaly. We welcome you to our home. Treff has told us a great deal about you, and we are very glad to meet you at last."

The magic spell was broken, and Hank was able to return to reality. All traces of his fatigue had disappeared. "Sir, I don't think I will ever be able to repay Treff for what he has done for me. First he saved my life after I was shot in the back, and then he recovered my stolen steers. I had given up all hope of ever seeing those steers again."

"Have you had a chance to see your cattle?"

"Well, yes and no."

Ace looked puzzled until Hank explained. "Yes, I did see the steers, but those steers no longer belong to me. Jeremiah and I worked out a deal, and he bought them. It didn't make sense for me to drive that small group all the way back to the Yellow River. And I mentioned to Jeremiah that I was seriously thinking of selling my ranch and moving this way. I've liked everything I have seen.

This is excellent cattle country."

"We think we're lucky to be here," Ace agreed. "The last twenty years have been very good for us. We have a few concerns right now because of the rumblings of another Seminole War and the increase in outlaw activity all around us. Treff has been working on these problems since you saw each other."

"Where is Treff? I'm anxious to see him again."

"He should be here any time now," Amaly said. "He's with Rusty, our son who manages this Central Division. They went to check on some things over near Payne's Prairie, but they promised to be back in time for supper."

Marv had been silently studying their visitor as he talked with her parents. She could see many similarities to her brothers, but neither the color of his hair nor his eyes was one of them. Her brothers were either blond or red-haired. Hank's hair was coal black and curly. His entire face lit up with each of his frequent smiles, and besides being incredibly handsome, he was soft-spoken and polite. He was different from any of the men she knew. When she finally detected a lull in their conversation, she spoke up: "How long do you plan to be with us, Hank?"

"Unless something changes my plans, I figure on leaving the first of next week. I'm anxious to get back so I can start looking for someone to buy my spread and cattle."

"We wouldn't be able to see the whole place in one day, but I'd like to show you some of the Leon Division tomorrow, if that wouldn't interfere with anyone else's plans. Then you would have seen a little bit of each division of the ranch." Marv did not add that she was frantically foraging for an excuse to spend some time alone with Hank, to learn more about this unusual man! She had never met anyone who excited her like Hank O'Mara.

Hank looked expectantly at Ace and Amaly to discern their reaction to Marv's invitation.

Ace looked at Amaly and noted her gentle nod of approval. "That would be an excellent idea," he said. Ace had no misgivings about his daughter's plans. Even in the short time he had known Hank, Ace judged him as a fine, upstanding young man with a proper respect for women, and he had no doubt that Marv was perfectly capable of taking care of herself under any set of circumstances. Even so, he could not resist adding a paternal stipulation. "If you do that, Marv, plan to be back here by the middle of the afternoon. All of your brothers are coming for supper, and we want them all to have a chance to become better acquainted with Hank."

The grass still glistened with dew when Marv and Hank left the next morning. The slight chill of the late October air made their ponies spirited, and they let the horses trot for several miles before they settled back into a steady, ground-covering walk. Hank drank in the beauty of the gently rolling countryside as the early morning sunlight crept over the tops of the trees. Wildlife seemed to abound everywhere; deer, wild hogs, turkeys, coons, all foraging for food before returning to the woods during the heat of the day. As they crossed a small stream on the north side of the Leon, he noticed the tracks of a large cat. "What kind of a cat track is that, Marv?"

"That's a panther track. We have several that travel in and out of our ranch. If you followed those tracks, they would probably lead you toward the saltwater marsh that lies off to our west. The cats will travel many miles to protect their territory."

Looking down the stream, Hank could see snow-white egrets stretched tall on spindly legs, searching the water for food. Some of them spread their wings and soared skyward as the two riders passed by. Bird songs filled the air, and Hank declared that he had never witnessed such beautiful surroundings.

As the sun climbed higher in the sky, the terrain became more hilly, shadowed with thick groves of moss-laden oak trees. Marv led the way through the dense woods until quite suddenly they emerged from the sheltering canopy of trees, and Hank found himself looking down at a long, flat, marshy area. A large herd of female stock, each seemingly with a young calf by her side, grazed peacefully, unconcerned with their two intruders.

"We separate our cows that have calves from other female stock to make sure they have access to good grass. These are next summer's calf crop. Our dry cows are kept together with the bulls in another part of the ranch. If they breed, they will be kept. If a cow doesn't have a calf during a two-year period, we will sell her. Our pastures are able to provide enough to eat so that they should have a calf at least every other year. We figure if the old girl doesn't give us a calf by then, she isn't the kind of cow we want for TSR."

Hank admired this healthy herd of cattle, but not half as much as he admired the woman who was showing them to him. Marvelous was certainly an appropriate name for her! He had never met a woman who knew so much about cattle, nor one who would dare to mention a subject as delicate as the breeding of them.

As they rode through the herd, Hank suddenly detected movement from the corner of his eye. "Marv, there is someone watching us from yonder oak trees."

"That's just a couple of our line riders, Hank. We have to keep a careful watch on our herds these days because of rustlers. You'll see more of our riders as the day passes."

Marv continued to lead the way, hoping to show Hank as much of the TSR as they could cover in one day. "I want to take you by Morgan Pond and let you see some of our steers. We usually sell our steers by the time they are four years old. Most of the time they are sent to Mobile, but once in a while a buyer wants a herd to go to Savannah. After we see the steers, we'll stop by Leon headquarters for a bite to eat before we start working our way back to the Central Division."

Hank was enchanted by this charming lady with the flaming hair, who was able to ride all day and still look as fresh as a daisy. Although she seemed to know as much about cattle as anyone he had ever met, no one could deny that she was completely feminine. He was enjoying the day so much that he wished it could go on forever!

Riding through the steers that were grazing around

Morgan Pond, Hank was suddenly startled to find himself face-to-face with a Seminole Indian. He jerked his pony to a halt. Where had the man come from, and what did he want of them?

Seeing the concern on his face, Marv laughed. "Hank, I want you to meet Paul Billy, one of our most trusted employees. He has worked for my father for many years. Billy is one big reason why we have such good relations with the Seminoles."

"I'm glad to meet you, Paul Billy. Treff has told me about the way you helped to recover those HO-Bar cattle."

As Marv completed the introduction, the men shook hands and Billy said, "It is good to finally meet the owner of that brand. Your cattle were a long way from home, weren't they?" Paul Billy immediately liked the young man from Yellow River with the firm handshake and brown eyes that looked directly at you when he talked.

"I never thought to see them again," Hank marveled. "Incidentally, I made a deal with Jeremiah yesterday, and the steers are now the property of the TSR."

The men continued to talk until Marv turned to Paul Billy and said, "We'd better get on our way. Hank and I are going by headquarters to get something to eat, and then we'll start back to Central."

"I'm very glad to have met you, Hank. I'll probably see you again this evening, because Treff has asked me to stop by to see him. I won't go with you now, though, because I have some work to do over on the west side." As Hank turned to leave, he looked back over his shoulder to voice a final good-bye, but to his surprise, the Indian had disappeared from his sight. He had only turned his eyes away for a fraction of a second! Where had Paul Billy gone so quietly and yet so quickly? It gave him an eerie sensation! Then he chuckled. "I'm sure glad that Indian is your friend, Marv. I've never seen anyone who could move so quietly in the woods, although your brother Treff runs him a close second."

"Treff grew up riding in the woods with Paul Billy, and he learned many of the ways of the Indians. He is probably the best tracker in the Territory, next to Billy. Treff knows all of the Indian trails that criss-cross the countryside, and he travels them without a sound."

They rode in silence toward the Leon headquarters, each absorbed in individual thought. Marv was having trouble understanding her sudden infatuation with the black-haired man from Pensacola! She had known him for only a few hours, yet she had never before met a man who affected her like Hank O'Mara. He was so good-looking, so polite, so charming! And those dark, twinkling eyes seemed to melt her heartstrings! Surely the sun must be affecting her brain. She was a sane and sensible woman, not at all like those silly girls who were always chasing after her brothers. She urged her horse to pick up the pace. She needed to get inside where she could have a cool drink of water and get her head together.

Riding beside her, Hank O'Mara was wrestling with some thoughts of his own. There was probably not another woman in the world like Marv Dover, and although he had known her for only a short time, it was all the time he needed to know that he had found the one woman for him. She reinforced his decision to move to this part of the Territory, where he hoped he could settle and make her his wife. Should he voice his feelings for her now? He didn't want to ruin his chances by rushing things, but he had to leave in a few days, and failing to speak up now might leave the door open for some other man to come along and sweep her off her feet.

Hank had little experience in courting. He had never had the time for it. Just how could he let Marvelous Dover know of his feelings for her without scaring her away?

"Marv," he began. "There is something important that I want to talk to you about while we are alone." They drew their ponies to a halt, and Marv could see the anxiety in Hank's face. She guessed what he was about to say, and she did not want to discourage him.

"Hank, let's sit here under this oak tree where we can talk." She slipped out of her saddle and tied her horse to a clump of palmettos. She sat on a grassy mound and leaned against the trunk of a massive oak tree. Moss swayed in the limbs overhead and rippled soft shadows across her face. She patted the ground and smiled, "Come sit here beside me and tell me what's on your mind."

She prepared herself to hear the sweet romantic phrases she had always discouraged from other men. How beautiful they would sound from the lips of Hank O'Mara!

Hank dropped his lean, muscular frame to the grass beside her and took her hand in his. "Marv, I have just never seen a woman who could ride a horse as well as you do."

"*What?!*" These were not the romantic words she had expected to hear!

"Oh, I know this is going to sound a little forward, but really, Marv, the way you handle cattle is something to behold. Why, you know as much about breeding cattle and ranching as most of the men I know!"

Marv withdrew her hand from his. "Really, Hank, I think we should be going. It's getting rather late."

"But wait, Marv. I want you to know how I think of you."

"I think I've already figured that out, Hank. Let's go." Marv untied her horse and threw her leg over the saddle. She spurred her horse into a gallop toward head-quarters. This man had no intention of whispering romantic words in her ear. He only wanted to tell her that she was a good cowhunter! Well, she already knew that. She certainly didn't need Hank O'Mara to tell her.

Hank was baffled. Had he said something to offend her? He had tried to think of the nicest compliments he could offer, and she seemed to have taken offense. He really did not understand women at all! He had no choice but to follow her to Leon headquarters.

When they reached the house, Marv spoke in a cool, polite tone. "Hank, if you will excuse me for a few minutes, I need to see some of the crew concerning some work. Make yourself comfortable on the porch, and I'll be back."

Hank watched her gather a group of cowhands around her down by the horse barn. He marveled at the efficient way she handled her business. He had never even heard of a woman managing a ranch before, much less one as beautiful as Marv. He guessed she just must not be attracted to him the way he was to her. Why, she wouldn't even let him finish his proposal! She must have known he had a reason for paying her all those compliments. Obviously, he needed a few lessons in courting.

❖   ❖   ❖

Late in the day, they arrived back at the Central in time for supper. In spite of his disappointment, Hank could not remember when he had enjoyed a day so much! As he and Marv unsaddled their ponies, he tried once again to tell her of his admiration for her. "Marv, I can't thank you enough for taking the time to give me a tour of the Leon. Your cattle are in excellent shape. I couldn't help but be impressed by the way you handle the cowhunters you have working for you. The whole day was just an outstanding experience, and you are a wonderful guide!"

The normally talkative Marv suddenly found herself unable to find the words to express herself. She could feel the color rising to her cheeks. Struggling to regain her composure, she said, "I am happy to have had the chance to show you the place." Without further comment, she excused herself and hurried to the house, while Hank remained at the stable, brushing his horse and trying to figure what he could do to win the favor of Marvelous Dover.

When he finished grooming and feeding his horse, Hank walked toward the house and saw Treff sitting on the front porch. Happy to see his friend again, he quickened his pace and took the steps two at a time. "Treff! I've been asking when I would see you again."

"Hank, I would like for you to meet my brother,

Rusty. He manages this division of the ranch. We've been over east, scouting the area for tracks of unshod ponies or anything else that might indicate Indian activity, but we didn't find anything to be alarmed about."

While they were talking, Hank saw another tall, blond man emerge from the house. "Hank, this is my brother Ten. He manages the Fannin Division to the west of here. And now, you have met the entire Dover family. Fellas, this is Hank O'Mara, from out near Pensacola."

"So you're the owner of the mysterious HO-over-bar brand! Welcome to the TSR!" Ten held out his hand. "Have you already met Jeremiah?"

"Yes, we met day before yesterday. In fact, he bought those HO-Bar steers from me. I didn't think it was practical to try to drive such a few head of cattle all the way to Yellow River."

Ace came out on the porch to join them, and Treff decided this was a good time to present his plan. "Hank, we've been working on a problem," he said. "We'd like to tell you about it to see what you think."

"I sure didn't see any problems today. Everything looked good to me," Hank said. "What's the trouble?"

Treff began to fill him in on the experiences of Paul Billy and Aldo during their trips to Jacksonville. "They are going back to Jacksonville in the morning to meet with the young man called Jake, to see if he has any cattle lined up for them. We thought it might be a good idea to send someone along with them; someone to pose as a wealthy cattle buyer. We'd like to get a look at his cattle, but it's liable to be a dangerous proposition; these men would shoot you in the back just for looking at them the wrong way! We are trying to decide if it's worth the risk. Paul Billy has to remain out of sight, because some of the group might recognize him."

"There should be less risk if there were two people instead of only one." Hank smiled. "I have always wanted to be a big cattle buyer. Why don't you let me go with them? There won't be anyone there who would know me from back at the Yellow River."

"Can you handle that six-gun you carry?"

"As long as I'm not shot in the back from ambush, I have no trouble taking care of myself. I've lived in the woods most of my life, and I've had to use this thing more than once," Hank assured him, patting the gun on his hip. "I don't use it unless I have to," he added. Hank did not think it necessary to tell the brothers that he had recently buried a couple of outlaws who had thought him an easy target to rob.

"Hank, we'll outfit you and Aldo with horses that don't carry the TSR brand and provide you with enough gold to impress the young man. Tell him you need a group of steers to take to Cowpens. Maybe nothing will come of this, but you can never tell what a little intrigue might uncover."

"What time will we leave?"

"We'll talk to Aldo about that, but I figure he'll want to get away about daylight tomorrow."

"This is asking a lot from a person who is supposed to be our guest," Ace said. "Me and Treff argued for most of the day about what we should do, and we're mighty beholden to you for your offer to help."

"Sir, it will be my pleasure to do something to help

the Dover family." And, he thought, it will be an even greater pleasure to have a few extra days in which to try to win the favor of the beautiful redhead who had stolen his heart.

17

"ZEKE," DRAG SAID, "I need a few days off."

"What do you need off for?" Zeke growled, even though he already had a pretty good idea what was on Drag's mind.

"When we was at the Three Springs Ranch frolic, that good-looking redhead just couldn't leave me alone," Drag bragged. "I promised her I'd come back and see her in three weeks, and I don't want to disappoint her. Besides, last time I was pickin' up supplies over at Wanton's Store, I overheard talk about some steamboat captain down around Fort Brooke who's looking for a load of cattle to smuggle to Cuba. After I make a little time with the Dover gal, I could go down and check that out. It might be a good connection for us to have."

Zeke rubbed his chin thoughtfully. "That's a good idea to follow up on that steamboat captain, but we're gonna need you here next Thursday when we start collecting them four-year-old steers from the southeast pasture. I reckon as how you can take off at lunchtime Friday, but be sure you're back here by next Wednesday night."

Drag was pleased. If he left after lunch Friday, he could get to Jacksonville early Saturday morning. If he was able to see Toke early enough, he could probably make it to the TSR by dark Saturday night. He could spend a long Sunday with Marv Dover and then drift down to the Fort Brooke area on Monday. One whole day alone with that redhead and she would be ready to fall in his arms! Chuckling in anticipation, he muttered to himself, "There ain't never been a girl yet that I couldn't get to fall in love with me. That redhead ain't no different!"

Lady Luck seemed to follow Drag. As he rode into Jacksonville on Saturday morning, he spotted Toke's buckskin tied to the hitching rail in front of the Cowhunters Saloon. With any luck, he ought to be able to take care of his business with Toke in short order. He'd like to get away from this town soon after midday and be on his way to make the redhead happy.

Tying his horse alongside of Toke's, he made a cautious survey of both sides of the street. He saw nothing unusual to alarm him. It was still too early in the day for most cowhands to be in town. Then suddenly, the hair on the back of his neck seemed to rise and tingle in a sign that was often a prelude to danger. This feeling had often saved his life during his rustling days, and he knew better than to ignore it now.

As he glanced up the street to discover a reason for

this warning signal, he noticed several strange horses in front of the sheriff's office. The heavy coating of dust on their hides indicated a long ride, and the riders' gear was still tied behind their saddles. It was a good bet that these were not the horses of local cowhunters.

Drag forced himself to appear nonchalant, as he sauntered into the saloon. He saw Toke at once, sitting at his usual table in the back corner with two other cowhunters. Drag ordered a beer and took it with him as he swaggered back to their table. "Do you fellers want to play a few hands of poker?"

"If you got the money, we got the time," Toke grunted without looking up. "Me and my boys just got into town. We want to relax and get the dust out of our throats."

Drag pulled up a chair and straddled it, plopping his mug of beer on the table. "I remember Jake here," he said with forced unconcern, "but I don't recollect meetin' this other feller. Are y'all from the same place?"

"Dino here is the only member of our group that you ain't already met," grumbled Toke. "Are we gonna talk or play poker?"

"We need to do a little bit of both," Drag replied, "because I ain't gonna stay here very long, and I need to tell you about a group of fat steers."

"Why are you in such a big hurry?" Toke asked, purposely taking his time to deal the cards around the table.

"There's a group of strange horses in front of the sheriff's office, and I don't want to be found in this saloon when they come to look around," Drag answered. "They may not be out-of-town marshals, but I don't want to take that chance. The hair on the back of my neck tells me not to linger here today."

For a long moment, Toke did not say a word. He was thinking about Marshal Mizell from north Georgia who was looking for *him*. Finally, he put down his cards and said, "We wouldn't want to keep you, then. Besides, I just remembered somethin' me and the boys forgot to do. I reckon we better go back to our place and finish up a little work we started. Did you have somethin' important you want to tell us?"

"I've located a group of real fat steers on Payne's Prairie, just northwest of the Brown Owl Ranch. They would go real good with the steers you already have."

Jake broke in. "Man, you must be crazy. Them is Seminole cattle. That's a good way to lose your hair." He raised both hands to his head as if to protect it.

"I been watching these steers for several weeks while riding the Brown Owl, and I ain't never seen the first Injun. The cattle are belly deep in grass; they stay in the same spot, and they're very quiet. A group of good cowhunters could move them at night with no trouble," Drag replied. "They could be drifted straight north to your other cattle. You ought to take a look at 'em and then make up your own minds."

"Where you be aheading fer now?" Toke asked.

"I'm fixin' to go to Fort Brooke to try to touch base with a steamboat captain; I think his name is Caleb. I hear he's lookin' for a load of cattle to smuggle into Cuba. He might be a good man for us to get to know. But I gotta be back to the Brown Owl Ranch by Wednesday night."

"Where could we meet to take a look at them there steers?" Toke asked.

"I could meet you Sunday morning after I get back to the Brown Owl. We could meet at that little store on the south side of Keystone Lake. It won't take too long to see the steers. You might even decide to take 'em out Sunday night. You could, easy enough. There'll be a good moon, and the Injuns will probably all be sleeping."

"We'll meet you in front of the store at daybreak next Sunday. Right now we gotta high-tail it north to finish some errands I forgot," Toke said.

"I'll see you then, a week from tomorrow," Drag replied, as he left the table and pushed his way through the swinging door of the Cowhunters Saloon.

Before Toke left the saloon, he turned to Jake and barked an order: "Kid, I want you to mosey up the street and learn who them horses belong to. Dino and me'll drift out of town and stop at that big oak grove this side of the Verdie Settlement. We'll wait fer you there, 'cause we need to come back into town tonight. We gotta see if that feller shows up that told you he wanted to buy some cattle." Toke pointed his finger in Jake's face to emphasize his next words: "Don't you come to us until you know fer sure if them horses belongs to some lawmen."

Toke stomped off to the bar, bought a bottle of whiskey for his saddlebag, and rode quietly out of town.

As Drag rode south along the Alachua trail, a satisfied smile spread across his long, lean face. Everything seemed to be working out perfectly according to his master plan. Now all he had to do was marry into the Dover family and he would be fixed for life! He knew the redhead would be no problem once he turned on the old Johnson charm! It worked every time!

At that same moment just forty miles southeast, Marv Dover drew her horse to a halt and rested beneath the shade of a sprawling oak tree. She took off her hat and shook her thick hair to loosen it from her neck. Wiping the sweat from her forehead, she thought how happy she would be when Treff could return to take over management of the Leon Division.

At first she had been eager to run this place on her own, to prove that she was just as good as any of her brothers when it came to running a ranch. And she was satisfied with the job she had done. It had been a busy week gathering four-year-old steers from the thick underbrush of the Rio pasture, but she and her men had found most, if not all, of the steers. But she missed spending time with her parents, and now she looked forward to the lazy weekend ahead. She would sleep in her own feather bed, eat Francesca's wonderful cooking, and feel like a woman again.

And she *was* a woman now, whether the rest of her family realized it or not. Wasn't this the weekend that tall, good-looking gentleman from the Brown Owl Ranch promised to come calling on her? She hoped he would come so that she could see if he was really as attractive as she remembered him.

In the distance, she could hear the occasional snap of a blacksnake whip as Paul Billy and his cowhunters began moving the cattle toward the Ocoee pasture three miles to the north.

Moments later, Paul Billy rode up beside her and drew his horse to a stop. "Are you all right?"

"Yes, Paul Billy. I just stopped to rest from the heat. Here it is the second weekend in November. You'd think it would begin to cool off. That would make it a lot easier to work these cattle out of the brush. This sure is a lot different from last winter when it was cold enough to spit ice!"

"My people tell me it will be cold on the next full moon," Billy replied. "That will be in about seven days."

"We've gathered one hundred thirty-seven head in this group. After we move them into the Ocoee pasture with the sixty-nine head we gathered last week, we'll quit for the day." Marv figured she would have time to get back to Central before dark.

"I don't know for certain whether these cattle are going to Mobile or Savannah," Marv continued, "nor do I know when they will be moved. But water is plentiful and the grass is good in the Ocoee and should take care of them for quite awhile,"

"I will have the men start at once to move them in that direction," Paul Billy assured her. "Is there anything else I can do for you before I leave?"

"Well, yes, there is one thing." Marv hesitated, trying to decide if this was the proper time and place to discuss her personal concerns, but her curiosity won out. "Paul Billy, tell me about the tall, blond man I met during our open house. What do you know about him?"

Billy fumbled for an answer that would be honest without betraying the confidence of one who trusted him. Finally he lowered his eyes and said, "I do not know this man."

"Paul Billy, I can tell by your eyes that you know more than you are telling me. What is it?"

Reluctantly, Billy admitted, "I have seen him meet a fat man in Jacksonville; a man that Treff thinks may be an outlaw. I have seen the two of them together more than one time, but I know nothing of their business."

"Treff has not told me about this," Marv murmured.

"He does not talk about such things unless he knows them to be true," Billy replied. "Treff is working to find out more about this man. I know he will tell you if he finds reason for concern."

Marv watched him ride away and thought about his words. She knew that he was right about Treff, and she was glad that her brothers loved her and tried to take care of her. But sometimes she felt smothered by their over-zealous protection. When would they realize that she was a grown woman who could take care of herself?

She wanted to see that blond gentleman from the Brown Owl Ranch again. She remembered the excitement of dancing with him and the warm feel of his arms as he whirled her around the barn floor. She didn't need Treff or anyone else to tell her what kind of man he was; she could make up her own mind about that. He was certainly attractive, and he knew how to talk to a lady and make her feel special. When he was close to her, he made her feel every inch a woman.

Not at all like Hank O'Mara, who seemed to be more interested in how well she could ride a horse or shoot a gun. A woman wanted to be treated like a—well, a *woman*!

Oh, Hank was kind and considerate, all right, and

she had to admit that his touch had sent tingles through her whole body. But why couldn't he whisper something romantic in her ear once in a while instead of telling her how great she handled a bunch of steers?

Marv was glad that Hank would be away this weekend, just in case Drag Johnson did come to call. Handling either one of these tall, handsome men was challenging enough, but two at once would be impossible! And to think that just a few weeks ago she was certain she would never find any man in the Florida Territory who could interest her, and now suddenly there were two! Life had become very confusing but very exciting as well! She would talk to Mama about it this weekend.

She put her hat back on her head and spurred her horse to a gallop. She didn't have time to waste mooning over men when there was work to be done. She joined the men who were herding the cattle northward. Riding alongside Paul Billy, she asked, "Are there any older steers in the south pasture?"

"Yes, ma'am, quite a few. They will be hard to gather because the palmettos are tall in that pasture."

"That will be a good pasture to work when the weather turns cool. If your people are accurate with their weather forecast, we will start there in ten days. Let's work the Muskee Pasture next week."

"We need to have one day to ride the borders of this division to make certain we have no problems," Billy advised.

Marv's brow creased with concern. "Have you detected any signs of poaching or rustling on the southern border?"

"I have seen tracks made by barefoot ponies that could be a sign of poaching, but I do not believe we have lost cattle," Billy answered.

"Then why don't you ride the borders on Monday? That will leave all the rest of the week to gather the steers in the Muskee Pasture."

They crossed a shallow stream that flowed from north to south through the ranch, and stopped to let the ponies refresh themselves with the clear, cool water.

"Paul Billy," Marv said, "if you don't need my help, I think I'll follow this stream for awhile and work my way to Central. I want to see what kind of signs I might find around the water holes. I'll see you again some time on Monday."

"I will be interested to hear what you find," Paul Billy answered, as Marv turned northward to follow the bubbling brook.

The stream began at one of the several springs located on the western boundary of the Central Division, and randomly wound its way to the Leon Division. Lined with occasional clumps of hardwood trees, the crystal-clear brook meandered through piney flatwoods where the ground was covered with tough wiregrass and a scattering of palmettos. Marv had learned from Treff and Paul Billy how to read footprints and animal droppings along the banks of the stream as though they were pages of an open book. Careful observation told her when animals or people had come onto the Dover property. Today, as she rode alongside the watering holes, she saw only deer, bear, turkey, coon, and cat tracks. She had almost reached the northwest corner of the division when she came upon the tracks of three unshod horses that had entered the ranch. She followed the tracks for a short way and found that they turned southeast and did not continue toward the Central Division, but she saw no indication that they had turned to leave the ranch. Paul Billy needed to know about this on Monday, if he didn't find it out for himself during the weekend!

As she approached the barns of the Central Division, Marv could already begin to feel the enveloping warmth and the sense of comfort she always experienced when returning home.

When she reached the pens around the barn, she was especially glad to find Treff there, brushing the dust from Rojo's back. She needed a chance to visit with him before going to the house to see her parents.

Treff held the reins of her horse as she dismounted, and gave her a brotherly hug. "Marv, what a nice surprise! We didn't expect to see you until later tonight, or maybe even in the morning. You must have had a good day."

"We gathered one hundred thirty-seven head from the Rio pasture, and I believe that pasture is now empty," Marv reported proudly. "I told Paul Billy to put them with the sixty-nine head in the Ocoee pasture and call it a week."

"That's a good number," Treff agreed. "We'll need about four hundred head for that next trip to Mobile, but we won't be making that trip until sometime after the first of the year. In the winter there won't be much good grass for the cattle to graze on the way over, but the buyer is anxious and willing to pay."

Changing the subject abruptly, Marv moved directly to the point of her concern. "Treff, do you remember that tall fellow from the Brown Owl Ranch who came to our open house?"

"Yes, I do," Treff replied noncommittally. "He seemed to be a pleasant fellow."

"I found him quite pleasant," Marv said tersely. "He will probably visit me this weekend."

Treff was silent for a few moments before he spoke, choosing his words carefully. "It will be nice to see him again. When do you expect him?"

"I really don't know. When he was here he asked if he could come back this weekend, and I told him he would be welcome to do so."

"I will welcome the chance to become better acquainted with him," Treff answered honestly. "I didn't get to meet him during the open house."

Marv would not be put off so easily. "Treff, have you been going around trying to find out about him?"

The question startled Treff, but this was not the first time he had been surprised by questions from Marv. She was always honest and direct, and he knew he owed her the same kind of consideration. "Do you remember when we were discussing the loss of few head of cattle from the Fannin?" he asked.

Marv nodded her head and waited to hear more.

"We had a new man in that division that we let go. His name was Ritta. I asked Paul Billy to follow this Ritta to see where he went. The man rode into Jacksonville and met up with a real fat man in the Cowhunters Saloon."

"I don't see what that has to do with us. If we've let

Ritta go, what he does now should be no concern of ours."

"Wait until you hear me out before you decide. Pretty soon they were joined by the tall man from the Brown Owl Ranch. They played a little poker, and the tall fellow left. After a little while, Ritta and the fat man left and rode into the Okefinokee Swamp. It appears that Ritta had gotten a new job."

"That seems to have turned out well for him," Marv said. "Is that all that happened?"

"For several weekends I've had Billy checking on the fat man from the big swamp. I felt that he might be involved some way in the cattle we lost, but Billy hasn't been able to find anything to prove that. It's interesting, though, that our tall man from the Brown Owl Ranch has met with the fat man in the Cowhunters Saloon every weekend since the first time Billy saw them together."

"Treff Ballowe, I'm surprised at you! I don't think it's fair of you to start accusing a man of something that you can't prove. It's not like you!"

"I'm not accusing anyone of anything, Marv. That's the reason I haven't bothered to tell the family about it. In all fairness, there may be nothing to be concerned about. If you hadn't asked me, I wouldn't have brought it up until we have more information. But you need to know that I do have a concern about the fat man. I think he may have a gang of rustlers in the Okefinokee Swamp."

"Are you concerned about Drag Johnson coming to call on me?"

"Marv, I realize that you're a grown lady with a very level head on your shoulders. You're certainly able to take care of yourself. You know that we'll all be courteous to your guest this weekend, and personally, I'm glad for a chance to get better acquainted with him. I'm glad, too, that you and I had this chance to talk, so you will understand why I am so interested in your Mister Johnson."

"He's not my Mister Johnson," Marv protested. Then she relaxed and gave him her prettiest smile. "Treff, I am also glad we had this chance to talk. It's good to know that you aren't just worrying about me; that you're looking at a bigger problem."

Treff removed the saddle from Marv's horse, and she led him into a stall.

"Perhaps you can help us decide what we should think about the man, Marv," Treff suggested.

Without making any commitments, Marv watched Treff lead Rojo in his stall. After giving both horses some hay and grain, they walked together toward the house.

Late Saturday afternoon, Ace and Amaly Dover sat relaxing on the front porch with Marv and Treff. Ace leaned forward in his chair for a better look at two riders on horseback, silhouetted against the horizon. When the two men approached the corrals, the family recognized Rusty at once and soon realized that the man with him was Drag Johnson. Marv jumped up from her chair and disappeared into the house.

After settling their horses in stalls with hay and corn, the two men crossed the yard to the house. Rusty exclaimed, "Look who I ran into about a mile north of here. You remember Drag Johnson, don't you? He visited from the Brown Owl Ranch during our last open house."

Drag smiled widely and returned the Dovers' greetings as if nothing bothered him. Fortunately for him, no one could possibly read his disappointment at being discovered while nosing around the ranch.

"It is mighty nice of y'all to let me come back for a visit," he said, as he shook hands with everyone. "You sure do have a mighty fine place."

"We are happy to see you again, Drag," Ace replied. "We've been looking forward to your visit."

"Would you like a cup of coffee?" Amaly asked.

"That would be mighty nice, ma'am," Drag replied, smiling broadly. A glass of beer or whiskey would have pleased him more, but that would have to wait until later.

Just as Amaly handed Drag his coffee, Marv came through the door and onto the porch. She had changed from her dungarees into a gingham dress which Amaly had made some time ago but which Marv had seldom worn. The wide flounce at the bottom twirled around her ankles when she walked.

Rusty gave a low whistle, and Marv glared at him before she turned her attention to the visitor. "Drag, how nice of you to come," she said, offering him her hand. "We weren't sure whether you would be here this weekend."

"Wild horses couldn't have kept me away, ma'am. I wanted to come sooner, but we have been very busy at the Brown Owl. It's too bad the two ranches are so far apart." While he talked, Drag never took his eyes off Marv. She sure was one beautiful lady! She was curved in all the right places, and that red hair was really something special.

Trying to ignore the stare from their visitor, Marv sat down beside Treff, who sat silently sipping his coffee and observing. "Isn't this a beautiful evening?" Marv commented, trying to stimulate the conversation. "I do believe this is my favorite time of the day!"

"Marv, did you see anything unusual on your way up from the Leon?" Treff asked, trying to recapture the real Marv who seemed to have been replaced by a frivolous substitute.

"The only thing I saw was three sets of pony tracks coming in from the west. I followed them a ways. I thought if Drag didn't mind taking a ride tomorrow, we might see where the tracks led."

That sounded like an invitation to Drag. Nothing would suit him more than to ride off into the woods with this redheaded filly. If he could just get her alone to himself for a while, he could turn on the old Johnson charm and make time with the lady. Trying not to appear eager, he said, "If I could help in some way, it would be my pleasure to do so."

After breakfast early the next morning, Amaly gave Marv a neatly wrapped package. "We'll have supper around four o'clock this afternoon, but you may want a snack before then. I'd like for you to be back in time for supper, Marv."

"We should be back before then," Marv assured her, "but these snacks will taste good around noontime. Thanks a lot, Mama." Amaly squeezed her hand and gave her a secret wink that let Marv know her mother understood how important this day could be for her.

Turning to Treff, Marv said, "The tracks we are going to check on came in near the northwest corner of Leon and traveled southeast. I followed until I was near the Kirk Hollow. Drag and I will head down toward the hollow and pick up the tracks. We'll leave there in time to be back home by three o'clock. If we don't find anything, we will leave it for Paul Billy to follow up."

There was a cool crispness in the morning air that announced the arrival of fall. Dew lay heavy on the grass, and a gentle breeze carried a fresh, clean smell that gave a pleasant start to the new day. The horses were full of energy, raring to go. Drag and Marv let them trot for a couple of miles before slowing them down to a leisurely walk.

"I'm glad we're going to walk our horses for awhile," Drag said. "It will give us a chance to talk as we go along."

"What shall we talk about?" Marv asked demurely.

"I know this will seem rather sudden to you, Marvelous Dover, but I have done nothing but dream about you ever since we first met. You are, without a doubt, the most beautiful lady I have ever seen. I couldn't hardly wait to come back to see you again."

Marv flushed and tried to change the subject. "How long will you be with us?"

"If I had my way, I wouldn't ever go, but I'm afraid I'll have to ride out before daybreak tomorrow. I want to make a business contact at Fort Brooke, and I have to be back to work at the Brown Owl Ranch by Wednesday night."

"That will be a short visit, but I—that is, my family

is very happy to have you here."

"Are you engaged to anyone?" Drag asked abruptly.

"No."

"You are such a charming lady; I know there must be at least a dozen men chasing after you."

Although his guess was accurate, Marv did not admit it, nor did she admit that she had yet to meet a man with whom she wanted to become romantically involved. That is, not until Drag Johnson and Hank O'Mara came into her life. She found it all very confusing.

"Look," she said, pointing to the ground, "Here are those pony tracks I was following yesterday."

Drag cursed silently to himself. He had a lot of good ideas in his mind, and following horse tracks was not one of them. Now they would have to follow those damn tracks and he wouldn't be able to get the romance underway. But he smiled as though following horse tracks was the thing he most wanted to do. "Let's follow them and see what we can learn," he said, encouraging Marv to lead the way. After following the tracks for about a mile, Marv held her hand up to signal Drag to stop.

"Do you see that tall pine tree in the distance, the one that has been struck by lightning?"

Drag nodded his head.

"Just beyond that tree is a dip in the ground that we call Kirk Hollow. There is a pretty little stream twisting along over the rocks, and it's a favorite spot to camp. It would be a perfect place to stop and rest while we have a snack. Aren't you getting hungry?"

Stop and rest? Drag's hopes soared. "Why, yes, I believe I am."

"We need to be quiet as we approach the place, in case someone is camping there. If no one is there, we can stop and see what Mama fixed for us to snack on."

Drag could hardly believe his good fortune. He was finally going to get this luscious lady down from her horse!

They eased their horses forward in silence until they had a clear view into the hollow. When they saw that the place was deserted, they rode down to the stream to give their horses a drink. Although they saw evidence that someone had camped there within the last few days, the place was clean and serenely beautiful. They led the horses to a grassy spot to graze while they chose a shady spot for themselves.

"After we see what Mama packed for our snack, we can follow the tracks a little further. If we don't find anything soon, we'll have to leave it to someone else to find out where those tracks lead."

Drag was no more interested in eating than he was in following horse tracks. Watching the redhead bounce along on her horse all morning had really gotten him all fired up, and he couldn't wait to get his hands on her. Very likely, he thought, she was of the same mind and only used the snack as a good excuse to stop and cozy up to him.

Marv spread her rain slicker on the ground and pulled out the cornbread and pork chops that Amaly had sent. She piled food on each of two tin plates and handed one of them to Drag. "Try this. I think Francesca is just about the best cook in the whole Florida Territory."

Drag settled himself close to Marv and tried to make

it seem accidental when he brushed against her as she handed him a plate of food.

"How can I concentrate on food when I look into your eyes that remind me of the brightest stars in the heavens, and your flaming hair has done set a blazing fire in my heart!"

Marv's cheeks turned a becoming pink, but her smile encouraged him to continue.

"I hope we can get better acquainted," he whispered, taking her hands in his and gradually pulling her closer.

Marv found the warmth of his body exciting, and she liked the romantic way he talked to her. He had not mentioned one word about how she handled her cows or her guns; he only spoke of her beauty and charm. He made her feel every inch a woman! She felt shivers run up her spine when his lips brushed her hair.

She rested her head on his shoulder and fleetingly wondered if it might be better to start following those tracks again. But before she had a chance to even consider it, she felt his lips on hers and she was lost in a new and pleasing sensation.

Drag's confidence mounted. This was going to be easier than he thought. Never had work been more pleasant! Gently he lowered her head down on the slicker and continued to kiss her. As he felt her willing response, he began to caress her sides, gradually moving his hands higher and higher.

Somewhere inside Marv's head she could hear a warning bell, but she blocked out its sound until she felt him groping for her breasts. At the same time, she felt his loins hardening against her leg, and she knew it was time to move.

She tried to pull away from him. "Please don't, Drag." But her protest only excited him further. He reached for the buttons of her shirt. He liked a spirited gal. It only added to the fun!

"Drag, stop it, damn you!" Marv pounded against his chest as her temper raged, but Drag had lost his reason and paid no attention. When he shifted the weight of his body in an attempt to position himself on top of her, Marv balled up her right fist and swung an upper cut that caught him just under the chin and reeled him backwards. Only then did he come to the full realization that the woman he had complimented on beauty and charm also possessed muscles of steel, the reward of a lifetime of working cattle. He cupped one hand to his chin and felt the trickle of warm blood. His mouth opened in one big question mark. "Why?"

"When I said to stop it, that's what I meant," she said.

"All you are is a damn tease," he said, grabbing for her again in an attempt to appease his anger.

Dodging his advancing arms, she placed her hands on his shoulder and, with one mighty shove, sent him sprawling across the ground. "I am not your kind of girl, Drag Johnson, and there's one thing you'd better realize: I will decide *whom* I want to love and *when*. Now is not the time nor the place, and *you*, Drag Johnson, damn sure aren't the man! Now get up from there and go get on your horse, and we'll get on with our business."

"You go on ahead," Drag said. "I'll be along in a few minutes."

"As far as I'm concerned, you don't need to come along at all. You can go on to Fort Brooke if you wish. But if you do come along, you can be sure that no one in my family will ever know what has happened here today, because you would not be safe in this part of the Territory if they did, and I wouldn't want to have that on my conscience." With that, she mounted her horse and followed the trio of unfamiliar tracks.

As Marv rode out of the hollow, neither she nor Drag knew how close he had come to death that afternoon. Hidden in the deep brush at the top of the hollow, Paul Billy kept a silent vigil, his rifle cocked and aimed. When Marv disappeared through the thickets, he quietly slipped his rifle back into its scabbard and rode away.

Marv followed the tracks another hour before deciding it was time to go home. As she turned north, she heard the whinny of a horse and turning, saw that it was Drag. "Marv, I want to apologize for the way I acted. I'm afraid I misunderstood and acted poorly."

"Forget it, Drag. I assure you that I have. Let's head on north, so we will be there when Mama puts supper on the table."

They rode side by side the rest of the way back. Several times along the way Drag tried to initiate a conversation, but Marv made it quite clear that she had too many things on her mind to talk to him.

They arrived back at Central Division in plenty of time to meet the supper deadline. Amaly raised questioning eyebrows at her daughter, but Marv's expression revealed nothing.

After dinner Drag talked briefly with Ace and

thanked him for his hospitality. "I mentioned to Marv that I needed to go to Fort Brooke, and I really think I should start this evening rather than wait until tomorrow morning. I've gotta be back to the Brown Owl by Wednesday evening, and it's gonna push me to make the schedule."

"We're sorry you can't stay longer, but we understand," Ace assured him. "Business sometimes gets in the way of socializing, doesn't it?"

As Drag shook hands with the rest of the family, Marv declined to offer hers but merely said politely, "It was good of you to come, Drag. I hope your business in Fort Brooke is successful."

❖   ❖   ❖

Leaving the Central headquarters that evening, Drag realized that an important part of his plan had fallen through. Where did he go from here?

Perhaps the time had come for him to leave the Brown Owl Ranch and drift on south to look for a lady who would help him reach his goals. That redhead wasn't the only toad in the pond!

The more he thought about it, the more convinced he became that he should give Zeke a week's notice when he returned to the BOR next Wednesday. That would leave him free to look for that boat captain down at Fort Brooke that he'd heard about.

18

ON SATURDAY AFTERNOON, while Drag Johnson was beside the brook flourishing his dubious charms on Marv Dover, Aldo and Hank O'Mara were just riding into the outskirts of Jacksonville. Clouds of dust devils swirled around their horses' legs as they plodded down the main street past the Cowhunters Saloon and came to a stop in front of the Widow Perkins' rooming house.

"Don't forget," Aldo cautioned, "you're H. H. O'Malley, a cattle buyer from South Carolina, and I'm Max Hagan from the same state. Miz Perkins is supposed to be holdin' a couple of rooms for us."

The cool air that swept down the central hall of the rooming house gave welcome relief after the long, hot ride to Jacksonville. Hank picked up a bell from the desk in the foyer and gave it a shake.

From the depths of the house, a perky voice called, "Just a moment."

"You'd think," Hank said, using his neckerchief to

blot the moisture from his forehead, "that the days would begin to cool off by now. Here it is mid-November, and it feels like the middle of July. This sure has been a hot fall!"

"Some of my friends say cold weather's coming on the next full moon," Aldo told him. "That's only about a week away. Maybe nature's trying to make up for that fierce freeze we had last February that killed all those orange trees over on the east coast."

Before Hank could comment, a slight, gray-haired lady came toddling down the hall, a pleasant smile creasing her cheeks. "Mr. Hagan," she said, holding out her small, wrinkled hand, "I see you made it back, just as you promised. It's nice to see you again!" Turning to Hank, she added, "And you must be the friend Mr. Hagan told me about. It is certainly a pleasure to welcome you both. How long will you be with us?"

Hank took the lady's hand and shook it gently. "My name is H. H. O'Malley, ma'am, and I'm mighty pleased to make your acquaintance. We'll pay you for two nights in advance. If we have to leave earlier, you will be the winner. If we find it necessary to stay longer, we'll pay whatever additional we owe." He plunked a twenty-dollar gold piece on her desk, hoping it would ignite a rumor of the cattle buyer who was in town paying his bills with gold coin.

"You sure do have a comfortable place, Miz Perkins. I've been telling my friend, Mister O'Malley here, all about it. We don't have lodgings this fine in South Carolina. You must work real hard to keep it so nice."

Widow Perkins blushed with obvious pleasure at the rare compliment. "Let me show you gentlemen your rooms," she said, leading the way upstairs. "I have placed you in my two best rooms at the back of the house, away from the noise of the street. Is that satisfactory?"

"That's perfect, Miz Perkins. Thank you very much."

"You'll find water for the wash basin in the big pitcher next to the table," she said, ushering them into the first bedroom. "The slop bucket for dirty water is under the table. The other room joins this one, right through that door yonder." She lingered in the doorway. "If there is anything else you need, anything at all . . ."

"We'll need a place to stable our horses," Aldo said.

"Of course. You remember where the barn is, out back of the house. Use whatever you need."

Making sure Widow Perkins heard him, Hank turned to Aldo and said, "Mister Hagan, if you would be so good as to take care of my horse at the same time you put yours in the stable, I will freshen up a bit and meet you down at the Four Amigos Café in about thirty minutes. I want to shake the dust off my boots before I eat. That will give you some time if you need to see anyone."

"As a matter of fact, I do, Mister O'Malley, but I won't be long. I'm hungry as a starvin' buzzard. And don't fret about your horse; I'll take care of him."

Aldo put his saddlebag in the adjoining bedroom, and the Widow Perkins scurried off down the hall.

As soon as he was alone, Hank propped a chair against the door, took off his boots, and stretched across the high poster bed. He wanted to allow Aldo time to make his connections and check things out in the Cowhunters Saloon before they met to eat. The mattress was so soft that he sank down into its depths. A cool autumn breeze drifted through the open window and gently swept across the room. He had to admit that he was a mite tired.

❖   ❖   ❖

An hour later, Hank woke with a start. He had not meant to sleep. He jumped up, pulled on his boots, splashed water on his face, and hurried down the street to the Four Amigos Café. To his great relief, Aldo had not yet arrived. Hank decided to sit on the front porch of the café and watch the darkness of the night slowly claim the town. Lights began to flicker in the saloons and stores, and wagons disappeared from the street as families made their way back home. Sitting there in the early darkness, his thoughts turned to the Dover family, and especially Marv. For the first time in his life, he wished that he had made an effort to learn how to sweet-talk a woman. Up until now, he had considered such tomfoolery to be a waste of time. But that was before he had met Marvelous Dover! He reckoned he must be falling in love! Any doubts he might have had about moving east were now completely dispelled.

He looked at the harvest moon growing in the sky. Everything he saw now reminded him of Marv. He was so absorbed in his thoughts that he did not see Aldo approaching until he was coming up the steps. With him was a young man with hair the color of sun-bleached straw.

"Mister O'Malley," Aldo greeted him, "I'd like for you to meet Jake. This-here's the young feller I was playing poker with last weekend; the one who told me his boss might have some steers to sell."

"I'm pleased to meet you, Jake."

"Mister O'Malley, my boss had unexpected business come up right at the last minute, and he couldn't be here. He sends his apologies. He wanted me to talk with you to learn just what it is you're looking fer."

"Max, let's go eat supper while we talk," Hank said. "Jake, how about joining us?"

"That sounds good to me," Jake said. "I ain't had a real good meal in a coon's age."

While they ate their steak and cornbread, Jake looked at Hank and asked, "Whatcha got in mind in the way of cattle?"

"I'm looking for about four-hundred-fifty four-year-old steers to deliver to Cowpens," Hank answered. "I've looked at quite a few this past week, but I haven't found just exactly what I need. Max has been telling me about your cattle and I wanted to see them, since they were closer to South Carolina than the ones I've been looking at. Do you have that many ready for sale?"

"We might have just what you need. The boss has about two hundred picked out for sale. He told me he planned to gather another two hundred, or maybe two-fifty, head durin' the next couple of weeks."

Hank speared a large piece of steak and put it in his mouth. He took his time, chewing before he spoke. "What's he asking?"

"Sixteen dollars a head," Jake answered.

Hank smirked. "I have looked at over two thousand head of steers this past week, and I have yet to see a single steer worth that much. I don't reckon there's any need in my talking with your boss. I have other steers I can buy." Hank pushed away his empty plate to indicate that the conversation was finished.

Jake's face revealed his panic. "Wait a minute. What have them others been askin'?"

"That depends on how good the steers are. A real good steer might bring eleven dollars, but most have been nine or ten dollars a head. Your steers are closer to Cowpens, and it wouldn't cost me as much to get them there, but even so, they would have to be awful good steers for me to pay twelve dollars."

Jake motioned to have his coffee cup refilled in an effort to prolong the table conversation. "When do you need to have the steers in Cowpens?"

"By the end of November or middle of December. It would take me ten days to get my crew here, and I want to get a herd on the trail by the end of two weeks."

"I really think you should take a look at what we've got and talk to my boss. I ain't heard him say if he'd be willin' to take less, but you know it's almost winter. Grass will start gittin' short, and cattle are gonna lose weight. He might be willin' to make a deal just to move them cattle afore it gits cold. I just ain't able to say."

"When can I see these cattle?" Hank asked.

"We can meet at daybreak and go see the cattle already picked out for sale. They ain't too far from here, about twenty miles, near the Georgia border."

"Will your boss be there? I don't want to ride that far and not have someone to talk with that can buy or sell." Hank didn't want to appear anxious to see the steers. He was beginning to like this cattle-buying game. Maybe he should consider doing it for real.

"He'll be there," Jake assured him, neglecting to mention that his boss was only a few miles away, staying out of sight until those unidentified lawmen left town.

Hank made a show of paying for the three meals with a gold coin. "Keep the change." Turning to Aldo, he said, "What do you think, Max? Should we go take a look at what they have, or should we just go back and make a deal with that last ranch we visited."

Aldo scratched his head and cogitated a bit before he answered. Finally he said, "We might as well take a look at 'em while we're in this area. We got an open day tomorrow."

"All right, Jake. We'll meet you in front of this café at daybreak, but if your boss says he can't come, you get word to us at the Widow Perkins' place so we won't waste our time. We have a lot of other business to take care of."

The two men stood on the café porch and watched Jake ride out of town. "We don't know what we'll get into tomorrow, Aldo. We need to be ready in case we're getting in with a bunch of outlaws. Be sure your guns are in good working order and loaded."

"That Okefinokee Swamp is a mysterious place," Aldo said. "They's a lot of people what's disappeared in that alligator pit. But if the cattle really be only twenty miles from here, they won't be in the swamp."

"I've been told there are a lot of bayous and marshes north of here. The cattle are probably located on a prairie in some good marsh grass. If they don't move the cattle soon, the first real cold weather will kill their food supply, and they'll start losing weight," Hank said. "Aldo, tell me how you work your branding system?"

"We brand our cattle on the right hip with TSR. Then

we put a division brand below. It will be S for Santa Fe, F for Fannin, C for Central, and L for the Leon Division. And all of our cattle has got a under-bit in the right ear."

"That should make them easy to identify. We won't let them know if we do see steers with our brand tomorrow, but we'll need to try and figure out how many of them they have."

❖   ❖   ❖

Next morning, in the dimness of first light, Aldo and Hank stood on the porch of the Four Amigos Café. Aldo patted his stomach. "Them fried eggs and grits and biscuits shore did taste good."

"Mighty satisfying," Hank agreed. "You reckon our friend is gonna show?"

As if in answer to his question, a cloud of dust in the distance signaled the approach of a rider on horseback. Jake rode in alone, halted his pony by the hitching rail, and walked up the steps.

"Would you like something to eat, or a cup of coffee, perhaps?" Hank asked.

"A cup of coffee'd be good, but I done et, and I know you fellers is anxious to git goin'," Jake replied.

"You two fellers drink your coffee," Aldo said. "I'll go saddle up our horses. We need to be ridin' if we gotta go twenty miles to look at them steers." Without waiting for an answer, he left them at the café and walked the short distance to their rooming house.

He went inside quietly, not wanting to disturb Widow Perkins or her sleeping guests. He picked up the two new rifles and carried them to the barn. After saddling their horses, he slipped a rifle into each off-side scabbard and led both horses back to the café.

Jake and Hank were standing on the porch, ready to go. "Just follow me," Jake directed, untying his horse and swinging his body into the saddle.

As the three men rode northward on their way out of town, they passed three men riding in the opposite direction. "I believe those gentlemen are United States Marshals," Hank observed. "At least, they were all three wearing badges."

"What you reckon they be doin' in Jacksonville?" Jake asked, displaying more than a casual interest.

"I can't say for certain," Hank replied, "but I understand they had several outlaws on their list. Rumor has it they're going down Saint Augustine way to check on a gang camped between there and the St. Johns River. That's getting pretty close to the Seminole Indians, though, so the gang may be gone by now."

"How's come you know so much about it," Jake asked suspiciously.

"Oh, I just keep my ears and eyes open, and my mouth shut, and I find out all kinds of things."

The sun rose higher in the sky and cast a pink glow over the horizon. The three men rode in silence, each wondering what the rest of the day would bring.

Leaving Jacksonville behind them, they wove their way around hammocks of hardwoods where white egrets and wood ibises rose lazily in the air. Passing a small stream, they paused to let their horses drink the crystal-clear water. In spite of the unusually mild fall, the leaves of the trees had begun to change color and blanket the ground in shades of red and gold. They saw tracks of raccoons and deer that had passed here before them, and they heard the occasional call of a sandhill crane and a bob white. Had their mission not been of such a serious nature, Hank was sure he would have enjoyed this ride immensely. He tried to absorb every detail so that he could relate it all to Marv when he saw her.

The day grew warm as the men continued following Jake deeper into the woods. The vegetation gradually began to change from heavy thickets to prairie and marsh where egrets and other water-loving birds flocked in great clusters.

"A feller could get lost in this place; it all looks the same," Aldo muttered.

"This is good cattle country most of the year," Jake said. "There's plenty of water, and these-here marsh grasses put weight on cattle. If we git a flood, it ain't too good, but if that happens, we just try and move our cattle to higher ground."

"When are we going to meet your boss?" Hank asked.

"You'll meet him directly. He'll be with the cattle. He and a couple of cowhunters is gonna gather most of the steers so you'll be able to see 'em easier."

"What's his name?" Aldo asked.

"His name is Toke," Jake said, without offering a second name. "We don't have much further to go."

As they circled a big cypress head, Aldo and Hank could see a large group of cattle in the distance about a mile away. "Them are the steers," Jake said, pointing. "It looks like Toke and the boys have 'em rounded up together where you can see 'em pretty easy."

Hank saw a man approaching them on horseback. The rider was so big and fat that Hank wondered how that poor red buckskin horse managed to carry him. The three men stopped and waited as the fat man rode up to join them. The stench that surrounded him made Hank glad that they had arranged to meet outdoors.

"Toke, this here's Max and Mister O'Malley. They been down around Fort Brooke looking fer about four hundred steers to deliver to Cowpens. Fellers, this here's Toke, the owner of these steers I been tellin' you about."

"We're glad to meet you, Toke," Hank said.

Toke looked the two newcomers up and down, ignoring Hank's outstretched hand and saying nothing. Finally, he muttered, "If you be looking fer steers to buy, why do you go all the way to Fort Brooke?"

Hank realized that Toke was making small talk while stalling for time to make up his mind about these two strangers. He decided to play his part tough. "We go wherever we learn about steers for sale," he responded tersely. "If we can make a good deal on steers this much closer to Cowpens, so much the better, but of course, it all depends on how the steers look and what they can be bought for. Jake told us you have some stock he wanted us to look at and discuss making a deal. If he was mistaken, just say so, and we'll turn around and go back to Jacksonville."

"How many steers you need?"

"We need somewhere between four and five hundred head. We located some that we like south of here, but Jake wanted us to see what you had. The price Jake said you were asking was a lot more than what we can buy steers for in other places, but being this close, we decided to come take a look at them anyway. How many do you have for sale?"

"They's about two hundred and fifty in this group," Toke replied.

"Do you have any more?"

"We got several hundred more steers, but it would take about a week to gather another two hundred." Toke's greedy mind was thinking about the fat cattle Drag Johnson was going to show him next weekend. "They're probably a little heavier than these-here cattle."

"Can we take a closer look at the steers in this group?" Hank asked. "Do you think we could ease through the cattle without disturbing them too much?"

"I ain't anxious to get 'em excited," Toke mumbled.

"But you can't expect us to make an offer on cattle we can't see."

"Well, I reckon if you-uns stay close with me, maybe the steers prob'ly won't notice nothin' strange." Toke did not intend to let these two get out of ear-shot if he could help it.

As the four men eased through the beginning of the herd, Hank thought that the cattle looked to be in surprisingly good condition. Hank and Aldo were able to observe a variety of brands on the cattle, while some had no brands at all. When they were less than half-way through the herd, they began to spot some TSR over S brands and a few TSR over F. Nearing a clump of oak trees, Hank suggested that they stop in the shade for a few minutes, to talk business. Actually, he wanted to observe some of the moving steers to get a better look at their brands.

"Toke, I wanted to give the steers a little time to get used to us before we went any further. It seemed like they were getting a little nervous."

"What do you think so far?"

"You have some of the kind of steers I'm looking for," Hank responded. "Then you have some smaller steers that I call Spanish cattle. I'd have a hard time using those. Now, you take a steer like that little brindle-colored steer coming toward us. Those kind of steers are harder to sell at the other end."

Aldo, who had been quiet most of the time since Toke joined them, spoke up. "Mister O'Malley, we'd best go ahead and look at the rest of the steers. We need to get back to Jacksonville by dark, and the sun goes down early this time of the year."

Aldo's suggestion spurred the men back into action, and they continued their ride through the herd. Although the animals bearing the TSR brand were sprinkled among the others, Hank and Aldo did not dare risk exchanging glances but kept their eyes focused on the cattle.

When they came to the end, Hank asked, "When can you put the rest of the cattle up where we can see them?"

Toke thought for a moment. "We can prob'ly have 'em gathered in ten days."

"You say they are bigger than these?"

"Yep, they been on better grass, and they ain't any of what you call Spanish cattle in the herd."

Hank pretended to give the matter serious consideration. "I'll tell you what. I can pay you nine dollars a head across the board for this herd, delivered into the Jacksonville pens, if you can get another two hundred head to go with them. Otherwise, I think I'd be better off to buy that group down south, where I can get the entire bunch from the same place. If your other two hundred or two hundred fifty head are bigger and in better flesh, I might be able to go as much as ten-fifty or eleven dollars a head."

Toke's face turned a bright crimson. "Hell, these steers is worth more'n any nine dollars a head. I'll take thirteen dollars a head." He pounded his fist in the palm of his hand to emphasize his point.

"I might pay you ten dollars, if you give me a twenty percent cutback to eliminate the Spanish cattle," Hank said. "The bigger steers in this group aren't too bad, and I think I could use them at that price."

Toke was not happy with Hank's offer. He wanted to spit in his high-and-mighty face and tell him to keep his damn money. Still, with winter coming, he needed to unload this herd, and where else was he going to come up with a customer with gold in his saddlebags? He figured to get eleven dollars a head for the Injun cattle, if they were really as good as Drag Johnson said they were. Toke sat on his horse and thought about his options.

In the long silence, Hank began to worry. Perhaps he had been a bit too hard. "Toke," he said, mellowing his voice, "I will be at Widow Perkins' house tonight. You think about my offer, and remember, I'll pay in gold coin. If you want to do business, get word to me tomorrow by the middle of the morning. If I don't hear from you by that time, I'm going back south to get that other herd." He turned his horse around.

"Max, we need to head back if we're going to reach town by dark," Hank said, swinging around to extend his hand to Toke. "I am pleased to have met you Toke. I hope we can make a deal, but if we can't get together this time, maybe we can next time."

"Do y'all need me to take you back to town?" Jake asked.

"Not if we start now while it's still daylight," Hank said, casting his eyes toward the horizon.

As the two men headed back toward Jacksonville, Hank turned once more and called over his shoulder, "I hope to hear from you, Toke."

Hank and Aldo found the tracks they had made coming north and followed them out of the marshland all the way back to Jacksonville.

Aldo looked at Hank and chuckled. "Man, I sure don't never want to sell or buy no cattle with you. You almost had me fooled with all that tough talk."

"That was an interesting ride, wasn't it, Aldo?"

"Now we know what happened to a few more of our steers, Hank. I figger I saw about forty head of TSR steers, mostly from the Santa Fe."

"It will be interesting to see if we can get them back. We'll have to talk to Ace and the boys right away about what we've seen today."

"Hank, where do you reckon they plan on gettin' another two hundred steers?"

"They may already have another herd hidden some

place. But if it's going to take them seven to ten days to get them gathered, that may mean they'll have to rustle some more. We need to warn Jeremiah and Ten to watch their borders. TSR has already lost enough cattle to that gang."

"If they try to get their hands on some fatter cattle for you, they may try to rustle some steers from Payne's Prairie."

"But, Aldo, I've been told those are Indians' cattle. That would be too dangerous, what with the Seminole War threatenin' to start up again."

"Well, I'm just trying to figger where they's a lot of cattle. Maybe the Brown Owl Ranch might have some, but I don't know nothing about that outfit."

Hank rode along in silence for a few minutes, putting his thoughts together. Finally he said, "Aldo, we need to be careful about the Brown Owl Ranch. We already know that Drag Johnson has been meeting with Toke. They may be in cahoots with each other. We can't let them find out who we are or what we've uncovered."

"We'd best not talk about this to nobody but Ace," Aldo agreed.

As they approached the outskirts of Jacksonville, Hank said, "Max, we didn't have any dinner today, and I am hungry. Let's get on into town and get some supper. We can sleep on all this and see if we hear from Toke in the morning."

On Monday morning, Hank was up and about early. He

wandered in and out of the stores that lined the main street, talking to anyone who would stop to pass some time with him. He wanted to learn everything he could about cattle in the area, and he liberally spread the word around that he was looking for cattle to buy. He wanted to establish his identity and his reason for being in town in case Toke decided to check up on him.

He bought several small items, letting his gold coins bounce and clatter on the counters. Around the middle of the morning, he strolled back to the café where Aldo was waiting with the horses saddled and ready to go.

"Max, I want another cup of coffee and some biscuits before we leave. Would you like to join me?"

"I'd be proud to. It'll be a fer piece down south to where we're headed, and we might not git another chance to eat before dark."

The men ate a hearty, unhurried breakfast, and while Aldo was drinking his third cup of coffee, Hank said, "Max, take your time. I want to walk back down and say a word to Widow Perkins before we leave." He was stalling for time, hoping that he would receive word from Toke about the cattle. The morning was fast slipping away, and still they had no message.

Mrs. Perkins was standing by the front steps with her watering can, trying to extend the life of her wilting purple petunias, when she saw Mister O'Malley coming up the path. "Land sakes, I do wish you and your friend could stay longer. It's surely a pleasure to have two gentlemen such as you!"

"I came back to thank you for all your hospitality, Miz Perkins. We sure did enjoy your nice, clean rooms.

Perhaps we will see you again."

Hank walked back to the café, tipping his hat politely to the people he passed. Already the merchants were beginning to recognize him and consider him one of their own, just as he had hoped they would.

When he returned to the café, Aldo told him that there was still no word from Toke, so he said in a voice loud enough for anyone to hear, "Let's go, Max. I guess we had best go look at that other group of steers we liked down south. Toke apparently didn't like my deal."

Disappointed, they mounted their horses and rode south down the main street. They were heading for the Alachua Trail when they were surprised by the sounds of rapid hoofbeats bearing down on them. Looking back, they were pleased to see Jake riding toward them at a brisk gallop.

"Where did you come from?" Hank asked. "When you didn't show up, we decided Toke must not be interested in dealing, and now we're on our way back south to look at some other cattle."

"I been watching you for a long time," Jake replied. "Since you were leaving, I wanted to let you know that Toke says he'll take your deal. He wants to move the whole herd you saw yesterday for nine dollars a head. He'll git you the fat steers like you want, and for them he wants eleven dollars a head. He'll have the cattle ready in ten days."

"You tell Toke it's a deal, but only if his other cattle are as good as he says they are. I don't want to bring my cowhunters all the way down here and find out they aren't good cattle, though. If the other steers are not better than what we saw yesterday, the deal is off."

"Mister O'Malley, if we're gonna deal with this Toke feller, we need to let that other man know we ain't gonna buy his steers."

"You're right, Max. It's only fair. We'll head that way now. Jake, you tell Toke we'll meet him at the Jacksonville cattle pens on Thursday of next week. We'll pay him on the spot in gold coin, if his cattle are good."

Without further conversation, Hank and Max turned to continue south toward the Alachua Trail, ostensibly to visit another rancher with steers to sell. "We'll see you later, Jake. Thank you for all your help."

19

CONCERNED THAT THEY might be followed, Hank and Aldo decided to return to Central by a roundabout way.

"That rascal Jake had the gall to admit he was watching us all morning," Hank fumed. "I don't know how we could've missed spotting him."

"Kinda makes a feller uneasy, don't it?" Aldo agreed. He pulled off into a thicket of palmettos to stop and listen, and Hank reined in beside him.

"Did you hear something?"

"Naw, I didn't hear nothin'. I just wanted to make sure nobody was followin' our tracks. When you deal with snakes, you gotta think like snakes," Aldo declared. The two men sat in silence for almost half an hour, watching and listening, before continuing south. Even though they felt certain they were traveling alone, they waited for the cover of darkness before turning west toward the Dover ranch, and did not reach their destination until well after midnight.

They rode straight to the barn, unsaddled their horses with as little noise as possible, and put them in stalls with hay and grain. Exhausted, they turned to the bunkhouse to claim a few hours of well-earned sleep.

❖ ❖ ❖

Early Tuesday morning, Hank and Aldo joined Ace and Rusty at the breakfast table and gave them a full report of their meeting with Toke and his crew. By the time they finished their story, Ace had made up his mind. "It's time for us to have a gathering of the family to decide on what action we should take. Rusty, send a rider to each division. Tell Marv and your brothers to come in for an important meeting tomorrow morning. And ask Marv to bring Paul Billy with her. We might need him, and besides, I don't like the idea of her riding through those woods by herself."

Rusty chuckled. "Better not let Marv hear you say that."

"I know," Ace agreed. "She doesn't like to receive special treatment, but that doesn't change the fact that she is a woman."

"What about Treff?" Rusty asked. "He should be here, too. How do we get word to him?"

"Treff has been checking on some trespassers in the Leon Division. I expect him to come back tonight, but if your man sees him along the way, tell him it's important for him to get home as quickly as possible."

"I'll get started on it right away, Dad," Rusty said, putting two biscuits in his pockets before pushing himself away from the breakfast table.

After Rusty left, Ace turned to his guest. "Hank, my family and I are mighty beholden to you for all your help. I know you're anxious to get back to your own spread, and I have no right to ask anything more of you, but if you could stay on with us another day or two, we would sure appreciate it."

"Ace, after that trip to Jacksonville, I'd be mighty disappointed if I couldn't stay around to see the outcome. It would be like starting a good book and not getting to read the last chapter."

Ace smiled. "I'd like to think we could write the last chapter. I don't know what we may be getting into, but at least we may shed some light on a lot of unanswered questions. Aldo, I owe you a vote of thanks, too. You and Hank both put your life on the line these last two days."

"Boss, I ain't never heard nobody bargain on cattle like Hank. He almost had *me* convinced he was big-time cattle buyer. Why, he had them outlaws completely hornswoggled!"

Ace chuckled. "Maybe he has a talent we didn't know about. We'll have to check into that. Anyway, I just want to thank both of you for what you've done, and I want to add a word of caution. For now, Aldo, don't discuss your trip with anyone. If word of this gets back to those scalawags in Okefinokee, your life won't be worth a chip of cow dung. Sometimes rumor travels mighty fast, almost like the wind. You better go now and see what Rusty wants you to do next, and if any of the fellers ask you where you've been, just tell them you had a couple of days off. They'll think you were up the trail sparkin' with that pretty little blond I keep hearing about."

The two men rose to leave, but Ace put a restraining hand on Hank's arm. "If you have a minute, Hank, I'd like to visit with you."

❖   ❖   ❖

On Wednesday morning, Francesca carried platters heaped with food into the Central Division dining room in anticipation of the crowd expected for breakfast.

Hank took his place at the table with all of the Dover family. His eyes were drawn to Marv, who sat directly across from him, and his pulse quickened. He had to make a conscious effort to keep from staring at her.

Marv was not unaware of his glances and several times caught him casting his eyes her way, only to turn them in another direction when she looked up at him. What was he thinking? That she could ride a horse and rope a steer, or shoot a gun like a man? He could sure use a few lessons in the romance department, but even so, she felt her heart turn flip-flops every time she heard his voice. Like Drag Johnson, he was tall and strong and handsome, but there the resemblance between the two men ended. Thoughts of Drag now only filled her with revulsion, while Hank—well, she just wasn't sure. All she knew was that he excited her in a way no other man ever had before. And she was purely delighted to see him today, romantic or not!

With Francesca moving in and out of the room and the cowhands noisily enjoying their breakfast just across the open breezeway, Ace chose to keep the conversation casual and light. Not until the table was cleared and the hands had gone back outside to work did he plunge into the business they had all gathered to discuss.

He told them about the weekend trips Paul Billy and Aldo had made to Jacksonville. He explained how each time they had observed Drag Johnson meeting there with a group of cowhunters, and how Aldo had contrived an alliance with one of the members of that group.

"The leader of the group seems to be a man they call Toke. Jake, the young man Aldo met, told him his boss had some steers for sale. We don't know what connection, if any, Drag has with this group, other than he likes to play poker.

"Anyhow, at that point, Treff and I started talking about what possible action we might take to follow up on it. We discussed the situation with Hank, and he generously agreed to go to Jacksonville, posing as a cattle buyer looking for four hundred or four hundred fifty steers to take to Cowpens. I'd like to ask Hank to tell you about his experience in Jacksonville this past weekend."

"Much of the credit goes to Aldo," Hank began modestly. With considerable care, he told them about the trip and how they had met Toke, who claimed to be the owner of a large group of cattle he was willing to sell. "When we rode near the Okefinokee, we were able to convince Toke to let us ride through his herd, and we were not terribly surprised to find that it contained TSR steers. Aldo estimated he saw about forty TSR steers in the group we bargained to buy."

An audible gasp was the only sound that interrupted Hank's story, as his audience listened in wide-eyed amazement.

"Most of the TSR steers were from the Santa Fe, but there were a few from the Fannin. There was a total of two hundred to two hundred fifty head in the group we looked at, and we saw several other brands in the herd. Some of the cattle were not branded. When we told him we needed four to five hundred steers, Toke was quick to let us know he could gather up another two hundred head or more for us to see in about a week or ten days. We sent him word to have all the cattle in the Jacksonville cattle pens on Thursday of next week."

Treff spoke up. "Where do you think he plans to find that many steers?"

"Aldo and I talked about that on the way back here. The only places we could think about that were big enough to have that many steers were the TSR, the Brown Owl Ranch, and the cattle on Payne's Prairie. We didn't think it would be wise to alert the Brown Owl people until we know more about Drag Johnson's connection with Toke. We don't want to chance word getting back to the Okefinokee group."

Ace placed his arms on the table and leaned forward. "Jeremiah, you and Rusty both need to increase your security for the next couple of weeks."

"That will be taken care of no later than tomorrow morning," Rusty responded.

"We'll double our riders on the north and east borders," Jeremiah said, "and make certain they're concealed in the woods so as not to advertise what we're doing."

"We'll do the same on the northern border of the Fannin," Ten added, "and we'll put some extra riders on the west side of the Santa Fe, too."

"That fella, Slim Ritta, that we let go is apparently riding for Toke. He may have told Toke where our cattle were located when he worked here," Treff reminded them.

"Most of the cattle in the Santa Fe have either moved themselves, or have been moved since he left," Jeremiah said. "We'll make sure we don't have any cattle near our borders."

"Do you think Toke can be planning on getting some of the steers on Payne's Prairie?" Ace asked. "I know people from Georgia have been coming down and rustling those Seminole cattle for years, but the animosity is growing stronger and more violent every day. Right now, it would be a mighty dangerous proposition for Toke and his gang to try to move in there."

Treff had been uncommonly quiet, but now he spoke up. "We have nothing to prove that Drag Johnson is involved in any wrongdoing, and we shouldn't accuse him until we have all the facts. But we do know that ever since our open house, he has gone to Jacksonville every weekend except this last one, and each time he meets this guy Toke. We need to find out why. Are they in cahoots with one another? I'm sure Drag could find a poker game closer to home. Can it be that Drag is locating cattle for Toke to rustle? Mind you, I'm not accusing him of anything," he said, glancing out of the corner of his eye at Marv, "but the Brown Owl Ranch is fairly close to Payne's Prairie, and he could have scouted the eastern edge of the Seminole cattle. He might have spotted a group of steers on the prairie that he thinks could be easily rustled, or he may know where Zeke Mongol keeps a group of steers that could be taken without too much trouble."

"Should we ask Paul Billy to alert some of his family about this?" Ace asked. "If Toke does try to rustle steers from the Indians, it could result in a massacre. At least, that would help rid the Territory of a few rustlers. Otherwise, we are going to have to face them ourselves when we go to Okefinokee to claim our cattle."

"I'll talk with Paul Billy and see what he thinks," Treff promised.

Marv listened in silence. As much as she despised Drag Johnson, she thought it best to keep her own experiences with him to herself. If her father and four brothers knew of his behavior, there was no telling what action they might take. She didn't want to cloud the outlaw issue with her personal concerns. Instead, she focused on the facts that might be helpful to them. "When Drag left me to go to Fort Brooke, he indicated he had to be back to the Brown Owl Ranch by this evening. It seems they are planning to work cattle for the next few days. I think he said they plan to do some branding."

"Marv," her father said, "I don't think you need to take any special precautions at the Leon, as far as cattle are concerned. I only asked you to be here today so that you would be aware of what has happened. But, honey, I think you should be very careful of your own safety for a while, in case Drag is involved in some way."

"Daddy, what Drag Johnson does is no longer any concern of mine, unless it involves the TSR."

"Well, I'd be lying if I said I was sorry to hear that. But anyway, please indulge your old father, and try to have someone with you anytime you're checking cattle or riding our border." Ace expected to hear a spate of protest from his daughter, but she only smiled at him.

"Ace, do you think we should make a trip up to the Okefinokee and get our cattle back, or should we wait until next Thursday and see what happens?" Treff asked.

Instead of answering, Ace turned to O'Mara. "Hank, can you and Aldo find your way back to those cattle?"

"I think so, Ace. And I believe Paul Billy can help us. They tell me he knows his way around that swamp."

"Well, let's wait until next week and see what shows up in the Jacksonville pens. If nothing comes in to the pens, then we'll go looking for the herd you saw, Hank. Each of you plan on taking four men from your division and drift into town next Wednesday night. Lie low until Thursday morning. We don't want to raise suspicion by having people see twenty or twenty-five horses from the TSR ranch all in one place. Maybe you can find some horses that haven't been branded. That would help. Thursday morning, drift out to the cattle pens. If anybody asks you what you want, just say that you work for Mister O'Malley, and you're supposed to get some cattle to take to Cowpens."

"I don't want to start an argument," Marv said, "but you might as well know right now that I intend to go to Jacksonville with you. I'm part of this business too, you know, and just because I'm someone's little sister doesn't give me special privileges. I will get four of the best men at Leon and meet you in Jacksonville!"

She looked around the table, waiting for someone to challenge her plans, but surprisingly, no one did. The

Dovers all knew that when Marv got that determined glint in her eyes, there was no point in arguing.

"I'm going now to talk with Paul Billy," Treff said. "I expect the rest of you should get about your business too, unless Ace wants to see us some more."

"No, we've gone over everything. I will see you all in Jacksonville. Be sure to bring men who know how to use a gun. Bring rifles if they have them, and make sure everyone has a good supply of ammunition. We may not have any trouble, but we should be prepared."

Hank had been silent while the family made their plans, but now he spoke up. "If there are no objections, I would like to ride back to the Leon with Marv. Paul Billy will be tied up with Treff, and I don't think she should ride back by herself."

Ace was not blind to the stars in Marv's eyes when she looked at Hank O'Mara, and Amaly had dropped a few hints his way. "If Marv has no objection, her mother and I would appreciate you helping out that way." Ace was not so old that he couldn't remember the pleasure of a couple spending a few hours together, without the intrusion of brothers or parents.

Marv's heart leaped, but she hoped her eager enthusiasm did not show. She tried to sound indifferent when she said, "I would be happy for Hank to ride back to the Leon with me, if he chooses. But first, I have a few details I must take care of. I should be ready in about an hour." There were times when a girl just had to talk with her mother, and this was certainly one of them!

While he waited for Marv, Hank cleaned his saddle gear and rifle. He brushed his horse, examined its feet, and saddled both of their horses, and still he waited. What was taking Marv so long? It seemed like it was taking her forever to finish her work. He was beginning to grow impatient when she suddenly appeared, carrying a pair of saddlebags.

"Mama is sending a little snack for us to have along the way, Hank."

Hank looked at her and tried to think of something pleasing and proper to say, but his tongue seemed to tangle between his teeth. Finally he uttered, "Everyone has left but us. I reckon we best get on our way." Then, seeing Marv look at him as though she expected him to say something more, he added, "The snack will taste real good."

Marv sighed. Hank was so nice, and handsome, too, but he sure wasn't the romantic type! She had spent the last hour prettying up, and he hadn't even noticed! Nevertheless, she felt an inward excitement as they rode side by side along the trail in silence.

They rode through the woods for about an hour, each engaged in private thoughts. Hank knew there was something different about Marv today. He stole another sideways glance. Finally he blurted out, "You sure look pretty today. Did you do something to your hair?"

His uncharacteristic remark caught her by surprise! A strange warmth surged through her body and turned her cheeks a becoming shade of pink. "Well, thank you, sir. Mama just trimmed it a little. Do you like it?"

"Your hair is always beautiful. It just seems unusually so today." Just as Marv's hopes soared, he added, "I guess all that hair gets in your way when you're working cattle. This shorter style will probably be better suited to you. I've just never seen a woman who could handle cattle the way you do."

Marv wanted to scream her rage at him, but then she remembered her talk with Mama this morning. Something about molasses catching more flies than vinegar. She took a deep breath and swallowed her anger. At least she could be glad that he didn't have a line like Drag Johnson, but she sure wished he would learn to improve his own line a bit. In spite of herself, she realized that she was falling in love with this hopeless man. She simply *must* find some way to teach him the art of sweet-talk.

"We're coming up on Kirk Hollow," she said, "and I'm beginning to get hungry. It's a good place to enjoy our snack."

When they reached the little stream, Hank hurried to help Marv from her horse. "That snack sure does smell good," he commented, as he helped her down from her stirrup. "It smells like it has vanilla in it. It must be something new to me."

Marv heaved an exasperated sigh. My goodness, she thought, didn't he know that girls sometimes put a little vanilla behind their ears to make them smell nice and romantic? This man sure didn't know much about women! She shook her head. "No, Hank, we're just having a little cornbread." She opened the bags and spread a small cloth on the ground. "Here," she offered, handing him a piece of cornbread liberally spread with fresh-churned butter. "Try some of this."

As they munched on the tender, moist cornbread, Marv asked, "When are you going back to your ranch?"

"Just as soon as this business in Jacksonville is finished next week," he answered. "I've been gone from home for three weeks. Folks back there are probably worried, wondering what happened to me."

"Will I—that is, will *we* see you again?"

"I've decided to sell my land near Pensacola and move over this way. This seems like much better cattle country." He paused before adding, "I would like to see more of you, too, Marv. That is, if you don't mind."

"I don't mind at all. In fact, I'd like that very much, Hank."

"Maybe you could help me find some land to buy," he said. "I've come to admire you and your family in the short time I've known you. You know a lot about the land out here, and I know you could be a big help to me getting a herd started."

The combination of genes that gave Marv her red hair had also endowed her with a temperament to match. Molasses be hanged! A girl could tolerate only so much!

"Hank O'Mara! Look at me!"

Her tone startled him so that he dropped his cornbread on the ground. "Wha—?"

"Right now I don't care a hoot about buying land or working cattle! Can't you tell when a woman is attracted to you? Can't you think about anything besides cows and horses and land? Have I got to tell you everything?" Oh my goodness, what have I done, she thought. Now he will probably leave and never come back. She blushed to think what Mama would say if she knew what Marv had just done. As her anger subsided, embarrassment took its place, and she folded her arms on top of her knees and buried her face in them.

Hank saw her shoulders quiver with her silent sobs, and he thought his heart would burst. "You sure are pretty when you blush like that," he said softly. "I didn't realize you could be so feisty." He put an arm over her shoulder. "Look at me, Marv." He tipped up her chin with his finger.

She raised teary eyes and looked into his wonderful face, savoring the words he spoke to her.

"From the first minute I saw you, I found myself falling hopelessly in love. I've been afraid to tell you for fear I might scare you away."

Now Marv was the one who was at a loss for words. "You—you mean—"

"I mean I love you, Marvelous Dover, and with your permission, I aim to speak to your father the first chance I get."

"Oh, Hank, you've made me so happy. And I think I already know what Daddy will say. But now we'd better get started to the Leon if we intend to get there before dark."

As they gathered up the remains of their snack and packed them into the saddlebags, Hank helped Marv to her feet. But when her feet were firmly planted on the ground, he did not let go of her hands. Instead, he pulled her into his arms and kissed her long and tenderly.

Marv felt her world spinning round and round. She had never known such happiness. She swung herself into the saddle and led the way toward Leon headquarters, humming as she rode through the woods, with Hank following close behind her.

Hank watched her red hair bob against the back of

her neck and knew that in all the world, he was the luck-
iest man alive.

20

ON SUNDAY MORNING, Drag left the Brown Owl Ranch in plenty of time to arrive early for his meeting with Toke. This was an important day, and he would not chance having anything go wrong. Not when success was just around the corner! He had already told Zeke that he wanted to leave the BOR next week, so it was important to wind up all the details in this neck of the woods and be free to move on with his plans.

Perched uncomfortably on an upturned keg, he sat on the front porch of the little store south of Keystone Lake and waited. And waited! By mid-morning, his rear end was getting sore, and his patience was wearing thin. Where was that fat slob?

As if in answer to his thoughts, he raised his eyes and saw the slovenly, foul-smelling man shuffling his way up to the store.

"Where's the rest of your crew, Toke?"

"I left 'em in the woods a little ways back. I didn't

see no reason for the whole bunch of us to ride up and make people ask questions."

"Are you ready to ride?"

"Yea, I reckon I am. Which way we be goin'?"

"We'll head east from here," Drag said.

"You go ahead. I'll git my horse and catch up with you in about a mile. I need to go inside and get me a chaw of tobaccy, and I don't cotton to havin' people see us leavin' together, no-how." Toke disappeared inside the store, and Drag tramped down the steps to untie his horse from the hitching rail.

Drag paced his horse at a slow trot and followed an easterly trail. Before he had gone far, he heard hoofbeats approaching from behind.

As soon as Toke caught up with him, Drag said, "Now we need to turn south." Without further explanation, he led the way toward the prairie where he knew prosperity was waiting for him.

The two men held to the woods and heavy brush all the way, in an effort to remain out of sight. When they were half a mile from the prairie, Drag reined in his pony under a dense cluster of oak trees and motioned for Toke to follow.

In silence, they watched and listened for signs of other riders. The cloudless sky showed no flurry of birds, and the ground was firm and stable. There was nothing to alert them to the recent presence of Indians. They waited for over half an hour before they felt confident enough to leave the cover of the trees. At last Drag felt convinced there was no one watching them, and that it was safe to get a closer look at the herd.

The cattle were still placidly grazing in the same place where Drag had seen them before. "Well, here they are, Toke, just like I promised you. You have to admit these are good-looking cattle. They're not restless or nervous, and I believe a good crew of cowhunters could move 'em out the northeast corner of the prairie and have 'em over the Georgia line before anyone knew they were gone."

"Mebbe so," Toke growled. "I need to look around a while before I decide if it's safe."

"Take all the time you need, but I have to get back to the Brown Owl. Zeke wants me to help move some female stock, and I'm already running late. Is there anything else I need to do with you before I leave?"

"Naw, Drag, not right now. You go on. I jist need to stick around here fer a spell to make sure there ain't no one watchin' the cattle. Then I'll talk to the fellers, and we'll decide what to do."

"I'll see you in Jacksonville next Sunday, Toke. It looks like we got us a good deal going. Don't let anything mess it up." Drag didn't trust this man as far as he could spit hot tobacco, and he hoped his tone implied a warning. He turned his horse and headed back to the Brown Owl Ranch.

Toke watched Drag until he rode out of sight. Then he took cover in the dense brush and spent the rest of the day watching the cattle, his eyes scanning the prairie for signs that Indians might be guarding the herd. Egrets flocked peacefully at the feet of the cattle, and wild ibises scavenged for food in the shallow streams. A pair of hawks flew over, and a group of prairie deer grazed placidly on the outer edge of the prairie, as the sun dipped lower in the sky.

Toke saw no indication of anything that tensed the cattle or wildlife and not the first sign of Seminole activity. The herd looked fat and healthy. Drag's idea of moving the animals out of the northeast corner of Payne's Prairie should not cause a problem. A few hammocks and a copse of trees stood between the cattle and the place where they would take them, but this was nothing Toke and his men couldn't handle.

As the sun slipped over the horizon and darkness blanketed the sky, clouds of mosquitoes rose from the prairie in great, whining swarms. Toke abandoned his hideout to return to the temporary camp where his men were waiting to receive his instructions.

"Them steers look pretty damn good," he told his men when he got back to camp. "We can't do nothing with 'em tonight, but right at daylight we oughta move 'em out to the northeast. If we git started early, we should be able to git the herd far enough to the north to be safe from Injuns by dark tomorrow. Git some sleep, and we'll start early enough to be with the cattle by daylight."

In the muted light of early dawn, Toke and his men eased onto the northern edge of the prairie, where cattle began their laggardly stir. Toke was relieved that his job would not be complicated by having to wake the cattle from their resting place.

"Slim, you and Dino work the west side of the cattle. Snake, you and Jake handle the south end, and me and Weasel will move the east side of the herd. Don't make a lot of noise, and don't use no whips. We ain't aimin' to send out no announcements to them Injuns to let 'em know we're here. We'll drive the herd between them two large hammocks in the northeast corner."

The rustlers slipped stealthily into the tall prairie grass and began to jostle the cattle with sticks. The steers were easy to handle, and soon the large herd ambled forward in a northeasterly direction, softly lowing their mild protest. The rustlers grinned at each other, happy with the way things were going. These cattle, once they left the prairie, would have enough grass in their bellies to keep them moving at a fast pace with little weight loss. As soon as they got them close to the Okefinokee, the animals could fill their bellies again before moving on to the Jacksonville cattle pens.

The first few steers worked their way up the slope from the prairie, drifting between the two hammocks, and Toke was certain there would be no difficulty in moving the herd northward.

As Slim and Dino moved in from the west side and reached the edge of the hammock areas, they could see Toke and Weasel riding in from the east. "Man, Dino," Slim boasted, with a big smile plastered across his face, "this here is almost too easy!"

Those were the last words he was ever to utter, as a rifle bullet seared his chest and knocked him from the saddle. The air around them seemed to explode with a heavy curtain of lead, and Dino, too, felt the sting of bullets before he dropped to the ground.

"Seminoles," he screamed, as he scrambled into a clump of tall grass.

At the first sound of gunfire, Toke and Weasel tried to escape by lunging their horses back into the tall prairie grass. Excited cattle stampeded all around them. Toke recognized the sound of the small-bore rifles that the Seminoles had been bringing in from Cuba, and he realized too late that he had ridden right into an Indian ambush.

Toke's years of experience as an outlaw had equipped him with the skill of a wild animal stalking its prey and a vicious desire to survive. He threw himself from his saddle and slapped his horse on its flank to make it run. Then, with remarkable speed for a fat man, he plunged into a tall stand of maidencane. As he lay motionless on the ground, he was surrounded by the continuing blast of gunfire and the thundering hooves of frightened cattle.

Weasel was not so fortunate. Just when he thought he had managed to escape, his horse stepped in a big gator hole. He heard the leg bone snap moments before the horse catapulted, carrying the rider down with him and pinning Weasel under the water with the heavy horse on top of him.

As abruptly as the explosion of bullets had started, the firing stopped and the world was ominously silent. Toke hunkered down on his belly in the tall grass. He did not dare to move. He would stay here in his hiding place and wait for the concealing cover of darkness. He wondered what had happened to Snake and Jake, who had been riding in the back of the herd, but he did not raise his head to look.

He did not have long to wonder. A hideous scream

pierced the air, and Toke knew that Snake had been captured by the Indians. His mind surged with hatred for Snake, because he knew the Indians could easily make that coward talk. The Seminoles would soon know that there were two other men on the east side of the herd and one more in the back. Toke put his hands over his ears to block out the agonizing screams that continued for several minutes and then abruptly stopped. Toke knew what that sudden silence meant: Snake was dead!

Moments later, he heard footsteps and frenzied jabbering among the Indians as they searched the area for the two remaining survivors. Toke scarcely dared to breathe. After minutes that seemed like hours, he heard the Indians excitedly call to one another and realized that they had found Weasel and his horse where they had fallen. He could hear them stripping the saddle and gear from the horse and the guns and ammunition from Weasel's body. He could not risk raising his head to look, but his ears told him the Indians had found his horse too, some distance away.

All morning he could hear the Indians plundering the grass in search of him, but they did not find him. Then the ground began to rumble like an earthquake, and a sea of pounding legs surrounded him. The steers were being driven back to their previous location. They trampled all around him but miraculously did not step on Toke as he remained motionless in the tall maidencane. At times some of the Indians came very close, but in their excitement they failed to see him.

As the sun began to sink below the horizon, Toke heaved a sigh of relief. He was going to escape from this nightmare alive! Then an acrid odor filled his nostrils. He took a deep breath and recognized the unmistakable smell of smoke. Without moving his body, he tried to determine the direction from which it came. The smell intensified, and from the corner of his eye, he saw a spiral of rising smoke. The Indians had set fire to a portion of the prairie south of his hiding place, and winds from the south were blowing the flames his way! The blasted Indians were going to burn him from his hiding place! He waited as long as he could, and then, choking and almost overcome by the smoke, he began to crawl through the grass, hoping against hope that the savages would not see him.

The flames crackled as they continued to gain on him, and he had to abandon his crawl and run to keep from being burned alive. As he ran toward the trees, he heard a guttural scream from the middle of the flames and knew that either Slim or Dino had been caught in the raging fire, unable to escape death in the blazing inferno.

By some miracle, Toke was able to reach the edge of the flames and dart into dense brush on the edge of the prairie. Collapsing into the bushes, he pulled great gulps of clean air into his lungs. His nose and eyes burned, and his chest felt as though a load of bricks rested on it, but he was alive! He could hardly believe he had escaped the ambush. He had always said he was smarter than those Indians, but now he would live to tell a story that proved it.

As he crouched in the brush, silently congratulating himself, a searing pain ripped between his shoulder blades and tore through his back, consuming him with agony.

Crimson blood spattered the bushes around him. His world darkened so quickly that he was barely able to see the Indian who cleaned his knife by wiping its bloody blade on Toke's trousers. Toke had finally been outsmarted.

Across the prairie, one lone rider was silhouetted against the fading purple horizon, riding north as fast as his horse would travel. The only survivor of Toke's group of rustlers was injured, but at least he was alive! What could have gone wrong, just when everything seemed to be going so right? Jake knew they had been tricked, and that Indians had ambushed them, but Toke had everything scouted out beforehand. Jake did not know if any of the others had escaped, but surely they would follow if they were able. His left arm was still bleeding from two rifle wounds, and his head was spinning from the loss of blood, but he did not dare stop or even slow down until he put some miles between himself and those wild red savages.

When darkness closed in, Jake pulled into the middle of a thick copse of oak trees and slumped in the saddle. He wrapped his bandanna tightly around his arm to stem the flow of blood. Fishing dried venison from his saddlebags, he forced himself to eat, while his pony nibbled on the sparse wiregrass.

After a time, he began to feel better and summoned the strength to ride through the night until he reached Jacksonville. He tied his horse outside the Cowhunters Saloon and went inside for a shot of whiskey and a chance to rest.

The bartender gave him a hard glare. "It looks like you musta had a hard day, pardner. Is everything all right?"

"Yeh, everything's fine," Jake muttered. "I'm looking

fer that fat man that comes in here now and then. You ain't seen him tonight, have you?"

"He ain't been here since last weekend, and he didn't stay long then. Said he forgot to do something and had to go back home."

Jake decided he should wait here until daylight. If no one showed up by then, it was a pretty sure guess they were either dead or captured by the Indians. He wasn't sure which would be worse. That would mean that Jake was now in charge! The thought excited him! He must come up with a plan.

Toke had left Uncle Amos in the Okefinokee camp on Black Oak Island, to look after things while the rest of the gang went to Keystone Lake. The old man wasn't able to do many things, but he wasn't completely useless. He claimed to have been a good cowhunter in his younger days, and he could still handle a herd of cattle fairly well. If nobody showed up here by tomorrow, Jake decided he would get Uncle Amos to help him gather up those steers and bring them to the Jacksonville pens Thursday morning. He might have to sell them a little cheaper than what Toke would have asked, but it would give him a stake to get out of this Florida Territory. Uncle Amos was an escaped slave, and he would want to go back to the Okefinokee as soon as possible. Jake would be shed of him and wouldn't have to share any of the money from the sale.

He slumped in a chair in the back corner of the saloon and slept fitfully for a short time. When the sun came up, and still none of Toke's men had shown up, Jake went to the café and ordered a hearty breakfast.

As he scarffed down a plate of grits and scrambled eggs, his strength began to return. He paid the man with the few remaining coins in his pocket and rode to the Jacksonville pens.

Jake made arrangements with the manager to use part of the pens on Thursday morning. He could hardly wait to get out of town and head for the camp where he could catch some sleep and have Uncle Amos fix up his rifle wound. His whole arm was beginning to throb, and his head felt like someone was pounding on it with a hammer.

As he neared their camp in the Okefinokee, Jake signaled with the whistle of the bobwhite. He had survived an Indian massacre, and he sure didn't want Uncle Amos to shoot him now. When he heard an echo of his call, he knew it was safe to ride into camp.

The old colored cowman stepped out from the palmetto patch where he had been hiding. "Law, Master Jake, I been skeert near out o' my mind. I ain't seen none o' the others. Will they be a-comin?"

"Uncle Amos, we was ambushed, and I think I'm the only one that escaped. We'll jist have to wait and see if any of the others make it back. I'm gonna rest this arm today."

"You let ole Uncle Amos take keer o' that arm. I knows how to make a sugar poultice that'll take the pizen right out, an' I got a pot o' rabbit stew cookin' on the fire."

"That sounds good. But listen, Uncle Amos; if no one gets back here by tomorrow morning, you and me gotta move that bunch of steers into the Jacksonville pens Thursday morning. Toke already made a deal with some feller to buy them cattle."

"Master Jake, I sho' don't wanna be seen in Jacksonville. I don't wanna be caught and sent back to Charleston."

Don't you worry, Uncle Amos. We can take them steers in just before dark on Wednesday. That way you can slip away and come back to camp in the dark, and nobody will see you." Jake stretched out under an oak tree and went to sleep with a smile on his face, dreaming about the success of his clever little plan.

Early Wednesday morning, Jake and Uncle Amos gathered the steers and began heading them toward Jacksonville. It was a slow job for only two men, but the steers had full bellies and were fairly calm. When occasionally one of the animals would dart into a hammock or a cypress head, they would simply let it go in order to keep the main herd moving south.

Just before dark, they reached the edge of Jacksonville. Jake left Uncle Amos to watch the herd while he rode into town to arrange to put them in the pens immediately instead of waiting until Thursday morning.

"There's no problem with putting them in the pens early," the manager assured him, happy to extract a larger fee. "There's plenty of space."

Jake rode back to deliver the good news to Uncle Amos, and together they drove their herd into town. Slowly, they urged the steers down the long corral leading to the pens. As soon as the cattle were safely inside the pens and the gates secured, the fearful escaped slave disappeared into the darkness and began his journey back to the secluded island camp in the Okefinokee Swamp.

It seemed to Jake that things could not have worked better. Tomorrow he would get his hands on a lot of money, more money than he had ever possessed at one time. And the best part was that there would be no one else around to demand a share of it. He would head west and begin a new life. He might even go all the way to the northwest. With the money from the sale of the steers, he would have a good stake. He could head out without turning back, so that he wouldn't even have to share with Uncle Amos.

The next morning, Jake was greedily wolfing down a hearty breakfast when he looked up to see Mister H. H. O'Malley entering the café with a good-looking redhead on his arm.

"Mister O'Malley," he said, rising to his feet, "I'm mighty glad to see you again."

"I'll bet you are, Jake. Are you alone?"

"Yes, sir. Toke's been held up. He asked me to come on down to meet you. He said to tell you he was terrible sorry he hadn't been able to git them other steers together. He said if you was interested in the cattle in the pens, I could go ahead and cut you a special deal on 'em."

"I wouldn't be able to pay you what I could have if you had brought the other two hundred head of better cattle. Those Spanish cattle are hard to sell."

Jake couldn't help stealing glances out of the corner of his eye at that good-looking woman Mister O'Malley brought with him. He hadn't ever seen anything like her before. It made it hard fer a feller to keep his mind on business!

"Jake, I would like for you to meet Miss Revod. She came with me today to look at your cattle. She may be interested in some of them."

"I—I'm pleased to meet you, ma'am," Jake stuttered.

"Are your cattle in the pens now?" Miss Revod asked.

"Yes'm, they are."

"Jake, I'll tell you what I'll do," O'Malley said. "I'm willing to pay eight dollars a head for that group of cattle. If that is not enough, we won't even go to look at them. I'm very unhappy that Toke didn't bring the other two hundred steers like he promised. If I had known that ahead of time, it would have saved me a trip."

Jake feigned disappointment with the offer, but in his mind he was already trying to calculate how much money he would have. "You said you would pay in gold coin, didn't you?"

"Yes, paying is no problem," Hank assured him.

"Well, Toke ain't gonna be happy, but I guess we'll let them go for that, seein' as how he feels so bad about not livin' up to his word an' all. You want we should go look at the steers now?"

The three of them walked to the pens and Jake proudly pointed out his cattle. "Ain't them a pretty bunch?"

"What do you think of the cattle, Miss Revod?"

"There are some good steers and some sorry ones," Marv replied. "I'll tell you what I'd like to do. Why don't we run the cattle down a chute and divide them into three groups. Put all the Spanish cattle in one group, put those nice-looking steers with the TSR brand in another pen, and put everything else in the third pen."

"Jake, if you'll run them down the chute, I'll handle the cutting gate. That will give Miss Revod a better chance to look at the steers."

Jake was glad for the extra helping hand, and he began to send the steers down the chute toward the gate. Hank separated the cattle as they came down, and they ended up with fifty-seven TSR steers, forty-one Spanish cattle, and ninety-eight cattle with various brands.

Jake had been too busy to notice the men who had drifted over to watch, and he was surprised when he looked up to find fifteen or twenty cowhunters looking over the top of the pens.

"Do you like the TSR steers, Miss Revod?" Hank asked.

"Yes, I like them very much," she replied.

Hank smiled at her and said, "Miss Revod, I would like for you to meet Mister Dover." He pointed to a gray-haired cowhunter sitting on the top rail of the pens.

"I believe we've met somewhere before," Miss Revod demurred.

The only problem we have here," Hank continued, "is that the TSR steers don't belong to Jake. Instead, they belong to Mister Dover. You'll need to talk to him."

Jake suddenly realized he had walked straight into a trap. As he started to reach for his gun, he heard a chorus of familiar clicks which he recognized as the sound of hammers lifted on at least a dozen handguns. Looking around, he saw that he was surrounded by twice that many men, each of whom held either a pistol or a rifle, and all of them pointed directly at him.

"I wouldn't reach for your gun, Jake," Mister Dover ordered. "Do you know where the other steers came from?"

"No, sir. I don't know nothin' about none of 'em. I just work for Toke. I thought all of these was his cattle."

"Do we have a sheriff in this town, or a marshal?"

"They've all gone to Saint Augustine," Hank replied.

"Well, men, what do you think we should do? Should we leave Jake here, or should we take him with us?" Ace asked.

"Let's take him with us," someone said, and a roar of agreement rose from the group.

"We can do that." Pointing toward two of his cowhunters, he said, "You men take Jake's gun and go with him to saddle his horse. While you are doing that, I'll arrange for the manager of these pens to handle the branded steers. Maybe he will recognize the brands and can let the owners know. Maybe some of them belong to Ito Bensen."

Ace continued to organize the activity. "Treff, you and the rest of the men can get the TSR steers, the Spanish steers, and any other cattle that don't have a brand and get them started on the way to the Santa Fe Division. Hank and Marv can help you. Leave four men here with me. We'll catch up with you before you reach the Santa Fe."

Rusty spoke to the men he had brought from Central Division. "Cotton, you and the other three men from Central stay here with Ace."

Ace left to find the manager of the stock pens and explain the situation to him. When he returned, the TSR cowhunters had Jake's horse saddled and were waiting for Ace to tell them what to do next.

"Has Treff left?" Ace asked.

"Yes, sir, he and the rest of the crew are on their way to Santa Fe."

"Let's ride out to the shade of those big oak trees and have us a little meeting," Ace said.

When they reached the trees, the men drew their horses to a halt and formed a circle, waiting to hear what Ace had to say. There was little doubt as to what he planned to talk about, but no one knew just exactly how he would handle the meeting.

"Jake, you were in possession of stolen cattle. I have asked these four cowhunters to act as a jury to decide what we should do with you. I'm going to ask you some questions. How you answer will help your jury decide whether or not to hang you."

Jake's eyes were wide with fear, and his face was as white as an egret's feathers. "I was just carrying out orders," he whined.

"Where are the rest of your crew?"

"I can't exactly tell you. They was gonna try to round up some more cattle for Mister O'Malley. He was wantin' about four hundred head."

"Do you know where they were going to get the other cattle?"

"No, sir, I don't have no idea. All's I ever do is stay home and tend to Toke's cattle. I don't never go after none myself."

"Where did you hurt your arm? It looks like a gunshot wound."

"I was cleaning my gun yesterday, and it accidentally went off."

Ace looked at his men. "Cotton, what do you men think about this fellow's story?"

The men huddled together and whispered before Cotton delivered their decision: "We think he is lying. He's got shifty eyes, and he don't look right at you when he talks. We heard about a group of rustlers that was killed by the Seminoles last Sunday, but rumor has it that one rustler escaped. I've talked it over with the boys here, and we think Jake is the one who got away. We think he is still lying, and we say he is guilty of stealing cattle and should be hung to this big limb above our head."

"No, wait, fellers! You got this all wrong," Jake protested, but his cries fell on deaf ears.

"All right, Cotton. If that's your verdict, tie his hands and pin this sign to the front of his shirt." Ace handed Cotton a hand-drawn sign that said STOLE FROM TSR RANCH. "Let's string him up and be on our way."

Ace turned to leave the hanging job to Cotton and his men. It was good to let people know what happened to outlaws who rustled cattle from the TSR. "When you finish, you might as well bring his horse and saddle. He won't have any further use for them."

❖   ❖   ❖

Later in the day, when Ace and his men caught up with the herd going to Santa Fe, he said to Cotton, "You and your men ride up and take the place of Rusty, Jeremiah, Ten, Treff, and Marv. Ask those five to drop back and ride with me. We need to talk about some family matters, and you'll have more than enough men to handle those few cattle."

Ace and his children dropped back from the herd to talk without having to shout over noises from the cattle drive.

"I wanted us to take a few minutes to reflect on all the things that have happened," Ace began. "It seems like we have done nothing but fight renegade Indians and outlaws for the last three months, but until we get law in the Territory it's going to be necessary for us to fight to protect our property. Things could get worse before they get better, what with the trouble developing between the army and the Seminoles again."

"We are fortunate to be on such good terms with most of the tribes," Treff reminded him. "But there are still a few red men who are against the white settlers, and you can't tell what they'll do if they begin to feel more pressure to move."

"I hear talk that some of the Seminoles have gone into hiding down south," Marv said. "They're getting ready to fight the new settlers and the army troops that are moving into the state."

"It seems like the Leon would be the most likely division to have problems, since some of the army outposts aren't far away. And some of the Seminoles are beginning to gather down in the Green Swamp area. Marv, you and

Treff need to keep your ears to the ground to stay on top of things."

"You're right, Dad. We need to be careful. But the Indians are not our only worry. Just last week we saw Joel and Sammy Godwin in our pastures again, even after I made a point of warning Grandma Godwin to keep her sons off our property."

"Yes, our troubles are far from over, but we've made a good dent in them this day," Ace said. "Now, is there anything else we need to discuss while we are all together?"

Now seemed a good time for Marv to speak to her family about something that was on her mind. She wasn't sure how to begin. "Well, you might as well all hear this now," she said, the color rising in her cheeks. "It looks like there may be another man in our family soon."

Treff suppressed a smile as he winked at Jeremiah. "Oh, is Cissy expecting again?" He couldn't let his sister get off without some good-natured ribbing.

"Not as I know of, Treff. Dad, if you and Mama are fixin' to take in some more strays, I sure hope they're better lookin' than Treff and Ten!"

"Just be quiet and let me finish, if you please," Marv said, her temper beginning to surface. "Daddy, Hank and I have become quite fond of each other. He plans to talk with you tomorrow before he leaves for his ranch." As she saw impish smiles spread over her brothers' faces, Marv knew that her troubles were only beginning. She tried to speak sternly, but her happiness spilled all over her face. "If you heathens can control yourselves until after he talks to Daddy, maybe he won't get scared away. I happen to love him very much."

Ace could see his sons' minds at work, and he knew that he needed to take quick control of the situation. "Marv, honey, we're all very happy for you, and I can assure you that these young men will control themselves unless they want to deal with me."

But even Ace had that devilish Dover gleam in his eyes, and Marv did not dare to guess what special tricks and surprises her wonderful, terrible family held in store for her future husband.

THE END

If you enjoyed reading this book, here are some other fiction titles from Pineapple Press. For a complete catalog or to place an order, write to Pineapple Press, P.O. Box 3899, Sarasota, Florida 34230 or call 1-800-PINEAPL (746-3275).

CRACKER WESTERNS:

Ghosts of the Green Swamp by Lee Gramling. Saddle up your easy chair and kick back for a Cracker Western featuring that rough-and-ready but soft-hearted Florida cowboy Tate Barkley—introduced in *Riders of the Suwannee*. ISBN: 1-56164-120-0 (HB); 1-56164-126-X (PB)

Guns of the Palmetto Plains by Rick Tonyan. As the Civil War explodes over Florida, Tree Hooker dodges Union soldiers and Florida outlaws to drive cattle to feed the starving Confederacy. ISBN: 1-56164-061-1 (HB); 1-56164-070-0 (PB)

Riders of the Suwannee by Lee Gramling. Tate Barkley returns to 1870s Florida just in time to come to the aid of a young widow and her children as they fight to save their homestead from outlaws. ISBN: 1-56164-046-8 (HB); 1-56164-043-3 (PB)

Thunder on the St. Johns by Lee Gramling. Riverboat gambler Chance Ramsay teams up with the family of young Josh Carpenter and the trapper's daughter Abby Macklin to combat a slew of greedy outlaws seeking to destroy the dreams of the honest homesteaders. ISBN: 1-56164-064-6 (HB); 1-56164-080-8 (PB)

Trail from St. Augustine by Lee Gramling. A young trapper, a crusty ex-sailor, and an indentured servant girl fleeing a cruel master join forces to cross the Florida wilderness in search of buried treasure and a new life.
ISBN: 1-56164-047-6 (HB); 1-56164-042-5 (PB)

OTHER FLORIDA FICTION:
Forever Island and *Allapattah* by Patrick Smith. *Forever Island* has been called the classic novel of the Everglades. *Allapattah* is the story of a young Seminole in despair in the white man's world.
ISBN: 0-910923-42-6 (HB)

The River is Home and *Angel City* by Patrick Smith. *The River is Home* tells of a Louisiana family's struggle to cope with the changes in their rural environment. *Angel City* is a powerful and moving exposé of migrant workers in the 1970s.
ISBN: 0-910923-64-7 (HB)

A Land Remembered by Patrick Smith. Three generations of the MacIveys, a Florida family battling the hardships of the frontier to rise from a dirt-poor cracker life to the wealth and standing of real-estate tycoons.
ISBN: 0-910923-12-4 (HB); 1-56164-116-2 (PB)